DARKNESS UNLEASHED

"Regan, you are certain?" Jagr demanded.

Certain? No. She didn't have a clue what was about to happen. Well, nothing beyond a great deal of pain when those huge fangs sank into her flesh.

Thankfully, she was no coward, and if Jagr needed blood to get him up and moving, then by God, he was going to get blood.

"Do you need an engraved invitation?" she taunted, not at all surprised when his mouth widened and his fangs slid smoothly into her wrist. Jagr was not a vampire to back down from a direct challenge. Regrettably, her plan had neglected one small detail.

She was braced for pain. She was even braced for the necessity of ripping him forcibly from her flesh if he lost his head and tried to take more than she was willing to offer.

What she wasn't prepared for was the realization that far from painful, the sensation that jolted through her was one of intense, relentless pleasure.

"Oh . . ." Her eyes drifted shut as she felt him suck deeply of her blood, every pull tightening the coiling bliss that was lodged in the pit of her stomach. Her entire body trembled, the same excitement that had set her on fire when he'd kissed her blazing through her body. Only this time it was more powerful, more driving, more . . . explosive. She was drowning, lost in the dark, intoxicating desire . . .

Books by Alexandra Ivy

WHEN DARKNESS COMES

EMBRACE THE DARKNESS

DARKNESS EVERLASTING

DARKNESS REVEALED

DARKNESS UNLEASHED

Published by Zebra Books

Darkness Unleashed

ALEXANDRA IVY

ZEBRA BOOKS
KENSINGTON PUBLISHING CORP.
http://www.kensingtonbooks.com

ZEBRA BOOKS are published by

Kensington Publishing Corp.
119 West 40th Street
New York, NY 10018

All Kensington titles, imprints, and distributed lines are available at special quantity discounts for bulk purchases for sales
promotion, premiums, fund-raising, educational, or institu-
tional use.

Special book excerpts or customized printings can also be created to fit specific needs. For details, write or phone the office
of the Kensington Special Sales Manager: Attn. Special Sales
Department. Kensington Publishing Corp., 119 West 40th
Street, New York, NY 10018. Phone: 1-800-221-2647.

Zebra and the Z logo Reg. U.S. Pat. & TM Off.

ISBN-13: 978-1-4201-0297-0
ISBN-10: 1-4201-0297-4

First Printing: November 2009
10 9 8 7 6 5 4 3 2

Printed in the United States of America

Prologue

Jagr knew he was creating panic in Viper's exclusive nightclub. The elegant establishment with its crystal chandeliers and red velvet upholstery catered to the more civilized members of the demon-world. Jagr was anything but civilized.

He was a six-foot-three vampire who had once been a Visigoth chief. But it wasn't his braided, pale gold hair that fell nearly to his waist, or the ice-blue eyes that missed nothing and sent creatures with any claim to intelligence scurrying from his path. It wasn't even the leather duster that flared about his hard body.

No, it was the cold perfection of his stark features, and the hint of feral fury that smoldered about him.

Three hundred years of relentless torture had stripped away any hint of civility.

Ignoring the assorted demons who tumbled over chairs and tables in an effort to avoid his long strides, Jagr concentrated on the two Ravens guarding the door to the back office. The hushed air of sophistication was giving him a rash.

He was a vampire who preferred the solitude of his lair hidden beneath the streets of Chicago, surrounded by his vast library, secure in the knowledge that not a human, beast, or demon possessed the ability to enter.

Not that he was the total recluse that his vampire brothers assumed.

No matter how powerful or skilled or intelligent he might be, he understood that his survival depended on understanding the ever changing technology of the modern world. And beyond that was the necessity of being able to blend in with current society.

Even a recluse had to feed.

Tucked in the very back of his lair was a plasma TV with every channel known to humankind, and the sort of nondescript clothing that allowed him to cruise through the seedier neighborhoods without causing a riot.

The most lethal hunters knew how to camouflage themselves while on the prowl.

But this place . . .

He'd rather be staked than mince and prance around like a jackass.

Damn Styx. The ancient vampire had known that only a royal command could force him to enter a crowded nightclub. Jagr made no secret of his disdain for the companionship of others.

Which begged the question of why the Anasso would choose such a setting to meet.

In a mood foul enough to fill the vast club with an icy chill, Jagr ignored the two Ravens who stood on sentry duty near the back office, and lifting his hand, allowed his power to blow the heavy oak door off its hinges.

The looming Ravens growled in warning, dropping their heavy capes, which hid the numerous swords, daggers, and guns attached to various parts of their bodies.

Jagr's step never faltered. Styx wouldn't let his pet vampires hurt an invited guest. At least not until he had what he needed from Jagr.

And even if Styx didn't call off the guards . . . well, hell, he'd been waiting centuries to be taken out in battle. It was a warrior's destiny.

There was a low murmur from inside the room, and the two Ravens grudgingly allowed him to pass with nothing more painful than a heated glare.

Stepping over the shattered door, Jagr paused to cast a wary glance about the pale blue and ivory room. As expected, Styx, a towering Aztec who was the current king of vampires, was consuming more than his fair share of space behind a heavy walnut desk, his bronzed features unreadable. Viper, clan chief of Chicago, who, with his silver hair and dark eyes looked more like an angel than lethal warrior, stood by his shoulder.

"Jagr." Styx leaned back in the leather chair, his fingers steepled beneath his chin. "Thank you for coming so promptly."

Jagr narrowed his frigid gaze. "Did I have a choice?"

"Careful, Jagr," Viper warned. "This is your Anasso."

Jagr curled his lips, but he was wise enough to keep his angry words to himself. Even presuming he could match Styx's renowned power, he would be dead before ever leaving the club if he challenged the Anasso.

"What do you want?" he growled.

"I have a task for you."

Jagr clenched his teeth. For the past century he'd managed to keep away from the clan who called him brother, never bothering others and expecting the same in return. Since he'd been foolish enough to allow Cezar to enter his lair, it seemed he couldn't get rid of the damn vampires.

"What sort of task?" he demanded, his tone making it clear he didn't appreciate playing the role of toady.

Styx smiled as he waved a slender hand toward a nearby sofa. It was a smile that sent a chill of alarm down Jagr's spine.

"Have a seat, my friend," the Anasso drawled. "This might take a while."

For an insane moment, Jagr considered refusing the order. Before being turned into a vampire, he had been a leader of thousands. While he had no memory of those days, he had retained all his arrogance. Not to mention his issue with authority.

Thankfully, he had also kept the larger portion of his intelligence.

"Very well, Anasso, I have rushed to obey your royal command." He lowered his hard bulk onto a delicate brocade sofa, inwardly swearing to kill the designer if it broke. "What do you demand of your dutiful subject?"

Viper growled deep in his throat, the air tingling with his power. Jagr never blinked, although his muscles coiled in preparation.

"Perhaps you should see to your guests, Viper," Styx smoothly commanded. "Jagr's . . . dramatic entrance has disrupted your charming entertainment, and attracted more attention than I desire."

"I will not be far." Viper flashed Jagr a warning glare before disappearing through the busted door.

"Is he auditioning for a place among your Ravens?" Jagr mocked.

Pinpricks of pain bit into his skin as Styx released a small thread of his power.

"So long as you remain in Chicago, Viper is your clan chief. Do not make the mistake of forgetting his position."

Jagr shrugged. He wasn't indifferent to the debt and loyalty owed to Viper. The truth was he was in a pissy mood, and being stuck in the *chichi* nightclub where there wasn't a damned thing to kill beyond a bunch of dew fairies wasn't helping.

"I can hardly forget when I am forever being commanded to involve myself in affairs that do not concern me, and more importantly, do not interest me."

"What *does* interest you, Jagr?" He held Styx's searching gaze with a flat stare. At last the king grimaced. "Like it or not, you offered your sword when Viper accepted you into his clan."

He didn't like it, but he couldn't argue. Being taken into a clan was the only means of survival among the vampires.

"What would you have of me?"

Styx rose to his feet to round the desk, perching on a corner. The wood groaned beneath the considerable weight, but didn't crack. Jagr could only assume Viper had had all the furniture reinforced.

Smart vampire.

"What do you know of my mate?" Styx abruptly demanded.

Jagr stilled. "Is this a trap?"

A wry smile touched the Anasso's mouth. "I'm not a subtle vampire, Jagr. Unlike the previous Anasso, I have no talent for manipulating and deceiving others. If there comes a day when I feel the need to challenge you, it will be done face-to-face."

"Then why are you asking me about your mate?"

"When I first met Darcy, she knew nothing of her heritage. She had been fostered by humans from the time she was a babe, and it wasn't until Salvatore Giuliani, the current king of the Weres, arrived in Chicago that we discovered she was a pureblood who had been genetically altered."

Jagr flicked a brow upward. That was a little tidbit that the king had kept secret.

"Genetically altered?"

"The Weres are increasingly desperate to produce healthy offspring. The pureblood females have lost their ability to control their shifts during the full moon, which makes it all but impossible to carry a litter to full term. The Weres altered Darcy and her sisters so they would be incapable of shifting."

Jagr folded his arms over his chest. He didn't give a damn about the worthless dogs.

"I presume you will tell me why you have summoned me, before the sun rises?"

Styx narrowed his golden eyes. "That depends entirely on

you r cooperation, :ny brother. I can make this meeting last as lon z as I desire."

Jagr's lips twitched. The one thing he respected was power. "Please continue."

"Darcy's mother gave birth to a litter of four daughters, all genetically altered, and all stolen from the Weres shortly after their births."

"Why were they stolen?"

"That remains a mystery Salvatore has never fully explained." There was an edge in the Anasso's voice that warned he wasn't pleased by the lack of information. "What we do know is that one of Darcy's sisters was discovered in St. Louis, being held captive by an imp named Culligan."

"He's fortunate that she's incapable of shifting. A pure-blood could rip out the throat of an imp."

"From what Salvatore could discover, the imp managed to get his hands on Regan when she was just a child, and kept her locked in a cage coated with silver. That is when he wasn't torturing her for a quick buck."

Torture.

The Dutch masterpieces hanging on the walls crashed to the floor at Jagr's flare of fury.

"Do you wish the Were rescued?"

Styx grimaced. "Salvatore already freed her from Culligan, although the damned imp managed to slip away before Salvatore could eat him for dinner."

Jagr's brief flare of hope that the night wasn't a total waste was brought to a sharp end. Slaughtering bastards who tormented the weak was one of his few pleasures.

"If the woman was rescued, why do you need me?"

Styx straightened, his bulk consuming a considerable amount of the office space.

"Salvatore's only interest in Regan was installing her as his queen and primary breeder. He is determined to secure his power base by providing a mate who is capable of restoring the purebloods' dwindling population. Unfortunately, once he freed Regan, he discovered she was infertile."

"So she was of no use."

"Precisely." The towering Aztec was careful to keep his composure, but even an idiot could sense he wouldn't mind making a snack of the Were king. "That is why he contacted Darcy. He intended to send Regan to Chicago so she could be under my protection until he established her in the St. Louis Were pack."

"And?"

"And she managed to escape while he was conferring with the local pack master."

Jagr grunted in disgust. "This Salvatore is pathetically inefficient. First he allows the imp to escape, and then the woman. It's little wonder the Weres are declining in number."

"Let us hope you are more efficient."

Jagr rose to his feet, his expression cold. "Me?"

"Darcy is concerned for her sister. I want her found and brought to Chicago."

"The woman has made it fairly obvious she doesn't want to come."

"Then it will be your job to convince her."

Jagr narrowed his gaze. He wasn't a damned Mary Poppins. Hell, he would eat Mary Poppins for breakfast.

"Why me?"

"I've already sent several of my best trackers to St. Louis, but you're my finest warrior. If Regan has managed to run into trouble, you will be needed to help rescue her."

There were no doubt worse things than chasing after a genetically altered Were who clearly didn't want to be found, but he couldn't think of one off the top of his head.

In the outer room, the sounds of a string quartet resumed, along with soft "ohhs" and "ahhs" from the audience as the dew fairies continued their delicate dance. Jagr could suddenly think of one thing worse than chasing after the Were.

Remaining trapped in this hellhole.

"Why should I do this?" he rasped.

"Because what makes Darcy happy makes me happy." Styx moved until they were nose to nose, his power digging into Jagr's flesh. "Clear enough?"

"Painfully clear."

"Good." Styx stepped back and released his power. Slipping his hand beneath his leather coat, he pulled out a cell phone and tossed it to Jagr. "Here. The phone has the numbers of the brothers who are searching for Regan, as well as contacts in St. Louis. It also has my private line. Contact me when you find Regan."

Jagr pocketed the phone and headed for the door. There was no point in arguing. Styx was struggling to force the vampires out of their barbaric past, but it wasn't a freaking democracy.

Not even close.

"I will leave within the hour."

"Jagr."

Halting at the door, Jagr turned with a searing fury. "What?"

Styx didn't so much as flinch. "Do not forget for one moment that Regan is precious cargo. If I discover you have left so much as a bruise on her pretty skin, you won't be pleased with the consequences."

"So I'm to track down a rabid Were who doesn't want to be found, and haul her to Chicago without leaving a mark?"

"Obviously the rumors of your extraordinary intelligence were not exaggerated, my brother."

With a hiss, Jagr turned and stormed through the shattered opening. "I'm not your brother."

Viper monitored Jagr's furious exit with a wary gaze.

Actually it hadn't gone as bad as he had feared. No death or mutilation. Not even a maiming.

Always a plus.

Still, he knew Jagr too well. Of all his clansmen, he had always known that the ancient Visigoth was the most feral. Understandable after what he'd endured, but no less dangerous. He was beginning to regret having brought the tortured vampire to Styx's attention.

Slipping past the seated demons who were once again enthralled with the dew fairies, Viper returned to the office, finding Styx staring out the window.

"I have a bad feeling about this," he muttered, his gaze taking in his priceless paintings, lying shattered on the floor.

Styx turned, his arms folded over his chest. "A premonition? Shall I contact the Commission and inform them they have a potential Oracle?"

Viper arched a warning brow. "Only if you want me to lock you in a cell with Levet for the next century."

Styx gave a sharp bark of laughter. "A nice bluff, but Levet has decided that he is the only one capable of tracking Darcy's missing sister. He left for St. Louis as soon as Salvatore informed me that Regan had slipped from his grasp."

"Perfect, now we have two loose cannons charging about Missouri. I'm not sure the natives will survive."

"You believe Jagr is a loose cannon?"

Viper grimaced, recalling the night that Jagr had appeared at his lair requesting asylum. He had encountered any number of lethal demons, most of whom wanted nothing more than to kill him. He'd never, however, until that night, looked into the eyes of another and seen only death.

"I think beneath all that grim control, he's a step from slipping into madness."

"And yet you allowed him to become a clansman."

Viper shrugged. "When he petitioned, my first inclination was to refuse. I could sense he was not only dangerously close to the edge, but that he was powerful and aggressive enough to challenge me as clan chief. He's a leader by nature, not a follower."

"So why allow him into Chicago?"

"Because he swore an oath to disappear into his lair and not offer any trouble."

"And?" Styx prodded.

"And I knew he wouldn't survive if he were without the protection of a clan," Viper grudgingly admitted. "We both know that despite your attempts to civilize the vampires, some habits are too deeply ingrained to be easily changed. A rogue vampire with that much power would be seen as a threat to any chief. He would be destroyed."

"So you took mercy."

Viper frowned. He didn't like being thought of as anything but a ruthless bastard. He hadn't become clan chief because of any sensitivity bullshit. He was leader because the other vampires were scared he'd rip out their undead hearts.

"Not mercy—it was a calculated decision," he growled. "I knew if the need ever arose, he would prove an invaluable ally. Of course, I assumed that I would need him as a warrior, not as a babysitter for a young, vulnerable Were. I'm not entirely comfortable sending him on such a mission."

Styx grasped the medallion that always hung about his neck, revealing he was not nearly as confident in his decision as he would have Viper believe.

"I need Regan found, and Jagr has the intelligence and skills that are best suited to track her and keep her safe. And he possesses an even more important quality."

"It can't be his sparkling personality."

"No, it's his intimate knowledge of the anguish Regan has suffered." Styx regarded him with a somber expression. "He, better than any of us, will understand what Regan needs now that she has been freed from her tormentor."

Chapter 1

The campground a few miles south of Hannibal, Missouri, was like any other campground.

Oversized RVs parked on the barren ground, a row of portable potties in the back, and a small shack near the front entrance where the humans paid for the privilege of being crammed next to people they wanted to throttle by the end of their vacation.

Regan Garrett knew all about the throttling thing firsthand.

Granted, she wasn't human, but she had spent the majority of her life in one campground or another. They were breeding grounds for homicide.

Indifferent to the threat of impending mass murder, Regan swiftly jogged through the neat columns of RVs. She had deliberately waited until it was late enough that the old folks would have their dentures in a glass and their wrinkled asses in bed, while the younger parents would be comatose after a day of unrelieved suffering at the hands of their children.

Midnight in Hannibal, and not a creature was stirring.

Reluctantly, she turned to jog back toward the shack that had its door closed against the late March air. The chill didn't trouble Regan, despite the fact she was wearing nothing more than a pair of jeans and a sleeveless knit top. She might not possess the ability to shift or procreate, but she did have most of the werewolf's talents.

She was faster and stronger than humans, temperatures didn't trouble her, she could see perfectly in the dark, and she had a remarkable ability to heal any wound not inflicted with silver.

Her feet briefly faltered. It was that ability to heal that had . . .

No. Not now.

She had to focus. She would grieve the past once Culligan was dead.

For the past ten hours she'd been on the imp's trail, following his scent from St. Louis to the edge of Hannibal. She could almost taste her revenge when his trail mysteriously vanished on the outskirts of town. She didn't know how the son of a bitch had managed to disappear into thin air, but it wasn't going to stop her.

One way or another, she was finding the man who had held her captive for the past thirty years, and paying him back a hundredfold.

Not bothering to knock, Regan shoved open the door to the shack and stepped in. It was a cramped space, the walls covered with glossy pamphlets proclaiming all the wondrous sights to see in Hannibal, and one narrow window that overlooked the park.

At first glance the place looked empty, but Regan didn't miss the cigarette smoke that hung in the air. Moving to the Formica counter at the far end of the room, she banged on the small silver bell.

There was the muffled sound of cursing, then a door behind the counter was shoved open, and a shaggy head poked out.

"Yeah?" The boy, who couldn't have been more than eighteen, with a nose too big for his narrow face, stiffened as his pale eyes skimmed over Darcy's long, golden blond hair and down her slender body. Slowly they lifted to study the green eyes that dominated her pale heart-shaped face. A goofy smile curved his lips as he stepped into the room and leaned against the counter. "Helloooo. What's up?"

"I'm looking for a friend."

"You just found him, doll. Give me ten minutes to lock up, and I'm all yours."

As if.

Regan resisted the urge to smash the overlarge nose, barely. Instead, she pulled out the folded page she had ripped from a magazine before leaving St. Louis.

"Have you seen an RV that looks like this?"

The kid barely glanced at the picture. "Do I look like that freak from *Monk*? I take the money, I give them a card to put on their dash, and that's the end of it. I don't give a shit what their RV looks like."

"You would have noticed this one. The driver has long red hair and eyes like a cat. He's very . . . distinctive."

"There's no one here who doesn't have gray hair and dentures." The boy shuddered. "I have nightmares that one day I'll look out there and nothing will be left but corpses and rotting RVs."

"Charming."

The goofy smile widened. "You could take my mind off the nasty geriatrics and their imminent death. I have a cot in the back."

Regan once again eyed the protruding beak. Targets didn't come more tempting. Unfortunately, she couldn't afford to attract attention. Humans always made such a fuss over bit of blood and a few broken bones.

"Not even if you came giftwrapped," she muttered, turning to leave.

"Hey . . ."

Whatever he had to say was cut off as Regan slammed the door and jogged toward the nearby road leading into Hannibal.

This was the last RV park in the area. Her only hope now was that she could pick up Culligan's trail somewhere in town.

He couldn't have just vanished.

Not only was Culligan a greedy sadist, but he was also a pathetic imp. Unlike many of his kind, he didn't have the skill to create portals to travel. Hell, he could barely form a hex.

Which meant he was either in his RV, or on foot.

Five hours later, she'd jogged through every street in town, finding nothing more than the usual drunken humans and a handful of sprites dancing in the gathering fog.

Damn. She was hungry, weary to the bone, and in no condition to battle Culligan, even if she did run across him. As much as it ticked her off, it was time to call it a night.

Angling back toward the main highway that snaked through town, Regan ignored the scent of food that wafted from the few fast-food restaurants that remained open. She had stolen money from Salvatore before leaving St. Louis, but it would only last so long. For now she preferred the protection of four walls and a locked door while she slept to easing the empty ache in her belly.

She returned to the hotel that she'd booked earlier (one of a dozen that had Mark Twain emblazoned in the name), in the hopes she would need a place to stash a beaten and bloody imp. That hope was shot to hell for the moment, but at least she could look forward to a hot shower and clean bed.

Keeping her head lowered, she limped across the nondescript lobby, nodding toward the nondescript front desk clerk, and climbing the nondescript stairs. No matter how tired she might be, she wasn't willing to enter the elevator. She'd been trapped the majority of her life in a tiny silver cell. Not an act of God, or a promised date with the Jonas Brothers could haul her back into one.

She reached the fifth floor, absently rubbing her arms as a chill crawled over her. Strange. She never felt the cold. Obviously, she was even more tired than she thought.

Halting at her door, she slid her card into the lock and pressed it open. It wasn't until steely arms wrapped about her that she realized the danger.

Shit. The cold prickling over her skin wasn't from the temperature, it was from a damned vampire. And she had waltzed into his arms as if she didn't have any more sense than a freaking human.

Momentarily frozen with shock, Regan was abruptly catapulted into action as the vampire kicked shut the door and attempted to drag her further into the dark room.

Calling upon her waning strength, Regan pretended to slump in her attacker's arms, pulling them far enough downward so that when she abruptly slammed her head backward, she managed to hit him flush in the face.

There was a muffled curse, but the arms holding her hostage didn't loosen. In fact, they tightened with a brutal force, hiking her closer as the heavy body slammed her to the carpeted floor, landing on top of her and knocking the air from her lungs.

She was well and truly trapped, but that didn't stop her from struggling. Okay, it was more like a fish futilely flopping on the bank of a river. Still, it made her feel like she was doing something. Just like she used to taunt and mock Culligan, despite the fact that he was bound to beat the hell out of her for it.

"What do you want?" she gritted. "Tell me now or I swear I'll stake you."

A dark, utterly male chuckle whispered over her face. "And they claim I have no social skills." There was a pause, and Regan sensed the vampire's mind reach out to brush against hers. "Hold still."

She tried to free a leg so she could knee him in the nuts. "That shit doesn't work on me, vampire."

He growled low in his throat. "Regan, stop this. I don't want to hurt you."

Regan stilled in shock. "How do you know my name?"

There was a prickle of power, and suddenly the lamp beside the bed flared with light.

"I was sent by Darcy to bring you to Chicago."

Regan barely heard the low, slightly raspy words. Holy . . . crap.

She was a woman who'd spent her life surrounded by demons, many who could make *GQ* models weep with envy, but none could compare to the vampire currently lodged on top of her.

A delicious, heart-stopping, edible hunk of eye candy.

His body was hard and chiseled with more muscles than any man had a right to possess. His long hair, two shades a paler gold than hers, was pulled into a tight braid, emphasizing the ice-blue eyes. His features appeared to be carved from the finest marble, the lines and angles so perfect they could only have been formed by the hand of a master. His nose was aquiline, his cheekbones angular beneath the smooth ivory skin, his brow wide, and his lips . . . they were hard, but precisely chiseled. The sort of lips that made a woman wonder what they would feel like exploring hot, intimate places.

A shocking heat clenched her lower muscles, infuriating Regan. Christ, the demon was here at the bidding of her interfering sister, not to offer relief to a lonely, sex-starved Were.

Not that she would spread her legs, even if this was just a random encounter, she sternly told herself. Okay, he was hot enough to make her bones melt, and the scent of raw male power was making her head dizzy, but . . .

Stop it, you idiot. This wasn't a man. He was a lethal vampire who could drain her dry in a heartbeat.

"Darcy sent you?" she snapped.

The frozen blue eyes narrowed, his nose flaring as if catching scent of her stupid awareness. Which was ridiculous. Wasn't it?

"Yes."

"Well, who died and made her queen?" she mocked.

"The Anasso."

Regan blinked in confusion. "What?"

His gaze briefly swept over her pale face before lifting to clash with her uneasy glare.

"You asked who died to make Darcy queen," he retorted. "Her mate Styx killed the previous King of Vampires, which made him the current leader, and your sister queen."

Well, of course she was a freaking queen.

She'd never met Darcy, or any of her three sisters for that matter, but she'd learned from Salvatore that Darcy was currently mated to a vampire who not only adored her, but had just purchased a flipping mansion on the outskirts of Chicago for her. No doubt she was also drenched in diamonds, and attended the opera on a regular basis.

Not that Regan wanted all that froufrou crap. She'd rather be stabbed in the eye than put on a dress. Still, her sister's cushy lifestyle was a thorn in Regan's side.

Her family had abandoned her to the hands of a psychotic imp who had relentlessly abused her for thirty years. As far as she was concerned, the entire bunch of them could go screw themselves.

"Awesome, my sister is married to a genocidal maniac," she drawled. "And people wonder why I'm not leaping at the chance to get to know my family."

"Styx is no more genocidal than any other vampire. Or Were, for that matter."

She snorted at the flat, emotionless tone. "Are you trying to reassure me? If so, you suck at it."

"My only duty is to escort you to Chicago."

"Duty?"

"Yes."

Freaking perfect. This gorgeous hunk of man was nothing more than a flunky for her sister.

She pressed her hands against the unyielding wall of his

chest. "Well, consider yourself officially off duty, because I have no intention of going."

"Your sister is concerned. She only desires to protect you."

His low, hypnotizing voice tingled down her spine even as his words pissed her off.

"Yeah, and where was all that sisterly concern when I was being held captive by a monster?"

His stark, beautiful face was without mercy. "You're free now, aren't you? Be grateful."

"I don't want to be grateful, and I sure as hell don't want to have my supposed sister pretending she gives a damn after all these years. Tell her to take her concern and shove it up her . . ."

His head swooped down, his lips claiming her mouth in a kiss that was raw and demanding, and shocking as hell.

Regan had braced herself for the familiar blow. Even a savage bite to her neck. She wasn't prepared for the sensation of cool, skillful lips parting her mouth, or the oddly erotic press of fangs.

The treacherous heat returned with a vengeance, flowing through her trembling body and tightening her muscles with the promise of beckoning pleasure.

He tasted of brandy and temptation, his hard body pressed against her most intimate places. She wanted to rip off the black T-shirt that looked spray-painted to his muscled bulk, and rub against the wide chest.

She wanted . . .

God, she just wanted.

With a groan, she allowed his tongue to slip between her lips, sucking it gently as her hips instinctively arched upward. Never in her life had she ever felt the touch of a man's hand. Not unless it was to dole out punishment. Now her body was changing, altering as his kiss deepened.

Her lips softened, her nipples hardened to tight points,

nearly begging to be stroked, her fingers spread across the chiseled muscles of his chest.

Then, as swiftly as he'd kissed her, the vampire pulled back to regard her with a strange expression of wariness. As if he was as caught off guard by her volatile reaction as she was.

Embarrassed, Regan smacked her hands against his chest. Damn the bastard. She'd just made a fool of herself, and it was entirely his fault.

"What the hell do you think you're doing?"

His features smoothed into an unreadable expression. "Darcy is my queen. You're not allowed to insult her without consequences."

"You consider rape a consequence?"

"It was a kiss, nothing more, and the only means to stop your childish whining without leaving a bruise."

"You bastard." Smack, smack, smack. "I have every right to whine after what I've suffered. You have no idea . . ."

"You're not stupid enough to believe that you're the only one who has ever suffered," he said, overriding her words, his voice edged with ice. "It's done. Move on."

Her jaw clenched. Damn the cold bastard. It was bad enough he had gotten her all hot and bothered while he remained Mr. Freeze, but now he was dismissing her years of torture as if she were nothing but a sulky child.

"I would love to move on, but it's a little difficult with freaking Hulk Hogan squashing me. Get off."

His eyes narrowed. "What do you know of vampires?"

"That you're evil, soulless bastards who care about nothing but yourself."

"We're also stronger, faster, and far more lethal than Weres."

"And your point?"

"I'm going to release you, but know that if you annoy me, I won't hesitate to tie you to the bed and shove a gag in your mouth."

She didn't doubt the threat. Not even for a minute. Of

course, in her life, being tied and gagged didn't rate high on the fright-o-meter.

"Charming."

"Do you understand?"

"I understand that someday I'm going to shove a stake up your ass."

A golden brow flicked upward. "That would not kill me."

"No, but it'll be funny as hell."

Something that could have almost been a smile touched his mouth before swiftly disappearing.

"Not nearly as amusing as seeing you try."

"Jackass."

He regarded her for a long, silent moment, almost as if he was searching past her defensive aggression to the terrified woman beneath.

It was unnerving as hell.

"Will you behave yourself?" he at last demanded.

She blew out a sigh, knowing she would never get the aggravating man off her until she agreed. And she really needed him off.

Her mind might be contemplating the best means of kicking some vampire ass, but her body was still enjoying the sensations of his hard parts pressing against her soft parts.

"Fine, just get off," she muttered.

With one smooth, fluid motion, the vampire was on his feet, looming over her. She had a brief moment to appreciate the faded jeans that molded to his powerful legs, and the motorcycle boots that covered his Shaq-sized feet, before he reached down to grasp her hand and jerk her upright.

With a gasp at the electric charge that jolted up her arm, Regan wrenched her hand from his grasp and backed away. She didn't give a damn if it made her look weak. She needed space.

And maybe a wooden stake.

"How did you find me?" she demanded.

He folded his arms over his chest, appearing even more dangerously beautiful now that he was upright.

"It wasn't difficult." His low, mesmerizing voice filled the room. "Once I reached St. Louis, I simply followed the trail of the imp, knowing you wouldn't be far behind."

"And how would you know that?"

The ice-blue gaze regarded her steadily. "As I said, you aren't the only one familiar with suffering. And I know when a demon, no matter how tiny, is released from captivity, the only thought on their mind is revenge. You want the imp dead."

Her chin tilted. What the hell would this vampire know of suffering? He lived smack-dab on top of the food chain.

"If you're so smart, then you know I have no intention of allowing Culligan to escape. You can go back to Chicago and tell my sister thanks, but no thanks."

"There is nothing that would please me more than to return to my lair and leave you to your business. Unfortunately, that's not an option."

"Oh, it's an option. Just turn around and walk out the door."

"I was commanded to bring you to Chicago, and that means I'm not allowed to leave here without you. Not unless I'm willing to face the wrath of my king. Which—" His gaze seared a path down her tightly clenched body, lingering a terrifying moment on the pulse fluttering at the base of her throat, before returning to her wide eyes. "I'm not."

Great. Her Knight in Shining Armor had not only showed up thirty years too late, but he was only there under threat of some horrible retribution.

It was enough to make a woman feel all warm and fuzzy. Not.

"Then we have a serious problem, Hulk freaking Hogan, because I'm not going."

"Jagr."

"What?"

"My name is Jagr."

"Of course it is," she muttered. The name was just as hard, dangerous, and beautiful as the rest of him.

"I could force you to come with me."

"Over my dead body."

That hit-and-run smile touched his mouth. "Don't tempt me."

Regan stomped her foot, at the end of her patience. "Dammit, would you just go away?"

"No."

"Fine." She marched across the tiny room that had been decorated in the seventies, all hideous swirling blues and greens, with cheap furniture and fading prints of flowers on the walls. Reaching the door to the connecting bathroom, she wrenched it open.

"What are you doing?"

She turned her head to stab the intruder with a frustrated glare. "You've managed to turn a perfectly rotten day into a masterpiece of misery, so either you truss me up and haul me to Chicago, or I'm taking a hot shower."

Jagr stood perfectly still as Regan stepped into the bathroom and slammed the door.

For the first time in centuries, he found himself . . . conflicted.

The grim logic—that was the only means of keeping his lethal fury in check—warned him to toss the Were over his shoulder and return her to Chicago. It was not only what he'd been commanded to do, but the sooner he was done with this stupid mission, the sooner he could return to his peaceful existence.

But another part, a part he hadn't experienced in years and was not at all pleased to discover he still possessed, was reluctant to take such an irrevocable step.

It was nothing more than common sense, he was swift to excuse his odd hesitation. What was the point of hauling her to Chicago when she was bound to flee at the first opportunity?

The gods knew he wasn't lucky enough for Styx to pick someone else to hunt her down.

Perfectly reasonable. Unfortunately, Jagr was too intelligent to entirely dismiss his chaotic reaction to the beautiful woman.

He was a vampire who preferred his life, his battles, and his sex uncomplicated.

Regan was anything but uncomplicated.

She was a tangled mess of fury, aggression, vulnerability, wry humor, and frustrated sensuality.

A sensuality that wakened a hunger that now roared through him with brutal force.

He wanted her. And he sure as hell wasn't turning her over to Styx until he'd had a taste.

Or two.

Counting to a hundred, Jagr was prepared when Regan cracked open the door and peered back into the room. He hadn't believed for a moment she intended to strip naked and take a shower while a lethal predator stood just a few feet away. She was furious, not stupid.

Yanking open the door, she glared at him with impotent anger.

"Christ, are you still here?"

He regarded her in silence. He'd discovered over the centuries that it rarely took more to rattle an opponent. For a crazed moment she tried to match him stare for stare, then with a muttered curse, she marched forward to stand directly before him.

"What the hell is it going to take to get rid of you? Money? Blood? Sex?"

His gaze drifted down to her small, perfectly rounded breasts. "Which are you offering?"

She took a hasty step back. "None of the above."

"A pity." He lifted his gaze. "Then it would seem that I am staying. Tell me of the imp."

"What?"

"I said, tell-me-of-the-imp."

Her eyes narrowed at his slow, deliberate words.

"Why?"

"You obviously won't leave until he's dead, so I intend to put an end to this farce so I can return to the peace of my lair."

"No." She planted her hands on her hips. "No one kills Culligan except me."

He arched a brow. "You expect him to stroll into your hotel room so you can beat him to death with a pillow?"

"I intend to rip out his throat with my bare hands."

"What are you waiting for?"

Her lips thinned. "I lost the scent of the damned bastard at the edge of Hannibal." There was a beat, then without warning, she stepped forward to grasp his arm. "Wait. You said you tracked Culligan to find me. Where is he?"

Jagr's expression never altered, but his entire body tensed as a scalding heat rushed through him at her urgent touch.

Regan wasn't the first woman he'd desired. Far from it. But never had his need been so ruthless, so raw, so primitive.

"So now you want my help?" he demanded, his voice as cool and controlled as ever. It was the ability to keep his emotions hidden that had allowed him to survive centuries of torture.

"If it leads me to Culligan." Her fingers tightened, revealing she possessed all the strength of a pureblood. "Do you know where he is hiding, or not?"

"No."

"But . . ."

"Like you, I lost his trail at the edge of town. That's where I picked up your scent."

"Damn." She dropped her hand and stepped back. Jagr swallowed his low growl of disappointment. "How could his trail just disappear?"

"Most imps can create portals to move through long distances."

"Not Culligan." Her lips twisted with a grim satisfaction. "He's a weak, pathetic bully who can barely cast a hex."

Jagr shrugged. "Then he could be dead, although it's far more likely he had assistance in covering his presence."

He watched the frustration ripple over Regan's delicate features. They weren't an exact replica of Darcy's. Her eyes were a darker emerald, her brows more gold than blond, and her expression was hardened by years of abuse. But overall, she shared Darcy's fragile, heartrending beauty.

The sort of fragility that made even a scarred recluse want to toss her over his shoulder and take her somewhere he could keep her safe.

Unaware of his shocking thoughts, Regan furrowed her brow. "How would he cover his presence? A witch?"

"A witch would have the power. But, of course, so would any number of demons."

"Great." The green eyes flashed with irritation. "You're a butt-load of help. So glad you showed up."

"It was because the imp's trail ended that I asked you to tell me of him. I need to know more before I can decide how best to lure him from the shadows." He lifted his brows as she regarded him with a stubborn expression. "Regan?"

"I don't want your help."

He narrowed his gaze, knowing he had to take a stand. This woman was so blinded by her need for revenge, she couldn't think clearly. If she wasn't to end up back in Culligan's power, or dead, he would have to find some means to keep her distracted while he considered the best means of flushing the imp into the open.

"And I don't want to be trapped playing nanny to a pint-sized Were with even less charm than myself." His voice was sheer ice. "Unfortunately we're stuck with one another until I hand you over to Darcy, and you can devote yourself to making her life a misery."

She quivered with rage. "Pint-sized?"

"I believe that's the current term used to describe a smaller than usual object."

"Why you son of a . . ."

The crack of gunshots interrupted the angry tirade, the sound so unexpected that the bullets smashed though the window before Jagr was able to launch forward and force Regan to the floor. His teeth clenched in pain, his thoughts dark with fury.

He had protected the more delicate Were, but three of the bullets had lodged in his back, the fourth slicing through his arm to create a nasty gash.

Not life-threatening injuries, but they left him too weak to battle whoever was attacking them.

Shit.

If he survived this, Styx was going to kill him.

Chapter 2

Shocked by the sudden attack, not to mention the six-foot-plus vampire that had just landed on top of her, Regan struggled to clear the fog from her mind.

What the hell?

She knew enough to realize someone had shot through the window. And that Jagr had quite likely saved her from a nasty injury.

What she didn't know was why.

It couldn't have been Culligan. The few times the imp had tried to use a gun, he hadn't been able to hit the broadside of a barn. Besides, if he'd come gunning for her, he would have brought a rocket launcher. The son of a bitch knew he had one chance, and one chance only, to kill her before she ripped out his throat.

Jagr's groan jolted her out of her inane thoughts, and Regan wriggled from beneath his heavy body. He was too weak to protest, lying face-down on the carpet to reveal the brutal injuries that were even now oozing with a frightening amount of blood.

A flare of terror raced through her.

Jagr might be an annoying ass, but he'd just taken a number

of bullets for her. She didn't want the guilt of his wounds on her conscience.

Besides, whoever was shooting at them was probably still out there. Or else headed up to the room to finish them off.

She couldn't just run off and leave the damned vamp to be murdered while he was injured. Which meant she needed him healed, and healed fast.

Struggling to recall what little she knew of vampires, she tensed at the sound of approaching footsteps, her heart stopping as the door to the room was suddenly thrown open.

Prepared for battle, Regan was caught off guard by the strange creature who waddled into the room. The thing possessed the grotesque features of a gargoyle—thick gray skin, reptilian eyes, horns, and cloven hooves. He even had a long tail that trailed behind him. But while Regan had never actually seen a gargoyle, she'd always presumed they were more than three feet tall, and that their wings were leather, not delicate bits of gossamer that were far too pretty for a ruthless savage.

Still, you didn't have to be a nine-foot fire-breathing demon to pull a trigger. The miniature creature might very well be the one taking potshots at them.

"Get out," she rasped, instinctively crawling to place herself between the intruder and the wounded Jagr.

Ignoring her command, the . . . thing moved forward to peer down at the vampire, and then, of all things, spoke with a lilting French accent.

"What happened, *mon ami?*"

Jagr groaned. "Damn Styx. If I live through this, I'm going to make him pay."

Somewhat reassured that the two seemed to know one another, Regan frowned at the stranger.

"Who the hell are you?"

"A masterpiece of misery," Jagr muttered, echoing her earlier words.

Shockingly, the creature blew a raspberry toward the vampire who could squash him without a thought.

"I am the demon who is about to save you and your Gothic friend's ass," he announced grandly. "Just lay there and bleed, Jagr, while I work my mojo."

Regan watched Jagr's eyes snap open with genuine horror, his hand reaching out to weakly grab at the creature. The tiny beast was too quick, and with a flick of his tail, he was hurrying to scramble onto the window ledge, his tiny arms outstretched.

"No." Jagr moaned, and then without warning, his arm snaked around her waist and she found herself yanked down beside him. "Stay down."

"What?" Regan glared at the vampire. "Dammit, Jagr, you're hurt . . ." Her lecture was once again interrupted as a brilliant flash of light filled the room, swiftly followed by a deafening boom. "Christ," she breathed, wondering if the Air Force had arrived and decided Hannibal needed bombing. "What the hell was that?"

She heard the patter of footsteps, and the gray creature returned to stand beside them.

"That was salvation, *ma petite,*" he assured her, leaning over Jagr. "How bad is it, vampire?"

Jagr reached up to grab the beast's arm. "Did you kill them?"

"They're most certainly toasty, if not dead. They will not be troubling us for a while."

A hint of relief touched Jagr's tight features. "Did you see them?"

The creature gave a flap of his wings. "No, but I smelled them. Yuck."

"Tell me."

"Cur."

Jagr frowned. "Cur, not Were?"

"Has your brain dribbled away with your blood, *mon ami?*

I am a gargoyle with exquisite skills. I know the difference between a Were and a cur."

"Why the hell would a cur be shooting at us?" Jagr muttered.

"The better question is: who wouldn't want to shoot you?"

Regan barely noted the sharp exchange, regarding the stranger with a disbelieving frown.

"You're really a . . . gargoyle?"

The gargoyle performed a small bow, his wings fluttering to create a dazzling rainbow of red and blue and gold.

"Levet, at your service, my beauty. I was sent by your sister to escort you to Chicago."

Regan struggled to a sitting position. "Jesus, was there anyone in Chicago she didn't send?"

Levet shrugged. "She's concerned for you."

Before Regan could respond, Jagr hissed with impatience. "We can discuss Darcy and her evil sense of humor later. For now we must concentrate on leaving this hotel before the humans call the police."

Levet snorted. "While I would be perfectly content to sign off on your death warrant, Jagr, there's the teeniest tiniest chance I might need you to help keep Regan safe. You can't be moved in your condition."

"Blood . . ." Jagr rasped.

Levet held up his hands and stepped hastily back. "Sorry, fresh out."

Jagr's eyes fluttered shut, as if he were on the verge of losing consciousness.

"The hospital . . . blood bank . . ." he murmured weakly.

Regan gritted her teeth. Damn. Jagr was right about the humans calling for the cops. And the last thing they needed right now was another battle with guns blazing.

"Screw that, we don't have time." Blowing out an aggravated sigh, Regan pressed her wrist to Jagr's mouth. As much as she hated to admit it, she owed the damned vampire. "Here."

His lids lifted to reveal those stunning ice-blue eyes. "Regan?"

"Just do it before I decide to leave your ass here for the cops to haul off to the morgue."

"Ew." With a flutter of his wings, the gargoyle hurried toward the door leading to the hallway. "I'll go keep watch and make sure your dinner isn't interrupted."

"Regan, you are certain?" Jagr demanded, his voice thicker, with an odd accent and strange speech pattern.

Certain? Christ, no. She didn't have clue what was about to happen. Well, nothing beyond a great deal of pain when those huge fangs sank into her flesh.

Thankfully, she was no coward, and if Jagr needed blood to get him up and moving, then by God, he was going to get blood.

"Do you need an engraved invitation?" she taunted, not at all surprised when his mouth widened and his fangs slid smoothly into her wrist. Jagr was not a vampire to back down from a direct challenge. Regrettably, her plan had neglected one small detail.

She was braced for pain. She was even braced for the necessity of ripping him forcibly from her flesh if he lost his head and tried to take more than she was willing to offer.

What she wasn't prepared for was the realization that far from painful, the sensation that jolted through her was one of intense, relentless pleasure.

"Oh . . ." Her eyes drifted shut as she felt him suck deeply of her blood, every pull tightening the coiling bliss that was lodged in the pit of her stomach. "Shit . . ."

Her entire body trembled, the same excitement that had set her on fire when he'd kissed her blazing through her body. Only this time it was more powerful, more driving, more . . . explosive. Her free hand landed flat on the floor as her body bent forward, nearly toppling her onto Jagr's prostrate form. She was drowning, lost in the dark, intoxicating desire.

In a distant corner of her mind, she heard Jagr's low moan of satisfaction, or perhaps it was pleasure. At the moment, she didn't care which it was. She was too caught in the sweet building tension that gripped her with breathtaking force.

He sucked again and again, forcing the pleasure to near pain. God almighty. She couldn't stand any more. There had to be something . . . something . . .

And then it happened. The pleasure reached a critical mass, and exploded with enough force to wrench a low scream from her throat.

Toppling forward, her face landed squarely on Jagr's hard chest, the rich scent of his male power mingling with the lingering convulsions that rocked her body.

Boneless and floating on a tide of sweet lethargy, Regan battled to regain command of her shaken body. Holy crap. She sucked in a deep, rasping breath. Then with an effort, she lifted her head and wrenched open her heavy lids.

Only to encounter Jagr's ice-blue gaze.

"Damn you," she husked, her heartbeat still thundering in her ear.

With a deliberate motion, the vampire gently licked the two pinpricks of blood staining her wrist before allowing her to jerk her arm from his grasp.

"You've never had the bite of a vampire?"

Still too weak to stand, Regan contented herself with scooting backward on her knees, rubbing her already healed wrist on her jeans, as if she could rub away the memories of her raw pleasure.

Fat chance.

She knew beyond all doubt that the sensations would be seared into her brain for all eternity.

"No," she muttered. "Culligan refused to share torturing me with anyone else."

He remained stretched on the floor, his fiercely beautiful features unreadable.

"Do you want an apology?"

"Are you sorry?"

"Not in the least. Your blood is far more potent than that of a human, and better yet"—his gaze swept down her tense body—"I now know the sweet cries you make when . . ."

"Shut up before I make sure you need another transfusion."

The distant sounds of sirens shattered through the thick tension in the air. In the blink of an eye, Jagr was on his feet, reaching down to jerk her upward in one smooth motion.

"The police. We must get out of here." Stunned by the vampire's remarkable recovery, Regan found herself being hauled toward the broken window. "Can you jump from here?" Jagr demanded.

She flashed him a glare at his ridiculous question, then careful to avoid the jagged shards of glass still stuck in the frame, she climbed through the window and leaped to the sidewalk below.

Slinking into the nearby shadows of the alley, Regan tested the air for any nearby dangers.

There was the usual stench of trash that filled the nearby Dumpsters, the scent of humans stirring to prepare for their early morning shifts, and the unmistakable tang of burnt flesh and blood.

A part of her knew she should cross the street and discover if any of the curs had survived the attack. She needed to know why they attacked. And if they had any connection to Culligan.

Another part, however, realized that she was too weakened by her hours of searching for the imp, not to mention her recent blood donation, to face her enemies alone. Especially not when they carried guns.

Even a cur could shoot her dead if his bullets were silver.

Cursing her current sense of impotence, Regan gave a small jerk when Jagr simply appeared beside her. One minute he wasn't there, and then he was. No sound, no stir of the air, not even a trace of his scent.

It was unnerving.

And maddening.

And . . . a whole host of other things that made her temper snap and snarl.

"What took you so long?" she hissed.

He tossed a heavy leather bag over his shoulder, indifferent to her foul mood.

"We have to go."

Without waiting for her agreement, Jagr grasped her arm and steered her back to the street and headed east. The wolf in Regan growled in protest at being manhandled, but she ignored her instinct to bite.

Not only was she smart enough to know she would need the aggravating vampire to fight off any attackers until she regained her strength, but there was a dark (frighteningly seductive) fear that he would bite back.

They had barely managed to reach the end of the block when there was the sound of flapping wings, and the tiny gargoyle landed directly in front of them. Regan halted, surprised to realize she was pleased to see the strange little beast. He was . . . endearing in his own way.

"Hey, did you think to trench me?" he demanded, his wings obviously ruffled.

"Trench me?" Regan demanded in confusion.

"I believe he means 'ditch me,'" Jagr translated, stabbing Levet with a cold stare. "You deceive yourself, gargoyle, if you think that you can play with me as you do with Styx or Viper. I don't fear any punishment the Anasso could inflict if I decided to put an end to you."

Far from wilting beneath the frigid warning, Levet puffed out his chest, managing to appear almost dignified as he met Jagr's terrifying gaze.

"You need my help, whether you like it or not, vampire.

Perhaps you will recall I was the one who frightened off those attacking curs." He cleared his throat as Jagr regarded him with that unnerving silence. "I can lead you to a cave. I can protect Regan. I have magic . . ."

"Enough." Jagr's clipped voice brought the litany of talents to an abrupt end. "I'm going to regret this."

"Regret what?" Regan demanded warily.

Jagr never allowed his gaze to stray from Levet. "Wait here with Regan. I'll be back."

The gargoyle saluted. "Yes, sir, Mr. Terminator, sir."

"Levet," Jagr breathed.

"*Oui?*"

"Taunt me again and I'll rip off those wings and shove them down your throat."

"You have hostility issues, you know that, vampire?"

"Just keep her safe." And with that, Jagr turned and melted into the shadows.

Regan leaned against the brick front of a local antique shop, too weary to be angered at Jagr's mysterious disappearance, or even at being passed off like a used car. Once she had the opportunity to gather her strength, she would rid herself of her intrusive guardians. Until then . . .

Well, she'd endured worse.

Worse in an epic way.

Her heavy lids drifted downward as she relaxed against the wall, trusting her keen sense of smell to warn of any approaching danger. Five minutes passed, and then another five. At last Levet, who clearly possessed the attention span of a gnat, could stand the silence no longer.

"Sooo . . . you're Darcy's sister," he murmured. "The resemblance is remarkable."

Regan lifted her heavy lids, ignoring the biting anger that flared through her heart at the mention of her sister. Family issues? Nah. Not her.

"I thought gargoyles were bigger?" she said, more to change the subject than to be insulting.

Levet's tail twitched. "I might be vertically challenged, but I assure you that I'm a highly respected warrior among the vampires. Indeed, I'm something of a Knight in Shining Armor. I can't count the number of damsels I've rescued from imminent death and dismemberment, which, of course, is why I was sent to rescue you."

A reluctant smile touched her lips. He looked more like a lawn ornament than a Knight in Shining Armor.

"Why would you help the vampires?"

"It's a way to pass the time until I land my dream position."

"Dream position?"

"Well, I've given up on the whole Vanna thing since Darcy pointed out that I'm not quite tall enough to reach the letters of the puzzle, so I've decided to take over *Deal Or No Deal*. Now that would be a sweet gig."

Regan choked back a laugh. Culligan had been a television junkie, rarely turning off the thing when he was in the RV. Not that Regan complained. It at least offered her a glimpse of the world beyond her silver cage.

"Does Howie Mandel know he's about to become unemployed?" she demanded, shaking off the savage memories.

"I thought I would keep it on the down-low for now. No need for him to go all Britney Spears before I've actually been offered the job."

This time Regan couldn't stop her chuckle. "Very thoughtful."

"That's me, a heart of gold. It's both a blessing . . ." Dramatic pause. "And a curse."

"Yes, I can imagine."

A silence descended, broken only by the song of crickets and distant frogs. It was a comfortable silence. So comfortable that Regan was astonished to discover she didn't mind the gargoyle's company. In fact . . .

No. She swiftly squashed the treacherous thoughts. She didn't want or need a companion. Not Levet, who could make her laugh, and certainly not Jagr, who could piss her off one moment, and the next, wreak sensual havoc with a single bite.

Against her will, Regan found her gaze searching through the darkness, her senses seeking some sign of the MIA vampire. She told herself she didn't give a damn if Jagr had run off and gotten himself killed. One less vampire in the world couldn't be a bad thing. Her only concern was . . . was . . . finding a place to sleep before the humans began filling the streets.

Yeah.

That was it.

Absolutely.

"You can trust him, you know."

Levet's lilting voice interrupted her dark broodings. She turned to find him regarding her with knowing gray eyes.

"What?"

"Jagr." His tiny face twisted in a grimace. "I might not like the coldhearted bastard, but he's a lethal warrior and he has made a pledge to return you safely to Chicago. He will give his own life before he will let you be hurt."

Her fur (metaphorically speaking) was instantly ruffled. "I didn't ask for anyone's help."

Levet snorted. "As if that ever stopped the pushy bastards."

"You mean Darcy?"

"*Sacrebleu,* no." The gargoyle was shocked by the mere suggestion. "I was speaking of the vampires. Darcy possesses the most gentle, most beautiful soul I have ever encountered. There's no one who doesn't love her."

Regan ignored the pang of envy that struck her heart.

"Gentle soul? How the hell did we come from the same womb?"

Levet shrugged. "Life has given you a hardened shell, but your soul is just as pure. Which is no doubt what has Mr. Cold as Ice so on edge. And of course, the fact that you're hot as hell does not hurt."

Regan choked at the ridiculous claims. "You are . . ."

"*Oui?*"

"Very peculiar."

The demon flapped his wings. "Well, that's a fine thing to say to the demon who helped save your life."

Regan shrugged. "I'm peculiar myself. It's not all bad."

"Yeah, well you'd never call Brad Pitt or McDreamy peculiar."

"Tom Cruise."

Levet considered, then nodded. "Valid point."

"Weren't you going to lead us to some caves, gargoyle?" an icy male voice demanded, the only warning that Jagr had silently appeared from the shadows.

The gargoyle squeaked, clapping a hand to his chest. "Holy mother of God, you nearly gave me a heart attack, and not in a good way."

Jagr's eyes narrowed. "The caves."

"And I thought Styx was a grump." With a flick of his tail, Levet turned and waddled down the street in an obvious snit. "This way."

Regan hurried to follow Levet. The last thing she wanted was to be alone with the grim-faced vampire.

Well, that wasn't exactly true.

The *last* thing she wanted was for him to sense the rapid pounding of her heart and the flare of awareness that stained her stupid cheeks with a blush.

What was wrong with her?

Okay, she'd reacted to his bite. And (as much as it griped her to admit it) to his kiss.

Jagr was a vampire. Everyone knew they used sex to lure their prey. And that even the most powerful of demons were susceptible. The only shocker would have been if she didn't respond.

So why was she acting like a freaking preteen with a crush on her teacher?

Pathetic.

Sensing Jagr move to walk by her side, Regan gave herself a mental shake and squared her shoulders. Time to start acting like a mature pureblood.

Whatever the hell that meant.

"Where did you go?" she demanded.

His cool glance slashed in her direction. "I disposed of the bodies."

"Oh."

"Levet was right," he continued smoothly. "They were curs. Three of them. Two were caught in Levet's blast and one managed to escape."

Her steps faltered. "Why aren't we following his trail? Culligan might have sent him."

"I followed the trail. It disappeared four blocks north of here."

"Just like Culligan's."

"Yes." The frosty blue gaze swept over her face. "Did the imp have a lot of contact with the curs during your imprisonment?"

"On occasion." Regan grimaced. "No more than any other of the lowlife demons we encountered during our travels."

"Travels?"

"Culligan never remained in one place more than a few nights. We crisscrossed the country a hundred times."

"What about Hannibal? Did you stay here often?"

"No." Regan shook her head. She'd heard of Hannibal, of course. Built on the edge of the mighty Mississippi River, it was the home of Samuel Clemons (Mark Twain), and the setting for many of his most famous novels. There was also some cave or another that had been the hiding spot for Jesse James (the History Channel was a wonderful thing). A charming town, but hardly a hot spot for demons. "He never even mentioned this place."

Jagr considered her words as they crossed through an

empty parking lot built close to the river. In the darkness, Regan could hear the waters that swirled and eddied around the tethered steamboat tied to the nearby dock.

"Then we can't be certain that Culligan was behind the attack," he at last concluded.

Great. New, mysterious enemies. Just what she needed.

"Why would the curs want to kill me?" she growled, as annoyed by Jagr's cool reaction to her obvious danger as being shot at in the first place. Wasn't he freaking sent to keep her safe? "I thought they worshipped pureblooded Weres?"

A golden brow arched at her churlish tone. "If there's a local Were pack, they might think you're a rogue. Weres are as territorial as vampires."

"But what about the trail disappearing?"

"It's a connection, but for all we know the curs slaughtered Culligan and covered his death with the same magic that hides their scent. We don't know enough to jump to conclusions."

He was right. Only a fool would ignore the possibility that there were other dangers beyond Culligan.

"Damn."

Jagr's icy expression softened at her weary concession. Never breaking stride, he thrust a paper bag into her hand and led her from the parking lot to the tangle of undergrowth that lined the river.

"Here."

Regan frowned. "What's this?"

"Food." His gaze drifted down to her wrist. "You'll need it to replenish the blood I took."

White-hot heat flared through her, squeezing the air from her lungs. She could almost feel his fangs sinking into her flesh, and the sensuous tugs as he took her blood.

Ducking her head down, she ripped open the bag to discover two still warm bagels and a container of orange juice.

Her stomach rumbled in pleasure.

"Thanks," she muttered, keeping her face hidden behind

the thick curtain of her hair as she rapidly worked her way through the bagels.

Jagr retreated to his familiar silence, wise enough not to offer help when they reached a narrow path that led to the high bluff overlooking the river. Her nerves were already on edge. It wouldn't take much to have her striking out, regardless of the consequence.

They climbed without speaking, and reaching the top of the bluff, Regan paused to throw away the empty bag, covertly leaning against the plastic trash can. The path had been a steep one, perilously sapping her waning energy.

In less than a heartbeat Jagr was at her side, his arm wrapping about her waist to haul her against the erotic power of his body.

"Why didn't you ask for help?" he demanded, his dark voice sliding down her spine, sending ripples of pleasure through her.

Oh . . . hell.

She wanted to lean into all that male hardness. To close her eyes and drown in his ruthless strength.

The need was as intense and unwelcome as the awareness that hummed through her body with tiny, electric jolts.

Placing her palms against his chest, she shoved. "I'm fine."

He frowned down at her, refusing to loosen his grip. "You might be dizzy . . ."

She shoved again. "I said I'm fine. Just stop talking about it."

"About what?" His hard lips twitched. "My feeding, or your reaction?"

Lifting her foot, she kicked him as hard as she could in the knee.

It couldn't have hurt. Even at her full power, it would be difficult to injure such an ancient demon. Still, it was enough to catch him off guard. Using the nanosecond of distraction, Regan ducked beneath his arms and rushed toward the gargoyle, who was disappearing into the thick tangle of brush and trees that ran along the bluff.

"I swear to God, one day . . ." she muttered beneath her breath.

She didn't know what she was going to do.

But it was going to be evil.

Chapter 3

The cave that tunneled through the bluff was not large. The main chamber was the size of a human living room, and low enough that Jagr was in constant danger of banging his head. On the plus side, the entrance was narrow enough to prevent more than one attacker from entering at a time, and there was a smaller chamber in the back that had a shallow stream of water that emptied into a basin.

It was not the fact that it was easily defensible, or that there was a ready supply of fresh water, however, that made the cave seemed like a paradise, Jagr decided.

It was the armful of warm Were he had tucked close to his body as he lay on the hard floor.

Leaning on his elbow, Jagr studied Regan's finely carved features. In sleep they appeared even more unbearably fragile. Her skin was a flawless ivory stretched over the perfectly formed brow and tiny nose. Her lips were lush, when not tightened with anger, and her lashes a thick curtain as they lay against her cheeks.

So lovely.

So breathtaking.

And so terrifying in her ability to fascinate him.

Jagr shook his head. He'd lived for centuries. Beautiful

women had drifted in and out of his life with predictable regularity. But none had possessed the golden innocence of her soul. An innocence that the tortured darkness in him craved. As if her purity could soothe away the festering shadows.

And of course, there was the fierce, relentless courage that had allowed her to survive her years of torture.

Culligan had wounded her, but he had never broken her.

He was one of the few who could truly appreciate what it had cost her.

She was completely and utterly unique. A creature like no other he had ever encountered.

A strange hint of warning whispered to his heart. An instinctive awareness that his behavior since arriving in Hannibal was . . . uncharacteristic. The grim control and cool logic that had ruled him for centuries was being undermined by the tiny, ferocious Were currently snuggled against him.

He wasn't sure whether he should be furious or terrified.

Certainly he shouldn't have been . . . smug. As if he'd found a treasure that he hadn't expected and didn't even know he desired.

Perhaps sensing his inner conflict, Regan stirred against his chest. Jagr tightened his grip.

They had barely arrived at the cave when Regan had collapsed in exhaustion. For all her power and stubborn determination, she'd pushed herself too hard for too long and her body had simply shut down.

Without hesitation, Jagr had carried her to the back of the cave, placing her against the wall and lying down so he was between her unconscious form and the distant entrance. Nothing would be allowed to get to her without coming through him first.

At the time he'd told himself it was for her protection. He had made a pledge to keep her safe, and by the gods, that's what he would do.

But no matter how he tried to twist logic, he knew it wasn't a mere need to protect that led him to tenderly cradle her in his arms, or to awaken well before sunset just so he could study her pale, perfect face.

With a flutter, she lifted her thick tangle of lashes, revealing the emerald eyes that were still clouded by sleep.

There was a moment as she struggled to recall why she was lying in a strange cave in the arms of a vampire, a renegade hint of sensual awareness darkening her gaze before reality crashed through her fog, and she was angrily shoving her hands against his chest.

"What the hell . . . let me go."

Jagr was caught off guard by the force of her blow, nearly losing his grip before he could roll on top of her and use his considerable weight to control her attempts to escape.

Her strength had returned with a vengeance.

Along with her temper.

A pity, since he could think of far better means of passing the next few minutes than fighting with the beautiful Were.

Ignoring the stirring of his body, Jagr met Regan's furious glare with a stoic determination.

"Not until the sun has completely set. I won't allow you to leave the cave until I can accompany you."

She sucked in a sharp breath. "You let me sleep the entire day?"

"Your mind is too strong. I can't control your sleep patterns. You were obviously in need of the rest."

"Dammit." She wriggled beneath him. Jagr swallowed a groan at the delicious friction. "Let me go. Culligan could be miles away by now."

It took his endless years of self-discipline and restraint to ignore the firm, deliciously female body beneath him. For now his biting need was secondary to keeping Regan safe.

Something he couldn't ensure if she bolted from the cave and into the lingering sunset.

"Then a few minutes won't matter," he pointed out with the

cool tones that seemed to set Regan's teeth on edge. So long as she was contemplating the best means to stick a stake in his heart, she wasn't plotting the means to escape him.

Predictably her face flushed with fury. "I'll never forgive my sister for inflicting you on me. I bet she sent you to get you out of her . . ."

Before he could leash the impulse, his head was dipping down to capture her mouth in a silencing kiss. How else could he halt the angry tirade without physical harm? A noble goal that was swiftly undermined by the intoxicating heat that flared through his body.

This kiss had nothing to do with silencing Regan, and everything to do with the ravenous hunger that flared through him with a painful force.

He wanted this woman.

He wanted to stroke his lips over every inch of her pure, ivory skin. He wanted to kiss and lick and nibble over every delectable curve. He wanted to be buried deep inside her as he sank his fangs into her neck and drank of her potent blood.

More than anything, he wanted to hear those low, husky cries as she reached her climax.

Her fingers dug into his chest as he deepened the kiss, her lips softening. The scent of arousal bloomed on her skin, lengthening his fangs and making his heavy erection twitch in anticipation.

This was . . . right.

She fit perfectly beneath him, her feminine body soft and yet strong enough to handle an ancient vampire's passion. Her scent was exactly blended to stir his deepest hungers. And her blood. Hell, his body still trembled with the power from his feeding.

Shifting his hands, Jagr tangled his fingers in the satin smoothness of her hair, drowning in sensations that were familiar, and yet completely unknown in their intensity.

After an eternity of hell, this was . . . paradise. There was no other word.

He teased at her lips, lightly nipping and stroking before exploring the stubborn line of her jaw. Her nails dug through the thin T-shirt, causing sharp darts of delicious pain, but his senses were too keen to miss the tiny moan of distress that was wrenched from her throat.

Regan's body might respond with intoxicating urgency to his touch, but her mind didn't trust him.

At this point, he doubted she was capable of trusting anyone.

Jagr lifted his head to regard her with a cool composure that disguised the frustration howling through his body.

"I did warn you not to insult my queen," he murmured.

Her face was flushed with a combination of embarrassment and anger at having responded so readily to his touch.

"I wasn't insulting my sister, I was insulting you."

A hint of a smile touched his lips. "My mistake."

She glared at him for a long moment, infuriated at her inability to toss aside his large body and flee as she desired. Then, with obvious effort, she wrapped herself in a brittle dignity.

"Where's the gargoyle?"

Jagr's smile faded at the mention of the tiny demon. He hadn't been pleased when he'd returned from disposing of the curs' bodies to discover Regan and Levet chatting as if they were old friends. He wasn't certain why he was angered by the sight of the two of them together. Not even a reclusive vampire who spent more time with books than other demons would believe that Regan could be sexually attracted to the ugly little beast.

It was only now that he could acknowledge the truth. He'd been jealous that the stupid gargoyle had made Regan smile.

"Still in statue form," he muttered. "Luckily for him."

"He did find us these caves," she countered, managing

to keep her expression aloof, as if she were lying on the hard cave floor by choice, rather than being pinned by his heavy body.

Jagr felt a stirring deep inside him. He'd never encountered a woman with such extraordinary courage.

"I'm a vampire. There isn't a cave I can't sense."

Her eyes narrowed. "Then why did you allow him to come with us?"

"Because my clansmen have several mates who are peculairly attached to the pest."

She blinked, caught off guard by his blunt confession.

"Surely big bad Jagr is not afraid of a few women?"

"I'm wise enough to fear a goddess, a Shalott demon, an Oracle, and even a pureblooded Were when she is enraged," he said dryly, his gaze lowering to the lush temptation of her mouth. "Besides, there are few creatures more dangerous in the world than a woman."

"You sound as if you have personal experience. Did some vamp babe break your heart?" she mocked.

With one fluid motion Jagr was on his feet, his features cold and unreadable. Regan couldn't know his past, or the female vampire who had tortured him for centuries, but her taunt released the flood of nightmares that never truly left him in peace.

"It's nearly dark. Do you need to feed?"

Regan scrambled to her feet, warily backing away as his icy power swirled through the cave.

"What I need is a shower and clean clothes."

"Very well. Give me a moment."

Jagr headed toward the back of the cave, cursing as he caught the scent of Regan's unease. Dammit, Styx had been a fool to send him after the Were. He was a volatile warrior who was feared by his own brothers, not a nanny. What the hell did he know about wounded, overly proud, vengeance-obsessed women? Jack shit, that's what.

So why wasn't he hauling Regan back to Chicago and washing his hands of the ridiculous situation?

Bending downward, he unzipped the leather satchel he had brought with him from Chicago.

He heard Regan impatiently shuffle her feet behind him. "What are you doing?"

Jagr pulled out two finely crafted silver daggers and tucked them into his boots. There were few things that could best an ancient vampire, but he hadn't lived so long by being stupid. If there were curs around, there were most certainly Weres. He would need the silver if they were attacked by an entire pack.

Straightening, he headed for the narrow entrance. "I'm ready."

Regan ground her teeth as the vampire disappeared through the entrance of the cave. Did he think she would scurry behind him like a well trained dog?

Heel, Regan. Sit, Regan. Roll over, Regan.

Arrogant bloodsucker.

Wasn't it enough that he'd pinned her to the floor and kissed her until she'd melted into an embarrassing puddle of willing flesh? And then topped it off by going into his Mr. Freeze act, one that would terrify any rational creature?

She hadn't asked for his interference. And she most certainly hadn't asked for his damned toe-curling, stomach-churning kisses.

Why wouldn't he just go back to Chicago and leave her alone?

Stomping across the cave, Regan slipped through the entrance and charged after Jagr's retreating form. As much as she wanted to plant a fat wooden stake in his heart, she was smart enough to realize that she wasn't strong enough to tangle with a vampire. Especially not when that vampire also happened to be a hulking freak of nature like Jagr. Christ, did the vampire tap the veins of steroid junkies?

No, if she were going to escape her current pain in the ass, it would only be with patience and a constant eye on opportunity.

It shouldn't be tough. She had thirty years of practice.

Muttering curses beneath her breath, Regan lengthened her strides, catching up with Jagr as he reached the bottom of the high bluff.

"What about Levet?" she demanded.

"We'd never be so lucky as to lose him. He will find our trail soon enough."

"Our trail? Where are we going?"

Jagr turned his head, his eyes capturing and reflecting the stars that sprinkled the velvet black sky overhead. Regan's heart gave an odd twist. She'd never seen anything quite so beautiful.

"You said you wanted a shower and clothes."

Her brows shot upward. He'd actually listened to her? And remembered the words that came out of her mouth?

Unnerved by the realization, Regan turned her attention to the street that lay just beyond the empty parking lot. There were the usual stores expected in a tourist town. Arts and crafts, souvenirs, antiques, a quaint coffee shop and bakery. All charmingly rustic, with large windows to display their wares.

Jagr led her past them without a word, thankfully missing her wistful gaze that lingered on a pretty necklace. She'd never possessed anything in her life but a few cheap clothes that Culligan tossed through the bars of her cage. Despite being a wolf by nature, she was still a woman at heart, and she couldn't deny an instinctive urge to browse and gather and . . . well, frankly just buy a bunch of junk that she could call her own.

Lost in her thoughts, Regan was caught off guard when Jagr came to an abrupt halt before a red brick building. Barreling into his massive form, she hastily stepped back and glared into his impassive face.

"Holy crap, warn a girl, why don't you?"

A golden brow flicked upward. "Will this do?"

"Do for what?"

"Clothing."

"Oh." She licked her suddenly dry lips as she glanced toward the elegant clothes displayed in the large window. "I . . . I don't think it's open."

Stepping forward, Jagr pressed his hand against the door. For a moment nothing happened, then with a low squeak, the door swung inward.

"It is now."

"What about the alarms?"

"They've been disarmed."

"Security cameras?" He regarded her with that flat stare. At last she threw her hands up in defeat. "Fine, but if you get shot again, I'm not offering a vein," she muttered, marching forward.

She had barely reached the door when Jagr wrapped an arm about her waist to haul her against his hard chest, whispering directly into her ear.

"You didn't seem to mind while I was feeding."

Regan wasn't sure what infuriated her more. Being manhandled by the brute, or the delicious heat that licked through her body at being manhandled.

"One more word about that . . . feeding, and you're going to get a lot more up close and personal with those daggers you're carrying," she hissed.

His lips brushed over the curve of ear, making her pulse leap and proving his complete lack of fear at her threat. She shuddered as his fangs lightly scraped down the curve of her neck, swallowing a moan as a thousand pinpricks of excitement tingled through her.

"You can get up close and personal with anything you want, little one," he murmured, his lips teasing at her skin.

"Damn you."

Wrenching free of his grasp, Regan stormed into the dark interior of the store, heading toward the back racks that held the expensive designer jeans and T-shirts.

What was wrong with her? Jagr was nothing more than an oversized, over-smug, obnoxiously gorgeous pain in her ass. So why did she keep letting him get under her skin?

Because she was an idiot.

Gritting her teeth, Regan forced herself to ignore his large form leaning against the doorjamb watching her every move with that too perceptive gaze. By God, this was her first, and perhaps only, opportunity to actually enjoy what most women took for granted. She'd be damned if the guardian from hell was going to ruin the moment.

Flicking the hangers around the circular stand, Regan occasionally paused to pull out whatever happened to catch her eye. Any of them would do, of course. The jeans were all faded and looked like they had been put through a meat slicer, while the shirts were cropped to show more than they covered.

Ah, the wacky world of fashion.

Still, she couldn't stop herself from fingering the various materials and imagining how each would feel against her skin.

Studying a tiny pink sweater with a metallic star stitched on the front, Regan stiffened as she felt the cool brush of Jagr's power as he stepped behind her.

"Do they not have your size?" he demanded.

Regan deliberately replaced the pink sweater and selected a tiny white T-shirt.

"Of course they have my size."

"Then the clothing isn't appropriate?"

"It's fine."

"Why do you keep searching?"

Heaving a sigh, she turned to glare over her shoulder. "Give me a break, will you? I've never been shopping before. I want to . . . savor it."

He stilled at her confession. "Never?"

She shoved the shirt back onto the rack. "In case you missed the news flash, Jagr, Culligan and I weren't exactly BFF. I was kept locked in a cage for the past thirty years."

"You must have been let out on occasion."

"Only when the bastard needed me to convince an audience he was a genuine faith healer."

Before she could react, Jagr turned her to face him, his features oddly tight.

"How did you convince them?"

Regan shifted beneath the intensity of his icy gaze. Dammit, she felt freakish enough without Jagr eyeballing her as if she'd grown a second head.

"Whenever we reached a town, he would set up a big tent in a field and start handing out flyers." She ground her teeth until they ached, refusing to acknowledge the brutal pain that twisted her gut at the mere thought of Culligan. She'd made a promise to herself a long time ago: she would never, ever give the damned imp the satisfaction of making her cry. Not one tear. Not ever. Regaining command of her emotions, she met Jagr's fierce gaze. "Before the show started, he would slice me open with his knife, or break a leg, and I would stumble into the tent he'd set up. Once I had the audience's attention, he would rush over to put his hands over me and start praying."

"And you would heal," he hissed softly.

"Right before their very eyes. The humans thought they were watching a miracle. They couldn't get their wallets out fast enough." Her lips twisted with disgust. "Chumps."

"Humans believe what they see."

"They're still chumps."

His hands lifted, lightly cupping her face and forcing her to meet his gaze. Regan's heart stuttered to a halt. Christ, she'd thought his frigid composure was unnerving, but now his eyes had lost their ice and smoldered with a savage, near feral fury. It was a forcible reminder that while this vampire had been sent to rescue her, he was still a dangerous predator.

"Jagr?"

"I'll skin him alive and feed his heart to the vultures," he rasped. "Or perhaps I'll chain him in the sewers near my lair for the rats to devour—slowly."

Regan didn't doubt his threat. Or his ability to carry it out.

What she didn't understand was the strange thrill that pulsed through her heart at his harsh words. As if she was . . . pleased by his arrogant assumption that he could interfere in her business.

Which was even more terrifying than his perilous fury.

Jerking from his touch, Regan glared at him in frustration. "I told you, Culligan is mine."

Chapter 4

Jagr's anger eased as he watched Regan hastily back away from him. Oh, he still intended to slaughter the imp. Slowly, painfully, and with exquisite skill. But he couldn't deny a hint of amusement at Regan's skittish unease at his grim announcement.

She'd spent the past thirty years being brutally taught that she could depend on no one but herself. Trust no one. Now her prickly independence resented the mere hint that someone else might fight her battles.

Just as she resented the thought she possessed a sister and pack who cared for her.

"We'll see," he murmured, turning to grab two armfuls of clothes off the rack. "This should do."

As he'd hoped, Regan was instantly distracted. He wasn't a particularly perceptive vampire. Unlike Viper, he couldn't sense other's most intimate thoughts. But not even an idiot could miss her covetous expression or longing sighs as she had searched through the racks.

She wanted the clothes, she would have them.

"I can't take all that," she protested.

"Then I will."

Without missing a beat, Jagr searched until he found the

large bags stashed behind the counter and filled them with his bounty. He even included several bras and panties that were piled in a large bin, refusing to consider what the bits of lace of would look like against her ivory skin.

Reaching into the pocket of his jeans, he pulled out a wad of cash and tossed it near the register, then headed out the door and into the dark street.

He knew better than to ask, or worse yet, demand that Regan accompany him. She needed to feel as if she were in control. He was willing to give her a sense of freedom so long as she didn't put herself in danger.

There was a tense pause before he heard Regan's soft curse, and soon she was hurrying to match his long strides.

"Why did you leave money?" she demanded. "You have a moral issue with stealing?"

Jagr allowed his powers to flow through the dark street, searching for any hint of danger.

"No, just a dislike for attracting unwanted attention. I left enough money to keep the owner from calling the cops and risk losing her sudden windfall."

"Now where are we going?"

"A shower."

Confident there was nothing more threatening than the usual humans and a few water sprites that sang their siren song from the river, Jagr turned the corner and headed toward the main highway that cut through town.

Despite his swift pace, Regan easily kept at his side, her gaze warily searching the shadows, her body tense, ready for any unexpected attack.

Jagr should have been pleased. The woman was obviously smart enough to keep up her guard, despite the seeming lack of danger.

But he wasn't pleased.

In fact, he was downright pissy. As if some latent, primitive part of his nature was offended she would question his right and ability to keep her safe.

Alarm trickled down his spine like ice, but Jagr grimly ignored the warning. Regan had been setting off alarms since he first caught sight of her. Instead, he slowed before the cheap chain motel with the blinking vacancy sign.

Regan frowned as he headed toward the far end of the building. "What are we doing here?"

"This is the nearest shower."

"We're checking into a hotel?"

"Tonight I prefer to skip the paperwork. The desk clerk is no doubt busy sharpening his skills at Guitar Hero."

"Christ, what is it with you?"

"What?"

She regarded him with a sour expression. "One minute you sound like you just crawled out of a medieval crypt and the next, you sound like you're a full-fledged member of Gen X."

He shrugged, hiding his smile at her fierce need to keep him at a distance. And people called him antisocial.

"I watch TV."

"Let me guess. You're addicted to *Dexter*."

"Actually I prefer *Gossip Girl*."

Her jaw dropped. "You've got to be kidding."

He moved toward the last door. "This one's empty." Placing his hand against the door, Jagr waited until he heard the click of the lock and pressed it open. Standing aside, he waited for Regan to march past him, her head high, her spine stiff.

Shutting the door, he held the bags toward the wary woman.

"Don't turn on the light until you've closed the bathroom door. We don't want to alarm the staff."

She inched forward, clearly suspicious of his motives in bringing her to the hotel room.

"What are you going to be doing?"

"Keeping guard." His brief amusement faded as the jasmine scent of her wrapped around him, stoking the hunger that smoldered deep inside him. The mere thought of her naked in the shower, with only a flimsy door between them . . . gods. Heat blasted through him, swirling through the air and making his voice thick. "Unless you have need of me?"

Snatching the bags, Regan backed toward the open door across the room.

"I've got it, thanks."

Her tone was sharp, but Jagr didn't miss the darkening of her eyes or the rapid beat of her pulse. He pushed from the door, the flames licking through his blood.

"My assistance would save time. I could scrub your back." His gaze swept down the delicate curves. "Or your front, if you prefer."

"Not even in your dreams, Jagr."

Oh, she was definitely going to be in his dreams. The only question was for how many nights.

Or centuries.

"You did say you were in a hurry to get on the trail of Culligan."

"Ha. Do I look stupid?"

The sweet, enticing scent of her arousal perfumed the air, but Jagr didn't miss the hint of panic that flared through her emerald eyes. She desired him, but she feared that desire as much as she feared any emotion that wasn't hate or revenge.

Damn. He moved forward, forcing himself to halt when a tremor shook through her body. She was going to bolt. He sensed it as clearly as if she'd tattooed it across her forehead.

"You look like a woman who has been knocked around enough to assume everyone is your enemy." His voice was deliberately cool, his hunger firmly leashed. "I will not hurt you."

She swallowed heavily, then predictably channeled her unease into anger.

"Because precious Darcy would be mad?" she sneered.

"Because I understand."

"Yeah, right. Just keep watch, Hulkster," she growled, her

wolf prowling beneath her skin. "And don't you dare come anywhere near this door."

The door in question was slammed with enough force to split one of the wooden panels. Jagr remained in the center of the room, pretending that the image of Regan stripping off her clothes and stepping beneath the pelting water wasn't searing through his brain. Then, confident she was actually taking the opportunity to bathe, he slowly backed out of the room and made a swift sweep of the neighborhood to make sure they hadn't been followed.

Finding nothing out of the ordinary, he slipped to the back of the building and pressed himself against the worn bricks.

Nearly half an hour passed when the window next to him was shoved open, and a number of large bags were tossed onto the pavement. His lips twitched at the realization that Regan couldn't leave behind her new clothes, even in her desperation to escape him.

Scooping the bags beneath one arm, Jagr straightened and turned, waiting for Regan to swing her legs (attired in a new pair of jeans), through the window. With a motion so fast not even a Were could follow, he scooped her off the ledge.

"The window, Regan?" he mocked softly. "You disappoint me. I thought you would be more creative."

Regan gave a squeak and then a shriek as he easily tossed her over his shoulder and headed swiftly back toward the cave.

"Jackass." Her fist slammed into his back with jarring force, reminding him that she was all pureblood, despite her inability to shift. "Put me down."

"No."

"Dammit, you're wasting my time with these stupid vampire games."

Moving with a speed that would defy human eyes, Jagr rapidly neared their temporary lair. He'd been a fool to believe that giving into her demands for clean clothing and a shower would ease her distrust.

He was still one of the bad guys.

She was determined to play the Lone Ranger (sans Tonto). And now he was once again forced to hold her close enough to torment him with the scent of her freshly scrubbed skin and hot blood.

His arms tightened around her legs as she continued to struggle. "This is no game, little one. I was commanded by my Anasso to bring you to Chicago, and that's exactly what I intend to do."

"I thought my sister was the one who sent you?"

"Darcy wants you in Chicago, and Styx wants Darcy happy. It's the way of mates."

The blows to his back abruptly halted. "And what about your mate? I can't imagine she's thrilled with this little road trip of yours."

Jagr halted before the entrance to the cave, abruptly setting the aggravating demon on her feet.

"I have no mate."

Something flashed through her eyes. Relief? Uncertainty? Indigestion?

Whatever it was, she was swift to squash it as she shoved her fingers through her damp hair.

"No mate? What a shocker." Her smile was taunting. "With your stunning lack of charm and habit of treating women like you're a Neanderthal, I would have thought the demon babes would be crawling all over you."

Jagr's fangs throbbed, his heavy erection ached, and his mood was taking a southward dip toward foul.

"It's not the lack of females that has prevented me from taking a mate," he icily denied.

"Then what is it?"

"My lack of interest in those females."

"As if. Men like you . . ."

Jagr was bending down his head and sealing her lips with a brief, searing kiss before he could halt the impulse. Perhaps because for the first time in centuries, his brutal self-control was being undermined by a tiny wisp of a Were with the tongue of a drunken harpy and the manners of rabid badger.

Abruptly lifting his head, he met her stunned gaze.

"Why the hell do you keep doing that?" she muttered, her cheeks flushed with a heat she couldn't hide.

Jagr growled deep in his throat. "If I knew, I would no doubt be falling on the nearest stake."

The emerald eyes flashed. "That can be arranged."

"There you are." Stomping from the cave, Levet regarded them with a jaundiced frown, his wings twitching in aggravation. "I thought you'd abandoned me. Again."

Jagr swallowed a snarl, resisting the urge to toss the gargoyle into the river below. His body might howl at the interruption, but the pea-sized part of his brain that was still functioning realized that he was allowing himself to be perilously distracted by his strange fascination with Regan.

Gods, he was going to get them both killed.

"Levet, I need your help," he commanded in frigid tones, allowing his warrior instincts to drown his seething frustration.

"Of course you do." Levet smirked. "You run off and do whatever vampires do, and I will be happy to keep Regan safe."

As if Jagr would allow Regan out of his sight for a second. Stupid demon.

"I need you to track down the local cur pack."

"Oh, I see." Levet narrowed his gaze. "I'm to do the grunt work while you get to stay with the beautiful woman. Typical."

"I suspect that the curs have a demon or witch who is helping to keep them hidden."

"And what does that have to do with me?"

"You're the only one capable of sensing magic."

Levet sputtered, wanting to argue but unable to deny the truth. At last he threw up his hands in defeat.

"*Sacrebleu.* Fine, I will do it."

"When you find the pack, do not approach them," Jagr warned. "I don't want them spooked before I discover why they were shooting at us, and what connection they have to the imp."

"Fine, but I expect payment for trailing after a bunch of stinking curs."

Jagr grasped one of the stunted horns and hauled Levet up to glare into his wide eyes.

"Your payment is that you get to keep your wings. Understood?"

"Hey, let go."

Jagr dropped the demon back to the ground. "Don't return until you've found the curs."

"Goth bully." With a flick of his tail, Levet turned to waddle away.

Jagr grimaced. No doubt both Darcy and Shay would rake him over the coals when he returned to Chicago. They possessed a bizarre fondness for the gargoyle. But for the moment, all he cared about was finding the curs and ending their threat to Regan.

At his side, Regan raked a glance over his large body. "Why does he keep calling you a Goth? I'd say you're more . . . ghetto chic."

Ghetto chic?

"I was once a Visigoth chief."

"Christ." Her eyes widened in shock. "Exactly when did you get changed into a vampire?"

With a flinch, Jagr turned to enter the cave, the bags of clothing banging against his legs. The night of his turning was something he never discussed.

Not with anyone.

With a snort of disgust at his retreat, Regan followed on his heels.

"Hello, Mr. Freeze. What the hell are you doing now?"

"I need to speak with Salvatore."

* * *

The elegant bedroom in the St. Louis mansion was a decadent feast for the senses. Gold-veined marble walls reflected the glow of the priceless chandelier, the lacquer furniture was designed for accommodating the most adventurous sexual fantasies, and even the high ceiling was painted with naughty satyrs seducing Rubenesque angels.

Lying in the middle of the Olympic-sized bed drenched in gold satin and black velvet, Salvatore Giuliani was jerked from his fleeting pleasure by the persistent buzz of his private cell phone.

His hand reached for the phone even as the woman straddling his naked body prepared to impale herself on his stiff erection.

"Don't answer it," the beautiful cur with long crimson hair and pale green eyes moaned, her lips trailing over his chest. "Please, lover."

"Get off, Jenna," he growled, his golden brown eyes glowing as the wolf inside him stirred with anger.

"Call them back later."

"Get the hell off."

With a sweep of his arm, Salvatore knocked the cur aside, rising from the bed in one smooth motion.

"Bastard," Jenna rasped, sprawled spread-eagle across the rumpled sheets, her eyes sparkling with excitement at his rough treatment.

"You have no idea," Salvatore drawled.

Turning his back on the woman, he reached for the phone, his brows drawing together at the unfamiliar number. Only a handful of people were allowed to dial his private line. Those who called without permission usually found themselves missing their throat. And occasionally their spleen. Flipping open the phone, he held it to his ear. "Who is this?"

"Jagr." The cold, dark voice was edged with the revolting

arrogance that was as much a part of a vampire as his fangs. Filthy leeches. "I was sent by Styx to retrieve the Were."

"Did you find her?"

"Of course. We're in Hannibal."

Salvatore curled his lips at the smug response. *Cristo.* He hated vampires.

"And?"

"And I want to know why your curs tried to kill us."

"Curs." With quick strides, Salvatore was standing beside the heavy desk across the room, clicking through the files on his laptop. "There is no Were pack near Hannibal."

"Then you have some strays taking potshots at the tourists."

Salvatore clenched his fist, his eyes glowing with fury. As King of the Weres, he kept his rules simple. Obey or die. No room for confusion.

"A problem easily corrected. I will be there tomorrow night."

"Once we locate them, I need at least one left alive to question."

Salvatore clenched his teeth at the cool command. One day soon . . .

"I make no guarantees."

With a flick of his wrist, he snapped shut the phone and headed toward the door.

"Aren't you coming back to bed?" Jenna whined.

Salvatore didn't bother to glance in her direction. "Get your clothes on, and get out." Reaching the door, he jerked it open to gesture toward the massive, shaven-headed cur that stood guard in the hallway. "Hess."

Dropping to his knees, the cur pressed his forehead to the crimson carpet in proper deference. "Yes, sire?"

"We have a problem in Hannibal. I want you to gather up three of our best soldiers, and pack the Humvee with enough arsenal to clean out a pack of rogue curs. We leave after my lunch with the mayor."

Chapter 5

Regan watched as Jagr slipped the cell phone into the pocket of his jeans. Jeans that hung low on his hips and clung to his powerful legs with yummy determination . . .

Crap.

Tilting her chin, Regan tried to ignore the constant awareness that buzzed through her like an electric shock. Okay, the damned vamp was the most beautiful creature she'd ever seen. And he oozed sex from the top of his golden head to the tips of his shit-kicker boots. And his kisses were making her so randy she thought she might scream if she didn't have relief soon.

But he was still the most obnoxious, arrogant, unpredictable, pig-headed brute it was ever her misfortune to encounter.

"If you intended to call Salvatore, then why did you send Levet to look for the curs?" she demanded, her voice sharp with . . . hell, she'd might as well admit it, if only to herself. Sharp with frustration.

He shrugged. "Salvatore has no greater ability to sense magic than I do. A gargoyle is a creature of magic. There's no spell, no matter how powerful the demon or witch, that he won't be able to track."

"Well, I'm not just waiting in this cave for Levet to return." She folded her arms over her chest, ready (no, aching) for a fight. "As you pointed out, we don't even know if Culligan is with the curs."

He flicked a golden brow upward, tossing her bags of clothing into a far corner. Clothes he'd bought for her just because he knew she wanted them. Her frustration became downright painful. Damn the vampire.

"And what is your plan?" he mocked. "To roam the streets, and hope you stumble over the imp?"

"Do you have a better idea, *chief?*"

"Yes. I think we should find the RV. The curs might be capable of hiding an imp, but they wouldn't expend the magic to hide his vehicle."

She snorted. "What does it matter if he isn't in it?"

"Culligan was no doubt in a hurry to disappear. He might have left something behind that will reveal why he chose Hannibal."

Against her will, Regan recalled those chaotic hours after her rescue. She'd been certain Salvatore Giuliani must be some sort of gorgeous guardian angel sent to free her from Culligan's clutches. It was exactly what she'd dreamed of for years.

Until, of course, the freaking Were had allowed Culligan to escape, followed by her being informed that she had an extended family who obviously hadn't given a damn that she was being used and abused, and then topped it off with the news she was worthless to him since he could *smell* her infertility.

Bastard.

"Why would Culligan be in a hurry?" She didn't bother to hide her bitterness. "Salvatore made it clear he wasn't going to waste his time tracking down a mere imp to punish him. Not when I'm barren and worthless."

His lips twisted. "Culligan wasn't afraid of the damned King of Weres. He was afraid of *you.*"

"He should be," she muttered.

His artic gaze flicked over her tense body. "Do you need to feed before we begin?"

She was starving, but she wasn't about to admit as much. Allowing this vampire to take care of her needs was . . . disturbing.

"I will later."

His eyes flashed with annoyance. "That's no answer."

"Well, too bad, because that's all you're getting."

"If you need to feed, then you'll do it now. You're no good to me weak."

Regan snapped. There was no other word for it.

One moment she was standing near the entrance of the cave, and the next she was flying through the air to tackle the six-foot-three, two-hundred-fifty-pound vampire.

When they tumbled to the hard ground, Regan wasn't certain who was the more astonished, her or Jagr.

She did know who recovered first.

She'd barely managed a smirk at the realization she'd landed on top when Jagr gave a low growl, and with one smooth motion had rolled her beneath him, his body pinning her to the hard dirt.

Regan felt her breath being squeezed from her lungs. Of course, who wouldn't suffocate with a massive vampire squashing them?

It didn't have anything to do with the thick hair that had loosened from its braid to tumble about them like a curtain of gold satin. Or the scent of raw power flooding her senses.

Nope. No way in hell.

So why were those blue eyes thawing as if Jagr could sense the hot rush of her blood, and the renegade softening of her limbs?

"We both know I could force you to Chicago if I wanted," he husked, his hand cupping her face in a gesture of pure possession. "Unfortunately I understand your thirst for revenge and I'm willing to indulge you for a day or two. But not if this is a death wish. You take one unnecessary risk or try to sneak away from me again, and I will stuff you in a bag and carry you to your sister."

Regan hissed, her body trembling with the need to rub against the hard thrust of his arousal.

"You're really pissing me off."

His gaze lowered to her lips. "Do we have a deal?"

"Screw you."

Muttering words she didn't understand, Jagr buried his face in the curve of her neck, the sensation of his fangs scraping her sensitive skin sending a shocking rash of pleasure through her body.

"You're playing with fire, little one."

Regan's lips parted, her fingers digging into his upper arms as his tongue lightly traced the line of her collarbone revealed by her new pink T-shirt.

"Jagr," she breathed.

"You smell of hot nights and jasmine." His mouth brushed her skin as he spoke, the cool stroke of his lips branding her flesh. "Exquisite."

Regan squeezed her eyes shut, desperately trying to halt the dark tide of need. Okay, her body wanted Jagr. Wanted him with a force that was close to going nuclear.

But it was just lust. The reaction of a woman who had been denied sex her entire life.

"I didn't say you could kiss me," she muttered, jerking with pleasure as his lips traveled up her neck to tease the hollow just below her ear.

"Do you want me to stop?"

Stop? Hell, no. She wanted him to rip off her clothes and lick her from head to toe. She wanted him to taste and nibble and bite until she screamed in pleasure. She wanted to wrap her fingers around his thickening cock and guide him into the aching void that refused to leave her in peace. She wanted . . .

She wanted.

And that was the problem.

"Please, Jagr."

He nipped the lobe of her ear. "Please what, little one? What do you want?"

"Christ." Calling upon the considerable strength of her heritage, along with a good dose of panic, Regan slammed her hands against the steel width of his chest, managing to gain enough space to wriggle from beneath his body. Scrambling to her feet, she brushed the dirt from her new clothes and glared at the vampire who gained his feet with a sinuous grace. "What is it with you? One minute you're giving me frostbite, and the next you have your tongue down my throat. Are you psychotic, or just a garden-variety wing nut?"

With a cold smile, Jagr prowled toward the entrance of the cave. "I think the better question is why a woman who is so obviously desperate for my touch would be so terrified of her own desire."

Chapter 6

The high ridge overlooking the Mississippi River south of Hannibal was perfectly suited to hide a pack of renegade curs. The abandoned wooden cabin was miles from its nearest neighbor, and the thick tangle of trees deterred all but the most determined hikers. But it was not only the isolation that had lured Sadie and her pack to the remote peak.

No, it was the echoing magic that lingered in the rich black earth, and the power of the churning waters below. In long-ago times, this land had belonged to the native Indians, and residue of their devotion to nature lingered with potent force, resonating through Sadie like a tuning fork.

Not that she wouldn't have preferred an elegant mansion, complete with acres of marble and priceless works of art. She might be an animal at heart, but she lusted for the finer things in life. Just as she had when she was turning tricks in the nasty alleys of St. Louis nearly thirty years ago.

That's where she had first encountered Caine, the cur who had promised to make her a queen before he'd bit her and changed her world forever.

She was still waiting on the whole queen thing, she acknowledged wryly, moving through the main room of the cabin shrouded in the gathering gloom. It offered nothing more than a ratty couch, two overstuffed chairs, and a stone fireplace. There wasn't even a picture hung on the rough wooden walls.

It was about as far away from the palace she dreamed of as the squalid boardinghouse she'd once shared with three other whores.

But then, revolutions were rarely without sacrifice.

Or blood, she was reminded as a hoarse scream reverberated from the attached shed.

A small smile touched her thin, some would claim cruel, features. Not that many men minded the hint of malicious fire that burned deep inside her. Humans might be attracted to her pale, still-smooth skin that contrasted with her waist-length raven hair and smoldering black eyes, but curs were brought to their knees by the hard muscles of her slender body and air of coiled violence that promised sweet pain.

Running her hands over the black leather pants that hung low on her hips and matched the barely-there halter top, Sadie was debating between returning to the shed and enjoying some quality torture with her captive, or going on the hunt, when a familiar scent had her rushing across the room.

Jerking open the door, she frowned as the tall, slender cur stepped from the thick shadows of the trees.

He was a tasty toy with dark hair he parted in the middle and allowed to brush past the line of his firm jaw. His eyes were indigo blue and surrounded by a tangle of thick lashes, and his features were carved with bad-boy perfection. An image only enhanced by his precisely trimmed goatee.

Black Irish.

Delectable.

Tonight, however, her first thought was not mounting him like a mechanical bull. It was pure fury that he'd obviously failed at his mission.

Stepping aside, Sadie waited for Duncan to enter the cabin before slamming the door and leaning against the wooden panels.

Outside, half a dozen curs and her personal witch roamed the woods, keeping constant guard on the area. She could catch the occasional rustle of underbrush as they circled the cabin. None would intrude without her permission.

"Where's the bitch?" Sadie growled. She'd never been one for pleasantries. Why use a scalpel when a sledgehammer was so much more fun?

With the familiarity of a longtime lover, Duncan strolled across the room to grab a bottle of whiskey from the mantel, taking a deep swig before turning to meet her glowing gaze.

"There were . . . complications."

"Do I look like I give a shit about complications? I told you to bring me the Were."

Duncan grimaced. "She wasn't alone."

Sadie hissed as she straightened from the door. "Salvatore followed her to Hannibal?"

Another swig of the whiskey. "Worse. She had a vampire with her."

"What the hell would she be doing with a bloodsucker?"

"Not just any bloodsucker." Duncan's sharp laugh ricocheted uneasily through the room. "I'd bet my ass it was the reclusive, legendary Jagr. I caught a glimpse of him once when I was in Chicago, but he's not a demon you forget."

"Jagr? I thought he was a myth."

"Tooth fairies are a myth. Jagr is a force of nature that even other vampires fear."

Sadie stormed across the room, yanking the bottle of whiskey from Duncan's hand and swallowing the remaining dregs.

Perfect. Absolutely freaking perfect.

It wasn't bad enough that Regan had slipped from her grasp, now she was being protected by the Hannibal Lecter of vampires?

Shit, Caine was going to skin her alive.

Literally, not figuratively.

"Why would he protect the Were?"

Duncan leaned against the stone mantel, folding his arms over his chest.

"Oh, I don't know," he drawled. "Perhaps it has something to do with the fact her sister is the current Queen of Vampires?"

The thought of Darcy being discovered after so many years, only to be snatched away by the King of the Living Dead, sent another wave of fury through Sadie, forcing her to battle the instinctive urge to shift.

"Interfering leeches. I warned Caine that leaving that ditzy Were in the hands of the vamps was trouble."

Duncan's lips twisted as his gaze skimmed down her tense body, lingering on the tattoo of a striking snake that coiled about her waist.

"I heard your complaints, but I noticed you didn't offer yourself to become fodder in the skirmish between the vampires and purebloods, Sadie, luv."

Sadie stepped back from Duncan's pulsing heat. Now was not the time to be distracted.

"Where are the others?" she demanded.

"Dead."

Sadie whirled to hurl the empty bottle of booze into the fireplace. The shatter of glass was satisfying, but it did nothing to soothe her scalding fury.

It wasn't that she gave a crap about the dead curs. They were nothing more than renewable resources. But the fact they had failed in their duty made her want to rip their corpses apart piece by piece.

"The vampire?"

Duncan rubbed his side as if remembering a painful blow. "No, we were hit by a spell."

Sadie sucked in a sharp breath. "They have a witch?"

"Not human. Some sort of demon."

"Shit. What kind?"

"I didn't wait around for DNA testing."

Sadie grabbed the front of Duncan's blue cashmere sweater he'd matched with black chinos. The male was addicted to *Project Runway.*

"You're certain you weren't followed?"

Duncan's jaw tightened, but he was smart enough not to struggle. "I still have the amulet the witch gave me, and just to be certain I headed straight south before doubling back. If there was anyone on my trail, they're in St. Louis by now."

Sadie briefly considered crushing her fist into the cur's face, if only to relieve the frustration that curdled in the pit of her stomach. A pity she still had need of the incompetent fool.

Tossing the cur away, Sadie paced the narrow room. "We have to get the Were before Caine returns."

"Don't look my way, luv." Duncan smoothed his sweater, his natural arrogance back in full force. "I've already had my near-death experience for the week."

Sadie curled her lips. "Be careful, Duncan. Your balls get any smaller, they might disappear altogether."

"At least I'll still have them intact." He cupped his impressive package. "You want the Were? Go get her."

"Oh, I intend to."

"And the vampire?"

Sadie shrugged, her cunning mind already plotting her next move. "Beneath all that fang and fury, he's just a man."

"Get over yourself, Sadie," Duncan drawled. "You might be a cur's wet dream, but you're way out of your league when it comes to vamps. Every demon knows they accept nothing less than perfection."

Sadie merely smiled. Her years as a whore had taught her that any man could be controlled. It was all a matter of finding what buttons to push.

"I could have the vampire on his knees if I wanted," she purred, "but men have more weaknesses beyond just an inability to think with anything besides their cock."

"And those would be?"

"Overblown ego, and an insatiable need to flex their testosterone." Sadie tossed her raven curls. "I set the trap, and he walks in. Bringing the sweet little Were with him."

"You're in over your head, luv."

"Unlike you, Duncan, I have a spine."

"Until Jagr rips it out."

Sadie's smile faded, a ruthless chill of unease inching down her still-attached spine. With a low growl, she thrust away the stupid sensation.

The years of her being a feeble victim were long gone. She was the hunter now, not the prey.

Shoving her hand into the front pocket of her leather pants, she pulled out a set of keys and tossed them to the startled Duncan.

"Here."

His brows lifted. "Babe, you shouldn't have."

"I didn't. The keys are to the imp's RV."

His teeth flashed white in the thickening darkness. "I'm more a Lamborghini man."

"Caine wants the RV torched before it's discovered by the humans."

An eerie glow came and went in Duncan's gaze. He was alpha enough to resent Caine's superior position in the pack.

"That's below my pay grade. Get one of the grunts to play pyro."

"Scared, Duncan?" Sadie taunted, turning to stroll toward the side door. She was itching to hurt something. And she had a tasty toy already tied up and waiting for her attention. How fortunate. "Don't worry, I'll send Silk with you. Her magic will keep the big bad vampire away."

"Bitch."

With a low chuckle, Sadie stepped through the door that connected the small shed. The bald lightbulb hanging from the open rafters by an electric cord swayed at her entrance, filling the cramp space with harsh light and revealing the broken shovels, axes, hammers, and coffee cans filled with nails left to rust in the corners.

Sadie had no interest in the abandoned tools or the thick dust that blanketed the interior of the shed. Her entire attention was focused on the imp with long red hair and green eyes who was stripped naked and chained to the wall.

A smile of anticipation curled her lips as her gaze ran over the tall, muscular body. Except for a few flecks of dried blood, Culligan's ivory skin had healed to smooth perfection. It made her hands twitch with anticipation. Slicing through unmarred flesh was just like dipping her finger into a new jar of peanut butter.

And speaking of peanut butter . . .

Her smile widened as she crossed to the overturned barrel where she'd left her favorite peanut butter fudge, wrapped in foil. She popped a large bite into her mouth before retrieving a silver dagger hanging on the wall and approaching the cowering imp.

He looked like an ancient sacrifice with his arms and legs spread wide, his flame hair flowing over his naked body. And, ah . . . his scent. Rich, plum-spiced, with a heady edge of stark, raving terror.

It was enough to make Sadie's heart pitty-pat with delight.

Halting directly before the quivering demon, Sadie slowly leaned forward.

"You've been a very naughty boy, Culligan," she purred, skimming the tip of the dagger down the center of his chest. "First you allow Salvatore to track you down and discover the girl, then you lead one of the most lethal vampires to ever walk the earth to my doorstep."

The green eyes rolled like he was a wild horse being bridled. "Please . . . mistress . . ."

She dug in the dagger until a bead of blood marred the ivory skin. "You wish to plead for your life, spineless worm?"

"I did what was asked of me." Culligan licked his lips, his

voice rough from his hours of screaming. "I was told to keep the woman alive, and not to allow her to escape. No one warned me that the pissed-off King of Weres was searching for the bitch."

"You were told what you needed to know." Sadie sliced a shallow cut from the imp's breastbone to his belly button, her ears singing from Culligan's cries of pain. Such a pathetic wretch. He couldn't even manage a proper hex, the simplest of imp magic. Still, he did make the loveliest sounds when he was being carved like a Thanksgiving turkey. "Did you think you could deal with the devil and not pay in blood?"

"What do you want from me?"

"For now, your pain will do. A pity I've been warned we might need you as bait. I can't permanently damage you, but I'm creative enough to keep you in one piece." With a smile she withdrew the dagger, only to plunge it back into his stomach, all the way to the hilt. "Well, perhaps not one piece, but a large enough piece to keep your heart beating."

When he was done screaming, Culligan struggled to speak. "Bait? What does that mean?"

Reminded that the imp had not only lost the Were, but had dropped a butt-load of trouble in her lap, Sadie twisted the blade.

"You, my pet, have managed to make an enemy of both the vamps and Weres," she hissed. "They would follow your scent to the gates of hell to have the pleasure of killing you."

His head sagged, the hair falling forward like a crimson river. "What does anyone care about the stupid girl? She's nothing but damaged goods. She can't even shift, for Christ's sake."

"What an idiot you are, Culligan. The girl's worth is beyond price. And you'd better hope your bumbling hasn't endangered my master's experiments, or you're going to be praying the Weres get you first."

"If she's worth so much, then why did you sell her to me?"

Pulling out the dagger, Sadie placed the bloody tip beneath his chin and forced his face upward. She leaned forward until their noses were nearly touching.

"She's . . . insurance."

"Insurance for what?"

Sadie chuckled. "The ruling elite in the demon-world is about undergo a change in management, imp. A pity you won't be around to enjoy the transformation."

With a smooth thrust, the dagger slid through the soft under skin of Culligan's chin, moving through flesh to pierce his tongue to the roof of his mouth.

The shriek of agony was muffled, but no less sweet.

The land south and west of Hannibal smoothed from high bluffs to rolling fields and heavily wooded acres. Squatting down to study the narrow dirt path, Jagr could hear the rustle of raccoons and opossums, as well as native deer. Precisely the wild game that would attract a pack of hungry curs.

Too bad there wasn't a hint of cur in the air. Not a scent, not a track, not even a stray hair.

There was a rustle beside him and the scent of midnight jasmine teased at his senses.

Regan.

His jaw clenched as his body painfully reacted to her proximity.

Gods, he thought his days of torture were behind him. He'd slaughtered his enemies and retreated to the barricaded safety of his lair. His life was supposed to be one of peace and quiet contemplation.

Yeah . . . right.

There was nothing peaceful in the way his body burned for a Were who couldn't decide if she wanted to rip off his clothes or stick a stake in his heart. Or in the knowledge he was risking a death sentence by ignoring Styx's order to return Regan to Chicago so the revenge-crazed woman could kill her enemy. Or even in having his hard-earned distrust for others slowly, relentlessly undermined.

It was no wonder he was in the mood to bite something.

Or, more particularly, someone.

Smoothly rising to his feet, Jagr turned his head to study the female at his side.

As if by magic, his fury and frustration eased to a rueful resignation.

Perhaps Regan had cast a spell upon him. Or perhaps the brutal barriers he'd built around himself were simply no match for the powerful attraction that roared through him.

Whatever the case, he knew he wasn't nearly as desperate to return to the dark solitude of his lair as he should be.

Shuffling her feet, Regan at last cleared her throat. Since leaving the cave, she'd grimly refused to utter a word. No doubt assuming her silence was some sort of punishment.

He hated to tell her that before the days of technology, he'd gone decades without a sound to disturb his studies. Besides, he'd known her silence wouldn't last. She was not the type of woman who could keep her emotions bottled inside.

She was more a spit-in-your-face, kick-your-ass type of gal.

Just the way he liked them.

"Well?" she demanded.

Jagr hid a smile at her sharp tone. "This is where I lost the imp's trail. What of you?"

She glanced around the empty field, her brow furrowed. "It was around here. Maybe closer to those trees."

"Then that's where we'll begin our search."

Before he could take a step, Regan had stubbornly folded her arms over her chest.

"This would go faster if we split up."

He lifted his brows at the suggestion. "So I can waste the rest of the night chasing you down? I don't think so. You stay at my side."

"Christ." Her eyes shimmered in the moonlight, not the glow of a Were on the point of shifting, but one of a pissed-off woman. Just as dangerous. "Wasn't it enough that I was imprisoned for the past thirty years? Do I have to go from one hell to another?"

His eyes narrowed. "My only purpose is to keep you safe, Regan, not to imprison you."

"Well, it feels remarkably the same."

With a hiss, Jagr grabbed her arms and regarded her with a flare of anger. He would endure many things, but not being compared to a spineless coward who would harm a young female.

"Take care, little one."

"Go to hell, big chief."

Abruptly he dropped his hands and stepped back. Just the feel of her soft skin beneath his fingers was making his body clench with hunger.

"You want to be rid of me, then let me take you to Chicago," he challenged with a cool control he was far from feeling. "You'll never have to set eyes on me again."

Her lips tightened as she absently rubbed her arms where he'd touched her.

"I'm not leaving until I've skinned Culligan and fed his heart to the fishes."

"Then it would seem we're stuck with one another." Turning on his heel, Jagr led the way toward the line of trees.

Regan fell into step behind him, muttering vile threats that included chopping off his more precious body parts, as well as a gruesome decapitation.

Jagr ignored her threats. Despite her unique ability to annoy the hell out of him, he understood her frustration. She'd just escaped from Culligan's clutches—she didn't want to depend on anyone. Even if his presence meant keeping her alive.

Nearing the tree line, Jagr abruptly halted, his senses flaring with life.

"Wait."

Regan flowed to his side, her body coiled to attack. "What is it?"

"I smell blood." He pointed toward the trees. "In there."

"Human?"

"Imp."

She sucked in a deep breath. "Is he still in there?"

"Impossible to say."

"Let's go."

Jagr bit back his instinctive protest. Regan had earned the right to battle Culligan. So long as he was near to prevent disaster.

"This way."

Without speaking, they entered the thick woods, their steps barely stirring a leaf as they moved in silence. In the distance, Jagr could hear the rustle of nocturnal animals and babble of a shallow creek, but there was no sense of human or demon in the darkness.

Following the intoxicating scent of blood, Jagr angled to the west. There was nothing but trees for several feet, then without warning they ended, revealing a wide path that had been carved through the very heart of the woods.

It was clearly a road for the local farmer to transfer his equipment from one field to another, but Jagr's only interest was in the long RV that was distinctly out of place.

"Shit."

Coming to a halt, Jagr was sharply aware of the savage emotions that assaulted the woman at his side.

"Regan?"

She shook her head, her arms wrapped protectively around her waist. "I can't. I . . . I just can't."

Before he realized he was moving, Jagr had gathered Regan in his arms. Strange. He'd never before felt the urge to comfort another, not even those of his clan, but in this moment there was nothing more vital.

Smoothing a hand down the knotted muscles of her back, he lowered his head to whisper in her ear.

"Stay here and keep guard. Can you do that, little one?"

There was a tense pause, then she gave a jerky nod. "Yes."

"Good."

Ignoring the irrational reluctance to leave her alone, Jagr loosened his grip and stepped back. This possessive sense of protection toward Regan was not only dangerous, it was distracting.

A warrior needed to be cold and logical, a master of his emotions.

This fermenting fear for Regan's safety could make him sloppy.

And sloppy meant death.

Ignoring his unwelcome instincts, Jagr stepped onto the rough path and approached the RV. Nearing the door, he withdrew a dagger from his boot. His senses might tell him the vehicle was empty, but he knew better than to walk in blindly. The curs had already proven they could hide their presence behind a spell. He wasn't taking chances.

Circling the long motor home, he cautiously peered through the windows. Empty. Unless the curs also managed to become invisible.

At last, Jagr approached the door, wrapping himself in shadows as he threw it open and flowed silently inside. He crouched low, prepared for attack. When one didn't occur, he straightened and allowed his gaze to slide over the built-in kitchen and living room that were crammed into the small space.

It all looked . . .

Human.

Not at all the lavish lifestyle preferred by imps.

Of course, Regan had claimed that Culligan was weak. If he couldn't produce hexes or portals, then he would have to depend on other means to acquire his wealth.

Such as abusing a vulnerable young Were in his sick sideshow.

With a low growl, Jagr moved toward the back of the RV, already knowing what he would discover when he yanked open the door to the bedroom.

Knowing, however, and seeing were two very different things.

The small room was surrounded by pure silver bars. The walls, the ceiling, the windows, and even the inside of the door. Even worse, there were silver shackles and chains tossed on a narrow cot that was the only piece of furniture, beyond a tiny TV and shelf of worn books.

This is where Regan had lived for the past thirty years. Where she'd been raised by a brutal master, and abused on a regular basis.

Had she been forced to wear the shackles whenever she was in this room?

The corrosive burn would have been near unbearable, and would have weakened her to the point where she could barely function.

Cold, lethal fury seared through him.

Someone would pay for this.

In blood.

Lost in his dark thoughts, it was the scent of jasmine that had him abruptly turning and heading back to the front of the vehicle.

"Regan. Do not," he rasped, his voice thickening with his native accent as he watched her climb through the door.

Sick fear swirled about her, filling the narrow space, but her beautiful face was hard with determination.

"I have to see."

"If there's anything to discover, I will find it. There's no need for you . . ."

"There's every need, Jagr," she interrupted, her voice low and ragged.

"Why?"

"To prove that I can."

Stepping forward, Jagr cupped her chilled face in his hand. "You have nothing to prove, Regan. Not to anyone."

"This is for me. I won't be haunted by my memories of Culligan, or the hell he put me through." She sucked in a shaky breath. "I won't give him that power."

A bleak, piercing memory of slipping through a deep cavern to slaughter his enemies without mercy flashed through his mind before he managed to scrub it away.

This was about Regan.

And the festering pain that ran like poison through her blood.

"He lost all power over you when you survived," Jagr husked, willing her to believe the truth of his words. "Your strength and courage overcame everything he could do to you. You've conquered your demon." His lips twisted, the ever present heat shimmering in his eyes. "Not the last demon you'll conquer, I'd bet."

As he intended, Regan was swiftly distracted, a blush staining her cheeks as she took a jerky step away from his lingering touch.

"You said you smelled blood."

"Yes." He moved to the very front of the RV, forced to bend over as he studied the driver's seat. "I don't know why Culligan came to Hannibal, but his welcoming committee was in a foul mood."

"He's dead?"

"He was alive when he left the RV, but he was hurting."

"Damn."

With an unexpected speed, Regan was moving deeper into the living area of the RV, punching holes into the faux wooden panels of the wall.

Jagr moved to her side, his lips curving as splinters

filled the air. There was nothing more arousing than a powerful woman.

"Not that I don't approve of wholesale destruction, but there are more satisfying means of exorcising your frustration," he murmured.

"Culligan kept his money and private papers in a safe . . . ah." Tossing him a smug smile, Regan tugged out a small metal box from the hole she'd just made in the panel. A smile that faded as she struggled to wrench the thing open. "Crap."

"Allow me." Without asking for permission, Jagr pulled the box from her grasp and wrenched the heavy lid off.

Not surprisingly, he was rewarded with a nasty glare. "Am I supposed to be impressed with your bulging muscles and mindless brute strength?"

"You can be impressed by anything you want, little one, although most women prefer my bulging . . ."

"Bleck." She held up a hand. "Enough."

Jagr might have been offended if he didn't catch the unmistakable scent of her desire whenever he was near.

Glancing in the box, Jagr grimaced and shoved it toward Regan. "I think you've earned this."

"Christ," she breathed, her eyes widening at the stash of jewels and watches and neatly stacked money. "Humans. You would think thousands of years of evolution would finally give them the talent of recognizing a blatant swindle." Regan shuddered, staring at the box as if it were contaminated. "I don't want this. It's tainted."

"Then give it to a charity or throw it in the river. Just so long as Culligan or his friends can't get their hands on it."

Regan grimaced. "You're right."

"I'm right?" Jagr pressed a hand to his heart in mock astonishment. "Blessed saints, did the sky fall?"

"Smart ass . . ."

Regan's eyes widened as Jagr flowed forward to press a hand to her mouth.

"Someone's approaching," he whispered close to her ear. She tugged his hand from her mouth, but was careful to keep her voice soft.

"Culligan?"

"I can't tell. They must be cloaked by a spell to cover their scent."

On the point of turning the hunter into his personal prey, Jagr stiffened. He had less than a beat to catch the scent of smoke before a bottle crashed through the window of the RV and exploded in flames. Instinctively, Jagr backed away. Fire was one enemy a vampire couldn't battle.

"Time for you to go, Regan." He shoved her toward the flames that were spreading with lethal speed. "Run."

Digging in her heels she whirled to glare at him. "Are you mental?"

"The fire isn't magical, you'll heal from the burns," he rasped, his body quivering with the need to rush her to safety.

"Yeah, only to be killed by the freaking King of Vamps when he discovers I bolted like a wuss and left his favorite pet to become toast."

"Styx would never harm you, and I am not the Anasso's favorite anything, let alone his pet. Now get the hell out of here."

The smoke thickened, the heat already bringing beads of sweat to Regan's face, but the woman stubbornly refused to flee.

"Forget it, chief. It's not happening."

"Damn."

Muttering ancient curses and more than a few derogatory comments on the brains of Weres in general, and one in particular, Jagr wrapped his arms around his personal thorn in his side, and with one mighty surge smashed through the side of the RV.

Chapter 7

Even buffered by Jagr's huge body, Regan's breath was wrenched from her lungs as they crashed through the side of the motor home and landed on the pathway with a hard jolt.

Before she'd managed to suck in the much needed air, Jagr had jerked her to her feet and turned to face the two attackers that appeared frozen in horror by their abrupt appearance.

There was a slender human woman with a mop of blond curls and innocuous blue eyes, as well as a tall, leanly handsome man that Regan instantly recognized as a cur, with dark hair and a goatee that somehow seemed perfect for his wicked features.

Regan had barely regained her balance when a cold blast of power filled the air, and Jagr had launched himself into battle.

The female screamed in terror, but rather than fleeing as any intelligent creature should have done, she threw out her hands, as if trying to shoo away the massive predator. Regan might have found it funny if there wasn't a brilliant flash of light that smacked Jagr in the center of his chest, sending him flying backwards.

Witch.

Regan rushed toward the vampire, who was sprawled on the hard ground, the front of his sweater charred and still smoking. Damn the witch to hell. No one was allowed to harm Jagr.

No one but her.

She was less than a half step away from the injured vampire when the hair on the back of her neck stood on end.

Allowing instinct to guide her, Regan crouched low as she whirled around, her leg striking out to trip the attacking cur.

Her dip allowed her to avoid a painful blow to her jaw as the attacker's fist swung over the top of her head, but he managed to leap over her kicking leg, his eyes glowing with the eerie light of a wolf. Spinning to face her, the cur held up his hands in a gesture of peace.

"Easy, luv," he soothed, his voice hinting at Irish origins. "I have no wish to hurt you."

Regan gritted her teeth, too furious to be properly terrified.

"Yeah, right." Her sharp laugh echoed through the trees. "I suppose you also have a bridge you're trying to unload?"

His lips curved in a well rehearsed smile. "I swear on my sweet mother's grave that I've been ordered to bring you alive."

"Bring me where?"

He held out a slender hand. "Come with me, and I'll show you."

Did she have stupid tattooed on her forehead?

Regan attempted to inch around the cur, plagued by a desperate need to reach Jagr.

"What do you want with me?"

"Nothing more than to keep you safe."

"Safe? You tried to shoot me in that hotel room, not to mention nearly roasting me alive just a minute ago."

"We were trying to kill the vampire in that hotel room, not you. We thought he was attacking you." His gaze slowly roamed down her body, his arrogant expression revealing he believed women enjoyed being checked over like used cars. Schmuck. "Weres and vampires don't usually mix."

"And tonight?" she demanded.

"I had no idea anyone was in the RV. I was sent to get rid of it, not to harm you."

Regan stiffened. She'd assumed that they had been followed by the cur to this remote spot. But if he was telling the truth, then he'd known about the RV.

And Culligan.

"Who sent you?" she hissed. "Culligan?"

The man snorted. "Don't be daft. As if I would take orders from a filthy imp."

"But you know where he is?"

He confidently stepped closer, his voice low and seductive. "Not only do I know, but I have him all tied up like a birthday present, just waiting for you to come and punish him."

Regan's thoughts churned. There wasn't a snowball's chance in hell of her actually going with the cur. Her every instinct shrieked in warning. Besides, she wouldn't leave Jagr. (Why she felt the need to protect an ancient vampire who was currently holding her hostage, not to mention driving her nuts, was something she wasn't about to consider.)

But if she could keep him talking, then he might give some clue as to where he was hiding Culligan . . . and why the hell he wanted to get his hands on her.

"How do you know Culligan?" she asked.

The cur shrugged. "Never met him before he arrived in Hannibal."

"Christ, is there a demon who comes through town who you don't try to kill?"

"We didn't try to kill the imp." The man stepped closer, as if hoping his potent heat would befuddle her mind. "It was a simple snatch and grab."

She continued inching toward Jagr. Her heart twisted. Why wouldn't he wake up? He would poof if he was dead, wouldn't he?

"Hardly simple," she accused. "Culligan didn't go willingly."

His lips curled into a snarl. "There might have been some blood involved."

"Why take him at all?"

"Beyond the pleasure of listening to him squeal?" The cur chuckled. "We discovered that he'd held a fellow wolf captive. That can't go unpunished."

He was lying. Regan had never been so certain of anything in her life.

"Fantastic. Where the hell were you when I actually needed your help?" she mocked, still circling the dangerous cur.

Suddenly, she was close enough to sense Jagr's power, though it was faint. Sheer relief crashed through her.

He was still alive.

She didn't know why, but it felt as if a truck had abruptly been lifted from her chest.

Unaware of Regan's distraction, the man smoothed a hand over the rippling muscles of his chest, his smile edged with a wicked smile.

"I'm here now. Ready and prepared to help with whatever you might need."

Ick, ick, ick.

Regan didn't feel any of the tingling excitement that she felt when Jagr regarded her with that heated awareness. All she felt was . . . revulsion.

Struggling to hide her less than flattering response, Regan was distracted as the witch grabbed the cur's arm.

"What are you doing?" she hissed, her eyes wide with panic. "The vamp won't be down forever. We have to go."

Regan growled, itching to knock the woman to the ground and beat the crap out of her. The witch squeaked, but before Regan could get her hands on her, the cur was shoving the terrified woman behind his back.

"Not without my pretty little wolf." He held out a slender hand. "Come with me, Regan. That's the only way you'll ever get your hands on Culligan."

"Tell me where he is and I'll join you later," she countered.

"No deal. You either let me take you to him now, or you'll never find him."

She clenched her hands. "How do I . . ."

There was a rustle as Jagr stirred on the hard ground, clearly shaking off whatever spell had hit him.

"Shit." Without warning, the cur reached out to grasp her arm, his charming expression hardening to one of ugly anger. "You just ran out of time, bitch. You're coming with me."

"Not in this lifetime," Regan hissed, yanking her arm free and taking a swing at the arrogant cur.

The man ducked, his fist hitting her in the center of the stomach before she could react. Regan grunted as the air was knocked from her lungs, but rather than battling against the painful momentum, she allowed it to take her to the ground, falling next to Jagr's legs.

She'd barely hit the dirt when the cur was on top of her, one fist catching her on the side of the head, the other grabbing her hair as he tried to yank her back on her feet.

Blinking back the wave of dizziness, Regan grimly reached out for Jagr's leg. She'd been battered enough times not to be distracted by a bit of pain. Not even when her hair was being pulled out by the roots.

Hissing in fury, the cur wrapped his hand around Regan's throat, squeezing her windpipe as he tried to force her to her feet. Regan gritted her teeth, aiming a kick at his knee as she ran her hand down Jagr's leg to his boot.

The attacker howled in pain as her heel connected with his kneecap with a sickening crack, but his fingers only tightened on her throat.

Regan struggled to breathe, her fingers at last closing around the dagger Jagr had tucked into his boot. Jerking it from the hidden sheath, she slashed at the arm holding her captive.

The silver blade slid easily through flesh and muscle,

scraping against the bone as the cur abruptly leaped backward, loosening his crushing grip on her throat.

Holding his arm, the man glared at her with a murderous fury before a shimmer of energy swirled about his muscular body, and he shifted. An echo of power tingled through Regan's blood as she watched the handsome face elongate, his clothes shredding as his body twisted and altered, at last becoming the shape of a huge wolflike creature with dark fur and gleaming red eyes.

Regan flowed to her feet, prepared for the imminent attack.

An attack that never came.

Even as Regan planted her feet and held the dagger at the ready, there was a low growl from beside her and Jagr was suddenly looming like an avenging angel behind her shoulder.

The cur snarled, snapping his teeth, but he wasn't so far gone as to believe he could battle a massive, infuriated vampire. Even one who'd been so recently wounded.

For just a moment they were frozen in a strange tableau, the violence trembling in the air, prepared to explode at the first movement.

Regan ridiculously found herself holding her breath, her gaze glued on the cur who remained poised to pounce. A mistake in the end. While the cur flashed his considerable fangs and rumbled deep in his throat, it was the witch who took matters into her own hands.

Literally.

Raising her arms, she muttered a low chant. Jagr cursed, and with a sharp motion knocked Regan to the side. A split second too late as the bright light flared, and a savage pain exploded inside Regan's head.

Jagr carried his slender burden through the silent streets and up the bluff to the hidden cave. Consumed with worry, he made no effort to control his icy power that flowed through the darkness and sent a feeling of cold dread through the hapless citizens of Hannibal.

What did he care? Let the humans stir uneasily in their beds, and the lesser demons flee the area in terror. His only concern was finding the gargoyle, and reviving Regan.

Easily sensing the tiny demon, Jagr slipped through the opening of the cave, already braced for Levet's shriek of horror as he settled Regan's unconscious form in the center of the hard floor.

"Regan." Wings flapping and tail twitching, Levet hurried to Regan's side. "What did you do to her, you undead reptile?"

Moving to the back of the cave, Jagr retrieved his long leather duster to carefully drape over Regan's too-still form. Then, kneeling on the dirt floor, he grasped one of her slender hands.

"She was hit by a spell." He stabbed his companion with a fierce glare. "Remove it."

"How . . ." Levet swallowed his question as he was nearly tumbled backward by a blast of Jagr's icy power. Instead, he closed his eyes and touched a gnarled finger to Regan's forehead. "Human witch. A defensive spell."

"I didn't ask for *CSI* bullshit," Jagr snarled. "Get rid of the spell."

"*Sacrebleu.*" Levet snapped open his eyes. "I have to know what magic was used to reverse it."

"Fine, it was a human witch. Now get on with it." Jagr pointed a warning finger in the gargoyle's ugly face. "And Levet."

"*Oui?*"

"Keep in mind that if you make a mistake, it'll be your last."

Levet narrowed his gaze, the fierce pride of his ancestors suddenly shimmering in the gray depths.

"I would stick a dagger in my own heart before I would

harm Darcy's sister," he swore. "Now shut up, and let me take care of her."

Jagr clenched his jaw against the fury that battered through him with brutal force.

The night had been a disaster.

Being trapped in the burning RV. Allowing himself to be knocked unconscious by a witch, a *human* witch, so Regan was forced to battle their attackers on her own. And being too slow to protect her against the spell that now held her in its grip.

A major screw-up from start to finish.

And it was Regan who was suffering for his failure.

Keeping his gaze trained on Regan's pale face, he paid scant attention as Levet muttered beneath his breath and occasionally waved his hands, but he recognized the moment the spell was broken.

It was in the easing of her body, and the soft sigh that fluttered through her parted lips. Levet rocked back on his heels, his wings drooping with weariness.

"I have removed the spell, but she will need a considerable amount of sleep to heal from the damage."

"But she'll heal? Completely?"

"Oui."

The tightness constricting his unbeating heart lessened, but it didn't disappear. Regan would heal, but those who wanted to hurt her remained alive.

For now.

Pressing her fingers to his lips, Jagr gently settled her hand on her chest that rose and fell with assuring regularity. Then ignoring the pain that lingered from the witch's blast, Jagr surged to his feet.

A voice of reason whispered in the back of his mind that he should be returning to the charred RV. Not only was there the hope that the wounds Regan had managed to inflict on the cur would overcome the witch's ability to mask his scent, but he needed to make sure that his own trail back to the cave was properly covered.

Reason, however, didn't mean squat while his protective instincts were in full roar. There was no way he was leaving Regan while she was unconscious and completely vulnerable.

No way in hell.

"Levet." With a narrowed gaze, he motioned toward the wary gargoyle. "I have a little task for you."

"Crap."

Regan wasn't certain how long she waged her battle with the clinging darkness. The thick shroud was nothing if not tenacious. But then again, so was she. (Some, especially a gorgeous Visigoth chief, might even claim she was stubborn as hell.)

Refusing to admit defeat, she shredded through the unconsciousness that held her captive, her senses slowly tingling back to life, though her lids remained too heavy to lift.

She was lying on a hard dirt floor. The cave, no doubt. She could smell cool, damp air and only a trace of gargoyle, as if Levet were no longer near. And overall, the cool, exotic scent of power that could only belong to Jagr.

He was near. Keeping watch over her.

Warmth flowed through her, banishing the lingering pain and bringing an odd sense of peace.

Peace?

From an arrogant vampire who thought he could put a leash on her?

Christ, she was mental.

Wrenching her eyes open, Regan glanced around the torch-lit chamber, assuring herself that she was safely tucked in the cave and not in the hands of the curs. Or worse, back in that damned silver cage.

Always assuming that the hideous thing survived the fire.

Confident she was in no immediate danger, Regan pushed herself to her feet, relieved when she didn't fall flat on her face. Or even stumble—much.

Running her fingers through her hair, she glanced around the deepening shadows. The cool wash of power that charged the air assured her that Jagr was near, but his considerable bulk was nowhere to be seen.

So either he'd used his vampire tricks to wrap himself in darkness, or he was in one of the attached caverns.

She briefly hesitated.

Pride told her that there was nothing keeping her in the cave. She could walk out the front entrance and continue her search for Culligan. Or if she were truly smart, she could hop on the nearest bus and simply disappear.

No imps, no Weres, no annoyingly gorgeous vampires . . .

Pride, however, wasn't in control of her feet. Instead of leading her out of the cave, they headed toward the openings at the back.

Ducking her head to avoid the low archway, she slipped into the cramped space that offered a natural cistern. As she straightened, she was prepared to find Jagr. His power was tangible this close. What she hadn't expected was to find him stark naked as he rose from the shallow water, tossing his wet hair over his massive shoulders.

The world stopped.

Or at least the little corner where Regan was standing.

Christ. She'd already accepted he was a magnificent specimen. The glorious mane of golden hair. The proud, masculine beauty of features. The relentless intelligence in the ice-blue eyes.

But stripped of his clothing, he was . . . holy moly.

Raw power molded into thick muscles and sinew were the only words that came to mind. Enough to halt the heart of any woman.

Briefly lost in the sheer perfection of his body, it took a

moment before Regan's avid gaze focused enough to realize that the smooth beauty of his ivory skin had been cruelly marred by a series of crisscrossing scars that ran from his chest to his groin.

Shocked as much by the pain that savaged her heart as by the sight of his gruesome injuries, Regan slowly lifted her eyes, clashing with the ice-blue gaze.

As always, his expression was impossible to read, but Regan wasn't stupid. Jagr would have sensed the moment she awakened. Which meant he could easily have covered himself before she stumbled across him.

Vampires weren't modest, but they abhorred any deformity. The scars would be a source of humiliation for such a demon.

So why had he revealed them to her?

And why now?

Struggling to clear her tangled thoughts, Regan forced a breath past her tight throat, her gaze shifting to the rippling water.

"Aren't you supposed to hang some sort of sign if you intend to shower in a coed cave?"

There was a rustle, and covertly glancing out the corner of her eye, Regan watched Jagr tug on a pair of faded jeans, pulling up the zipper but leaving the button undone.

Yow.

Her mouth went dry. And it had nothing to do with his scars.

Did all men have such large . . . man parts?

And were they supposed to make a woman pant like a hound in heat?

"How do you feel?" he demanded, prowling until he stood directly before her.

"Headache, dry mouth, hair from hell." With effort, she lifted her head to meet his guarded gaze. "How long was I out?"

"You lost a day."

Frustration simmered deep in her gut. At this rate she

would be signed up for AARP by the time she managed to track down Culligan.

"Crap. I remember crashing out of the RV and being attacked by that cur . . . then everything's a blank."

"The human." His tone was clipped, icy. "She hit you with a spell."

"Bitch. Is she dead?"

"No. You managed to injure the cur, but they both escaped."

Regan grimaced. She didn't have to ask to know that Jagr had chosen to carry her to safety rather than slaughter the cur and witch. Or even to capture them so they could be questioned.

The knowledge should have infuriated her.

She didn't need his protection. She certainly hadn't asked for it.

But she wasn't infuriated.

She was stupidly pleased. As if she wanted to have someone concerned for her welfare.

Dangerous, Regan. Very, very dangerous.

As dangerous as wanting to run her hands over the scarred skin of his chest to prove they did nothing to lessen his fierce beauty.

Her tongue had touched her dry lips when she abruptly realized she had been staring at that wide, delicious chest for far too long. Wrenching her gaze back to his eyes, she felt a blush stain her cheeks.

"I . . . wonder what a witch would be doing with a pack of curs . . ."

"No," he rudely interrupted, stepping close enough so that she was forced to tilt back her head.

"What?"

"That's not what you're wondering. Is it?" His voice was cool, detached. "If you want to know, just ask."

With a start of astonishment, Regan realized that Jagr had

mistakenly assumed her preoccupation with his scars was crass curiosity. Not . . . fascination.

Two very different things.

Of course, curiosity seemed the wiser course when she was alone in a cave with a half-naked vampire she suddenly wanted to lick from head to toe.

"I didn't know that vampires could scar," she muttered the most obvious question.

"It's not a natural process." His eyes darkened with an ancient fury. "It takes savage effort and twisted perseverance to permanently mar a vampire's skin. It's certainly not for the faint of heart."

"Why would . . ." Her hand lifted to press against her heart. "Oh, my God, you were tortured."

"Tortured and then starved so my body could not heal."

"How long?"

"Three centuries."

Her gut twisted in horrified sympathy. Three hundred years of endless torture? How had he survived? And more importantly, how had he survived with his sanity intact?

Christ, she couldn't even comprehend the strength it must have taken.

And she had bitched at him for swinging from hot to cold? He should have been a raving lunatic.

"Was it a demon?" she rasped.

His lips twisted in a humorless smile. "A vampire."

"Jeez." She slowly shook her head. "So the rumors are true."

"What rumors?"

"Culligan was twitchy as hell whenever he had to approach the local vampire clan and pay tribute for doing business in their territory." Her gaze skimmed over the thick scars. "He claimed that vampires are vicious beasts who will slaughter anyone, even each other."

He shrugged, and Regan wished he hadn't. The ripple of

muscles beneath that ivory skin made things twitch and tingle in the pit of her stomach.

"Any creature can be vicious, especially Weres, but vampires have a particularly exquisite talent for terror and pain."

Her gaze was jerked upward at the implication in his cold words.

"They tortured you for fun?"

"Certainly hearing my screams provided entertainment for my captors, but I was tortured for revenge."

"Revenge for what?"

"The truth? I don't remember."

Chapter 8

Jagr watched the predictable astonishment ripple over Regan's beautiful features. Ah, if only his own emotions were so easy to analyze.

For centuries, he'd refused to speak of his endless torture. Most of his brothers sensed the violence of his past, and Viper knew that Jagr's torturer had been a vampire, but nothing more. And none were stupid enough to ask questions.

So why had he deliberately forced this confrontation?

And it had been deliberate.

He could easily have covered his scars before she entered the back cavern. There had been no need for her to ever suspect the truth.

And even now he left them exposed, as if daring her to react to the ugly testament to his past.

So . . . why?

Thankfully Regan managed to recover her voice before he could consider his motives too deeply. They no doubt were something that should remain a mystery.

"You were tortured for three centuries, and you don't remember why?" she husked, the sympathy shimmering in her beautiful eyes not nearly so repulsive as it should have been.

"When a human is turned into a vampire, they have no

memory of their previous life. My sins were committed while I was still a Visigoth chief."

"They must have been doozies."

Jagr shuddered. It didn't matter how many centuries passed, he would never forget the vampire who had held him captive.

Kesi had been a member of the Egyptian royalty before being turned, and she had retained all the proud beauty of her ancestors. The dark almond-shaped eyes, the smoothly burnished skin, the sleek black hair that had flowed like a curtain of satin down her slender back.

Ah, yes, she had been lovely.

And as poisonous as an asp.

She might have captured him in the name of revenge, but she had kept him out of a twisted, obsessive need to inflict pain. He hadn't been her only victim in her private pits of hell.

"The vampire who turned me claimed that I led my clan into the local lair and slaughtered a dozen vampires, including her mate," he explained, pleased as always by the thought that he had dealt Kesi a painful blow, even if he couldn't remember it. "Unfortunately, I was captured during the raid."

"I'm surprised they didn't just kill you. Why make you a vampire?"

"Obviously you missed the Saw movies. Humans are far too fragile to survive more than the vanilla brand of torture. To be truly creative, you need a creature that can endure pain. And, of course, there's always the bonus of making me immortal, so my punishment could last an eternity."

"Dear God." She sucked in a sharp breath, her eyes shimmering with tears. "How did you escape?"

The memory of blood-soaked tunnels filled with vampires and demons he'd ripped apart with his bare hands was washed away by the glitter of tears trickling down her cheeks.

Bemused by the odd phenomenon, Jagr cupped her face in his hands and wiped the dampness with his thumbs.

"I killed them," he murmured, his voice thickening with something other than ancient anger.

"All of them?"

"Yes."

"Good."

His lips twitched. "They weren't nearly so pleased."

A silence descended as Regan studied him with a searching gaze. Jagr didn't flinch. He'd always feared that confessing the truth would make him feel vulnerable, exposed. Instead, he felt . . . cleansed.

Perhaps it was Regan's sweet tears that washed away a portion of the bitterness that festered in his soul.

At last, she sucked in a deep breath. "I'm sorry."

"Why? It wasn't your fault."

"I meant I'm sorry that I didn't believe you when you said you understood. You do." Her lips curved in a watery smile. "More than anyone."

"Yes."

"And that's why you haven't forced me to Chicago."

Jagr hid his flare of wry amusement. If she wanted to believe that was the only reason he hadn't tossed her over his shoulder and hauled her to Chicago, then so be it.

"The thirst for revenge is a powerful force," he agreed. "Nothing will keep you in Chicago while Culligan lives. I would just have to come hunting you again."

"Hunting?" The emerald eyes darkened, then shockingly, she lifted a hand to lightly trace one of the scars that marred his skin. "Do you think I'm your prey?"

With a hiss, Jagr jerked from the searing temptation of her touch. By the fires of hell, what was she doing? Even a complete virgin should be able to sense that his legendary control wasn't so legendary. Not when it came to this emerald-eyed Were.

"Regan," he warned softly.

Deliberately she followed his retreat, her hand once again boldly stroking over his chest.

"What?"

He grasped her wrist, his fangs lengthening as scalding pleasure poured through him.

"Don't toy with me."

She didn't try to tug her wrist from his grim grip. Instead, she simply lifted her free hand and continued to torment him with light, searching fingers.

"Why did you show me your scars?" she demanded.

Jagr shivered, his body swiftly going up in flames. "You're playing a dangerous game, little one."

She met his gaze squarely, ignoring his warning as she stepped close enough to wrap him in midnight jasmine.

"Did you think they would bother me?"

"Do they?"

"Only what they represent." Leaning forward, she trailed her lips over a thick scar. "The fact that you were forced to endure such pain for so long."

Jagr's fingers loosened on her wrist, his thumb brushing the rapid beat of her pulse. Fine. Obviously she wanted to play. Already he could catch the scent of her arousal perfuming the air.

Who was he to be the voice of reason?

Soon enough she would discover you couldn't dance with the devil without getting burned.

Sliding his hand up the elegant sweep of her back, he grasped the tender nape of her neck.

"Like you, little one, I survived," he murmured. "And for the first time, in a very long time, I'm very glad that I did."

"Me, too," she whispered, her head bending forward to brush her lips over his chest.

Convulsively, his arms wrapped about her, tugging her tight against his hard body.

"Do you understand what you're starting, Regan?" he rasped, his senses stirring with an intensity that was almost painful.

"Not really." She trailed her tongue down the dip over his breastbone. "But I like it. Do you?"

His soft groan rumbled through the cavern as his hands shifted to cup her hips, compulsively pressing her to his thickening cock.

"Shit, if I liked it any more I would go up in flames," he muttered, for the first time fully appreciating the powers that had become his when he'd been reborn a vampire.

He could hear every beat of her heart, feel the finest of tremors that shook her slender body, smell the midnight jasmine of her skin . . . the temptation of her rich blood.

His fangs throbbed in concert with his aching erection.

"I never knew . . ." She arched back to meet his hungry gaze. "Does it always feel like this?"

Unable to resist the sight of that slender neck arched in open invitation, Jagr lowered his head to nibble his way down the satin skin.

"No," he rasped, his voice thick with need. "Never like this."

She quivered as his tongue ran a searing path along the line of her collarbone.

"Then what's happening?" Her fingers dug into his upper arms, as if her knees had suddenly become too weak to support her. "One minute I want to punch you in the nose, or at the very least get a restraining order, and the next . . ."

He nipped her earlobe, careful not to break the skin. One overwhelming lust was enough.

"And the next?"

"I want to strip off my clothes and feel your hands on my skin."

Before she could even guess his intention, Jagr grasped the hem of her shirt, and with one smooth jerk had it pulled over her head. She gasped as he tossed it aside and just as easily rid her of the tiny white bra.

"Like this?" he rasped, his hands moving to cup her breasts with a reverent care.

By the gods of his mother, she was beautiful. Perfect. Edible.

His thumbs stroked the rosy tips of her nipples, rumbling in pleasure as the peaks hardened and she shivered with excitement.

"Yes," she whispered. "Exactly like that."

His head lowered, his lips closing over the tip of her breast. "And like this?"

Her head dropped back, her hair brushing over his arms that he had wrapped about her like a warm spill of satin.

"Oh . . . God, yes."

Grimly reminding himself of her innocence, Jagr leashed his desperate hunger. Falling on her like a ravaging beast probably wasn't the best seduction tactic. Not yet.

Continuing to torment her nipple with his tongue, Jagr deftly slid down the zipper of her jeans, longing for the sensation of her naked body pressed against his. When there was no protest from Regan, he slowly began to peel them downward, lowering himself to his knees as he efficiently tugged off her running shoes and socks before removing the jeans.

Then, still kneeling, he simply drank in the sight of her.

Her legs were long and slender. Her waist narrow enough he knew he could span it with his hands. But it was the firm muscles that rippled beneath her smooth skin that sent a jolt of excitement through him.

Well, that, and the tiny triangle of silk that was at his direct eye level.

His fangs were fully extended, ready and willing to cut through the delicate material to reveal the sweet treasure beneath.

Once again, however, he restrained his sharp-edged need.

Instead, he slowly worked his way back to his feet, trailing his lips up the curve of her stomach, the hollow between her breasts, and the frantic pulse at the base of her neck.

She groaned, her lips parting willingly as he at last claimed her mouth in a demanding kiss.

"Jagr," she moaned.

"You smell of midnight jasmine. I could drown in that scent."

"You smell of power," she whispered against his lips. "Like a strike of lightning."

"Does lightning have a scent?" he teased, his hands compulsively caressing the curve of her back. He could have her in his arms for an eternity and still it would not be long enough.

Because this is where she belongs.

Where she will always belong.

The disturbing words floated through his mind before he could halt them.

"Raw energy," she retorted, moaning as his tongue traced the edge of her lower lip. "Dangerous . . . unpredictable . . ."

"Oh, I can be very predictable, little one," he corrected, grasping her hand to gently place it against his pulsing arousal.

Her breath caught as her fingers traced his hard cock straining against his zipper, her eyes darkening with awareness of her feminine power.

Desire clawed deep within him. He wanted to make this a slow, delicate seduction, but the thought of being buried deep within her was swiftly undermining his control. At heart, he was still a barbarian. A wild, pagan coupling was becoming a more viable option by the second.

Regan couldn't have missed the sudden heat that filled the cavern, or the tension that clenched his muscles, but as if deliberately seeking to push Jagr over the edge, her searching fingers slowly tugged down the zipper of his jeans, releasing the heavy thrust of his erection.

"Gods," Jagr managed to croak, shuddering at the hot surge of desire.

"Do you like this?" she demanded, lightly skimming her fingers down his thick length.

"Yes," he growled, his hands clutching her hips as he sought to remain in control of his building need.

"And this?" she whispered, her hand moving steadily lower.

"Regan . . ." He muttered a curse, his eyes clenching shut as he battled to hold off the surging climax. "Yes."

She discovered his tender sack and lightly squeezed. "And this?"

"Enough," he choked, grasping her wrist to halt the exquisite torment.

"Why?"

Forcing his eyes open, he met the glittering emerald gaze. "Because just your touch is enough to make me explode."

The sweet scent of her arousal deepened at his blunt words. "And that's a bad thing?"

"Bad?" His sharp laugh echoed through the darkness. "By the saints, I would walk through the fires of hell for the feel of your hands on my body."

Her lips curved in a smile of pure temptation.

A natural born Eve.

"Then why are you stopping me?"

Good question.

Oh, it wasn't uncommon for him to deny himself pleasure.

His lair was a cold, barren series of cement tunnels beneath an abandoned warehouse. It had none of the luxuries that most vampires craved. His only concession to comfort was his vast collection of books, his high-tech computer, and his plasma TVs.

And certainly he never allowed himself to wallow in the self-indulgent pursuit of physical pleasure that many demons craved.

He never questioned his monkish existence. What did it matter if it was an obsessive need to feel in control after years of being in the power of others? Or some obscure hatred for being turned into the same monster as those who'd tortured him? Or even a boorish distaste for the company of others.

In this moment, he wanted to plunge into the swirling sensations that heated his blood to a fever pitch. He wanted to . . . feel. To melt the ice that had held him captive since he'd left those blood-soaked caves.

He wanted Regan in any way she would have him.

It was obvious that despite her innocence, this Were possessed a playful curiosity. Why not allow her to explore her potent effect on his body?

They had an eternity to satisfy any number of fantasies.

Endless, decadent, wicked fantasies.

With a slow, deliberate motion, Jagr released her wrist at the same moment he branded her lips with a searing kiss. She readily opened her mouth to allow the invasion of his thrusting tongue, her hand moving on him with awkward but shockingly blissful strokes.

He didn't know why she'd suddenly lowered her stiff barriers. Why she'd accepted the passion that had pulsed between them since their first meeting. And to be honest, he didn't give a shit.

Fate was rarely kind to him. He intended to take advantage while it was willing to smile on him.

Dragging his lips over the heated skin of her cheeks, he nuzzled the hollow just below her ear, his fingers trailing a determined path down the sleek line of her waist. She shivered in response, her heart pounding so loudly that Jagr didn't need to be a vampire to hear it.

He used her telltale responses to guide his touch, intent on her pleasure even as his hips began to pump forward as her strokes became more assured, forceful.

Oh . . . hell.

In over a thousand years, nothing had ever felt so good.

Reaching the edge of her panties, Jagr ripped the fragile silk away, well beyond subtle.

He wanted to explore the damp heat he could already

sense. He wanted to feel her tremble in need. He wanted to hear those tiny cries of pleasure as he made her come.

Allowing his hand to slide over the curve of her thigh, Jagr gently parted her legs to allow his fingers access to her most tender flesh.

Growling low in his throat, he parted her folds and discovered her moist and eager for his touch.

"Holy crap," she muttered, her fingers unwittingly tightening on his erection.

Not that he intended to protest. Instead, he muttered soft words of encouragement as he caressed her with a growing urgency.

His fangs ached, his hunger roaring through him, but Jagr ignored the burning need to take her blood. The blissful pressure clenching his lower body was swiftly reaching the point of no return. He was fiercely determined to ensure her pleasure before claiming his own.

Dipping his head lower, Jagr sucked the tip of her nipple in his mouth, using his tongue to tease and torment her as his finger dipped into her slick channel. She whimpered softly, her hand stroking him with greater speed in response to his persistent caress.

She was close.

So close.

Her breath halted, her back arching, and with a soft cry she shuddered in completion, her last lingering tug of his erection causing him to shout as the sensations gathered and the world exploded in pleasure.

Folding her close, Jagr had to smile.

Maybe Regan hadn't been wrong when she claimed she smelled lightning.

The gods knew he'd just been struck.

* * *

Floating on a little cloud of paradise, Regan made no effort to struggle as Jagr swept her off her feet and waded into the chilled water that ran through the back of the cavern. Not even when he gently but thoroughly scrubbed her with the expensive soap and shampoo he'd obviously brought from Chicago.

For the first time in her existence, she felt . . . deliciously pampered.

Just like a normal woman who was being spoiled by her current lover.

Lover.

Regan shivered. Yes . . . lovers.

Oh, she wasn't stupid (okay, that might be debatable), but she understood the basic principles of intercourse, and the fact she was still technically a virgin. Who could watch Pay Per View and not have waaaay too much info?

Still, it had been . . .

Wow.

Yeah, that about summed it up.

And while a part of her wanted to blame her bout of insanity on mere pity for a creature who had suffered such agony, she couldn't make it stick. Not when she'd wanted to have her way with the gorgeous vamp since his orgasmic bite in that hotel room.

There, she'd admitted it, if only to herself.

She might not understand why a vampire who was arrogant, aggravating, and only with her because he'd been commanded by his mighty Anasso to protect her, could make her entire body quiver whenever he was near, but there it was.

And obviously the quiver factor didn't disappear even after a mind-blowing climax.

With every sweep of his hands, tiny jolts of awareness tingled through her, stirring the wondrous lethargy that held her captive.

"You're very quiet," he murmured.

"And no one's allowed to be the strong silent type except you?" she demanded, keeping her eyes closed. One glance at the impossibly beautiful face and she would be flat on her back, begging for mercy.

A woman had to have *some* pride, didn't she?

He chuckled softly. "You're certainly strong enough, but you haven't struck me as being particularly silent."

Her breath caught as his hand outlined the curve of her hip. "I spent thirty years forced to keep my mouth shut while Culligan blathered for hours on end. From now on, I intend to say what I want to say, when I want to say it, and as often as I want to say it."

"So I've noticed."

Unable to resist, she opened her eyes to meet his coolly amused gaze.

"If you don't like it, you can always . . ."

Regan didn't even try to avoid the starkly possessive kiss that stole her words.

"I didn't say I didn't like it," he muttered against her lips. "Besides, I know how to silence you when I want."

"Arrogant jackass."

"Always."

With one last burning kiss, he rinsed off the lingering soap, and hauled her out of the water. Then leaving her to dry off with his discarded shirt, he pulled on the faded jeans, a clean black T-shirt (that stretched with oh-my-God results over his wide chest), and a pair of heavy biker boots before disappearing into the outer cave.

Regan had barely managed to wipe off the dampness and pull on her bra and panties when he returned, his brows pulled into a frown as he held out the bags of her new clothing.

"I took half the store and there isn't one decent shirt in there."

Well, so much for the considerate lover who had bathed her with such tender care, she wryly acknowledged.

Yanking the bags from his hands, Regan pulled on a pair of hip hugging jeans, then dug through the mound of shirts to pull out a pretty yellow knit top with a scooped neckline and lace about the hem that barely reached her belly button.

Pulling it over her head, she smoothed it down and regarded him with a challenging smile.

"What's wrong with my shirts?"

He scowled as his gaze studied the tiny top that clung to her curves.

"They've all been chopped off at the waist and cut so low you might as well not even bother with them."

"In case you haven't noticed, the dark ages of keeping women covered from head to toe are long over, chief." Her eyes narrowed. "And what business is it of yours, anyway?"

He folded his arms over his chest, appearing big and dangerous and . . . Christ, so heartstoppingly beautiful it made her mouth water.

Damn vampire.

"I . . ." His words came to an abrupt halt at the same moment that Regan froze—an unmistakable scent floating through the air. "Were," he growled, turning with impossible grace to flow into the outer cave.

"Salvatore," Regan clarified, her hackles rising as she followed with less grace and a great deal more stomping.

Stepping into the large cave, Regan ignored Jagr's attempt to keep her hidden behind his massive form, instead moving so she could have an uninterrupted view as Salvatore Giuliani boldly stepped through the entrance.

As always, the King of Weres was elegantly attired in a designer suit, this one in a slate gray with a matching silk tie and pale ivory shirt. His thick black hair was pulled into a tail at the nape of his neck, and his sensuous Latin features were a polished bronze. It was his golden eyes, however, that caught and held attention. They were eyes that held a ruthless intelligence and lethal willingness to do whatever necessary to achieve his goal.

Including tossing her aside like a piece of non-recyclable trash.

Strolling arrogantly into the cave, Salvatore deliberately sniffed the air, the wicked glint in his eyes revealing his awareness of their earlier passion.

"Am I intruding?" he mocked, his voice accented with a hint of Italian. His lips twitched as Jagr regarded him in a frigid silence, his gaze shifting to Regan. "Ah, Regan. As exquisite as ever."

Regan didn't hesitate.

"You son of a bitch," she rasped, launching herself across the cave with a speed that caught both men off guard. Slamming into the startled Were, she knocked him flat on his back and perched on top of his chest, glaring into the too handsome face. "You let Culligan get away."

The golden eyes glowed, but it was pure male arousal rather than anger that stirred his inner wolf.

"*Cristo,* you are magnificent. Such a pity you can't bear me an heir. You would have been a worthy mate." His smile was slow, seductive. "Of course, that doesn't mean we couldn't enjoy each other's company. You haven't lived until you've been bedded by a pureblood . . ."

Her eyes narrowed in disgust. "Even think about it and I'll castrate you."

His husky laugh echoed through the cave as he gave a mighty shove and rolled Regan beneath him. Now on top, he smiled into her startled eyes.

"Oh, I'm thinking about it."

He didn't think about it long.

The cold blast of fury was the only warning before Jagr had Salvatore by the throat, and was shoving him against the wall of the cave.

"Touch her again, dog, and they'll be finding your body

parts from here to New Orleans," he informed Salvatore in artic tones.

The golden eyes blazed. "Release me, vampire, or you'll have a war on your hands Styx does not want."

Indifferent to the threat, Jagr leaned forward, whispering something too low for Regan to catch before abruptly stepping back and releasing his death-hold on the Were.

Salvatore growled low in his throat, but oddly didn't attack. Instead, he smoothed his hands down his Gucci suit and ensured his tie was still immaculate.

"Have I mentioned how much I hate vampires?" he purred with sweet venom.

Regan rose to her feet, wondering what the hell Jagr had whispered in Salvatore's ear.

"Why are you here?" Jagr demanded. "I called you to Hannibal to take care of your rabid curs, not to socialize."

Salvatore met the ancient vampire's glare without flinching. "I'm here because there's no proof there are any curs in the area, despite the fact my men have searched for hours. A suspicious Were might begin to conjecture that this is a trap."

"I don't need a trap to kill a Were, king or not."

Regan shivered, feeling as if she were standing in the middle of a brewing thunderstorm.

Not surprising.

Salvatore was throwing off the natural heat of a furious pureblood, while Jagr's power was a frigid blast.

Just like a hot- and cold-weather front clashing together.

"Christ, I'm choking on the testosterone in here," she muttered, shifting to stand between the two men. About as smart as stepping between a rabid wolf and feral tiger, but nothing would get done while the two played "who has the biggest balls" game. She regarded Salvatore with an annoyed glare. "You didn't find the curs because they're being concealed by a witch's spell."

"Have you actually seen any of them?" the Were

demanded, his gaze tracking Jagr as the vamp pressed his large body against Regan's back and wrapped a possessive arm about her waist.

Regan swallowed a sigh. It always looked so sexy in the movies to have two men snarling and snapping over a woman. Now she just wanted to punch them both in the nose.

"One attacked us last night," she said.

Salvatore stiffened in surprise. "A moment."

Turning toward the entrance of the cave, the Were gave a low whistle. Immediately, two curs entered the cave. One a huge, hulking cur with a shaved head and pit bull face. The other smaller, leaner with short blond hair and a startling intelligent expression.

In tandem they fell to their knees and pressed their foreheads to the hard ground.

"Yes, your majesty?" The bald-headed cur spoke for the groveling pair. "How may we serve?"

Regan gagged as she turned toward Salvatore. "Oh, you've got to be freaking kidding me. I thought Culligan was full of himself."

A smile curved the Were's lips. Smug bastard.

"Hess has lived among the hunting grounds north of here. It's possible he will recognize your attacker if you can describe him."

"I can do better than that if you have a pencil and paper," she said.

Salvatore snapped his fingers. "Max, go back down to the Humvee and find what the lady needs."

"Yes, sire."

Jumping to his feet, the young man charged out of the cave at full speed. Regan shook her head.

"You really get off on the whole royalty thing, don't you?"

"It's good to be King."

"Yeah, I bet."

His smile softened to a wicked invitation. "But not as good as it is to be the King's . . ."

Jagr tightened his arm around Regan's waist, his power making the hair on the nape of her neck stand on end.

"Careful, dog," he hissed.

"Feeling a little territorial, vamp?" Salvatore mocked.

"Regicidal."

Chapter 9

A tense silence descended as the two predators huffed and puffed and did all the stupid things males did when they weren't allowed to kill one another.

Regan rubbed her hands over her arms, shivering at the painful prickles that brushed over her skin. Holy crap. Things could go nuclear in a hurry, and there wasn't a damn thing she could do about it.

At last the gathering storm was broken by the return of Max, who had barely broken a sweat despite his swift run up and down the high bluff.

"Thank God," Regan muttered, struggling free of Jagr's arm to snatch the notebook and pencil from the cur.

Vividly aware of the tension sizzling between the males, Regan moved to perch on a flat rock. Christ, the air in the cave was so thick she could barely breathe. And it didn't help that the two curs had moved to flank Salvatore as if preparing for a battle. Why didn't they just wave a red flag in front of the ancient, lethal vampire?

Morons.

Clearing her mind, Regan forced herself to concentrate on the memory of the cur that had attacked them. What was the point in fretting over Jagr and Salvatore? If they wanted to rip each other apart, then so be it.

She wasn't about to play *Super Nanny*.

Sliding the pencil across the paper, Regan lost herself in her sketch. She was no Picasso (well, who was?), but over the years she'd discovered the trick of capturing an image with the minimum of strokes.

She had completed the basic outline of the cur's face and was working on the narrow goatee when she felt Jagr move to stand at her side, his power carefully muted.

"That's perfect," he murmured, a hint of surprise in his voice. "You have a true talent."

Regan shrugged. "Not talent, just practice. There's not a lot to do in a cramped cage besides watch TV, read, and sketch." With a few more strokes of her pencil, Regan was satisfied and held out the notebook toward Salvatore. "Here."

Salvatore moved forward with the hulking Hess at his side.

"Do you recognize him?" the Were demanded of his companion.

The cur snarled in recognition, his eyes glowing. "Duncan."

Salvatore frowned. "What do you know of him?"

"He's a disciple of Caine."

Shock rippled over the Were's handsome face. "*Cristo*."

"Who's this Caine?" Jagr demanded.

Salvatore snapped his teeth, his thoughts obviously distracted. "Internal Were business."

"It becomes my business when one of your hounds nearly barbeques me," Jagr snapped. "Why are they trying to kill Regan?"

"I don't know."

Jagr stepped toward Salvatore, his body coiled to attack, his fangs glinting in the dark.

"Don't try me, Were."

Regan shivered, but Salvatore merely arched an arrogant brow. Courage or stupidity?

Impossible to say.

"You can flash all the fang you want, vamp, I have no explanation for why the curs would be in Hannibal, or why they would have an interest in Regan."

"Then what the hell do you know?"

Salvatore gritted his teeth, but obviously aware that Jagr was preparing to beat the truth out of him (with as much pain as possible), he abruptly turned to pace across the cave.

"I've had reports that a cur by the name of Caine has been gathering curs into a secret society."

Regan swallowed a ridiculous urge to laugh. "Like the Masons?"

Salvatore continued to pace. "From what little information I've been able to gather, it's more like a fatwa."

"A holy war?" she demanded.

"A handful of curs have convinced themselves that the Weres are deliberately diluting their powers."

She shook her head. Being raised in a silver cage with only occasional encounters with other demons, she was remarkably ignorant of her people. Something that had never bothered her until a bunch of mangy curs decided to steal Culligan.

"Which powers?" she demanded.

Salvatore shrugged. "Their strength, their ability to control their shifts, their lack of immortality. Nonsense, of course. A cur might take on greater strength and a prolonged existence, but in the end they're merely a human infected by our bite. They are not resurrected to become a full demon as vampires are."

So the curs got a glimpse of glory, only to fall short. Kind of like her.

A mutant with no real place in the demon-world.

Who wouldn't want revenge? Especially if it meant dethroning the smug, overbearing, *GQ*-addicted King of Weres?

Of course, Caine of the curs couldn't be very smart if he

thought for a moment a ragtag pack would have any chance against any pureblood, let alone one of Salvatore's power. And why Duncan would imply they were somehow interested in her . . .

Her breath tangled in her throat. "Oh."

Jagr flowed to her side, as if sensing the outrageous suspicion that flowed through her mind.

"What is it, little one?"

"I . . ." With a shake of her head, Regan turned to meet Salvatore's searching gaze. "The curs believe a Were could offer them the powers they want?"

"As I said, a few idiots are convinced we are deliberately altering the amount of venom in our bites to lessen their abilities. Once I track down Caine, I intend to bring an end to his dangerous claims." His sensuous lips curved into a terrifying smile. "A painful end."

Regan grimaced. "Very *Rambo* of you, but have you considered the possibility that this Caine has decided to do more than just complain about the fate of curs?"

Salvatore snorted. "He doesn't possess enough followers to strike against the Weres. He prefers to hide in shadows while stirring the seeds of revolution."

"Yeah, well, maybe the Benedict Arnold routine is just an act."

Jagr hissed, reading her mind with unnerving ease. "Yes."

Salvatore frowned, thankfully not capable of rummaging around in her thoughts.

"What the hell do you mean?"

Regan struggled to put her vague suspicion into words. "If this Caine truly believes he can transform himself into a Were, why would he bother plotting a fight he can never win? Wouldn't it make more sense to spend his time finding the key to enhancing his gifts?"

"He's already gone through the change . . ." Salvatore bit off his words, his eyes glowing with that eerie fire. "*Cristo.*"

"And if he believes that he can still get the powers he lacks, what would he need?" Jagr rasped.

Salvatore toyed with the heavy signet ring on his finger. "If his theory wasn't completely illogical, completely unscientific, and completely crazy, I suppose he would need a pureblood."

Four pairs of male eyes turned to regard Regan as if she were a nasty bug beneath a microscope.

"Surely they would need her alive?" Jagr rasped, the edge of ice in his voice assuring Regan he wasn't nearly so calm as he appeared.

She was swiftly discovering the stronger his emotions, the deeper he coated them in permafrost.

"Actually, I think they have been trying to take me alive," Regan admitted, deliberately catching Jagr's fierce gaze. "It's *you* they want to kill."

"Imagine that," Salvatore drawled.

Jagr's attention never wavered from Regan. "How can you be certain?"

"I'm not certain, but Duncan was trying to convince me to come willingly with him while you were still unconscious."

"The terrifying Jagr knocked unconscious by a cur?"

This time Jagr flashed an icy glare toward the provoking Salvatore. "A witch."

"Duncan said that he wanted to keep me safe." Regan hurriedly headed off yet another squabble between the two. "He didn't say what danger I was supposedly in, but it was obvious he was desperate to take me somewhere, no matter what he had to do get me there."

Salvatore snarled a low curse. "I look forward to meeting this Duncan. We have a great deal to discuss."

Something that might have been frustration hardened Jagr's beautiful face.

"At this point, it's all nothing more than speculation. Leaping to conclusions could put Regan in danger. For now, all that matters is that she remain protected."

She instinctively bristled at his possessive tone. Okay, she was ready, willing, and able to take advantage of his bodacious body. Why not? She'd been forced into celibacy for too long. And he'd already proven he possessed the sort of skills a woman in rampant lust could appreciate.

But the last thing she wanted was an overbearing keeper.

She already had one of those on her list to kill.

"I can take care of myself, thank you very much," she snapped. "And the only thing I'm interested in is the fact that Duncan claims they have Culligan."

Jagr's frustration became a tangible blast of frozen air. "It's a trap."

She rolled her eyes at his flat accusation. "Ya think?"

"I think when it comes to the imp, you tend to act first and think of the consequences later."

Salvatore's soft laugh replaced Jagr's chill with a brush of warm velvet.

"I see he knows you in more than just the carnal sense, sweet Regan."

She tossed him an annoyed frown. "Shut up."

"Is that any way to speak to your king?" he mocked.

She was about to inform her freaking king she'd talk to him any way she pleased when the sudden entrance of Levet had everyone spinning toward him in shock.

Ignoring the various guns, daggers, and flashing fangs that were aimed in his direction, Levet waddled forward, his tiny snout twitching.

"*Sacrebleu.* What's that stench?" He blatantly glanced toward Salvatore. "Oh. Dogs. I should have known."

Salvatore merely smiled, reaching out a hand to catch the bristling cur at his side.

"Easy, Hess. Do you not recall the stunted gargoyle who so kindly led Darcy into our trap?" The smile widened to reveal the white, white teeth. "I never did have the opportunity to offer my thanks."

"Not much of a trap since Darcy is currently the Queen of Vampires, not Weres," Levet smoothly countered.

Salvatore's eyes flashed, but his expression remained mocking. "Her loss."

The words had barely tumbled from his lips when there was the distant sound of shattering glass.

Within the cave everyone stilled, the very air shimmering with a sense of foreboding. Then with a movement that was too swift for Regan to follow, Jagr had launched himself forward, knocking her to the ground and covering her with his large body, as the concussion of an explosion far below rocked the bluff.

Jagr ignored Regan's fists that pounded his chest, as well as her colorful descriptions of what should happen to oversized oafs who tackled hapless women, not willing to move until he was certain that the cave wasn't on the edge of collapse. Only then did he lift himself high enough to run a searching gaze over Regan's wriggling body, needing to be certain that she wasn't hurt.

Dodging a fist aimed directly at his chin, Jagr flowed to his feet, hiding his smile.

If she could throw a punch like that, she couldn't be badly injured.

Sensing he might lose a hand if he offered to help her off the ground, Jagr turned to join Salvatore and his curs at the entrance to the cave. He would no doubt pay for his violent instinct to protect Regan, but there had been no choice. He could no more have halted his reaction than he could halt the sun from rising.

A knowledge he shoved to the back of his mind as he stepped beside Salvatore and studied the expensive Humvee that was now a ball of flame in the parking lot far below.

"*Dio,*" the Were breathed. "Hess. Max. Bring me whoever is responsible."

Looking as if they'd been shot from a cannon, the two curs bolted down the steep slope of the bluff, their low growls echoing through the darkness.

Jagr folded his arms over his chest, not entirely displeased to watch Salvatore's vehicle go up flames. Not just because of his overly intimate manner toward Regan (although that was reason enough to rip out his filthy heart), but because the Were had wounded Regan when she was at her most vulnerable.

The bastard had freed her from the nightmare of Culligan, only to toss her aside when she couldn't provide him what he desired.

It was no wonder she found it impossible to trust.

"Your curs have a peculiar means of welcoming their king." He studied the burning Humvee. "Unless this is some ritual I'm unaware of?"

Salvatore ignored the taunt as power rippled beneath his skin. As a pureblood, he was capable of controlling his shifts, but the wolf was obviously struggling to break free.

"I should have sensed them," the king rasped, his voice low and thick.

Jagr grimaced. "The witch."

"She's starting to wear on my nerves."

"Agreed, but being rid of her is easier said than done. Only the gargoyle can sense her magic, and he seems incapable of tracking her down."

"Hey." There was a snap of angry wings as Levet exited the cave, followed closely by Regan. "I'm the one who's been out tromping through the nasty boonies while you were playing splish-splash with our beautiful guest."

Jagr took a second to savor the sudden heat that stained Regan's cheeks before returning his attention to the gargoyle with a lift of his brow.

"Tromping that obviously led the curs straight back to this lair."

"Or maybe they followed Mr. Lord and Master over there. Did you ever think about that?" Levet challenged.

"In either case, they've left warning that they know Salvatore is in Hannibal. And more importantly, they know this is our lair." This time he turned to directly meet Regan's guarded gaze. "We're no longer safe here."

Salvatore muttered a curse. "I have no pack in the area. I will have to return to St. Louis for reinforcements."

"Why don't you just call them?" Regan demanded.

"I prefer to give my commands in person. It helps to avoid any confusion."

She rolled her eyes. "Yeah, I bet."

Jagr frowned. "Do you have a magic-user among them?"

"No, but I can negotiate with the local coven." Salvatore toyed with his heavy signet ring, his expression hard. "Unfortunately, it will take time. Witches are notoriously reluctant to offer their services to demons."

"What am I?" Levet threw his hands in the air. "Chopped gall bladder?"

Jagr narrowed his gaze, in no mood for the annoying gargoyle. "What?"

"I think he means liver," Regan wryly translated. "Chopped liver."

"Gall bladder, liver . . . whatever." Levet puffed out his chest. "I am a magic-user. What could a witch do that I can't?"

"Track the curs? Weave an enchantment to hide our own presence? Ward this cave from intrusion?" Jagr smoothly pointed out.

"Bah, I will find the curs, and if you want an enchantment . . ." The tiny gargoyle lifted his hands.

"No," Jagr and Salvatore bellowed at the same time.

"Fine." With a twitch of his tail, Levet was marching down the steep bluff. "You want curs, I'll find you curs."

Regan spread her annoyed glare between both Jagr and Salvatore as she called out softly.

"Levet."

With a stiff dignity, Levet turned to face her. *"Oui?"*

"Please, be careful."

The ugly features softened. "For you, *ma cherie,* I will take the greatest care. Be assured that I will return in magnificent, vigorous, and virile health."

Jagr swallowed his urge to snarl. "You can return any way you want, but we won't be here. We have to find a new lair."

"Do not fear, I will find you."

"That was my fear," Jagr muttered.

Levet blew a raspberry in Jagr's direction before continuing down the slope.

"That creature is an embarrassment to gargoyles everywhere," Salvatore said with a shake of his head.

For once, Jagr could actually agree with the Were.

Not that he was about to admit as much.

Especially not when he could smell Salvatore's henchmen approaching.

The two curs appeared from the woods behind the cave, a matching expression of frustration on their faces.

"We followed their footprints to the river, then they disappeared," the larger, bald-headed Hess grudgingly confessed. "We searched the area, but there was no sign of them."

Jagr clenched his fists in annoyance. He didn't like being taunted by a pack of worthless dogs.

"They can't have gone far."

"No, but without a scent we're incapable of hunting them." Salvatore gestured toward his companions. "There's nothing more to be done here. I will return as soon as possible."

Jagr didn't attempt to halt Salvatore as he disappeared into the surrounding shadows. What good was the Were if he couldn't track the curs?

Besides, having two alpha predators in the same territory

was never a good idea. Jagr doubted that Styx would be pleased to learn one of his vampires had the pelt of the King of Weres nailed to the wall of his lair.

"Well, this is going just peachy," Regan muttered, her damp hair fluttering like strands of silver in the night breeze. "Christ. All I wanted was to find Culligan and kill him, not get mixed up in some stupid war between the curs and the Weres."

Jagr reached out to capture one of the silky strands, his expression somber.

"You would be safe in Chicago, Regan. Not even this Caine and his renegade pack of curs would be suicidal enough to attack a vampire stronghold."

"A really stupendous idea if I wanted to be buried alive," she mocked. "Thanks, but no thanks. I'm not exchanging one prison for another."

He gave a tug on her hair. "You would be an honored guest, never a prisoner."

"Oh, I'm sure my cell would be something out of the latest episode of *Cribs,* and my guards would be oh so kind while they explained why it was too dangerous for me to go out alone, or spend a weekend in Vegas."

His brows lifted. "You have a particular desire to visit Las Vegas?"

"I have a particular desire to go where I want, when I want, without asking for permission."

Jagr considered his words as his fingers shifted to brush down the seductive line of her throat. What could he say? There was no way in hell that Styx would allow Regan to come and go as she pleased. At least not as long as there was any threat to her.

Styx was by nature a control freak, and while Darcy had gone a long way to soften his rigid instincts, he couldn't change centuries of habit overnight.

"Even if it puts you in danger?" he at last demanded.

"Yes."

"Independence is one thing, Regan, and stubborn foolishness another."

"Do you live under the roof of the Anasso?" she challenged.

His fingers lingered on the pulse at the base of her throat, the rush of her blood teasing his senses with sweet temptation.

"I have a private lair, but I owe fealty to the Anasso, as well as Viper," he murmured, unwittingly lowering his head to drink in her intoxicating scent.

Her pulse leaped beneath his fingertips.

"Viper?" she rasped.

"Clan chief of Chicago. When either commands my service, I must obey."

"Like coming to Hannibal to collect a dysfunctional Were?"

His lips twitched. "Yes."

She sucked in a shuddering breath, as conscious as Jagr of the potent awareness that jolted between them.

"Why give them such power?"

Abruptly realizing his fingers had drifted to the distracting fullness of her lips, Jagr dropped his hand and stepped away.

What the devil was he doing? His highly honed senses might assure him that there were no dangers in the area, but that didn't mean they weren't sitting targets.

Where was his ruthless self-discipline? His icy logic? His barren disinterest in others?

When it came to Regan, he was as easily distracted as a dew fairy high on honey.

"A vampire without a clan is always seen as a threat," he retorted, taking her arm to steer back through the narrow entrance into the cave. "My only hope for a measure of peace was to find a chief who controlled a stable clan with no thirst for war. Nothing is without cost. Even freedom."

Shaking off his hand, Regan folded her arms over her chest and dug in her heels.

"Well, I'm not willing to become a pampered hostage to

my sister in exchange for safety. I'd rather take my chances with the curs."

His lips twisted at her predictable response. "Hardly a logical decision."

"I don't want to be logical. I want to find Culligan and kill him. Speaking of which . . ."

With a blur of speed, Jagr had moved to block the opening. "Wait, little one."

A frustration that Jagr fully appreciated tightened her beautiful features.

"Now what?"

"Unless you want to leave behind your clothes, you will need to take them with us. We can't risk returning here."

"Why bother finding a new lair? They'll just track us down again."

"Trust me."

Emerald eyes sparked with irritation at his command for her blind faith, but astonishingly, she spun on her heel and marched toward the back of the cave rather than try to rip out his heart.

Jagr wasn't sure whether to be pleased or terrified as he followed in her stormy wake.

In silence, she gathered the bags that were so obviously precious to her, stoically ignoring Jagr as he placed his own belongings into the leather satchel he'd brought from Chicago.

Tossing it over his shoulder, he moved to halt Regan as she reached for the rumpled clothes he'd peeled from her delectable body such a short time ago.

"Leave a few behind."

Her brows snapped together. "Why?"

"I thought you were going to trust me."

Chapter 10

I thought you were going to trust me . . .

Regan clutched the stuffed bags to her chest, her jaw clenched at Jagr's soft words.

She wanted to laugh at his words.

She'd spent thirty years being tormented, betrayed, and abused by everyone she had ever known. Now, a lethal vampire she'd met only days ago wanted her to blithely put her life in his hands?

Yeah, right.

So . . . why wasn't she laughing?

Maybe because her every instinct told her that Jagr would do everything in his power to keep her safe.

Whether out of fear his Anasso would mount him on the wall of his throne room or for some more personal reason was impossible to say.

"Here." Reading her conflicting emotions with annoying ease, Jagr moved forward, holding out a silver box in an obvious effort to distract her.

It worked.

Her eyes widened as she took Culligan's private safe. "I dropped this when you went juggernaut and launched us through the back of the RV." She met his searching gaze. "How'd you get it?"

"I had Levet retrieve it. There are papers in the bottom we haven't looked through yet."

"You think they might be important?"

"We can only hope."

Contemplating what papers Culligan could possibly have that he considered worth keeping, Regan lowered her guard. A stupid mistake. Before she could blink she found herself hauled off her feet and firmly cradled against his chest.

Damn vampire speed.

"What are you doing?" she hissed, cursing the bulky bags and metal safe that tangled her arms and made it impossible to struggle. "Put me down."

He ignored her command (big freaking surprise), moving with fluid ease across the cave.

"We can't be sure that the explosion wasn't a ruse to draw you out of the cave. We'll have to sneak out."

She held herself stiffly, vividly aware of the cool power washing over her skin. Dammit, she wanted to be furious, not . . . aroused.

"And if the curs are out there?" she snapped. "Won't they sense us?"

He shrugged, the long hair he'd left free to frame the haunting beauty of his lean face flowing down his back like liquid gold.

"Salvatore was mocking, but Caine has reason to resent the Weres," he said softly. "Unless a cur has fully shifted, their senses are not equal to most demons. Our scents are already spread through the area, so unless they actually see us leave the cave they won't know we've slipped beneath their noses."

"Oh." She abruptly felt like an idiot. "That's why you made me leave the clothes behind."

"They should keep your scent lingering for days."

"Fine, Mr. Smarty Pants . . ."

"Mr. Smarty Pants?"

She ignored his interruption. "If they're actually watching the cave, then how are we supposed to leave without being seen? Unlike you, I can't wrap myself in shadows."

He paused at the entrance of the cave, an almost smile hovering around his lips.

"You can as long as you stay close to me. Hold still."

Regan frowned.

Well, hell.

Was there anything vampires couldn't do?

Walk on water? Unlock the secret of cold fusion?

Create world peace?

Her annoyance at the injustice of vampires' position at the top of the demon-world was forgotten as she suddenly felt like she'd been dipped in an icy pool of water.

She sucked in a sharp breath.

This wasn't the cool surge of Jagr's power.

"Holy crap, what are you doing?" she demanded with a shiver. "I'm freezing."

"I've wrapped you in my shadows. They will hide us from prying eyes, but not from prying ears." Before she could guess his intention, he bent downward to place his lips against hers. "Not a word, little one."

Sadie smiled as she watched the expensive Humvee being consumed by flames. Standing several blocks away on the roof of a restaurant that had once been a bordello, she had a perfect view to watch Salvatore leave the cave with his neutered curs scurrying behind him.

Sniffling, spineless dogs.

Their blind subservience to the self-proclaimed King of Weres sickened her. Why didn't they just put a leash around their neck, and be done with it?

Of course, they had managed to lead her to where Regan

wa hidden with the vamp, so perhaps they weren't entirely useless.

Her smile widened as she leaned against the decorative brick wall that lined the rooftop.

"I do love a roaring bonfire. A pity I forgot to bring the marshmallows."

Standing at her side, Duncan growled with impatience. "Did you also forget to bring a point for this little exercise in futility?"

"Careful, Duncan." Sophie slid her companion a warning frown. "So far you've proven to be as incompetent as you are spineless. Twice now you've allowed our quarry to slip through your fingers."

Duncan's jaw tightened, his pride obviously still pricked at having been bested by the young, untrained woman.

Again.

"At least I've had her in my fingers. Which is more than you can say."

"Only because I was stupid enough to assume my merry band of morons could manage to capture one little Were." Sadie shrugged. "I won't make that mistake again."

An ugly smile twisted his lips. "Oh, no, you've done much better. Now we not only have the most dangerous vampire in the entire world hunting our sorry hides, but you've managed to piss off the King of Weres. A real bang-up job."

Sadie bit back her snarl. It had been an unpleasant shock when the unmistakable scent of Salvatore had invaded her territory. Caine had sworn that the king had no interest in Regan, and wouldn't so much as lift a finger to help her.

Easy for him to say when he was safely hidden miles away.

Bastard.

And to top it off, she'd followed the scent of the curs to the cave, only to discover that not only was Regan being guarded by a vampire, the King of Weres, and his curs, but there was a damned gargoyle in residence.

A lesser woman would have thrown in the towel. Sadie, however, had always been able to think on her feet, and it had taken only a moment to devise yet another brilliant plan.

"Pissed off or not, I've managed to separate Regan from the Weres, as well as the gargoyle," she pointed out, her annoyance easing as she smugly turned her attention back to the fire below.

Duncan snorted. "That still leaves the vampire."

Fear skittered down her spine. God, she hated vampires. Bloodthirsty beasts.

"He can be dealt with," she muttered.

Duncan's short, ugly laugh set her teeth on edge. "So you're not only arrogant, you're delusional?"

"What I am is smart enough to have a plan."

"So did the wolf in the *Three Little Pigs,* and you know how that worked out."

Sophie curled her lips. "What are you, twelve?"

"Just tell me this brilliant plan."

Reaching into the pocket of her leather duster, Sophie pulled out a small flask and screwed off the lid.

"Culligan was kind enough to donate his blood to our cause."

Never the sharpest tool in the shed, Duncan scowled in confusion.

"Not that I'm opposed to draining the nasty imp, but what good is his blood?"

Sophie waved the flask beneath his nose. "Such a poignant, fruity scent. Quite unique."

"Yeah, Calvin Klein should bottle it for his fall collection."

She chuckled in anticipation. "I'm glad you think so."

"Just tell me what the hell you're going to do with it."

"I've at last found a use for you outside my bed." With a casual motion, Sophie dumped half the blood onto the cur's silk shirt. "Congratulations, Duncan, you've just been promoted to bait."

Jumping back, Duncan stared at his stained shirt in fury. "What the hell?"

With an efficient motion, Sophie closed the flask and tucked it back into her pocket. She would need the rest of the blood to lure Regan into her trap.

"Circle around the gargoyle and let him catch a scent of Culligan's blood. Once he's on your trail, lead him away from here," she commanded. "Without his ability to sense magic, the vamp and Regan will be powerless to find us."

"Lead him where?"

"I don't give a shit, you idiot. Just away from here."

Duncan's eyes glittered with fury. "And what are you going to do?"

She turned back toward the bluff. She'd ordered two of her curs to keep watch on the cave from the woods behind the entrance, but she needed to find a closer position to set her trap.

"I'm going to wait for the sun to rise."

Without warning, Duncan was standing at her side, his head bent to whisper directly in her ear.

"A small warning, Sadie," he growled softly. "The early cur doesn't get the worm . . . she gets eaten by the big bad vampire."

A spike of unease tightened her stomach before she pushed him away with a violent burst of temper.

"Just go, Duncan. And try not to screw this up."

Ignoring the warning glow in her eyes, Duncan swaggered across the roof, and with one motion leaped over the low wall. She heard the faint scrape of his landing in the alley behind the building, followed by the fading sound of footsteps.

Waging war against the instinct to shift, Sadie clenched her teeth and dug her nails into the palms of her hands. It was a futile effort, of course.

Unlike purebloods, a cur was always at the mercy of their nature. Once they reached a critical point, there was no halting the transformation.

"You owe me, Caine," she swore on a low growl. "You owe me big."

With an effort that should earn her sainthood, Regan managed to hold her tongue as Jagr streaked through the darkness. His blinding speed (not to mention the icy shadows he'd wrapped around them) made her eyes water and her lungs struggle to function properly.

It was impossible to believe that anything lacking jet propulsion could be capable of following them, but Jagr clearly wasn't in the mood to take any chances, and she wasn't overly anxious to distract him while he charged across the empty fields at sonic speed.

Still, her patience wasn't endless. As ten minutes became twenty, Regan had had enough.

They were miles from Hannibal.

Hell, they were miles from anything resembling civilization.

"Hey, Sacagawea, I didn't sign up for the Lewis and Clark Expedition. Where are we going?" she demanded, her teeth clenched to keep them from chattering.

"North."

Smart ass.

"Yeah, I got that much." She forced her gaze from the empty fairgrounds they were passing to the austere beauty of his face. Her heart skipped a familiar beat. "Why don't we just go back to one of the hotels? There're two of them that not only have our scent all over them, but come complete with a bed and hot shower."

"A hotel is too easily surrounded." Jagr slowed his pace, his eyes shimmering like sapphires in the darkness. "And along with the bed and shower come very large windows that are perfect for allowing in the morning sunlight."

"Seems like a reasonable price to pay," she muttered,

aggravated by the insistent, merciless awareness that refused to leave her in peace.

A ghost of a smile played about his lips. The bastard knew precisely the effect he had on her treacherous body.

"You would miss me if I were reduced to a tiny pile of ash."

"Oh, I don't know. I think you might look good in shades of gray."

"Harsh, little one," he chastised. "Your manners leave a great deal to be desired."

"As if yours are any better?"

"Obviously, we deserve one another."

Her heart didn't skip this time. It came to a complete, perfect stop.

We deserve one another . . .

The words were harmless, nothing more than a casual joke. But there was nothing amusing in the poignant longing that flooded her heart.

"Not freaking likely." She squirmed in his arms, suddenly more afraid of the sensations jolting through her body than being dropped. "I'm freezing. Put me down."

Miraculously, Jagr came to a halt and gently lowered her to her feet. Not that she believed for a moment he was actually following orders. She wasn't *that* stupid.

A rabid tiger would be more likely to dance the rumba.

Obviously it suited his purpose to stand in an empty field, staring at the large, abandoned building. A building that looked as if it could be some sort of creepy asylum.

A suspicion that became absolute certainty when Jagr tilted back his head as if testing the air.

"Remain close to my side," he muttered.

Regan rubbed her arms, as much from the brittle tension radiating from Jagr as from the chill still clinging to her skin.

"You think the curs are chasing us?"

His gaze continued to scan the darkness. "There's always a possibility that we've been followed, but I'm more concerned with the vampire who has a lair in the area. I wouldn't want any misunderstandings by bringing a Were into his territory."

Regan stiffened in wariness. Another vampire? Just what she needed.

"There's a clan here?"

"No. Tane has no connection to a clan, although he no doubt has a number of guards with him. He's a Charon."

"A Charon." She shook her head, dredging up the little Greek mythology she'd read. "You mean a ferryman?"

"Not quite." His expression had settled into those cold, remote lines that always meant trouble. "A vampire assassin."

Well, this just got better and better.

"Just to clarify, does that mean he's a vampire who happens to be an assassin, or that he's an assassin who kills vampires?"

"He hunts vampires."

"He's some sort of cannibal, and you intend to invade his territory? Are you nuts?"

"Tane's not a cannibal. He's a part of an elite group of warriors that Styx founded long before he became the Anasso, their sole purpose being to destroy those vampires who have become unstable."

"Unstable?"

"It's rare, but not unknown."

Regan shuddered. The thought of a powerful, predatory vampire becoming unhinged wasn't a pretty one.

Actually it was downright terrifying.

"Should I ask?"

His expression was grim. "No."

Good enough for her.

"So this Tane hunts them down and kills them?" she instead demanded.

"It's his duty."

"Lovely." With a grimace, her attention shifted toward the nearby building. At a distance it looked as if it had once been a handsome structure. Three stories, with a large verandah on the ground level and a balcony with a decorative railing running along the second floor, it boasted the type of high arched windows popular before air-conditioning, and six fluted columns that added an air of graceful dignity. The darkness, however, couldn't disguise the fact that the red bricks were crumbling into slow oblivion and the windows were missing most of their panes of glass. "Why does he live out here in the middle of nowhere? Does he give the other vampires the heebie-jeebies?"

"A Charon must always remain above the politics and loyalties of various clans," Jagr said, his tone distracted as he continued to remain on guard. "The killing of a vampire, even one who is beyond salvation, has started too many wars."

"So he has to live in isolation?"

"Beyond his servants, yes. It helps avoid complications."

"Jeez." Regan grimaced. "What a crappy job."

"Tane took his position willingly. Many vampires prefer solitude."

"Vamps like you?"

His head turned, his brilliant eyes narrowed as if her soft question had struck a nerve.

"I can't deny that I've spent the past centuries preferring the company of books to that of my brothers."

"Did you blame them for leaving you in the hands of Kesi?"

Jagr tensed, his fangs flashing as his features hardened with a frozen fury.

"I blamed them for allowing me to be turned into the same sort of monster who tortured me in the first place."

"You . . ." Regan was forced to halt and clear her throat. "You resent being a vampire?"

"I did." The cold bitterness slowly thawed as he studied her wary eyes. "But I'm beginning to discover being turned isn't without a few benefits." His finger brushed her cheek, the cool caress leaving a trail of fire in its wake. "Do you want me to tell you some of those benefits, little one?"

Her mouth went dry.

She knew those benefits in intimate detail.

And she wanted more.

God almighty, did she want more.

"Did Styx try to make you one of his Charons?" she abruptly demanded, jerking away from his lingering finger. Holy crap, did all vamps possess the ability to seduce with a touch?

"Jagr as a Charon?" a dark, oddly hypnotic voice floated on the warm night breeze. "Our Anasso is far too wise to send one feral vampire after another. The idea of a Charon is to prevent a bloodbath, not create one."

Jagr smoothly turned as Tane at last revealed his presence.

He'd sensed the dangerous vampire lurking near the dilapidated building since they'd crossed into his territory, but it was never wise to acknowledge a Charon unless they invited you to do so.

"Tane."

The assassin remained wrapped in shadows, keeping enough distance to warn he wasn't pleased at the unexpected intrusion.

"You're trespassing, Jagr. A dangerous mistake that has been a death sentence for more than one creature."

Jagr held out his hands in a gesture of peace. When he'd traveled from Chicago to Hannibal, he'd sensed Tane's lair was in the vicinity but he hadn't intended to drop by for a visit. He'd met the assassin nearly a decade before and wasn't overly anxious to renew their acquaintance. All vampires were lethal, but Tane possessed an edgy, restless hunger that made even Jagr's skin crawl with warning.

Necessity, unfortunately, was a bitch, and for the moment Tane was the lesser of two evils.

He didn't need to use his senses to detect the wards and traps that were woven around the assassin's lair. Although

Charons were in theory under the protection of Styx, they weren't stupid. Any vampire living in such a remote spot would go to infinite lengths to ensure his own security.

"My presence is at the command of the Anasso," Jagr warned, knowing that any Charon was forced to take oaths that bound them tightly to Styx.

He could only hope that Tane was willing to honor those vows.

"And the woman?" Tane drawled. "Is she a gift for disturbing my peace? I prefer my females with more curves and less tongue, but she'll do."

"Hey, you piece of . . ."

Swiftly wrapping one arm around Regan's waist, Jagr placed his free hand over her mouth. Gods, the woman was going to get them both killed.

Leaning down, he spoke directly in her ear. "Regan, remain here while I negotiate with my brother."

She glared at him until he dropped his hand from her mouth. "Negotiate what?"

"Whether you live or die," Tane taunted from the shadows.

Her emerald eyes flashed, and Jagr could sense the wolf in her snarling in fury.

"You tell me to trust you, and this is where you bring me?" she hissed. "If I wanted to have my life threatened by a dirtbag demon, I could have stayed in Hannibal."

His arm tightened around her waist in a silent warning. "Little one, you're only making this more complicated."

"And?"

"And it would save a great deal of trouble if you would allow me to speak with Tane in private."

"So, I'm just supposed to stand here twiddling my thumbs while you parlay with Jack Sparrow?"

Tane's dark laugh floated on the breeze. "You could join me in my lair and twiddle my . . ."

"Enough, Tane," Jagr growled in warning.

Regan muttered a foul curse. "I really, really don't like this guy."

Pressing a brief kiss to her lips, Jagr released his hold on her tense body and turned. He needed Regan in the safety of a lair. The sooner the better.

"Stay here and trust me," he murmured, flowing toward the nearby building and waiting vampire.

"Someday, Jagr, I swear to God I'm going to . . ."

His lips twitched at her furious tirade, but wisely his attention swiftly moved to the assassin who waited on the wide terrace.

Approaching the steps, Jagr was brought to a sudden halt as a silver-tipped spear suddenly struck the ground a mere inch from the toe of his boot.

"That's close enough."

Jagr allowed his fangs to lengthen, his power dropping the temperature. Tane was a powerful vampire who'd been trained by Styx's Ravens, but Jagr wasn't feared by demons far and wide because of his less-than-sparkling personality.

"I'm not your enemy, Tane."

"Neither are you my friend." Allowing his shadows to drop, Tane stepped into a wash of silver moonlight.

Although smaller in bulk than Jagr, the vampire was smoothly muscular, with the golden skin of his Polynesian ancestors, his thick black hair shaved on the sides into a long Mohawk he braided to hang past his shoulders. His face was as lean and hard as the rest of him, with faintly slanted eyes the precise color of warm honey. Wearing nothing more than a pair of khaki shorts, Tane folded his arms over his bare chest and regarded Jagr with suspicion.

"What are you doing here? The last I heard you were in Chicago, cloistered in your lair and shunning your clan."

"I don't shun them," Jagr denied with a grim smile. "It's more a mutual agreement that I shouldn't bother to join the clan bowling league."

Tane's short, startled laugh did nothing to ease the menace thickening the air.

"Hardly a surprise. You never did play well with others, Jagr."

"No, but I serve the Anasso when I'm called."

"Don't we all?"

"Yes, which is why I have come to you." Jagr casually plucked the spear from the ground. "I assume you honor your pledge to Styx?"

"I'll decide if assisting you is included in my duty to the Anasso or not."

It was the best Jagr could hope for, and with stark precision, he revealed his purpose in coming to Hannibal and the events leading to seeking out this private lair.

Tane listened in silence, his gaze shifting toward Regan, who paced a small patch of ground, muttering her opinion of arrogant, ill-mannered, bloodsucking leeches.

"A Were that doesn't shift?"

"Yes."

"The miracles of modern medicine."

Jagr was quite willing to believe that Regan was a miracle, but not because of any modern medicine.

"The genetic alterations might have halted Regan's ability to shift, but she possesses most of a Were's skills, and more than her fair share of a Were's nasty temper."

Tane turned back to study Jagr with a taunting smile. "And she's twin to Styx's mate?"

"One of four."

"I thought Styx must have been crazed with his grief at the loss of the previous Anasso when I learned he bound himself to a Were, but now I begin to understand his obsession. She's . . ."

"Off limits," Jagr interrupted, the spear snapping in two as his fist clenched.

Tane tested the air, his smile widening. "You haven't claimed her."

Jagr tossed the broken weapon aside, not bothering to hide the possessive fury that whipped through the air.

"That won't stop me from ripping off your head if you so much as touch her."

Tane narrowed his eyes. "Threatening my life isn't going to get you any favors."

"No, but it will avoid any nasty misunderstandings."

Proving that he wasn't easily intimidated, Tane stepped forward. "Is Styx aware of your fascination with his sister-mate?"

"Styx is only concerned with her safety."

"While you're only concerned with keeping her away from her family and in your power?"

Jagr jerked at the smooth taunt. "Careful, Tane."

"Why haven't you taken her to Chicago?"

"I have allowed her to remain in Hannibal because she won't be satisfied until she's killed the imp," he growled, refusing to consider the accusation he might be deliberately postponing the moment he would have to turn Regan over to the protection of her family. "If I force her to Chicago, she'll only escape at the first opportunity and take off on her own. The demon-world might not survive the havoc she'd wreak before I could track her down again."

"And the Anasso has agreed to this plan?"

"He requested that I deal with Regan, and that's what I'm doing," Jagr snapped, angered by the mere thought the Anasso had any say over Regan. A dangerous, perhaps fatal, sensation. "Now, will you help us or not?"

There was a beat as Tane weighed the pleasure of battling a vampire with Jagr's skill against the certain punishment of interfering in the Anasso's business. At last he shrugged.

"Get your woman and follow me."

Chapter 11

Regan wasn't happy as she allowed Jagr to lead her into the crumbling building.

Maybe it had something to do with the stench of rotting mattresses that had been piled into what once had been a front lobby. Or the plaster that crumbled from the ceiling as they headed down the narrow flight of stairs to a basement that, frankly, was creepy as hell.

The small, cramped rooms they passed by, as well as the broken canes and walkers shoved in a storage room, pointed toward an abandoned old folks' home, but whatever charm it once might have claimed had long ago faded into oblivion.

Or maybe it had something to do with the large, edgy vampire who led them through the moldy darkness.

Oh, Tane was melt-worthy.

He was all smooth, golden planes, and honey eyes.

Yummy tropical heat in a pair of low-riding khaki shorts.

But the wolf in her wasn't fooled by Tane's promise of paradise. Like Jagr, the vampire carried the potent scent of danger. Unlike Jagr, however, Tane didn't try to disguise his lethal threat behind a wall of ice.

No, his menace was as blatant as a flashing neon sign.

Moving through what looked like an empty laundry room,

Tane halted to shove aside a heavy metal rack, revealing a narrow opening in the wall.

Regan swallowed a sigh as she followed in his wake, more resigned than surprised to discover the stairs that led deep underground. Vampires were nothing if not predictable in their love for the dark and dank.

Battling to keep her bulky bags from tangling her legs as she negotiated the steep steps and then the long passageway that ran beneath the surrounding fields, Regan only vaguely noticed when the tunnel transformed from dirt to stainless steel.

It was only when Tane slid open a heavy door blocking the path that she realized there was nothing dark or dank about the hidden lair.

Wide-eyed, she took in the banks of high-tech equipment that lined the long room. There were monitors with live feeds of at least a dozen cameras spread throughout the nearby countryside, sleek computers keeping track of God-only-knew what, and complex, sophisticated machines that Regan didn't even recognize.

"Holy crap," she breathed, instinctively edging closer to Jagr as the two large vampires scanning the complicated equipment sent her an impatient scowl. Even for a vampire, the over-the-top security system seemed a little paranoid. "Do you have a space shuttle tucked in a nearby cornfield?"

Tane glanced over his shoulder as he continued through a far door that led to yet another steel lined passage.

"I have many things tucked in the cornfields. I'll be happy to show them to you once we get my elderly brother settled into his bed."

"Tane," Jagr growled, predictably rising to the bait.

The taunting vampire turned down yet another corridor, making Regan wonder just how extensive the tunnels were.

"She is yet unclaimed, and I'm as capable as you to offer her protection. Actually it would appear I'm more capable since it's my lair keeping her safe."

Regan rolled her eyes. Not again.

"You know, I thought Culligan was a jackass because he was an imp. Turns out that the whole jackass thing comes with being a male," she drawled in overly sweet tones. "Now let me make one thing perfectly clear . . ." She shared her annoyed glare between the two vampires. "I don't need to be protected by Dumb or Dumber. I can take care of myself."

Halting next to a door set in the steel wall, Tane turned to regard Jagr with an unexpected amusement.

"You're right, Jagr, her temper is foul."

Regan hissed in annoyance. "Oh, it can get a whole lot worse than foul."

"She isn't exaggerating," Jagr added, the half smile playing about his lips. "Wise demons tremble when her wolf is on the prowl."

She clutched her bags to her chest. "Are you done?"

The two men shared a glance that would make any woman consider the pleasure of ridding the world of males, but wisely Tane shifted to open the door, waving a hand for them to enter the room beyond.

Regan stepped over the threshold, flipping the switch on the wall. It wasn't that she needed the soft light that spilled through the room, but it helped dismiss the sensation of being trapped underground.

She moved forward, then halted in shock. Good . . . Lord. It looked like it had been decorated by Hugh Hefner on crack.

Her brows lifted as she studied the rich crimson wallpaper and framed pictures of naked women. The ceiling was painted with satyrs in full arousal, dancing in the shimmering light of the large chandeliers. Even worse, there wasn't a stick of furniture, but instead a dozen large pillows spread over the acres of ivory carpeting, and an honest-to-God whirlpool humming and splashing in the center of the room.

"This is my guest apartment," Tane said from the doorway, the mocking amusement in his voice revealing he was thoroughly enjoying her appalled expression. "You should find what you need. However, if you decide to leave, don't stray from the path I've shown you. There are any number of nasty surprises for the uninvited."

Jagr gently tugged the bags of clothing from her stiff fingers, tossing them into a corner along with his own leather satchel.

"Speaking of uninvited, the Anasso sent his pet gargoyle to be a very persistent pain in my side," he warned Tane. "If he makes an appearance, you might want to avoid killing him."

"I've heard rumors of the creature."

"Rumors can't prepare you for the real thing," Jagr said dryly.

Tane made a sound of disgust. "I will allow him to perch on the roof if he can behave himself, but if he tries to invade my lair I make no promises."

Jagr shrugged. "Your funeral."

Appearing remarkably unconcerned, Tane stepped back into the corridor. "I have business to attend to, but my guards will remain on duty. You won't be disturbed."

Without warning, Jagr offered a bow of his head. "I'm in your debt, Tane."

"Yes, you are. Someday I'll collect."

His warning delivered, Tane shut the door, enclosing Regan and Jagr alone in the gaudy apartment.

For a minute, Regan simply enjoyed the absence of Tane's unnerving presence, but eventually the realization she was completely alone with Jagr, in a place custom-built for sex, made her . . . twitchy.

With jerky steps, she moved across the ivory carpet, peeking into the compact kitchen with its expensive appliances before moving through the connecting door to the bedroom beyond.

Not her smartest decision.

She'd barely switched on the light when Jagr slipped

past her, his brows lifting as he prowled toward the round bed draped in black satin that was reflected in the mirrors above it.

It was like one big bachelor pad cliché.

Her cheeks burned with a ridiculous heat. "I can't imagine why Tane would need guest chambers. Who the hell would want to visit?"

Jagr tugged open a drawer of the lacquer nightstand. "Unlike you, little one, most women find Tane inexplicably charming. Even among vampires, his reputation is that of a . . ."

"Hound?"

"Not the word I was looking for, but it'll do." Jagr plucked a pair of handcuffs from the drawer and dangled them from his finger. "Well, well."

"Good grief." She frowned as he studied her with an expectant expression. "Don't even think about it."

His soft, almost tangible chuckle feathered over her skin. "I don't need toys to please a woman. Of course . . ."

"I've seen enough."

Spinning on her heel, Regan marched into the kitchen, her back ramrod straight, even as all sorts of delicious sensations fluttered in the pit of her stomach.

No, Jagr most certainly didn't need toys.

Not when his touch was pure magic.

Only a step behind her, Jagr moved toward the built-in refrigerator and tugged open the side freezer.

"You should eat something. Do you have a preference?"

Refusing to reveal her childish unease, Regan moved directly to his side and peered into the freezer. Her mouth instantly watered at the sight of the neatly stacked packages from some of the most famous restaurants in the world.

Chicago style pizza . . . New Orleans gumbo . . . Kansas City barbeque . . . Maine lobster . . .

"Everything," she muttered, reaching to pluck a few of the top boxes from the freezer and handing them to Jagr to defrost in the microwave. "Tane at least knows how to feed his guests."

In a remarkably short amount of time, the small glass dining table was overflowing with pizza, bread sticks, minestrone soup, and a warm apple tart.

Taking a seat, Regan didn't even try to pretend she was one of those ridiculously skinny women she watched on TV. Why the hell would she starve herself to please some man?

Savoring the delicious food that had nothing in common with the cheap frozen dinners that Culligan used to feed her, Regan at last realized that Jagr was leaning against the counter watching her with an unwavering intensity.

"What about you?" she demanded, wiping her mouth with a linen napkin. "Aren't you hungry?"

His brooding gaze slid down to the curve of her neck. "Not for what's currently on the menu."

Desire, sharp and biting, clenched her body as Regan surged to her feet and began tossing the empty containers into the trash can. Oh, man. She didn't want to think about how her skin suddenly seemed way too tight for her body, or how her heart was pounding against her chest, or the heat pooling in the pit of her stomach.

She wanted . . .

Okay, that pretty much summed it up.

She wanted. She wanted bad.

"How often do you need to feed?" she demanded, her mushy brain unable to come up with anything better as a distraction.

"It depends on whether I'm wounded, or if I've gone without feeding for an extended period of time," he murmured, his voice low and husky. "It also depends on the potency of the blood. A Were's blood is prized for its rare power. Unfortunately, they prefer not to share with vampires."

Her Were blood abruptly warmed as it flowed through her veins, as if already anticipating the erotic tug of his fangs.

She instinctively bristled at the troublesome sensations. "Maybe that's because the vamps have nearly made them extinct by keeping them caged in cramped hunting grounds that have stolen their ancient abilities."

"Did you drink Salvatore's Kool-Aid?" he demanded, coolly.

It took a moment for her to realize he was accusing her of being brainwashed.

"No, but he's very convincing that the vamps are at least partially to blame for the lack of pureblood children."

Jagr flowed forward, easily sensing her rising desire despite her best attempts to appear indifferent.

"His grievance has been brought to the Oracles," he murmured, halting close enough for her to be wrapped in the cool wash of his power. "They will determine the ultimate fate of the Weres."

Her mouth went dry as her gaze was ruthlessly drawn to all those muscles rippling beneath his too-tight T-shirt. Christ. She should be given a medal for not having him down on the kitchen floor to have her way with him.

"I don't care how powerful the Oracles are, I won't be fenced into some sort of Were reservation," she muttered, referring to the years that the American Weres had been forced to live on land designated by the vampires.

Not that her thoughts were actually focused on the ancient feud between the two species. No, she was far more interested in the temptation of running her fingers through the long, golden hair.

Jagr seemed just as distracted, his eyes warming to a deep blue as his hand lifted to stroke down the curve of her throat.

"The hunting grounds were created as much for the protection of the Weres as for the humans," he said, his fingers wrecking a path of distraction as they followed the plunging neckline of her shirt. "Without a strong leader, the curs were out of control and attracting far too much attention. The demon-world was preparing for genocide before the previous Anasso stepped in and created the necessary boundaries. If Salvatore can prove he's capable of taking command of his people, then the Oracles will no doubt step aside and allow him to rule without interference."

Regan had to remind herself to breathe.

Air in. Air out. Air in. Air out.

"I don't care who's in charge as long as they leave me alone."

His fingers continued to tease and taunt, stroking over the curve of her breasts until her nipples hardened to painful peaks.

"Always supposing that's possible, what will you do?"

"Enjoy my freedom."

"It's more than just freedom." His hand lifted to cup the nape of her neck, gently messaging her tense muscles. "You'll have to survive in a world you know very little about."

She struggled to be annoyed by his patronizing words. Something that would be a hell of a lot easier if she weren't drowning in a flood of sensuous need.

"I can learn. I'm not stupid."

"No, you're extraordinarily intelligent." His lips brushed her temple. "Intelligent enough to know that a lone wolf is the most vulnerable. Why not accept the assistance of those who only want to help you?"

She swallowed a groan of pleasure. Damn, that mouth was wicked.

"My beloved sister? Thanks, but no thanks."

"Darcy is not your only option." He nipped the lobe of her ear. "My lair is well protected, although not nearly as elegant as Styx's estate."

Regan stilled. "Jagr?"

"Hmmm?"

"Are you asking me to move in with you?"

Jagr hesitated, then with a wary expression, he pulled back to meet her shocked gaze.

"Yes."

"Have you ever shared your lair before?"

"Not willingly, no."

"Then why would you offer now?"

His lips twisted. "Couldn't I just be a good guy with a generous heart?"

"Not flipping likely." She shook her head, strangely disturbed by his unexpected offer. "What do you get out of this?"

"I wish I knew."

"What?"

His hand slid from her nape to the curve of her lower back, urging her against his stirring hardness. Regan sucked in a ragged breath as his thick cock pressed into the tender flesh of her stomach.

"I know I want you. Desperately," he said, a fierce hunger flaring through his eyes. "I know that you fascinate me even when you're behaving like a lunatic."

"Hey."

"What I don't know is why the thought of watching you walk away is . . ." He grimaced.

"Is what?"

"Unacceptable."

"Unacceptable?"

"Completely and utterly unacceptable."

She licked her lips, unnerved by the stark satisfaction that flared through her heart. Surely she couldn't be pleased by his blatant claim of possession?

"It's also inevitable," she forced herself to mutter. "Once Culligan's dead, I'm out of here."

His lips twitched as he shifted to lightly scrape his fangs down the line of her throat.

"We'll see," he husked, his clever hands grasping the hem of her shirt to pull it off in one smooth motion. Her bra swiftly followed, fluttering to the ceramic tiles. "I can be very persuasive when I want something."

She made a choked sound as his thumbs brushed over her straining nipples. Holy . . . crap.

Persuasive?

He was downright mind-blowing.

Desperately trying to latch onto the reason this was a bad idea (and anything that felt so damned good *had* to be a bad idea), Regan sucked in a deep breath. Unfortunately, Jagr was one step ahead of her and, before she could form a coherent thought, his mouth was skating over the curve of her breast, closing over the tip, as his tongue teased her to near madness.

"Damn you," she muttered, her fingers shoving into the tempting silk of his hair. He kissed and nibbled his way down her body, peeling away her remaining clothes between caresses.

"No, not damned," he countered, straightening to meet her dazed gaze with an unreadable expression. "Redeemed."

With a motion too swift for Regan to anticipate, Jagr swept her off her feet and was moving through the apartment. She barely managed to realize what was happening when she was tossed in the center of the *Austin Powers* bed, her arms and legs splayed like a sacrificial virgin.

"Jagr."

Kicking off his heavy boots, Jagr pulled the T-shirt over his head and dropped his jeans to reveal the breathtaking glory of his male form.

"Yes, little one?" he demanded, lowering to cover her with the cool weight of his body.

She lifted her hands to push him away, only something went wrong. Instead of shoving against the hard planes of his chest, her fingers were stroking over the pale skin so ruthlessly marred by his scars.

"Shouldn't we be planning what we intend to do next?" she demanded, her voice a husky rasp.

Lowering his head, Jagr nibbled at the corner of her mouth. "I know exactly what I intend to do next."

An exquisite shudder shook her body. Oh, Lord, she hoped

that his intentions included spreading her legs and finishing what he'd started.

Suddenly, she no longer cared that Culligan was out there still alive and breathing . . . the bastard. Or that there was a pack of demented curs that might or might not be hunting her.

Or even that Jagr's determined seduction might very well be an elaborate scheme to lure her back to Chicago and into Darcy's trap.

Sometimes a woman had to have her priorities in order.

And at the moment, Regan's priority was satisfying the gnawing hunger that threatened to consume her.

As if sensing her capitulation, Jagr growled low in his throat, his hands skimming restlessly over her bare skin as he scattered tiny kisses over her face.

"Sweet midnight jasmine," he muttered, his tongue outlining her lips. "Your scent drives me mad."

Regan gave a small squeak as one roaming hand slid between her thighs to stroke through her growing dampness.

"That's ridiculous," she protested, breathless. "If I smell of anything, it's damp cave and horseweeds."

He crushed her lips in a searing kiss. "Always arguing, little one." He moaned as his finger slid into her tight flesh. "Is it a compulsive need to keep me at a distance, or are you just quarrelsome by nature?"

Regan instinctively dug her heels into the black silk sheets as she arched her hips upward.

"If you weren't always wrong, I wouldn't have to . . . to . . ." Oh, Christ, his finger was creating the most delicious friction as he dipped it in and out of her. "To argue."

His lips brushed over her cheek, then down the line of her jaw. "I'm never wrong." He pressed a kiss to the pulse racing at the base of her throat. "Never." His mouth trailed down her collarbone. "Never." He covered the aching tip of her breast. "Never."

He wasn't playing fair. She couldn't think when her entire

body was quivering with a near painful need. She didn't *want* to think.

She just wanted to once again feel that glorious release that hovered just out of reach.

Fisting her fingers in his thick hair, she instinctively wrapped her legs around his hips.

"Fine, you're always right. Now stop talking and do something."

Pulling back, he regarded her with an almost smile. "Quarrelsome and demanding."

She deliberately rubbed herself against the granite-hard length of his erection.

"Is that a problem?"

His eyes darkened, his fangs glinting bone white in the light spilling from the living room.

"No problem." Bracing himself on his elbow, he shifted until the tip of his cock pressed against her entrance. "No problem at all."

She gritted her teeth at his deliberate torture. Innocent or not, her body understood what it needed. And having it so close was making her crazy.

"Then why are you still talking?" she demanded, tugging his hair as he regarded her with an oddly watchful expression.

"You know, little one, there's no going back."

"Jagr, if you don't get on with it, I'm going to . . ."

She wasn't entirely sure what she was going to do, and in the end it didn't matter. With a low hiss, Jagr tilted his hips forward, sliding into her with a slow, relentless thrust.

Shifting her hands, Regan clutched at Jagr's shoulders, her nails digging into his skin. There wasn't pain. Even with Jagr's considerable size, her body readily accommodated his entry. But there was a delicious sense of fullness, and a startling intimacy, that she hadn't been expecting.

In this moment, she was connected to Jagr. Connected in

a way that seemed far more poignant than two bodies simply having sex.

It was . . .

Her mind instantly shied from pondering the dangerous sensations. No. She didn't want this to be more than a fleeting pleasure.

"Regan," he whispered close to her ear. "Are you okay?"

"I'm fine, just don't stop," she muttered, burying her face in the curve of his neck.

"There's no way in hell I could stop now," he muttered, withdrawing from her body before pushing back in with a growing urgency. "You are perfect."

Once again, Regan felt that instinctive urge to argue. She wasn't perfect. Far from it.

But before she could form the words, he was once again pulling out and thrusting forward with a rhythm that stole her breath. Yes. Oh, yes. This was what her body had longed for in the depths of the night. This was what she needed.

Squeezing her eyes shut, Regan raked her nails down his back, pleased when he growled in pleasure. She dug her nails deeper, rewarded as his lips found hers in a wild, demanding kiss.

His hips rocked faster, his hands tilting her hips upward to meet his deep, steady thrusts.

"Jagr . . . please," she muttered against his lips, her body clenched so tightly she felt as if she might shatter.

"Patience, little one." Dipping his head downward, he teased her aching nipple with his lips and fangs, his hips pumping faster and faster as she arched off the bed to meet him.

Regan's breath rasped in the silent air, her world narrowing to the point where Jagr's body surged in and out of her.

She was so close. So exquisitely close.

And then . . . it happened.

With one last surge he tumbled her over the edge, sending her into a vortex of dizzying bliss.

He swallowed her scream of pleasure with a searing kiss, continuing to pump into her shuddering body until he stiffened with his own release. Then, as he arched beneath the force of his climax, the lewd pictures exploded from the walls and the crystal decanter shattered.

Wrenching open her eyes, she regarded him in astonishment. "Christ."

Chapter 12

It's not easy to vanquish a vampire who was as old as Jagr.

His powers were terrifying, his intelligence formidable, and the sheer force of his will could overcome the most fearsome adversaries.

But there was no getting away from the fact that he had been well and truly brought to his knees by a bad-tempered, unpredictable, aggravatingly beautiful werewolf.

Tucking Regan's head beneath his chin, Jagr wrapped her tightly in his arms, his gaze ruefully taking in the shards of glass and shattered pictures scattered over the rugs.

He never lost control. Certainly not during sex.

Not that what he'd just shared with Regan was just sex.

It was . . . hell, he didn't even have a word for the astonishing sensations that continued to quake through his body.

A vampire would sacrifice everything (clan, sanity, his very soul), to claim such joy.

Unfortunately, Regan wasn't anxious to have anyone lay claim to her. Especially not an arrogant, overprotective vampire who had the social skills of a bad-tempered cobra.

"Regan . . ."

His soft words were cut short as Regan slapped her

hand over his mouth, shifting so she could glare at him with an unexpected annoyance.

"No."

So much for the tender, intimate cuddling he'd envisioned.

Peeling her fingers from his lips, Jagr regarded her beautiful face surrounded by the tangle of golden curls. A smug pride stabbed through his heart at the lingering heat that darkened her eyes, and the flush of pleasure she couldn't disguise. She might never admit she'd found satisfaction in his touch, but it was etched on her face.

"Isn't it a little late for no?"

"I mean, I don't want to Dr. Phil what just happened."

His brows lifted in amusement. "Do I strike you as a Dr. Phil kind of vampire?"

With a sudden motion, she jerked the black sheet over her slender body.

"I just don't want to discuss it."

Jagr wryly resisted the urge to press the issue. He might not understand the mysterious workings of the female mind, but he did know his stubborn Were. If she decided she didn't want to discuss what they'd just shared, then there wasn't a damn thing he could do about it.

"Whatever makes you happy, little one." Dropping a kiss on the top of her head, Jagr slid from the bed and pulled on a silk robe Tane had left draped over a nearby chair. "Do you have Culligan's safe?"

Regan pressed herself to a seated position, ridiculously keeping the sheet wrapped around her. As if he hadn't kissed every delectable inch of her body.

"It's in my bags. Why?"

"For the moment it's the only connection we have to Culligan."

Returning to the living room, Jagr gathered Regan's precious bags along with his own satchel, then returning to the bedroom he tossed the bags on the bed and searched until he discovered the small safe tucked among her clothes.

Regan frowned. "You think we might have overlooked something?"

Jagr turned the safe in his hands, running his fingers over the smooth metal. "Imps are notoriously paranoid when it comes to their treasures. There has to be at least one hidden compartment we haven't found."

"So you're what? Going to try and play Rubik's Cube with it?"

"I prefer a more straightforward approach." With one smooth motion, Jagr ripped off the bottom of the safe.

"You're a very destructive demon," she muttered, glancing toward the shattered glass spread across the floor before returning her attention to the smashed safe.

He wisely hid his smile. He'd managed to slip past her fierce defenses, to stir her most intimate yearnings. Now she was desperate to push him away.

"But effective."

"Yeah, yeah."

Reaching into the gaping hole, Jagr pulled out a thick envelope and tossed it into her lap.

"I think I've made my point."

She rolled her eyes, ripping open the envelope. "Fake IDs . . . credit cards . . ." She paused as she unfolded a piece of paper. "Ah, now this is interesting."

"What is it?"

"It's a message . . ."

The Clemens Tea Shop. Saturday. Midnight.

Her head lifted, her eyes wide. "Culligan left St. Louis on Saturday."

"I remember seeing a sign for the place. It's a restaurant west of town."

"This might explain what brought Culligan to Hannibal."

"It's worth investigating," Jagr slowly agreed.

"Yes, it is." She scooted toward the edge of the bed. "And that's exactly what I intend to do."

His brows drew together. "Now?"

"Of course now."

"Regan, we can't be certain we weren't followed."

"For God's sakes, your Jason Bourne wannabe friend has half of Missouri wired like the Pentagon. If there was anything out there, he would already have vaporized them with his ray gun."

His scowl deepened. He couldn't deny that Tane had gone above and beyond the usual defenses. Or that he would have easily discovered any stray cur in the area.

He couldn't even argue the necessity of discovering who had sent the message to Culligan.

But his every instinct screamed to keep her safely tucked in the lair where nothing could reach her.

Almost as if sensing the refusal that trembled on his lips, Regan scooted off the bed, grabbing one of the bags and scurrying toward the bathroom. Jagr had only a brief glimpse of her tasty backside before the door shut behind her and he heard the sound of the shower kick on.

Left alone in the bedroom, Jagr wrenched off the robe and tugged on a pair of jeans and black sweater he pulled from his satchel. A lesser vampire might be offended by her desperate desire to pretend she hadn't just given him her innocence. Or her embarrassing haste to chase after shadows rather than linger alone with him in the secluded lair.

Thankfully he wasn't a lesser vampire.

Just one who was suddenly in the mood to finish destroying the porn-chic pictures that lined the walls.

Braiding his hair, Jagr tied it off with a leather cord and tugged on his heavy boots. His weapons followed. The two daggers he slid into the sheaths in his boots, and the handgun he shoved into his waistband at the small of his back. The silver bullets would come in handy if they ran across a cur.

Then, desperate to ignore the tantalizing scent of soap and sweet jasmine filling the air, he returned to the kitchen and drained a bottle of the blood left in the refrigerator. He didn't particularly need to feed, but he didn't want to risk his hunger stirring while they were on the hunt.

Even if Regan were willing to donate a vein, he wasn't a masochist. The aggravating woman was a threat to more than just his sanity.

There was a very real danger Regan could be his true mate.

Cursing a fate that seemed determined to torture him, Jagr stiffened when she appeared in the doorway, her damp hair pulled into a ponytail, her slender curves covered in a pair of low-riding jeans and a too-tight knit top.

Heat, raw and primitive, flared through him. Damn. When he returned to Chicago, he intended to kick Styx's ass.

The ancient vampire had a great deal to answer for.

Thankfully unaware of his dark thoughts, Regan studied him with a guarded expression.

"Shouldn't you get rid of the mess in the bedroom?"

Jagr shrugged, turning to head for the door leading out of the apartment. Now wasn't the time to dwell on the intense pleasure that had caused his power to shatter Tane's repulsive works of art. Not when he needed his few remaining brain cells to make sure he didn't lead them into yet another disaster.

"Tane's servants can toss it into the trash. That's where the junk belonged in the first place," he muttered, opening the door and waiting for her to step past him before closing it and heading down the narrow hallway.

She walked at his side, her dry glance her only reaction to his surly mood.

"So you don't have your own lair decorated with *Hustler* rejects?"

"I haven't bothered decorating at all."

"Why doesn't that surprise me?"

"It didn't seem necessary." Coming to an abrupt halt, Jagr cupped her face and stole a swift, frustrated kiss. Lifting his head, he met her startled gaze. "Until now."

Her lips parted with a scathing remark, but before she could catch her breath, he was stepping into Command Central and speaking to the dark-haired vampire on guard.

"We need transportation."

The warrior with his dark hair shaved close to his head, and his large body covered with a variety of weapons, rose to his feet, clearly under orders to offer Jagr whatever he needed.

"Follow me."

Wryly wondering what Tane would demand in repayment for his hospitality, Jagr followed the vampire across the room.

Waiting for the servant to push open a narrow door, he wasn't surprised to discover the vast underground garage that held a half dozen gleaming cars. Many vampires possessed a fascination with expensive automobiles. Regan, on the other hand, sucked in a shocked breath.

"Jeez. No Batmobile?"

"It's having its tires rotated." He led her across the paved garage toward a shadowed corner.

Her hand reached out to stroke over the elegant curves of a silver Mercedes they passed.

"I wonder if Salvatore needs a Were assassin. I could use a pay grade that's obviously in the Donald Trump territory."

Jagr bristled. Salvatore might not be willing to take Regan as his queen, but he was more than interested in taking her to his bed. Jagr would see the king in hell first.

"There's no need for Salvatore. The Anasso would willingly offer you whatever luxury you want." His lips twisted. "I can promise you that his pay grade is much higher than Donald Trump."

"I don't need the Anasso's charity." She jerked her arm from his grasp. "Or the strings attached."

"No, you'd much rather cut off your nose to spite your face," he growled, ignoring her glare as he stopped next to a battered red truck. "This should do."

"This?" She wrinkled her nose. "Are you kidding me? There's a Lamborghini, a Porsche, an Aston Martin, and two Corvettes just begging to go for a drive, and you want to take this piece of junk?"

Opening the passenger side door, he eyed her with a lift of his brows. "I prefer not to attract any unwanted attention. How many Lamborghinis have you seen in Hannibal?"

"Fine." She folded her arms over her chest. "Then why don't we just go back the way we came? I'd rather run than be jolted around in this thing."

"The curs won't be looking for a red truck," he pointed out. "And we might need it if either of us is injured."

"Killjoy," she muttered, grudgingly grabbing the handle of the door to vault into the high cab.

"So I've been told."

Jagr waited until she was settled on the worn leather seat before closing the door and rounding the front of the truck to take his place behind the wheel. Ignoring the key in the ignition, he used his powers to start the powerful engine and headed toward the tunnel that led out of the underground complex.

They exited the tunnel in the middle of a thick tangle of trees and underbrush that hid the opening from prying eyes. Or at least from human eyes. Regan possessed enough wolf to spot the numerous cameras concealed among the branches, and the occasional vampire that slid through the dark shadows.

"Crap." Her gaze lingered on the heat detectors hidden in a clump of wild daisies. "What happens if someone accidentally stumbles into this little Area 51?"

Jagr shrugged. "They're removed and their memories altered."

"Just like the other Area 51."

His lips twitched. "Not quite."

He took the narrow path through the surrounding fields, keeping the lights off until they reached a paved road heading south. Then ignoring any claim to intelligence, he gunned the engine and they hurtled their way toward Hannibal.

For long minutes they traveled in silence, Jagr brooding on his plunge into insanity and Regan watching the passing scenery with an odd sort of curiosity.

At last, Jagr chalked up his peculiar behavior to the onset of dementia and allowed his attention to return to the woman at his side.

"You're frighteningly quiet. Are you plotting general mayhem, or just my own demise?"

"I'm enjoying the scenery."

His gaze lingered on the fields that would eventually be planted with corn and soy beans and the occasional patch of sorghum. The recently tilled fields were no doubt a lovely sight for the local farmers, but hardly one of the Seven Wonders of the World.

"The scenery?"

Her lips curved into a wistful smile. "Culligan used to drive through the back roads when we traveled from town to town. I always envied the humans tucked safely in their beds with no idea of the monsters lurking in the dark."

Jagr grimaced. He didn't have a memory of his time as a human, but the rumors of his brutal rampages were legendary. There hadn't been many tears shed when he'd mysteriously disappeared.

"Humans are not without their own share of monsters."

"Maybe not, but the countryside always seems so peaceful. Especially at night."

"Obviously you haven't read *In Cold Blood*."

She rolled her eyes. "Spoken like a true city vamp."

"I haven't always lived in cities, you know," he drawled.

"I've spent centuries hidden in lairs so remote I had to travel hours to feed."

"Centuries of solitude?" She sucked in a deep breath. "It sounds like heaven."

"At times." He slowed the truck as he turned to study the smooth perfection of her profile. "There are also times when it's lonely and tedious and frightening."

She turned to catch his intense gaze. "Frightening?"

"Without a connection to the world, it becomes far too easy to question the purpose in continuing to exist."

Even in the darkness he had no trouble seeing the shock, and something that might have been horror, that rippled over her face.

"Did you . . . ?"

"If I hadn't discovered a passion for my research, I would not have struggled against the lure of ending it all," he readily confessed. "It's a temptation that all immortals must battle."

Without warning, she shivered, wrapping her arms around her waist as if warding off a sudden chill.

"You'd better not do anything so stupid while I'm around, chief," she muttered. "I intend to be the only tragedy to befall you."

A stab of satisfaction rushed through him at her unmistakable distress. She didn't like the thought he had very nearly put an end to his empty existence.

"Don't worry, little one, you won't get rid of me that easily."

She deliberately turned her head to stare out the window, pretending an interest in clumps of houses and car lots and gas stations that replaced the fields as they skirted the edge of town. Jagr allowed her to wrestle with her emotions in silence, forcing himself to concentrate on where he'd seen the sign for the tea shop.

Crawling through the sleeping residential streets, he nearly missed the refurbished three-storied house that was set behind two towering oaks.

"This is it," he said, abruptly pulling the truck to a halt on the opposite side of the street. It was nearly two in the morning and, in the finer neighborhoods of Hannibal, the citizens were safely tucked in their beds.

Leaning forward, Regan studied the pretty white structure with pink trim, and all those curly doodads that Victorians were addicted to.

"No." She shook her head. "This can't be right."

He deliberately glanced at the gold letters painted in the bay window. "It claims to be the Clemons Tea Shop. Do you think there's more than one?"

"It's way too upscale for any of Culligan's friends," she muttered. "He hangs around with bottom-feeders like himself."

"Fine. We can return to the lair, and . . ."

He hid his smile as she hastily shoved open her door and jumped out of the truck.

"We might as well have a look while we're here."

He caught up with her as she vaulted over the white picket fence, his senses assuring him that there was nothing in the house but a prowling cat. Of course, his senses were worthless when it came to the curs and their damned witch, he reminded himself, tugging the handgun from his waistband as they rounded the house and entered the tiny rose garden at the back.

Reaching the edge of the patio dotted with tables, they both came to a sharp halt.

"Do you smell that?" Regan demanded, her eyes glittering at the distinct scent of peach that had nothing to do with the tarts or scones served from the nearby kitchen.

Jagr nodded. It wasn't the distinct plum scent of Culligan, but definitely fey.

"Imp. And male." His fingers tightened on the handle of the gun. "Do you recognize the scent?"

"No." She sucked in a deep breath, using her Were senses

to test the air. "I don't think Culligan was ever in contact with the imp while he held me captive."

"So why would this mysterious imp contact him with an invitation to meet in Hannibal?"

Her gaze widened. "A trap?"

It had been Jagr's first thought as well. "An imp would sell his own mother if he could get a profit."

Her lips curled in anticipation. "I think I'd like to meet this imp."

Jagr scowled, rebelling at the mere thought of Regan hunting an imp that might possess all sorts of nasty skills.

"I'll track him." He was careful to keep his words closer to a request than a demand. "You return to Tane's lair, and I'll . . ."

"Don't even start with me." Her hands landed on her hips, her expression at its most stubborn.

"Regan, we know nothing about this imp or how closely he's associated with the curs."

"Look, I've let you hang around because you're occasionally useful, but I don't take orders from you." Her eyes narrowed. "Got it?"

He muttered a low curse. "So you're willing to put yourself in danger to prove you can?"

"I'm willing to do what's necessary to track Culligan. In case you've forgotten, that's why I'm here." Turning, she marched toward the back hedge, her back stiff as she followed the trail of the imp. "It's the *only* reason I'm here."

Jagr held himself still, waging war with his predatory nature that was stirred to a fever pitch by Regan's brash challenge.

If he'd already claimed her, then these skirmishes would be nothing more than the delicious games played between mates. But, without the bond . . .

Damn.

He'd assumed Kesi was the expert on torture.

She was an amateur compared to Regan.

* * *

Levet kicked a stray rock as he wandered along the edge of the Mississippi River.

He'd caught the plum scent of an imp two hours ago, and had eagerly been on the hunt since. *Mon Dieu.* He'd been so certain that this was his opportunity to show that frozen Visigoth chief who was the better demon.

His mood of elation, however, was swiftly spiraling down to weary annoyance as the trail led him on a seeming goose chase through the mud and muck that Missouri produced in astonishing abundance.

Not for the first time, he considered washing his hands of this whole vampire-helping-business and retiring to a nice quiet church in Florida.

Or maybe Arizona.

The humidity did nothing for his skin.

After all, it wasn't like the cold-blooded bastards actually appreciated his spectacular skills. *Sacrebleu,* they barely acknowledged he was a full-blooded gargoyle, let alone treated him with the respect or dignity that was his due.

So why was he tromping through the nasty weeds, following an even nastier imp, when once again the damnable vampire was busy sweeping the beautiful damsel in distress off her feet?

Because he was an *imbecile,* that was why.

An *imbecile* with sore feet, an empty stomach, and a sinking certainty that he was doing nothing more than walking in circles.

He needed a pizza. An extra large, meat-lovers, double cheese, thick crust . . .

"Psst."

Startled by the unexpected sound, Levet jerked his head to discover a woman swimming in the powerful waters of the river, her pure white skin, slanted blue eyes, and pale green hair revealing she was something other than human.

Water sprite.

And one that he'd encountered before.

Cursing the hideous luck than had crossed his path with Bella, the-pain-in-the-ass sprite, Levet attempted to ignore the flighty fey.

"Hey. Hey, you." Swimming closer to the shore, she waved an arm, as if he were too stupid to notice a water sprite bobbing a stone's throw from him. "Over here. Psst."

"Stop pssting me," he growled, continuing his path along the edge of the river.

"I know you."

"*Non,* you do not," he denied.

"I do. You're Levet, the stunted gargoyle."

He halted at the insult, spinning to point a gnarled claw at the stupid pest. "I am not stunted. I am vertically challenged."

She batted her long lashes, her beauty near breathtaking in the silver moonlight. Of course, it was that beauty that had been leading sailors to their doom since the beginning of time.

Levet had learned his lesson when the sprite had crawled through his portal when he'd been attempting to save Viper and Shay from the previous Anasso who'd gone completely nuts.

"I made you big before, when you fought that icky vampire," she whispered, reminding him of the pleasure he'd felt in commanding the stature that most of his brethren took for granted. *Mon Dieu.* It had been such a lovely thing. "Do you want me to make you big again?"

"I didn't summon you. Go away."

"I'm bored."

"Then go pester the fishes." He puffed out his chest. "I am on important business."

"What kind of business would a miniature gargoyle have? Are you hunting leprechauns?" she mocked, her laughter tinkling through the night air. "Oh, I know, I know. You're hunting hobbits."

"Very amusing . . . not." Clenching his claws, Levet resumed his trek through the mud. "I happen to be hunting a very dangerous, very cunning imp."

"Imp?" She kept pace with his angry stride. "There's no imp around here."

"Is too."

"Is not."

"Is too."

"Is not."

Levet threw his hands in the air. "I smell him, you annoying creature."

"The only thing that's gone past here besides a raccoon was a cur."

"A cur." Levet halted in shock. "You are certain?"

Pleased to have his full attention, Bella ran a tempting hand through her hair. "I know a dog when I see one. He was far more handsome than you, but covered in blood." She grimaced. "Bleck."

A cur covered in blood?

Had one of them been injured?

And why did they smell like an imp . . .

Levet smacked his forehead with his clenched claw.

"*Sacrebleu.*" Smack, smack. "I have been such a fool."

"Well, your brain isn't very big," Bella sympathized.

Lifting his head, Levet glared at the water sprite. "One more word out of you and I'm turning you into a carp."

"Why do you want a stupid imp?" she pouted, blithely ignoring his threat. "They're nasty, tricky beasts. Sprites are much more fun. Don't you remember how you liked me rubbing your wings? Summon me and I'll make you the happiest gargoyle in the world."

"Enough, you make my head hurt," Levet snapped.

It wasn't that he wasn't tempted. Bella was lovely, and he

was a healthy male who liked having his wings stroked as well as the next gargoyle. Still, he understood the dangers of playing with the fey.

They always ended up being more trouble than they were worth.

Squaring his shoulders, Levet concentrated on the fading scent of plums. The damned cur may have tricked him, but that didn't mean he couldn't use the situation to his advantage.

"Wait." Breaking into his concentration, Bella swam closer to the shore. "Where are you going?"

He muttered a curse at the interruption. "I have a cur to capture."

"I can help."

"Bah."

"I know where the imp is."

Levet scowled. "How would you know?"

"I see things."

"See things? What could you possibly see? You cannot be in this world unless you're summoned . . ."

He stumbled to silence as his words sank through his thick skull. She couldn't be here. Not unless she'd already been summoned.

She was nothing more than another bit of bait. Just like the scent of imp that had led him to this precise spot.

"Oh, shit," he breathed, whirling just in time to watch the tall cur step from behind a tree.

His hands lifted to conjure a hasty spell, but the words didn't have time to form before he was struck by a brilliant explosion.

The world went black.

Chapter 13

Regan shivered, absently rubbing her hands over her bare arms. The chill in the air had nothing to do with the brisk spring breeze and everything to do with the very large, very annoyed vampire stalking silently behind her.

Not that she was about to apologize.

She hadn't asked for his interference, dammit. And she most certainly didn't ask to be treated like a helpless bimbo who had to be tucked away in a safe lair while Jagr played superhero.

She was the one who Culligan had tormented and tortured for three decades. She was the one who had dreamed night after night of ripping out the imp's throat. She was the one who'd tracked the bastard to Hannibal.

This was her fight, and by God, she was going to see it to the bitter end.

And her stubborn reaction to his protective instincts had nothing at all to do with the fear that the stunning pleasure she'd felt in Jagr's arms had given him a power over her that was as ruthless and eternal as Jagr himself.

She shivered again.

Christ. She needed a distraction.

And a freaking jacket.

"What is this place?" she demanded, gazing around the

wide stretch of open land that was surrounded by a handful of large, elegant homes. "A park?"

Quickening his pace to walk beside her rather than glowering from behind, Jagr deliberately pulled back his power, easing the chill in the air.

"A golf course," he corrected.

"Ah." Her lips twisted. No wonder she didn't recognize the place. Culligan had never spent much time around the country club set. "That would explain the lack of teeter-totters."

"And the manicured greens with holes cut in them."

She shot him a startled glance. "You golf?"

"There are few things I haven't tried over the centuries."

"Yeah, I can imagine," she said dryly.

Heat flared through his eyes, burning away the lingering ice. "I'd be happy to demonstrate a few of them later."

Regan hastily turned her head, following the peach-scented trail that led toward a line of woods at the back of the golf course. Not that she hoped for a minute the damned vampire couldn't see the blush staining her cheeks.

"What would an imp be doing out here?" she muttered.

Half-expecting Jagr to pounce on her obvious vulnerability, Regan breathed a sigh of relief when he instead turned his attention toward the thicker shadows gathered ahead.

"My first guess would be that he's hiding."

"From us?"

Jagr tilted back his head as if sensing the night air. "His trail is fresh. And he's near."

Regan abruptly halted, realizing the scent of peach had grown considerably stronger. She pointed toward the line of trees along a barbed wire fence.

"I'll circle to the right," she whispered so softly only a vampire could catch the words. "I'd rather not have to chase him through the trees."

"Regan."

She stiffened, sensing his grim frustration.

"What?"

He muttered a low curse. "Just be careful."

Regan lifted her brows.

No grim pronouncement that it was too dangerous?

No squawking that he was the only one capable of dealing with the hidden demon?

No growling, hissing, or chest thumping?

Not willing to press her luck, Regan slipped silently down a cement path she assumed was for the golf carts.

She didn't believe for a moment that an ancient vampire could actually learn new tricks. At least not this ancient vampire.

So either he didn't believe the imp posed enough of a threat to make a fuss over, or more likely, he was confident he could protect her even if she was stubborn enough to charge into danger.

The rueful thoughts had barely skimmed through her mind when there was a rustle of noise and a slender form darted across the closely mowed green, heading directly for the nearby bushes.

"Oh no, you don't," Regan muttered, launching forward to tackle the fleeing imp.

She had a brief impression of reddish blond hair that was cut short and styled to emphasize the narrow, handsome face and pale green eyes. His thin body was hidden beneath an elegant blue suit that made him look like a banker.

Or a gigolo.

No doubt the old ladies at the tea shop fluttered over him like a clutch of infatuated hens.

Tackling the imp from behind, Regan drove him to the ground, intending to land on his back. Of course, the best laid plans of mice and men . . . yadda, yadda . . .

The impact was enough to knock her to the side, and the imp struck out desperately, his fist hitting her square in the stomach. The breath was wrenched from her lungs and before she could move, the imp landed a blow that would have broken her jaw if she'd been human. Thankfully Regan wasn't a human. She was a pissed-off pureblood who'd just been sucker-punched.

The imp swung his arm again, but this time Regan was prepared. Grabbing his fist, she squeezed until he was squealing like a . . . well, pretty much like an imp in pain. Then wrenching his arm behind his back, she rolled him face-first into the ground.

He kicked out, connecting painfully with her knee as she climbed to straddle his lower back. Regan cursed, jacking his arm even higher up his back as she grabbed a fistful of his hair and smacked his face into the dirt.

There was a cool brush of air, and suddenly Jagr was crouched at her side, his gaze on the imp whimpering beneath her.

"I think he's subdued, little one."

She turned her head to spit the blood from her mouth. Damn, the freaking idiot had made her bite her tongue. She hated that.

"You could have helped," she muttered.

Jagr arched a golden brow. "And be accused of overstepping my place as your meaningless sidekick? Thanks, but no thanks. Besides, it looked like you had everything under control."

"Crazy bitch," the imp whined, his eyes rolling toward Jagr as if hoping to get a bit of sympathy from a fellow male. "Get her off me."

Jagr's chuckle chilled the air. "If I were you, I wouldn't insult the pissed-off werewolf holding you in a half nelson."

"Who are you?" the imp demanded. "What do you want?"

"You're confused, imp. We'll ask the questions, and you'll answer them," Jagr warned. "Understand?"

Regan tightened her grip on his hair. "And you'll give us the truth if you want to keep your head attached."

The imp hissed in pain. "What is this? The demon version of good cop, bad cop?"

"I'm afraid that Regan has a few issues with imps," Jagr drawled.

The imp stiffened beneath her. "Regan?" he breathed.

Jagr narrowed his gaze. "You recognize the name?"

"No . . ." His denial was cut short as Regan banged his head on the ground. "Wait, dammit. All I know is that Culligan had a pet Were called Regan."

"Pet?" Her temper snapped as she banged his head over and over. Christ, she hated imps.

Jagr gently touched her arm. "Careful, little one, we need him alive if he's going to answer our questions."

Regan forced herself to halt, sucking in a deep, calming breath as she met Jagr's steady gaze.

"Can you sense if he's speaking the truth?"

"Yes."

Regan leaned forward, deliberately twisting his arm higher. "What's your name?"

"Damn you, I . . . arrg . . . Gaynor. My name is Gaynor."

She eased the pressure. "How do you know Culligan?"

Gaynor licked his thin lips, the scent of peach thick in the air. "We both lived in New Orleans during the Civil War. Culligan never had much magic, but the looting was easy, and the humans were ripe to be plucked of what few valuables they had left."

Jagr growled deep in his throat. Even Regan shivered at the sound.

"That doesn't explain how you knew about Regan."

Despite the chill of Jagr's power, the imp began to sweat. "We crossed paths in Chicago thirty years ago. He told me he'd fallen into a sweet deal with a baby Were that he intended to take on the road in some sort of freak show. Lucky idiot."

Regan sucked in a startled breath.

Chicago?

Culligan had always claimed he'd found her abandoned in a ditch near Dallas.

Of course, Salvatore had tried to convince her that Culligan had lied, and that her family would never have willingly abandoned her.

Still . . . the suspicion had continued to rankle deep in her heart.

"Who offered him this sweet deal?" she rasped.

"A cur. I think Culligan said his name was Caine."

"Christ." She gave a stunned shake of her head, her stomach twisting with a sick sensation. "This is nuts. How did the curs get a hold of me? And why would they give me to Culligan?"

Easily sensing her distress, Jagr stroked her arm in a comforting motion.

"We'll discover the truth, little one. That I promise." Jagr turned his attention to the imp, his eyes glittering like frozen chips of sapphire in the dark. "Didn't you think the Weres might want to know about a missing child?"

"Culligan swore the dogs were the ones who gave him the baby in the first place."

"You couldn't possibly be stupid enough to believe any Were would willingly hand over a pureblood child to an imp," Jagr accused.

Gaynor tried to cringe from Jagr, obviously more afraid of the looming vampire than the angry Were perched on top of him.

Smart imp.

"He said she was damaged, that she couldn't even shift," he desperately tried to excuse his betrayal. "Besides, he had to make a blood oath that he wouldn't allow her to suffer any permanent harm."

"A blood oath?" Regan directed her question to Jagr. "What's that?"

He grimaced. "A promise bound in blood and magic."

"If Culligan had failed to protect you from serious damage, he would have dropped dead in a New York minute," Gaynor swiftly added, as if hoping for brownie points.

Regan ground her teeth, recalling how obsessive Culligan had been to keep the occasional demon visitors from wandering too near the back of the RV. At the time she'd thought he was protecting his cash cow. Now it was obvious he was simply terrified for his own life. "So that's why he was so careful to keep his disgusting friends away from my cage. Pig."

"And you haven't seen or heard from him in thirty years?" Jagr charged.

"No, I swear."

"Then how did you know he was in St. Louis?"

Gaynor licked his lips. "The word was already buzzing in the chat rooms that an imp had been busted by the King of Weres for holding a pureblood captive, and that he was hiding in St. Louis. I suspected it might be Culligan, so I sent a hell-hound to track him down with a message to meet me."

"Imps have chat rooms?" Regan mocked, envisioning a bunch of imps huddled over their keyboards.

"Hey, we're more tech-savvy than most demons."

Regan's lips twisted. Clearly the imp hadn't been into Tane's version of the *Death Star.*

"So the chat rooms were buzzing about an imp being in trouble, and you decided to contact Culligan out of the goodness of your heart?" she demanded. "Give me a break."

"I thought if it was Culligan, he might be willing to pay for my help." He shuddered beneath her. "Do you think I like peddling tea and cake to fat old ladies?"

"He's lying," Jagr breathed softly.

Regan smacked the imp on the back of the head, hard. "Well, I believe he hates peddling cakes to old ladies, so he must be lying about his reason for contacting Culligan."

"Ow . . . I'm not a Whack-a-Mole," he protested.

"No, you're a breath away from being dinner," Regan

informed him, not above using the imp's instinctive fear of vampires. "Did I forget to mention Jagr didn't have time to eat before we came looking for you?"

Jagr readily fell into his role as enforcer, his fangs suddenly shimmering in the moonlight.

"And I'm not hungry for cake."

"She'll kill me if I tell you."

"Then you're screwed, Gaynor, because we'll kill you if you don't," Regan assured him.

There was a pause, then straining his neck, Gaynor attempted to turn his head to speak directly to Regan.

"Maybe we can make a deal? The information has to be worth something to you."

"You want a deal? Fine." She grabbed his face to turn it directly toward Jagr. "You tell me everything you know about Culligan, and I won't feed you to the hungry vampire."

He swallowed heavily. "Fair enough."

"Why did you send a message to Culligan?" Jagr pressed.

"Can I at least sit up?" he whined. "You're giving me a cramp."

She shoved his arm high enough that it threatened to snap out of its socket.

"I'll let you up, but I'll give you more than a cramp if you try anything stupid."

Releasing his arm, Regan slipped off his back to kneel next to Jagr. Gaynor muttered a curse and scrambled to sit upright, straightening his silk tie even as he studied the grass stains on his jacket.

"Son of a bitch. Do you know how much this suit cost?"

"Do you know how much I don't care?" Regan snapped. "Start talking."

Giving up on his tie, the imp threw his hands in the air. "Fine. I did hear about Culligan in the chat rooms like I said, but I didn't send the message because I thought he could pay me. The worthless slug never did have the talent or intelligence to earn more than a few bucks. Even when he was handed a windfall like you."

Jagr's powers whipped painfully around the imp, making the short strands of his hair stand upright.

"So, why?"

Gaynor shivered. "A week ago a cur came into the tea shop and asked for me to invite Culligan to Hannibal."

Jagr beat her to the obvious question. "Who was this cur?"

"She called herself Sadie." His lips curled. "Damn, she was hot. Tall and dark with the kind of body that makes a man think about whips and chains. Very tasty."

Regan frowned. She'd assumed the cur would be Duncan or perhaps the mysterious Caine. Who the hell was this Sadie?

"Had you ever seen her before?"

"No, and she wasn't a woman a man would forget. Not ever." A leer touched the imp's too-pretty features. "Maybe her rack was a bit small, but . . ." His disgusting words were cut short as Regan threw a rock at him with enough force to snap his head back. He glared at her as he raised a hand to the bleeding lump on his forehead. "Shit."

"My suggestion would be to stop digging your own grave, imp," Jagr said dryly.

"She asked."

Regan regarded the imp in disgust. "You sold out your friend because you thought the cur was hot?"

"No, I sold him out because the cur handed over a butt load of money."

"Nice."

"Hey, Culligan would have done the same in my position."

Regan couldn't argue with his logic. Culligan was an amoral, spineless turd who would sell his soul for a buck.

"Did the cur say what she wanted with him?"

"She said he'd failed in his duty to the curs, and that he needed to be punished."

"That's not all she said, is it?" Jagr abruptly insisted.

"She might have mentioned using him as bait."

"To lure Regan to Hannibal?"

Gaynor flinched at the ice edging the vampire's voice. "She didn't say. I'm not precisely her confidant. More like her stooge."

"Where is she?" Regan demanded.

"I don't know, but it must be near the river."

Jagr frowned. "Why do you say that?"

"I could smell it on her."

Jagr's frown deepened. "Her scent wasn't masked?"

"Masked?" Gaynor widened his pale green eyes. "How does a cur mask her scent?"

Regan didn't need to be a mind reader to know the imp was lying. Casting a covert glance toward Jagr, she held her tongue as he gave a faint shake of his head. For whatever reason, he didn't want to challenge Gaynor.

"Did she come alone to meet you?" he instead asked.

"She came inside alone, but there were a half dozen curs surrounding the shop." There was no pretense in the flash of anger that rippled over his face. "The dolts completely ruined my daffodils. Oh, and the bitch took off with an entire batch of my peanut butter fudge."

Regan blinked. Okay, that was . . . weird.

"Why would she take your fudge?"

Gaynor stiffened, as if offended by the question. "Because it just happens to be the most famous fudge in the state. Perhaps in all of America."

Jagr snorted. "And it's hexed to compel the unwary to crave it like a drug."

"You can't prove that," Gaynor hissed.

Regan glanced toward Jagr. "Can curs be hexed?"

"They're more susceptible than pure demons," he answered before turning back to the imp. "Has she been back for more?"

Gaynor shifted nervously closer to the bushes. Idiot. Did he actually think he could outrun a vampire?

"When I opened the shop two days ago, she was waiting for me," he grudgingly confessed.

"For fudge?"

"For fudge, and to make another offer," he said slowly.

Regan gave a lift of her brows. "An offer for what?"

There was an odd pause, then with a movement so swift that it caught both Jagr and Regan off guard, Gaynor knocked aside a pile of branches to reveal a shimmering, swirling mist that seemed to hang in the darkness.

Although Culligan had never had the power necessary to create a portal, Regan had witnessed other imps weave a doorway in thin air. She'd always been fascinated by the magical gateways when they'd been at a distance. She wasn't nearly so delighted to have one close enough to tumble through.

"The offer is for you, Regan," the imp admitted, reaching to grasp her arm.

More astonished than frightened, Regan felt herself being yanked toward the swirling portal. She instinctively struggled, but the imp was unexpectedly strong as he planted his feet and scooted backward, inching her closer and closer to the opening.

Intent on their private battle, neither heard the warning growl from the furious vampire, not until he was lunging forward.

"No," he roared, shoving Gaynor with enough force that it wrenched Regan's arm from his grasp.

It also tumbled both of them backward.

Straight into the waiting portal.

"Jagr."

Crawling on her hands and knees, Regan watched in horror as Gaynor disappeared into the shimmering mist, still entangled with the furious vampire. Oh, God, no. She reached out, her fingertips brushing the tip of Jagr's heavy boot just as the portal pulsed, flared, and then disappeared with an audible snap.

Suddenly alone in the darkness, Regan stared at the spot where Jagr had disappeared, as if stupidly waiting for him to jump out of thin air.

Christ. He was gone. He was really, really gone.

And she didn't have a chance in hell of following him.

"Shit, shit, shit."

Regan jumped to her feet, running through the night at full speed. Culligan had never shared the secrets of imp magic, but there had to be someone who knew how to trail a person through a portal.

Indifferent to the dangers that might lurk in the shadows, Regan returned to the truck still parked in front of the tea shop. Hopping into the driver's seat, she switched on the key that Jagr had left in the ignition, and struggled to force it into gear.

She'd never actually driven before, but how hard could it be?

The thought had barely passed through her mind when she stomped on the long pedal that made the car go forward (at least it did on TV), and with a squeal of tires she slammed straight into one of the lovely dogwoods that lined the quiet street.

Well, crap . . . maybe it wasn't as easy as she'd thought.

Turning off the engine, she tumbled out of the truck and sprinted between the nearest houses, heading directly north. Her head throbbed from where it had banged into the windshield and the neighborhood dogs were already howling at her presence, but at least she wasn't in danger of massacring any more innocent trees.

Leaping a wooden fence, she briefly considered Jagr's annoyance when he'd discovered she was running like a maniac through the streets without a care to any curs that might be lurking nearby. No doubt she'd have to listen to his furious lecture on her lack of brains if he . . .

A sharp pain ripped through her heart.

No, there were no ifs.

She would find him.

And he would be okay.

Nothing else was acceptable.

Refusing to contemplate the panic that churned through her stomach, Regan weaved her way through town. She caught the distant scent of a dew fairy and the even more distant scent of a hellhound prowling through a Dumpster, but nothing leaped out to eat her, so putting down her head, she called upon her considerable powers and plunged through the fields and meadows with a speed only a vampire could match.

The scenery was no more than a blur as she concentrated on retracing the path back to Tane's isolated lair.

At last she could see the crumbling red brick chimney in the distance, and ignoring the growing stitch in her side, she dodged past an abandoned barn and leaped over a small creek.

It never occurred to Regan that she might not be welcomed at the vampire stronghold without Jagr at her side. At least not until Tane's massive form abruptly vaulted from the second-storied balcony to block her path to the door.

Skidding to a halt, Regan barely avoided colliding into the very broad, very bare chest.

"Tane." She pressed a hand to her thundering heart. "God, you scared me."

Pinpricks of pain stabbed into her flesh as Tane allowed his power to be released into the night.

"Where's Jagr?"

She was smart enough to feel a jolt of fear at the fierce expression on Tane's beautiful face, but she was too concerned for Jagr to truly appreciate just how dangerous her position might be.

"He was taken through a portal by an imp," she said in a

rush, too rattled to spell out more than the most pertinent information. "I can't find him."

Thankfully, Tane didn't press for details. It was enough to know a brother was in trouble.

His long, lethal fangs emerged, along with a dagger he pulled from the waistband of his khakis.

"Stay here. I'll try to pick up his trail."

"Wait, I want to go . . ."

Ignoring her urgent demand to be taken with him, Tane slid past her and silently disappeared into the dark.

Regan clenched her teeth, knowing she'd never catch him. "Damned vampires."

Briefly considering her limited options, Regan at last heaved a sigh and climbed the steps to the wide verandah.

She could return to the golf course and hope to stumble across a means to follow Jagr, but she wasn't so full of herself to believe that she would have better luck than a trained vampire assassin, who no doubt had had several hundred years to perfect his skills. The painful truth was she would likely be more a burden than help.

There was also the option of simply walking away and washing her hands of Jagr and everyone else determined to force her into a family she didn't want or need.

It wasn't as if she owed them anything.

Okay, Jagr had come in handy a time or two. Hell, he'd just saved her from being pulled into the damned portal.

And no woman, no matter how innocent, could deny that he was a world-class lover who'd made her first experience one she would remember for all eternity.

Still, he was possessive and bossy and ruthlessly worming his way into her heart. That alone should be enough to send her screaming into flight.

She didn't . . . of course.

Mere logic couldn't overcome the desperate need to rescue the aggravating beast.

Even if that meant doing the one thing she'd sworn she would never, ever do.

Squaring her shoulders, Regan entered the abandoned building, easily finding her way down to the basement where she was met by a military looking vampire guarding the opening to the lair.

Since he didn't attack at her approach, Regan could only assume that Tane hadn't left standing orders to kill on sight. In fact, the vampire actually bowed, making Regan halt in shock.

Was she supposed to bow back?

Curtsey?

She shook away the inane thoughts as the vampire straightened and regarded her with a stoic expression.

"May I be of service?"

Regan briefly struggled against the bitterness she'd nurtured for thirty years. It was an ugly battle filled with less than admirable emotions.

Pride, envy, festering resentment.

Yeah, ugly. But thankfully short.

Less than a heartbeat passed before she was sucking in a deep breath and taking the irrevocable plunge.

"I need to contact the Anasso," she said, relieved when the words came out almost steady.

"Here." Without hesitation, the vampire pulled a cell phone from the pocket of his camouflage pants. He flipped it open and scrolled through his contacts before handing it to her. "It's a direct line."

Regan took the phone and, not giving herself time to consider the consequences, punched the send button.

There was a buzz on the other end, then before Regan was entirely prepared, a low, commanding voice came on the line.

"Tane?"

"No." Regan was forced to stop and clear the lump from

her throat. It had to be Styx. Who else would have a voice even more arrogant than Jagr? "No, this is . . . Regan."

There was a shocked pause, then the leader of all vampires softened his tone.

"Regan, I cannot tell you how good it is to hear your voice," he murmured. "Darcy has been most anxious to speak with you."

Her jaw clenched, but she refused to be distracted. "Maybe later."

She could sense the moment he realized that this was not a social call.

"Tell me."

She did.

Chapter 14

Jagr hated magic.

As a vampire, he'd become accustomed to being firmly on top of the food chain.

He was the bump in the night that scared all the other creatures.

For all his powers, however, he had no defense as Gaynor plunged the two of them into the portal, and he was surrounded by the relentless sting of the strange mist that seemed to bite into his skin with malicious glee. He had a brief moment to savor the knowledge he'd managed to keep the imp's filthy hands off Regan before he was flung out of the portal with enough force to slam his head into a cement wall.

Briefly disoriented, he didn't realize that magic wasn't the only danger. Not until he heard the slam of a heavy metal door and he turned to discover he'd been locked in a cell that was custom-made to hold demons.

Any demon.

Including vampires.

Furiously wiping the blood from his forehead, he slowly turned, allowing his senses to flow outward.

His first realization was that they were deep below ground (which at least meant no early morning sunrise), and that the cement walls and ceiling were several feet thick. His next realization was that there were a number of hexes etched on the walls, and thick steel doors that were specifically created to drain the strength of any demon stupid enough to become trapped.

A dark, vicious dread curled through him.

It had been centuries since he'd been locked in a cage, but the memory was still vivid.

Starkly, painfully vivid.

He clenched his jaw, curling his hands into fists. Madness threatened to consume him. The same madness that had led to the bloody slaughter of his previous captors.

For a perilous moment he teetered on the edge, his ancient torment surging through him like a destructive wave. Then without warning, the image of Regan flashed through his mind and the panic receded.

Grasping onto the thought of the beautiful Were, Jagr pulled back from the darkness.

By the gods, he would not allow himself to lose control when Regan needed him. Nothing mattered but finding a means to escape so he could protect her.

His thoughts cleared until he was once again in command, although that didn't keep him from being seriously pissed off.

Trapped by a worthless imp.

He'd never live it down. With a hiss of frustration, he moved to swing his arm against the door, belatedly discovering there'd been enough silver mixed with the metal to make his forearm smolder.

"Gaynor, let me out," he roared, able to smell the imp on the other side of the door.

"Damn you, vampire," the imp's muffled voice echoed through the air. "Why did you have to interfere?"

"You have just signed your death warrant, imp."

"Shit." Jagr could pick up the sound of Gaynor's anxious

pacing. "I didn't ask to get involved in this mess. I wish that stupid cur had never come into my shop."

"Your regrets are just beginning," Jagr growled, his frustration deepening as he sensed his powers beginning to weaken. Dammit. Regan was out there alone. He had to get free. "Let me out and I might just consider letting you live."

Gaynor laughed bitterly. "Do you think I'm stupid? I may be a pathetic imp living in a podunk town, but even I've heard of Jagr, the crazed Visigoth chief who slaughtered an entire clan of vampires. If I let you out, I'll be dead before I can blink."

The imp wasn't entirely wrong. On any other night, Jagr would be foaming at the mouth and unable to consider anything but the need to rip the imp into a hundred pieces.

Tonight, however, his only concern was Regan.

"Allow me to leave here unharmed, and I swear . . ."

"Forget it, vamp. I'm not opening that door."

"Then what do you intend to do. Kill me?" he challenged.

"And have a rabid posse of vampires out for my head? No, thank you."

Jagr was forced to take a step from the door as the burn of silver seeped through his clothing.

"You think my clan is not already on the hunt?" he rasped.

Even through the thick door, Jagr could hear the imp's rapid heartbeat. His fear was tangible.

"They can't track me through a portal."

"It doesn't matter, the world isn't big enough for you to hide," Jagr deliberately taunted.

"Holy freaking hell." There was more pacing. "None of this is my fault."

Jagr hissed. "You endanger a pureblooded Were and kidnap a vampire, and you claim it's not your fault?"

"All I did was invite Culligan to Hannibal," he whined. "I didn't force the damned Were to follow. And for your information, I didn't have any intention of trying to capture Regan, no matter how much money Sadie offered."

"You spineless liar." Jagr's fangs ached with the need to sink deep in the imp's throat. "You deliberately led us to that spot where you had a portal waiting."

"Only after you tracked me to the tea shop," he desperately argued. "You came after me—I didn't go looking for trouble."

"But you were swift to try and take advantage."

"Give me a break, vampire," Gaynor muttered. "I'm an imp. What did you expect when you dropped the Were into my lap like an overripe plum? The curs are offering a damned fortune to get their hands on her."

The curs. Always the curs.

Someday soon he intended to rid the world of the mangy dogs.

Someday *very* soon.

"And instead of a fortune, all you've earned is a death sentence."

Gaynor's heartbeat raced to the point where Jagr wondered if it might burst. Then, without warning, the imp was moving swiftly away from Jagr's cell.

"No, I'm not taking the fall for this," he swore as he left. "Sadie got me into this, she can damned well get me out."

Left alone in the darkness, Jagr tilted back his head and screamed in fury.

Standing in the middle of the empty cave, Sadie viciously kicked the young male cur curled into a tight ball of misery on the ground.

She'd crouched for hours in the darkness, watching for some sign of Regan and the vamp to emerge from the cave. Or at least to make some indication that they were preparing for the coming dawn.

At last she'd grown bored with the waiting.

Patience was for losers, not for curs destined to make their mark in the world.

Creeping up the steep bluff, Sadie motioned for the cur she'd commanded to keep guard to join her. She didn't have an actual plan in mind. She only knew that she was tired of hiding and plotting with nothing to show for her efforts.

Despite the lingering scent of vamp and Were, Sadie didn't have to reach the entrance of the cave to realize that it was empty. Infuriated, she realized that not only had her prey escaped, but she'd been well and truly fooled by a few scraps of clothing.

With a sharp motion, she'd knocked her companion to the ground. Someone was going to pay for this latest disaster.

"You worthless piece of crap. How dare you let the Were escape." She punctuated her words with kicks, readily ignoring the fact that she was equally responsible for allowing the two to disappear. Shit rolled downhill. It was never her fault if there was someone else to blame. "I told you not to take your eyes off this cave."

"I didn't, I swear." The cur grunted as her foot connected with his cheek. "The vampire must have used his shadows to hide behind."

Sadie clenched her fists. She didn't like being reminded that there were demons out there who possessed skills far beyond a mere cur.

"I don't need your lame excuses. It was only luck that we stumbled across the Were's trail that led to this lair in the first place. How the hell are we supposed to find them now?"

The cur tried to dig deeper in the dirt, as if that would protect him from the brutal kicks.

"I thought you intended to lure her to the cabin with the imp."

Sadie growled. For God's sake, was the cur suicidal? He was pushing every kill-me button she possessed.

"And just what do you expect me to do with her pet vampire while I'm busy capturing her?" she gritted, her skin crawling with the need to shift. "Politely ask him not to kill me? Maybe I should invite Salvatore along as well?"

Belatedly sensing Sadie was at the edge of her control, the cur wisely resorted to shameless pleading.

"Forgive me, mistress, I beg of you."

"Forgiveness is not in my nature, stupid bastard." Preparing for another kick, Sadie was interrupted by the buzz of the phone she'd stuck in her pocket. "Saved by the bell, worm. Or should I say, the vibration?" Ignoring the useless cur cowering on the ground, Sadie pulled out the phone and lifted her brows as she read the name flashing across the screen. Snapping open the phone, she pressed it to her ear. "Gaynor, tell me you have good news."

He didn't.

Her already strained temper threatened to combust as she listened to his stumbling, bumbling confession of capturing Jagr by mistake.

"God, I'm surrounded by morons," she gritted, her mind already sifting through the implications of this latest mess. "Where are you?" He offered hesitant directions, clearly not overly anxious for their impending meeting. Which proved he wasn't entirely stupid. "You'd better hope I can use this to my advantage, imp, or I'll eat your heart for breakfast," she warned before cutting the connection and shoving the phone back into her pocket. Reaching down, she grasped the cringing cur by the hair and yanked him to a kneeling position. "I have a new task for you."

He nervously licked his lips. "How may I serve?"

"Regan is separated from her vamp. I want you to take the remaining curs and find her."

"But . . ."

She tossed him backward, watching as he slammed into the wall and slid to the ground.

"Don't screw this up."

"Yes, mistress," he managed to croak.

Regan's conversation with Styx was nothing if not to the point. She revealed no more than the fact that Jagr had been taken by an imp and, in turn, he promised he would be at Tane's lair within twenty-four hours.

Short and sweet.

But Regan wasn't gullible enough to believe that it was a simple phone call.

Or that it wouldn't have long-term consequences.

Having accomplished all she could, Regan returned to the rooms Tane had offered them, and over the next few hours she learned every inch of them.

She clocked in a dozen miles pacing from one end to the other. She rearranged the small kitchen, she folded her new clothes, and placed them neatly back in the bags. At last she lay down on the bed, desperately hoping to catch the lingering scent of Jagr, only to discover whoever had come in to clean the lair had changed the sheets.

Not that a change of sheets could erase the memories of Jagr's tender touch, or the icy-fire of his kisses.

There wasn't a power in the world that could accomplish that feat.

Ignoring the clang and whistle and outright screams of alarm that sounded in the back of her mind, Regan snuggled deeper into the mattress, allowing the image of Jagr poised above her, his expression one of fierce bliss as he thrust in and out of her body, to fill her thoughts.

Once he was safe, she would return to her futile battle

of pretending she could walk away from him and all his unwanted complications without a twinge of remorse.

For now she simply needed to hang on to the ruthless certainty he would be rescued.

Time passed until Regan could feel the heavy sensation of the approaching dawn. Although she didn't fear the sun like the vampires, she possessed the blood of Were. She was by nature called to the night.

She shoved herself off the bed, a horrible dread lodged in the pit of her stomach.

Christ, if Jagr didn't return soon, he would be trapped until sunset.

Always assuming he wasn't being held somewhere that the sun could . . .

No.

Enough of this waiting. She might not possess the skills of an ancient vampire, but at least she could function during the day.

Storming into the hideous living room, Regan skirted past the whirlpool and was a mere step from the door when it flung open to reveal Tane's massive form.

"Well?" she demanded, knowing the answer before he even shook his head.

"I could find nothing."

"Damn."

The golden features tightened. "As soon as the sun sets, I will return to the hunt."

"I called Styx," she absently muttered, her thoughts centered on Jagr and the overriding need to be doing . . . something. Anything. "He'll be here tonight with the cavalry."

Unexpectedly, Tane reached out to touch her cheek, his touch almost gentle.

"Jagr will be found, Regan."

Frustration flooded through her at the flat certainty in his voice. "Yeah, but before he's been staked or beheaded or tossed into the sun?"

The vampire shrugged. "The curs want you. They'll keep him alive if they think they can use him to lure you into a trap."

She clung to that hope, but it didn't ease the desperate need to find and rescue Jagr.

"Even if that's true, he'll be kept locked up. Maybe even tortured." She held the dark gaze, willing him to understand. "Tane, he can't go through that again. It might break him."

Only the lengthening of his terrifying fangs revealed that Tane not only understood, but was infuriated by the thought of his brother being harmed.

"Even if he could be found, there's no way to rescue him now. The sun's already rising." His tone indicated his opinion of the sun. It wasn't good. His fingers brushed down her cheek, before he dropped his hand and stepped back. "I know you're concerned, but our hands are tied until darkness falls."

She made a restless motion, her inner wolf at the end of its patience. "I can't just wait."

The dark, faintly slanted eyes narrowed. "You do know that Jagr will decapitate me if anything happens to you?"

"Do you intend to keep me from leaving?"

His lips twisted, no doubt sensing the impending battle. "No, pretty wolf, I suspect that Jagr isn't the only one who's had enough of prisons." His voice hardened with warning. "Just don't get yourself killed. My health depends on it."

"I'll do my best," she dryly promised.

Stepping back into the hall, Tane paused to send her a speaking glance.

"If you decide to drive, wolf, take one of the Hummers. It at least has a chance of surviving."

Regan ignored the slur to her driving ability. She had, after all, trashed his truck. Instead, she turned to make her way back to the bedroom.

Moving directly to a distant corner, she knelt before Jagr's heavy satchel.

Just for a moment, she hesitated.

After thirty years of being denied even the pretense of privacy, she possessed an intense dislike for the thought of invading anyone else's. Especially Jagr's, who had shared her endless humiliations.

Still, she wasn't so foolish as to go in search of him without some sort of weapon. Unlike other purebloods, she couldn't depend on shifting to fight her battles. She needed something sharp. And big.

Sucking in a deep breath, she forced herself to open the satchel, her fingers stilling as they encountered smooth leather instead of the cold, hard steel she'd been expecting. With a rueful smile she pulled out the heavy book that was written in a language she didn't recognize.

She wistfully trailed her fingers over the aged leather of the cover. She'd encountered various demons and warriors and even powerful leaders during her travels with Culligan, but none had offered such a fascinating mixture of contrasts.

Icily aloof and yet so terribly vulnerable. Strong and yet tender. Raw, ruthless power with the soul of a scholar.

With a shake of her head, Regan set the book on the floor and returned her attention to the satchel. This time, she had no trouble finding one of the numerous daggers that were stacked in the bottom.

Careful to choose one without silver (with her current luck, she'd probably stab herself), and big enough to put a nice-sized hole in an enemy, she tightly gripped the handle and headed out of the private rooms.

She half-expected to be halted as she retraced her steps out of the lair, but while the vampires watched her pass in creepy silence, not one leaped out to try and block her exit.

Thank God. She didn't think her dagger, no matter how big or shiny, was going to do much good against them.

Regan jogged across the open fields, keeping her senses alert for any scent of Jagr.

If the imp had a brain, he would have taken his hostage halfway across the world, but Culligan had taught her that the flighty demons were content to leap first and consider later. If ever.

Of course, hoping she might stumble across Jagr was something like hoping she might find a pot of gold at the end of the rainbow. Still, she had to . . .

Regan halted, suddenly struck by a crazed thought.

Why search for a needle in the proverbial haystack when she could go directly to the source of her troubles?

If she could track down the cur that had ordered Gaynor to capture her in the first place, then eventually the imp would make an appearance. The one thing that Regan was certain of was that the imp wouldn't want to be stuck with a furious vampire for long.

And she suddenly realized that she might actually possess the means to find the bitch.

Ignoring the urge to race as fast as possible back to Hannibal, Regan forced herself to maintain a steady pace that allowed her to continue her search for Jagr, as well as to keep guard for any lurking danger.

There was no use getting herself killed for what might very well turn out to be a wild-goose chase.

As she jogged, the sun crested the horizon, bathing the landscape in a soft haze of pale peach and rose. The light glittered off the dew clinging to the grass, fragmenting until it appeared the world was drenched in pastel.

Regan barely noticed the dazzling display. Or the dampness

clinging to the hem of her jeans. She was on a mission, and nothing was going to distract her.

Choosing a more direct route back to the tea shop, Regan hid in the bushes and studied the pretty structure for long minutes.

There was a gradual stirring in the quiet neighborhood. A woman dressed in a power suit climbed into her Lexus and roared down the street. An elder man swept his front porch. A child pressed his eager face against the window.

All mundanely human, without a beastie to be seen.

Regan straightened and dashed across the street, knowing it was now or never.

Skirting the house with all its froufrou trellises and cheesy birdbaths, she allowed her nose to lead her to the kitchen window, using her considerable strength to shove up the sash a few inches and breathe in the various scents.

She grimaced at the intoxicating aromas. Holy crap. Jagr hadn't been wrong when he accused Gaynor of hexing his food. Even with her immunity to the magic, she could feel her mouth watering in response.

Damn imps.

Closing her eyes, she concentrated on sorting through the various teas, pastries, and candies. At last, she caught and held the scent of peanut butter fudge.

As she had hoped, the smell was distinctive. Rich, creamy peanut butter with a hefty dose of imp magic.

Which meant that she wouldn't mistake it for any other fudge that seemed to be one of the basic food groups in Hannibal.

Circling the tea shop one last time, even knowing it was a futile effort to discover some hint of Jagr or the damned imp, she at last turned on her heel and began jogging toward the east.

Gaynor had admitted that he'd smelled the river on Sadie,

and since Jagr hadn't detected a lie, she was going with the hope the cur would still be near it.

Refusing to consider the knowledge that the Mississippi River ran over two thousand miles, she jogged through the near empty streets, ignoring the howling dogs and occasional car that whizzed past.

Briefly, she wondered if Levet found a safe place to turn into stone. Although she'd heard over the years that gargoyles were close to indestructible, she didn't know if that was true for miniature ones, and unlike Jagr, she found the tiny demon oddly charming. She would hate for him to be injured trying to help her.

Thoughts of Levet were driven from her mind as she reached the quaint, historic section of town. She turned right at the steps that led to the lighthouse on top of the bluff, and hurried past the antique and gift shops that now filled the old buildings. Thank God she'd taken the time to sniff out Gaynor's particular recipe for fudge. The entire area reeked of the stuff.

Turning again she passed by the bed-and-breakfast that had once catered to the passing steamboats, and climbed the levee behind it. From there it was an easy jog down to the edge of the river.

She briefly hesitated before she turned south, grimly refusing to glance toward the bluff where she'd shared the cave with Jagr. The curs would want a place outside of town where they could easily hunt away from prying eyes.

If she didn't find some sign of them within a few hours, she would backtrack and try her luck north of town.

Not much of a plan, but it was better than sitting in Tane's lair and pacing holes in the carpet.

Well, at least marginally better, she acknowledged three hours later, tugging her jeans free of yet another thornbush from hell. Scouring the banks and steep bluffs along the river was not only time-consuming, but it was wearisome work, even for a pureblooded Were. Clearly the whole Huck Finn lifestyle was far more romantic in books than real life.

With a sigh, she leaned against a rock that jetted from the river. She was only a handful of miles south of Hannibal, but she might as well have been in the middle of nowhere.

There was no sound of traffic, no laughter of children, no barking dogs. In fact, there wasn't even the call of a bird . . .

Regan shoved herself upright.

She might be in the middle of nowhere, but there should have been the usual wildlife scurrying through the dense trees. A bird, a squirrel, a curious raccoon.

The fact that there wasn't could only mean that there was something dangerous in the area. Something that had been around long enough to drive them away.

Feeling her strength return, along with a flood of hope, Regan grimly headed up the steeply angled bank, using the dagger to hack through the thicker foliage. At least the damned thing was going to come in handy for something.

Regan reached the top of the bluff and slowed her pace to a mere crawl. If she were right (not at all a certainty), there was a pack of curs roaming these woods and they had the witch's spell to keep then hidden from her senses.

It seemed a good idea to try to avoid tripping over one.

Slipping silently from tree to tree, she listened carefully, depending on her superior sight and hearing to warn her of any danger. The sun slowly moved overhead, warning that time was passing, but Regan ignored the urge to rush. This was supposed to be a . . . what did they call it? A recon mission. A search and get-out-alive sort of deal.

On the point of accepting she was wasting her time, again, she was hit by the unmistakable scent of peanut butter fudge. Yes! She continued forward and at last caught sight of a tin roof through the trees.

A cabin. It had to be.

Her heart lodged in her throat as she edged cautiously closer. Yep. Definitely a cabin. Peering through the trees, she studied the wooden structure. It wasn't much. Just a few unpainted boards slapped together with a door and two windows. The attached shed wasn't much better, only without the windows, and leaning to the point it threatened to become detached from the rusty tin roof.

A place that had gone past charming, straight to rustic.

And not at all the setting she would have pictured for a pack of curs with authority issues.

Of course, that's what usually made a good hiding place a good hiding place.

Crouching behind yet another bush, Regan kept a watch on the building, her nerves stretched tight by the uncanny silence. The place appeared deserted, but she wasn't stupid.

Isolated cabin. Seemingly abandoned.

It was a trap waiting to happen.

It was also the closest thing to a clue she'd found all day.

Gathering her courage, Regan slipped silently toward the cabin, her heart pounding so loudly she feared it would give her away. Astonishingly, nothing attacked (wonders of wonders), and pressed against the rough planks, she carefully inched up high enough to peer into the window.

A battered chair, a heavy dresser, a fireplace that looked like it had been recently used.

No howling curs. No magic-wielding witch.

No Sophie. No Gaynor.

She gritted her teeth, too stubborn, or maybe it was too stupid, to concede defeat.

Straightening, she inched her way toward the attached shed, keeping herself pressed against the cabin, as if that somehow made her invisible. Hey, it was how they did it in the movies. Then pausing only a moment to lean her ear against the door, she pushed it open.

Preparing to bolt at the first hint of danger, Regan scanned the shadowed interior, not surprised to find a handful of rusting tools collecting cobwebs in the corners, or the wooden barrel that had been overturned to play table for a kerosene lamp.

The whip and numerous daggers, swords, and handguns placed on a rickety shelf were a bit more unexpected.

It was the bedraggled, nearly unrecognizable imp chained to the wall, however, that was the real showstopper.

Culligan.

Chapter 15

Just for a moment, Regan remained frozen in the doorway.

After days of endless, grueling, relentless searching, she'd stumbled over her damned prey when she wasn't even looking for him.

How was that for irony?

She clenched the dagger, studying the imp who'd made her life a living hell.

He looked . . . ghastly.

Blindfolded and leaning heavily against the chains, as if he couldn't hold his own weight, his red hair was matted into disgusting clumps, and his white skin was marred with dirt and dried blood.

Gone was the brash, conceited demon who had taken such delight in tormenting her, and in its place was a sad, pathetic waste of a creature wearing nothing more than a red thong.

A smile of absolute pleasure curled her lips as he weakly attempted to lift his head, clearly sensing someone had entered the shed, but too disoriented to recognize her scent.

"Who's there?" he croaked. "Please, help me. I'm being held against my will. Please . . ." His plea was cut short as she crossed the narrow space to rip off the blindfold. He blinked against the sunlight that spilled into the room, then his eyes widened in horror as he recognized his rescuer. "Oh, shit."

"Hello, Culligan," she purred, her gaze lowering to the small medallion tied around his neck. The witch's amulet. And the reason she hadn't sensed the bastard when she'd first approached the cabin.

"You," he rasped, struggling against the heavy chains that held him.

"Surprise."

"What the hell are you doing here?"

"I told you that you couldn't escape me." Reaching out, Regan ripped the amulet from the leather thong around Culligan's neck and tucked it into her pocket. Immediately the shed was filled with the overpowering smell of plums, while her scent disappeared. Well, well. Wasn't that convenient? Her smile widened with wicked pleasure. "Of course, at the time I didn't expect the curs to be so rude as to steal my toy and hide him from me. I hope they didn't break you."

Sweat bloomed on his forehead, visions of his death dancing in his head.

"There are curs crawling all over the place," he desperately attempted to frighten her away. "Are you trying to get caught?"

He did have a point.

A smart Were would cut out Culligan's heart and escape before the curs returned.

Unfortunately, her mission was no longer one of simple revenge. Jagr needed her. And if it meant keeping this bastard alive and risking her neck . . . then so be it.

Of course, that didn't mean she couldn't have some fun with the jackass.

Lifting the dagger, she drew a thin line over his heart, watching the blood drip down his chest.

"Actually, there's not a cur to be found," she mocked.

He shuddered, although she hadn't truly hurt him. Yet.

"It's a trap. They'll be here any minute."

She pressed the dagger deeper. "Not in time to keep me from carving out your heart."

"Wait." He struggled to breathe, his eyes wild with delicious fear. "Let's not be hasty, Regan."

"Hasty?" Fury made her blood boil. "I've waited thirty years to kill you. It's all I dreamed of night after night."

"How can you say that? I've been like a father to you." He squealed as the dagger slid deeper. "Okay, maybe not a father, but don't forget I saved you from that ditch. You could have died if it weren't for me."

Her eyes narrowed. "Ditch, eh?"

"Maybe it was more of a culvert."

"You worthless piece of shit, I've talked to Gaynor," she hissed. "I know the curs gave me to you in Chicago."

Terror flashed through the pale green eyes before Culligan was frantically attempting to cover his ass.

"Gaynor? You can't believe a word he says. He deliberately tricked me into coming to Hannibal." His face tightened. "Treacherous bastard."

"I'd believe that treacherous bastard if he told me the sky was green before I would believe a word that came from your filthy mouth."

He glanced down at the dagger stuck directly over his heart, licking his lips.

"Right, I get it. You're angry. I didn't treat you as well as I should have. That doesn't mean we can't come to an . . . understanding."

Her sharp laugh echoed through the small shed. "Understanding?"

"Anything. Just tell me what you want."

A few days ago what she wanted was this imp dead. Slowly, painfully, and by her hand.

Now she had to accept that there were more important things.

Jagr.

And the truth of her past.

"What I want is answers," she rasped.

"Fine. Whatever."

"Tell me how you got your nasty hands on me when I was a baby."

"I told you I found you in a . . ." He screamed as Regan pushed the dagger a hair's breadth from his heart. "Shit."

"One more lie, and you're dead," she warned. "You didn't find me in a ditch."

Cowering with a fear that warmed Regan's vengeful soul, Culligan gave up on his lame story.

"Okay, okay." He sucked in a careful breath. "I was in Chicago, minding my own business, I might add, when I was approached by a cur who claimed he had some hot cargo he needed to unload in a hurry."

"I was the hot cargo?"

"You and your sisters," he clarified. "The curs had blundered and attracted the attention of the local social services agency. The humans had already taken one of the babies, but the curs managed to slip away with the other three."

Regan stiffened. Well, that little tidbit would please Darcy. According to Salvatore, her sister had never been able to discover how she'd ended up in the hands of humans. And of course, she now knew how Culligan had managed to get a pureblooded Were in his power, if not how the curs had gotten a hold of her and her sisters in the first place.

"They tried to hush it all up, but the rumors hit the streets, and the curs were afraid that the word might reach the ears of the Weres. They needed to get rid of the evidence before they were caught red-handed."

"What happened to my sisters?" she demanded, astonished to discover that the answer actually mattered.

What happened to the lone wolf who didn't give a crap

about her family? The one who would rather have her eyes clawed out than be invited to Thanksgiving dinner?

Jagr happened, a soft voice whispered in the back of her mind.

He'd made her . . . soft. Damn him.

Unaware of her inner conflict, Culligan gave another glance at the knife stuck in his chest.

"One stayed with the humans, and one they smuggled to curs out of state. They gave you to me, and the other . . . I don't know."

Her teeth clenched. "The curs have one of my sisters?"

"I haven't seen her, but they claim to have one. They're supposedly doing some kind of experiments on her."

The air was squeezed from her lungs. "What kind of experiments?"

"Do I look like a scientist?" The petulant words became a screech of agony as she twisted the knife. "Ow. Damn you, it's something about making the curs more powerful. That's all I know, I swear."

So the suspicion that the mysterious Caine was obsessed with creating the cur version of Frankenstein wasn't as far-fetched as it seemed. Christ. Was the man a nut job? Who knew what could happen if he started screwing with the ancient magic that turned a human to a cur.

Of course, had Salvatore been any different? He'd deliberately altered the DNA of her and her sisters to produce females who wouldn't shift. And he did it so they could become some sort of broodmares to resurrect the fading Weres.

Damn arrogant men and their God complexes.

In a perfect world, women would be in charge.

"If the curs have my sister, then what do they want with me?" she gritted.

"My only guess is that you're the backup in case your sister kicks the bucket before they're done experimenting with her."

"Bastards."

Culligan shivered. "You have no idea. Release me, Regan, and I can help."

"You know where they're holding my sister captive?"

"I . . ." His ready lie faltered on his lips as her eyes narrowed in warning. "No, not . . . exactly, but . . ."

"Worthless," she muttered, abruptly realizing that was the perfect word to describe this sorry excuse for a demon.

Culligan was a weak, greedy fool who offered nothing to the world.

He didn't even make a decent villain.

Her grip tightened on the handle of the dagger, her bitter, choking thirst for revenge somehow lessened by the thought. It was as if she'd just hauled the boogeyman out of the closet, and discovered he was nothing more than a spineless slug.

Culligan quivered as she unwittingly dug the knife deeper. "Dammit, watch that thing."

In answer, Regan leaned forward, her expression ruthless. She'd pressed her luck far enough. It was time to get the information she'd come for.

"This is my last question. And believe me when I tell you, your life depends on your answer." The tip of the blade rested against his throbbing heart. "Where's Jagr?"

"What? Who?"

"The vampire who . . . who Darcy sent to Hannibal." She struggled to hide her aching dread. Culligan would only try to use it to his advantage. "Gaynor took him through a portal. Where would he go?"

Culligan glared, although he was smart enough not to struggle. "How the hell would I know? In case you missed the memo, I've been a little tied up since coming to Hannibal."

Without warning, Regan yanked the knife from the imp's chest and pressed it to his most precious jewels.

"Gaynor's been your friend for centuries. You have to know something."

Panic flashed through the green eyes. As expected, the idiot was far more afraid of being castrated than killed.

"Are you a complete psycho?"

"That's what thirty years of torture will do to a perfectly nice girl." Her voice could have rivaled Jagr's for ice. "Now start talking, or lose it."

Sweat poured down his body as he struggled to find his voice. "All I can tell you is that in the past, Gaynor always had an underground lair with a cell he could use to trap lesser demons."

She frowned. "Why would he trap demons?"

"You can make a fortune in ransom if you find demons with clans or families who are willing to pay to get them back."

"Christ." She shook her head in disgust. There should be an open season on imps. "Would this cell be strong enough to hold a vampire?"

Culligan shrugged. "If he has it properly hexed."

"Where would it be?"

A cunning expression slid over the lean features. The jackass intended to try and con her. Or at least he intended to until she dug the knife into one of his danglies.

"Arrg."

His eyes crossed, and Regan waited to see if he would pass out. When he didn't, she leaned close enough to touch nose to nose.

"Where would it be?"

"It would be close to his business . . ." The words came out in small, pained gasps. "That tea shop he's running."

Regan froze, a sick sensation clutching her stomach. "How can you be certain?"

"Gaynor might be able to conjure a portal, but he barely has any more strength than I do. He can't travel over a few hundred feet if he has a passenger. If he took your vampire, he couldn't have gone far."

"If he was there, why wouldn't I sense him?"

"The hexes would block any scent."

"Damn."

Regan straightened abruptly, stepping away from Culligan as she cursed her stupidity. What an idiot she was. If she hadn't been in such a panic to find Jagr, then maybe she wouldn't have overlooked the most obvious.

God, he might have been right beneath her feet while she was creeping around the tea shop . . .

She gave a sharp shake of her head.

Dammit, she'd wasted enough time.

She had to get to Jagr.

Whirling on her heel, she headed for the door, intent on returning to the tea shop. Even if she couldn't move Jagr until night fell, she needed to find him.

To be near him.

How frightening was that?

Regan was stepping from the shed when a voice behind her abruptly reminded her that Culligan was still chained to the wall.

"Hey, wait, where are you going? You can't leave me here."

Turning, she regarded him with a hint of surprise. In her hurry to reach Jagr, she'd simply forgotten him.

The imp who'd made her life a misery for thirty years.

The imp who she'd pledged to torture and kill.

It no doubt revealed some deep, earth-shattering change in her psyche, but she didn't have time to care.

"Actually, I can," she retorted, consoling whatever thirst for revenge that might linger with the knowledge the curs seemed to be doing a bang-up job of making Culligan miserable.

As if reading her mind, Culligan struggled frantically against the shackles that held him.

"They'll kill me. Do you want that on your conscience?"

She slowly lifted her brows. "Frankly, Culligan, I don't give a damn."

As exit lines went, it was pretty damned excellent, and Regan couldn't halt a smug smile as she stepped out of the shed and slammed the door behind her.

Later she might regret not slicing him open and using his entrails as fish bait, but for now she was content to leave his torture in the hands of the curs.

The smile and contentment lasted all of two seconds.

Just long enough for the familiar male cur to step from the trees.

Duncan.

For an odd, timeless moment they simply stared at one another in shock. Then without warning, he lifted his arm to throw something directly at her face.

Regan instinctively ducked, expecting a knife or sword to lodge itself in the door behind her.

Instead, there was a brilliant explosion, and she had only a second to acknowledge that she'd failed Jagr when the world went black.

The sun was painting the horizon with its last fading rays when Regan struggled to shake the painful cobwebs out of her head.

Freaking hell. She felt as if she'd been hit by a cement truck.

At last, ignoring the bursts of agony in the back of her head, she forced open her reluctant eyes. Well . . . shit. She should have kept them closed.

Not that pretending this was all a horrible nightmare would change the fact that she was currently tied to a tree with chains that held enough silver to sap her strength and leave raw burns on her skin. Or that she'd been moved from the cabin to one of the small islands covered in trees and underbrush that dotted the middle of the river.

Still fuzzy, Regan watched as Duncan stepped out of the canvas tent stuck in the center of the small clearing.

She swallowed her instinctive growl.

Damn the bastard. It was bad enough he'd given her a headache from hell and tied her to a tree like some sort of animal, but she'd been in la-la land the entire afternoon.

She was never going to get to Jagr at this rate.

The handsome cur came to a halt directly before her, looking considerably worse for the wear with his long hair hanging in tangles around his lean face and his black pants marred with dirt. His shirt was missing altogether.

She scowled in frustration, ridiculously pleased when he took a wary step backward.

"What did you do to me?" she rasped.

With an effort, the cur managed a brittle hint of his former arrogance.

"Just a little spell bomb I borrowed from Sadie's pet witch before I ripped out her throat."

Regan blinked, strangely shocked by the blunt confession. "You killed the witch?"

"The amulets hold a spell to mask the scent of anyone wearing it." Duncan grimaced. "Unfortunately, it also holds an added spell, so the witch can track it from anywhere in the world. Sadie's nasty way of keeping control of her pack. No witch, no GPS."

"Christ, you couldn't just take it off?"

"And announce my scent to every Were and vampire who has flocked to Hannibal? Not bloody likely. Without the witch, I have all the benefits of the amulet, without any of the unpleasant side effects."

Her lips twisted. "Who says there's no honor among thieves?"

"You should be thanking me, luv." His gaze deliberately dropped to the pocket where she had hidden the amulet she'd stolen from Culligan. Obviously he'd searched her before tying her up. "Besides, I lost any claim to honor when I threw my lot in with Caine thirty years ago. I should have known better, but the man does have a way with words. He's kissed the blarney stone, as my mum would say, and he convinced me that his crazy ideas were actually possible."

"Caine." Her eyes narrowed in fury as she futilely struggled against the burning chains. "You were with the cur who stole us. You bastard. How did he get his hands on four pure-blooded children?"

Shock rippled over his face. "How did you . . ." He cut off his words as he shoved his hands through his tangled hair. "Never mind. Caine has never been willing to admit how he got a hold of you and your sisters. All I know is that he showed up at the Illinois hunting grounds with the four of you, claiming that he'd been given a prophecy that the blood of the Weres would make us whole."

Ah, yes, the cornerstone of every great cult. Some mysterious prophecy . . . the promise of greatness . . . yadda yadda.

"A prophecy from whom?" she demanded.

Duncan shrugged. "That's one of those questions no one had the balls to ask. Or maybe we just didn't want to ask. He promised power, immortality. The opportunity to go from the bottom of the dung heap to the top." The cur snorted in self-disgust. "Blimey, I should have known he was full of shit when he took us to Chicago and nearly got us arrested."

His story confirmed what she'd learned from Gaynor and Culligan, but it didn't explain how or why the cur had managed to steal four pureblooded Weres.

Regan turned her mind away from the past. She might never discover how Caine had gotten his filthy hands on her, and for the moment it didn't really matter. All she truly cared about was finding some means of getting free so she could get to Jagr.

"If he's so full of shit, then why have you kidnapped me?" she snapped.

His expression tightened with annoyance. "I didn't intend to kidnap you. I went back to the cabin to capture Sadie. Of course, the bitch is never around when I actually need her."

Capture Sadie?

Okay, that made about zero sense.

"I thought the two of you were packmates?"

"She's as psychotic as Caine, and I'm not taking the fall for either of them."

Regan shook her head. Obviously the spell bomb had left her as thick as a stump. She didn't have a clue what he was yammering about.

And in truth, she didn't really care.

Within minutes the sun would disappear. She had to get to Jagr.

"So if you wanted Sadie, why did you kidnap me?"

Yanking his hands through his hair yet again, Duncan paced the small clearing.

"I have to hope you'll do."

"Do for what?"

The cur halted, sucking in a deep breath before slowly turning to stab her with a hard, ruthless gaze.

"I want to negotiate a deal."

"A deal with Caine?"

"No, Salvatore."

Yep. Definitely thick as a stump.

"You . . . want to negotiate with Salvatore?" she at last managed to sputter. "Why?"

Resignation chased away the brittle arrogance, offering the first genuine glimpse of the cur.

"Because I'm weary of this suicide mission. Not to mention being Sadie's whipping boy," he confessed, his voice harsh. "I'm willing to trade everything I know about Caine and his plot against the lair if I can get a promise the Weres will offer me protection."

Regan suddenly didn't doubt his sincerity, just his sanity.

"Have you ever met Salvatore?" she demanded. "He's not the forgive and forget type. I doubt a bit of gossip about Caine is going to change that."

Duncan's eyes snapped with fury. "Fine, if he doesn't care about Caine, then what about your sister?"

Against her will, Regan's heart halted, easily revealing to the cur's sensitive ears just how much the information about her sister meant to her. Damn, she knew that the unwelcome emotions would be a pain in the ass.

She gritted her teeth. "You know where Caine's holding her?"

He paused, as if considering a lie, then with obvious reluctance, confessed the truth.

"He moves her around a lot, but I know where most of his labs are hidden. It would only be a matter of time before you could corner him."

Regan frowned. The information was just the sort of vague, unreliable crap that anyone could make up. Still, she couldn't dismiss even a remote possibility of rescuing her sister.

She, of all people, understood that miracles could occasionally occur.

That didn't mean, however, that the arrogant King of Weres would be willing to make a deal with the treacherous cur.

"Why would Salvatore trust you?" she demanded. "You've already proven to be a traitor."

"That's why I wanted to capture Sadie," he growled in frustration. "I intended to hand her over as a gesture of goodwill, but you came out of the cabin instead of her. Now I have no choice but to hope that by not handing you over to Caine when I could have, I've proven my intentions are pure."

She snorted. If Duncan's intentions were pure then she was the freaking Queen of England.

"Yeah, right."

He shrugged. "Okay, my intentions are completely self-serving, but if you want your sister back, I'm your best hope."

Regan gritted her teeth. It might piss her off to give into blatant blackmail, but at the moment she'd do anything, including selling her soul, to gain her freedom and get to Jagr.

Besides, if there was even a remote chance that her sister could be rescued, then surely she should take it.

"Fine, let me go, and I'll contact Salvatore . . ."

"No," he rudely interrupted, his expression hard.

She struggled against the chains, ignoring the searing pain that jolted through her body. She'd endured far worse over the years.

"I don't have time for this crap," she hissed. "Release me or I swear to God Salvatore will be the least of your concern."

He paled at the stark threat in her voice, but stubbornly held his ground.

"I need his word that he'll give me his protection before I release you."

"And just how the hell is he supposed to give you his word?" Regan narrowed her gaze. "Did you kidnap him, too?"

"The next best thing." With two long strides, Duncan was reaching to yank aside a blanket that had been draped over a nearby bush.

Only it wasn't a bush.

Her eyes widened in horror as she recognized the tiny gargoyle currently encased in stone.

"Levet," she breathed, her gaze shifting to stab Duncan with fury. "Damn you."

"He's not hurt. In a few minutes he'll awake and he can contact Salvatore directly."

Her brows snapped together. "He's a gargoyle, not a cell phone."

"All gargoyles, no matter how tiny, can open a portal in another's mind."

She grimaced at the thought of that strange rip in space that Gaynor had conjured opening in someone's head.

"Ew."

Duncan regarded her with a hint of surprise, as if startled she could be so clueless.

"Not a physical portal. More like a . . . wireless connection. Which means it can't be overheard or traced even by magical means." His hand absently lifted to stroke the amulet hung about his neck. "No one will know about this call except the three of us and Salvatore."

"Paranoid much?" she muttered, feeling stupid she hadn't known about Levet's skill.

He glared at her taunting, his expression tight in the thickening shadows.

"You haven't met Caine. He might be a mystical freak, but he's smart as hell and he has his personal spies everywhere. There's never been anyone who's tried to double-cross him who's lived to tell the tale."

About to inform the cur that Caine couldn't begin to compete with Salvatore when it came to ruthless cunning, Regan was distracted by the unmistakable crack of stone.

Turning her head, she watched in awe as the granite crumbled from the statue image of Levet to reveal the gargoyle beneath.

"*Sacrebleu.*" With a mighty shake, Levet rid himself of the clinging bits of stone, waddling forward and waving his arms in anger. "You mangy, lice-ridden dog, I'm going to . . ." Belatedly spotting Regan tied to the tree, Levet widened his eyes in alarm. "*Ma cherie,* what are you doing here? Are you harmed?"

"What I am is pissed off," she muttered.

Levet frowned as he glanced around the island. "Where's your vampire?"

Regan turned to glare at Duncan. "He's waiting for me and he's not going to be happy if I'm late."

Duncan planted his fists on his hips. "Get the gargoyle to contact Salvatore, and you're free as a bird."

She ground her teeth, knowing she was between a rock and a hard place.

Of course, a voice whispered in the back of her head, it wasn't the first time.

Hell, it wasn't even the first time today.

And with her luck, it wouldn't be the last.

"Christ." She turned her attention to the wary gargoyle. "Levet, I need a favor."

Chapter 16

Despite Jagr's grim determination to keep the howling demons at bay, the passing hours began to take their toll. Pacing the cramped prison, he felt his powers being ruthlessly drained even as the walls seemed to close in around him.

Memories of the endless years of torture seared through his mind, clenching his muscles until he was curled into a shuddering ball in the corner.

At last, not even the image of his beautiful Regan could hold back the hovering insanity.

In desperation, Jagr sank into the deep, death-like sleep only a vampire could achieve.

The comatose state left him vulnerable to attack, but it conserved his strength and, more importantly, it muted the black rage that threatened to consume him.

He was unaware of the passing hours. At least he was unaware until the soothing blackness was stirred by the sound of approaching footsteps outside his cell.

Slowly he allowed his consciousness to rise back to the surface, careful to keep his body perfectly still. At a glance he would look like a corpse, no heartbeat, no pulse, not even a breath. It was an ability that had served vampires well over the years.

Who would fear a dead man?

There was a scraping at the door, almost as if whoever was on the other side was unfamiliar with the lock. At last, there was a distinctive click and the door slid open.

Jagr's fangs lengthened as the footsteps edged toward his seemingly unconscious form.

His first thought was that there was no scent. An impossibility without the assistance of a witch. His second thought was that the intruder hadn't bothered to close and lock the door.

Freedom.

With grim effort, he leashed his brutal surge of hope.

There would be no escape until he'd dealt with the enemy who was stalking slowly toward him.

With his eyes closed and the creature's scent masked, Jagr silently measured the sound of the footsteps.

Closer, closer, closer . . .

There was a stir of air as the intruder knelt beside him, clearly believing he was dead, or at least incapacitated.

It would be the last mistake the fool ever made.

Preparing to attack, Jagr allowed the bloodlust he'd so desperately tried to keep at bay to flow freely through his body. With his strength muted by the damned hexes, he needed the fury to fuel his powers.

"Jagr."

The soft voice cut through the silence, but Jagr was past hearing. His only thought was to kill the enemy so he could reach the door and escape.

With a movement too swift for even the most skilled demon to avoid, Jagr shot his arm upward, grasping his enemy around the throat.

There was a gurgling moan as he wrenched his eyes open, staring at the pale, beautiful face poised above him.

Something flickered in the back of his mind. Some strange alarm that clamored for attention, but the bloodlust made his

gaze flicker with a haze of red, obscuring the delicate features
and drowning out the distress that clutched at his heart.

Kill.

He had to kill to be free.

With a low roar, he surged to his feet, still holding his prey
by the neck. It was surprisingly slender. As easy to snap as a
twig.

"Jagr," a voice rasped. "It's Regan."

Regan.

The bloodlust faltered.

That name . . .

With a rough motion, he jerked the squirming captive
closer, burrowing his head into the curve of her neck. Nothing. No scent. No explanation for why he was halting his
killing blow.

"Jagr . . . please," the voice pleaded, a hand touching his
face in with a soft, familiar touch.

Jagr shook his head, dropping the creature as he struggled
to clear his mind.

Instinct howled for blood, but a more powerful force refused to give into the screaming need.

He knew this woman, a voice whispered in the back of his
fogged mind. She was . . .

His.

His to protect.

Shuddering against the fierce desire to attack, Jagr wrapped
his arms around himself. Shit. He truly was going mad.

"Jagr?" The woman painfully struggled to her feet, either too
courageous, or too stubborn, to remain down. "Are you hurt?"

"Stay back," he growled in warning.

"What's wrong?"

"I . . ." He gave another shake of his head. "Why can I not
smell you?"

Beautiful green eyes widened, then with a jerky rush she

reached into the pocket of her too-tight jeans to reveal a small amulet. She licked her lips as he tracked her every movement, his fangs exposed and his eyes no doubt glowing with hunger. He didn't need to smell her fear to recognize it.

Careful to keep her motion slow and unthreatening, the female tossed the amulet toward the open door.

Immediately the sweet scent of midnight jasmine filled the cell, threading its way through the crimson veil of his bloodlust.

Drinking in the heady aroma, Jagr felt a stirring of excitement deep in the pit of his stomach.

"That scent," he breathed. "I've smelled it before."

"Yes." With a frown she stepped forward, as if to touch him.

Jagr took a hasty step back, knowing that he was far from stable. Just as he knew that something would break inside him if he accidentally injured the woman.

"Do not."

As if sensing the danger throbbing in the air, the female stood perfectly still, her expression troubled.

"I'm here to help you," she said softly. "But we don't have much time. I managed to slip past the curs on guard, but without the amulet they'll soon catch my scent and come to investigate."

Jagr growled, his fangs aching. Curs. Yes. He'd always hated the bastards.

"Where?"

She frowned. "What?"

He snapped his teeth with impatience. "Never mind. I will find them on my own."

Whirling on his heel, Jagr headed for the open door. His rage pulsed and the bloodlust still thundered through his body. He needed to kill. And if he didn't want it to be the woman in front of him, then he needed other prey.

The curs would do just fine.

The woman called out, but he ignored her plea to remain. He was a vampire on the hunt, and anything foolish enough to cross his path was dead.

Four long strides took him through the outer chamber and to the narrow flight of stone steps. Those he consumed in two swift bounds. A wooden door blocked his path at the top of the stairs, but one swing of his arm smashed through the fragile barrier.

Splinters flew through the air, spreading before Jagr as he stepped through the mangled frame. There was a yip as a cur keeping guard was hit with the small, but painful missiles. A yip that became a howl of agonized pain as Jagr grabbed him by the hair and tossed him across what appeared to be a kitchen.

Jagr watched the slender man smack painfully into the wall, leaving a trail of blood as he crumpled to the floor. The cur lived, but before Jagr could concentrate on yanking the bastard's heart out, there was the sound of footsteps from outside the house.

Bending down, Jagr yanked out the silver-bladed daggers he always kept hidden in his boots. A part of him might relish the thought of ripping apart his enemies with his bare hands, but bloodlust didn't equal stupidity.

Until he knew just how many curs were prowling around the place, he wasn't going to take any chances.

There was a low snarl and Jagr listened as one of the approaching sets of footsteps shifted from two legs to four. Jagr widened his stance, a dagger clutched in each hand, his lips pulling back to reveal his lethal fangs.

Showtime.

The shifted cur entered first, crashing through a set of French doors that led to a back terrace. It was large by cur standards, the height of a good-sized pony and thickly muscled beneath the shaggy brown fur. But it was the long, razor sharp teeth that could slice through bone that was the true danger. Even a vampire could be killed if his head was snapped off.

There was another snarl as the cur launched his heavy body directly at Jagr. The brainless animal was too far gone to have the sense to realize it was a suicide mission.

Which suited Jagr just fine.

Braced for the impact, he barely moved when the cur smashed into his body. Instead, he easily avoided the teeth aimed at his throat and slid the two daggers deep into the beast's chest.

The glowing eyes of the cur widened, a death rattle in its throat the only sound it made as it slid off the daggers and tumbled backward. He was changed back to a man, a very dead man, by the time he hit the floor.

Jagr had no time to admire his handiwork as two more curs appeared through the destroyed French door, both rushing forward in unison.

With deadly accuracy, Jag threw one of the daggers. It spun through the air, end over end, shimmering with brilliant flares of silver as the slanting moonlight caught it. The charging cur, stuck midway in his shift to wolf, had no chance to avoid the blade as it sunk deep into his chest.

The second attacker screamed in fury as his companion dropped to the ground. But he did, astonishingly, have enough sense to avoid a direct attack.

Slowly circling Jagr, the cur battled his instinctive need to shift. His eyes glowed and his skin rippled as his wolf struggled to free itself.

Jagr flashed a taunting smile. "Are we going to dance or fight, dog?"

The cur snapped his teeth, reaching beneath his shirt to pull out a large handgun.

"In a rush to die, vampire?"

"Not before dinner."

With a slow grin, Jagr released his coiled power. The frigid blast exploded through the room, knocking pans from the shelves and shattering the windows. The remaining cur screamed as he was tossed through the air and pinned to the wall by the tangible force.

Ignoring the bullets that his enemy desperately fired in his direction, Jagr prowled forward. He could easily kill the cur with his powers. Or even with the dagger still clutched in his hand.

His bloodlust, however, demanded more.

With a surge of desperate hunger, Jagr grabbed the cur by the hair and jerked his head to one side. There was the sound of someone calling his name, and the tantalizing scent of midnight jasmine, but he was too far gone to be distracted.

His fangs ached for soft flesh and warm blood. Nothing less would satisfy him now.

Roaring his victory, Jagr struck with painful force, his teeth sinking deep into the cur's throat.

The man briefly struggled, dropping the now empty gun as he pummeled Jagr's chest. Jagr didn't even feel the blows. Not with the rich, soothing taste of blood filling his mouth and the potent heat washing away the lingering effects of the hexes.

It took a few minutes to actually drain the cur dry, although his struggles ended after only a few deep sucks.

At last dropping the lifeless body to the floor, Jagr roared as the power rushed through him.

Although not a full demon, the cur's blood was far more potent than a mere human, bringing with it a satisfying rush that eased the black rage.

Shuddering in relief, Jagr allowed the madness to recede. Slowly, the red haze dissipated from his mind, clearing his thoughts and relaxing the knotted muscles.

As the fog lifted, he glanced around the ruined kitchen with a frown.

What the hell?

Painful minutes passed as he struggled to recall where he was and what had happened.

His last true memory had been of himself in a small, cramped cell. The imp—Gaynor, yes that had been his name—had yanked him through a portal. That's when things began to get fuzzy.

There'd been pacing and cussing and futile attempts to break down the door. That he damned well remembered. Then he'd gone deep inside himself to avoid the looming panic, hadn't he?

So how did he get out of the cell?

"Jagr?"

Regan's soft voice, along with the tantalizing scent of midnight jasmine, was nothing more than a whisper, but both slammed into him with the force of a two-ton truck.

Oh . . . shit.

The lingering fog was blasted away as images of his escape from his prison seared through his mind with cruel clarity.

The invader entering the cell. Leaning over him. And then . . .

Spinning on his heel, Jagr frantically studied the slender form standing in the door leading to the basement. Even through the shadows he could detect the faint marks that marred her slender neck.

Marks *he* had put there.

Regan wasn't a coward. Granted, she didn't have one of those hero complexes that demanded she always dash around proving her courage, but she could face pain and even danger when necessary.

So it wasn't fear that kept her in the basement as Jagr charged out of the cell and headed upstairs to battle the curs.

At least, not fear for herself.

For the moment, Jagr was at the mercy of his rampaging emotions. No big freaking surprise there. The vampire had to have a major case of PTSD after enduring centuries of torture, and being locked in the tiny cell had obviously pushed all his buttons.

And while she refused to believe he would seriously hurt her even in the midst of his bloodlust, she knew that during battles anything could happen. Friendly fire wasn't just a human danger.

If she were accidentally injured, the stupid man would hold himself responsible for rest of eternity.

So ignoring the desperate urge to rush up the stairs and make certain Jagr didn't allow his blind rage to get himself killed by the guards she'd slipped past only a short time ago, Regan hovered near the bottom of the stairs, clutching the dagger and hating the feelings of helplessness.

Thank the gods that the marks from Duncan's damned silver chains had already healed. At the time, she had been infuriated that it had taken so long for Levet to convince Salvatore to meet with the stupid cur. She might sympathize with the King of Were's reluctance to strike a bargain with an out-and-out traitor, but her only concern was being released so she could get to Jagr.

And of course, there had been long minutes wasted as she'd argued with Levet. The gargoyle had been determined to return to Hannibal with her, but while Regan would have taken any assistance she could get, she couldn't dismiss the thoughts of her sister.

If Duncan could honestly reveal where she might be hidden, then she didn't want the bastard out of sight for a moment. He wouldn't be allowed to disappear before Salvatore could get the information out of him.

With a shake of her head, Regan returned her attention to the cramped basement.

Distantly she could sense the bothersome drain of the hexes that lined the cell, and the lingering scent of Jagr's desperation, but she concentrated on the crashes echoing from above. One hint that Jagr was in danger, and she would be up those stairs and kicking some cur butt.

At last the sounds of the short, brutal battle came to an end, and sucking in a deep breath, Regan made her way to the top of the steps.

What she discovered as she stepped into the trashed kitchen didn't particularly surprise her. Windows shattered, one wall cracked, pots and pans scattered, three injured or dead curs on the floor, and the fourth being rapidly drained by the infuriated vampire.

Still, she couldn't help but admire Jagr's brute strength.

No wonder Culligan was always so nervous when it came time to negotiate with the local clan chief.

Watching from a relatively safe distance, Regan sensed the moment Jagr's maddened fury began to slip away. It was in the hint of warmth that threaded through the biting chill in the air, and the loosening of the warrior's bunched muscles.

Of course, she wasn't stupid enough to run and throw herself in his arms as she strangely ached to do.

Instead she softly called his name, careful not to startle him by moving forward.

For a moment, she thought he meant to ignore her, then slowly he turned, his expression wary as his gaze slid a searing path over her.

Sharp relief flared through Regan as recognition flared in those beautiful blue eyes. He was back. And lucid.

Taking a step forward, she abruptly halted as the ice-blue

gaze landed on her neck and recognition morphed to black regret.

Christ.

She resisted the urge to lift her hand and hide the telltale marks. Instead, she held herself perfectly still as he walked toward her, his movements jerky, as if his mind and body were at painful odds.

"Regan," he breathed, not stopping until his cool power wrapped around her like a welcomed blanket.

Regan licked her lips, unable to bear the look of shame that twisted Jagr's stark features. Since their first memorable encounter, she had ruthlessly fought to keep this man from tromping over her defenses. Even when her own body had betrayed her.

In this moment, she knew if she truly wanted to be rid of him and his aggravating interference in her life, all she had to do was keep her lips shut and allow him to drown in his own guilt. It was etched on every line of his face.

But even as the thought fluttered through her mind, she was already shoving it down the black hole where it belonged.

No freaking way.

And she didn't give a shit what it might reveal about her pathetic emotions.

"Are you okay?" she demanded, resisting the urge to wrap her arms around him and offer the comfort that he so obviously needed. He wasn't ready. Not yet.

Proving her point, he gave a slow shake of his head. "No, I'm damned well not okay," he rasped, his eyes never leaving her throat. "I hurt you."

"I'm fine." She waited a beat, but when his eyes refused to leave the fading bruises, she reached up to grasp his face in her hands and forced his head up. "Jagr, look at me." Grudgingly his gaze met hers. "I. Am. Fine. Got it?"

"I very nearly killed you."

"Ha." She narrowed her gaze, her tone angry. This was no time for touchy-feely crap. Not with a wounded warrior bent on self-flagellation. "I might not be an oversized oaf like some I could name, but I'm not that easy to get rid of. I would have stopped you if I truly thought I was in danger."

His jaw tightened. Annoying, stubborn vampire.

"No, Regan, you couldn't have. If I hadn't hesitated . . ."

"But you did," she interrupted, squeezing his face as if she could squeeze in a bit of sense. "No harm, no foul."

"And the next time the madness overtakes me?" he rasped.

"Next time? Does it happen often?"

"It did in the beginning."

Well . . . duh. She'd be worried if he hadn't gone Rambo after what the Kesi and her merry band of torturers had done to him.

"And now?"

His gaze abruptly dropped. "It doesn't matter."

Regan snorted. He didn't want to answer because he must know it would only prove her point.

"How long since the last time you . . ." She caught herself, not willing to call him mad. He might be maddening, but he was the sanest demon she'd met in her entire life. "Lost control?"

"It doesn't matter."

"How long?" She growled low in her throat as he remained mute. "Jagr?"

"It's been several centuries," he grudgingly confessed.

There. She knew it.

"Fine. Then I'll start worrying a few hundred years from now."

His expression hardened as his fingers dropped from her neck. No doubt telling himself he might accidentally hurt her.

"This can't be dismissed. I'm dangerous."

"Only because you were imprisoned." Damn, she wished he

wasn't too huge to shake. Trust her to get entangled with the biggest, most difficult demon to ever walk the earth. "Christ, anyone would have gone a little nuts. It wasn't your fault."

"This isn't about fault, it's about consequences."

"And what are these dire consequences?" she demanded. "A few bruises that I know damned well have already healed?"

His eyes flashed a frigid blue. Regan smiled ruefully. His anger, and even power, was always coated with ice rather than fire. His means of controlling the rage inside, she was beginning to suspect.

The heat he kept for his passion.

Which suited her just fine.

"Why won't you take this serious?" His brows snapped together. "Dammit, Regan, you should be afraid of me."

"You don't get to tell me what I should feel, chief." Lowering her hands, she poked his chest with a finger. "I'm perfectly capable of deciding if I should be afraid or not."

"Then you're a fool."

Her temper, always ready to be set off, exploded.

Fine. He wanted to be a dick? Then he was going to get treated like one.

"Oh, yeah?" Knowing she would have only one opportunity to catch him off guard, Regan leaned into his hard body, deliberately rubbing her softer curves against him. Temporarily distracted by her ploy, Jagr was unprepared when her foot slid behind his leg and she suddenly pushed for all she was worth against his chest. The vampire grunted in surprise, unable to halt the inevitable fall. He landed hard on his back, but giving no mercy, Regan was swiftly perched on top of his chest, the dagger she'd yanked from the waistband of her jeans shoved directly above his heart. "Well, fool this," she gritted.

She held her higher ground for less than the beat of a heart. With a low growl, Jagr twisted to the side, reversing their position so that she was pinned to the ground by his massive body.

"I think I've made my point," he rasped.

"Not even close, chief. I would already have carved out your heart if I wanted."

His expression was the perfect example of an exasperated male who'd reached the end of his rope.

Even his fangs were showing.

"Dammit, Regan."

"No, damn you, Jagr," she hissed, not about to back down. Jagr had isolated himself for centuries, pushing everyone away who might get too close. He wasn't going to get by with it this time. "I get that you're not a boy scout. Yippee kiyah. I don't need a freaking saint. I need a warrior. I need . . ." She swallowed the uncomfortable lump in her throat, and forced herself to admit the truth. "You."

He stilled, his eyes briefly revealing the stark, aching loneliness that was echoed deep within her before they were abruptly shuttered.

"Little one, I swore a vow that I would protect you." His jaw twitched, as if he struggled to contain his emotions. "Even from myself."

Her eyes narrowed. "And I swore a vow that I would never be at the mercy of another man."

Jerking as if her words had struck a nerve, Jagr abruptly flowed to his feet, glaring down at her with an offended expression.

"You're not at my mercy."

"No?" She scrambled to her feet with a great deal less grace than Jagr, planting her fists on her hips. "You want to make my decisions for me. You want to tell me what's best for me. You want . . ."

"I want to protect you, God dammit."

"Maybe in your mind, but it feels like shackles to me."

Without warning, his hands lifted to scrub his face in a gesture of utter weariness.

"God, you drive me crazy."

She smiled wryly. She hadn't won the battle, but she hadn't lost.

Not yet.

"Welcome to my world," she muttered.

Lowering his hands, Jagr gave a shake of his head, his gaze sweeping over the destroyed kitchen.

"This is not the time or place for this discussion."

"Well, at least we can agree on one thing." She grimaced. "We need to get out of here. Eventually someone is going to come looking for the guards."

"You can return to Tane's lair. I'll . . ."

"You'll come with me," she interrupted.

His eyes narrowed as a cold blast of air filled the kitchen. "I have a few debts to pay off first."

Already expecting his response, she smiled sweetly. "Do you really want me running around the countryside by myself, Jagr? Who knows what I might take it in my silly head to do?"

For a moment he struggled with his furious need to seek out vengeance. He'd been tormented in the worst possible way, and he needed to make those responsible pay.

At last his hands clenched as he accepted she couldn't possibly be trusted to make her own way back to Tane's lair. Typical male.

"You don't play fair, wolf," he muttered.

Her brows lifted. "And your point, vampire?"

He threw his hands up in resignation. "Let's go."

Stepping toward the door, Regan abruptly halted. "Wait there, I forgot something." Turning, she headed for the door to the basement.

"Regan."

She ignored his warning growl as she sprinted down the stairs and scooped up the amulet she had tossed near the door of the cell. The damned things had caused her nothing but headaches since coming to Hannibal. It seemed only fair that she have one to return the favor.

Shoving the amulet into her pocket, she raced upstairs to find Jagr pacing by the French doors that had seen better days.

"I'm ready."

Offering her a frustrated glare, the vampire stepped through the busted window.

"You know, little one, for a woman who bitches about shackles, you're willing enough to wrap them around me," he accused in low, rough tones.

Regan refused to feel guilt for having manipulated Jagr as she followed his large form across the terrace and around the silent tea shop. At the moment he was in no condition to be out hunting curs. Not when his furious need for payback was greater than his sense of self-preservation.

Besides, she didn't intend to allow his guilt over hurting her to fester into some big, freaking wound he would carry along with all his other scars.

Of course, that was easier said than done.

Flowing through the darkness at a speed he had to know would take all her efforts to match, Jagr headed directly toward Tane's lair, his expression bleak in the silver moonlight.

She snapped her lips together and grimly kept pace. Let him pout for now. Once they reached the lair . . .

Well, she wasn't exactly sure what she intended to do, but it was going to include shaking some sense into that thick skull.

And maybe ripping that shirt off his wide chest, and licking her way down . . .

Allowing the fantasy to fill her mind, Regan ran through the dark fields, managing not to falter despite Jagr's punishing pace.

Unfortunately, she was so lost in the erotic imaginings that she was unprepared when Jagr came to an abrupt halt just as they reached the crumbling building that marked Tane's lair.

"Shit."

Ramming into his back was like running face-first into a brick wall, and rubbing her injured nose, she glared at her aggravating companion.

"What is it?"

Tilting back his head, his expression hardened. "Styx."

"Oh." Damn. She'd forgotten her frantic conversation with the King of Vampires. "I called and asked him to come."

His head snapped round to regard her with a shocked frown. "*You* called?"

"I was worried."

As swiftly as the shock had appeared, it was being replaced by an expression of resignation.

"Of course." His lips twisted in a humorless smile. "A good choice. There are no warriors more powerful than the Anasso. You will be safe in his care."

Her mouth fell open as she realized he assumed she called for Styx as some kind of replacement vampire when Jagr had been captured.

Before she could halt the impulse, she moved forward to punch him squarely in the chest. A wasted effort. The damned man didn't even flinch.

"I didn't call him to be in his damned care." She shook her hand. Crap, she'd almost broken her fingers. "Hell, I've done everything possible to avoid that fate."

"Then why?"

"Because I would have done anything . . ." She was forced to halt and clear the lump from her throat. "Anything to find you."

The blue eyes briefly darkened at her soft confession, but

before he could speak, a large form detached from the shadows of the looming building.

"Jagr. Sister-mate."

Wanting to scream with frustration, Regan turned to cast an impatient glance at the unwelcome intruder.

Only to freeze in shock.

Holy shit.

As big as, or even bigger than Jagr, the vampire possessed the features of an ancient Aztec, with raven black hair pulled into a braid that hung well past his waist and golden brown eyes that seemed to sear right through her.

But it was more than his stark beauty and the way his leather pants and loose silk shirt caressed his heavily muscled body that made her instinctively step toward Jagr.

His power was a thick, tangible presence in the air, prickling over her skin with a near painful intensity.

Christ, her sister must have nerves of steel to bind herself to the dangerous demon.

At her side, Jagr offered a stiff bow. "My lord."

That unnerving golden gaze shifted to run a searching path over Jagr's stiff form, narrowing as he caught sight of the vampire's brittle expression.

"I am pleased to discover you unharmed, if not unscathed, brother," the Anasso rumbled, a hint of question in his deep voice.

"You will not be pleased to discover I have failed in my duty," Jagr retorted, offering another bow. "Forgive me."

Before Regan could guess his intent, Jagr was heading for the nearby stairs to the terrace, his back stiff and his shoulders bunched with tension.

"Jagr, wait." She stomped her foot as he deliberately ignored her plea and disappeared through the open door. "Dammit. He is . . ."

"Complicated," Styx helpfully supplied. "Yes, I know."

Forgetting the fact that she was confronting perhaps the most lethal demon in the world, not to mention her current brother-in-law, Regan clenched her fists and headed in Jagr's wake.

Walk out on her?

Not gonna happen.

"Well, I'm just about to uncomplicate him," she muttered. "Excuse me."

"Regan."

The dark voice was pleasant, but edged with enough of a command that she instinctively halted to glance over her shoulder.

"What?"

His beautiful face was somber in the moonlight. "I would ask to meet with you and discuss your future."

Future? Shit. She didn't want to deal with the expectations her call had no doubt raised in her sister. Or any future that might include a family she'd never wanted.

Not when she had an obstinate, mule-headed, world's most aggravating vampire to straighten out.

"I . . ." She halted her instinctive denial as she met the steady golden gaze. He wasn't budging on this. It might as well have been tattooed across his forehead. She sighed. Great. Just what she needed. Another ruthless vampire with an agenda. "Yeah, fine. But later." She headed for the door. "Much later."

Sadie was beyond pissed off.

Nothing unusual.

Being pissed off was a constant state of mind lately.

No. Not *lately*.

She could pinpoint the precise time her life had gone into the shitter.

The moment Regan-freaking-Princess-of-Weres had hit town.

Damn the bitch.

This was all her fault.

She was the one who had called the wrath of the vampires down on the curs. She was the one who had brought Salvatore snooping around where he didn't belong. She was even responsible for that damned gargoyle who was proving to be such a pain in the ass.

And yet, Sadie knew *she* would be the one held to blame for the entire fiasco.

Caine was not a cur who accepted failure.

Hell, the last person to fail him was stuffed and mounted to stand as a gruesome reminder of what happens to those who disappoint the self-proclaimed leader of the curs.

Which, no doubt, explained why Duncan had done a disappearing act, along with the witch.

Well, screw them.

Sadie didn't run. She didn't hide.

Not any more.

Caine commanded she capture Regan, come hell or high water, and that was exactly what she was going to do.

Unfurling the whip, she sliced another ribbon of flesh off Gaynor's back as he cowered in a corner of the basement.

When they had returned to the tea shop, after yet another futile search for the pureblood, to discover her guards dead and the vampire missing, Sadie had lost no time in taking out her frustrations on the imp.

She couldn't think straight with her temper blazing and her lust for pain clogging her mind.

Besides, she couldn't risk shifting. Not when her time was running out.

"Stupid bastard," she gritted, clenching the whip as she

watched the blood pour down the imp's shredded back. "You swore to me the vampire couldn't escape from your prison."

"He didn't."

"Ah." Another crack of the whip. "You have him hidden in the closet?"

The imp screamed. "No."

"The Dumpster?"

"No." Gaynor pressed even tighter to the wall, looking remarkably like Culligan, as he whimpered and cowered beneath her strikes. "But he didn't get out on his own. I can smell that female Were all over the cell."

The knowledge that Gaynor was right did nothing to ease her fury. While Sadie had been out tracking the damned Were so she could convince her to concede defeat peacefully, Regan had outwitted them all.

Now Sadie didn't have her prize, and her one bargaining chip was gone.

Regan would pay for that.

In blood.

"And how did she find this place?"

"I don't know."

"Liar." Needing her punishment to be a bit more personal, Sadie stepped forward to kick the imp in the head. There was a satisfying thump as he reeled to the side. "You must have revealed something when you spoke with her. After all, no one would suspect that a demon with half a brain would be stupid enough to hide his most private lair directly beneath his very public tea shop."

"Please . . ." Ridiculously, the imp tried to drag himself across the floor. "I said nothing, I swear."

She followed his painful path, kicking him in the side. "So a clueless Were barely out of diapers managed to outsmart a centuries-old imp?"

Curling into a ball, Gaynor managed to gather enough balls to glare at her.

"She also managed to get past four of your curs."

Sadie stilled, distracted by a sudden, unpleasant thought.

"Yes, she did," she said slowly. "And her scent wasn't outside the building. Why?"

There was a long pause as Gaynor struggled to breathe with his collapsed lung.

"Maybe she's found a witch of her own," he at last panted.

"Or taken mine," Sadie growled, her eyes glowing in the dark as she considered the various possibilities. "Of course, all she really needed was to get her greedy little hands on one of the amulets."

Gaynor grunted as he received another kick to the head. "Why are you punishing me? I didn't give her a damn amulet."

"Why am I punishing you?" Leaning down, she grabbed the imp by the hair and glared into his ruined face. "Because I can, you pathetic worm."

Chapter 17

Jagr wasn't surprised to discover his hands shaking as he braided his hair and slipped on a clean pair of jeans. The hot shower might have been capable of washing the filth from his skin, but it did nothing to wash away the lingering effects of his madness.

Or the horrifying memory of his fingers squeezing into Regan's throat.

Nothing would ever wash that away.

He had come so close . . .

Too close.

Leaning against the wall of the bathroom, Jagr banged his head with enough force to crack the marble.

In his mind, the images of blood-soaked corridors tormented him. Those hours of slaughtering Kesi and her clan were still wrapped in fog, but not the long journey out of her lair. Or the unstable years that followed when his rampages would strike without warning, leaving anyone in the vicinity slaughtered.

Over the past centuries he'd allowed himself to believe that those days were behind him. He'd buried his rage deep, and carefully honed his control. Oh, he would always possess a dangerous temper and a ready willingness to use violence when necessary. But he never unleashed his full fury.

Not until tonight.

Again the image of Regan, her eyes wide and her lips parted as he crushed her throat, seared through his mind.

No.

He would never, ever take such a risk again.

Ignoring the unexpected wrench of agony at the mere thought of walking away from Regan, Jagr forced himself to leave the bathroom and returned to the connecting bedroom.

He tossed his satchel on the bed, digging out his remaining daggers before shoving his used clothes into the bag.

He was reaching for the clean shirt he'd left on a side table when the unmistakable scent of jasmine had him spinning toward the door.

Stepping into the bedroom, Regan allowed her gaze to skim over the open satchel on the bed before returning to linger on his still bare chest.

A heat flushed through Jagr as her emerald eyes flared with awareness, tracing the scars that ran the length of his stomach.

Before Regan, he'd always kept his scars well hidden. They were a badge of shame that no one was allowed to witness. But standing before this beautiful Were, he felt nothing but searing pleasure as she studied his hard body. There was no disgust, no pity, no aversion.

Just pure appreciation.

Wanting nothing more than to yank off the jeans that were the only thing covering him, Jagr instead forced himself to turn back toward the bag.

His desire for Regan might be a brutal force, but it was nothing in comparison to his driving need to keep her safe.

For the first time in centuries, someone else's existence mattered more than his.

With an impatient click of her tongue, Regan moved to perch on the end of the bed, her expression impossible to read, though there was no missing the anger that snapped in the air around her.

"I thought I would find you here, you big lummox."

He didn't look up. It was bad enough to have her so close. To be wrapped in her exotic scent and feel the heat of her body.

To actually see her on the bed where he'd so recently spread her legs and plunged into her damp heat . . . damn, it was enough to snap what little control he had left.

"Lummox?" he muttered.

"It's a word." He sensed her shift on the bed. Gods. His jeans tightened painfully over his growing erection. "What are you doing?"

Don't look. Do. Not. Look.

"I would think it's rather self-evident."

"I guess it is. Hard to miss a six-foot-plus sulking vampire. Or is it pouting? Difficult to tell," she taunted. "I assume you're leaving?"

"First I intend to go imp hunting."

"And then?"

Pain ripped through his chest, nearly sending him to his knees. "Then I will return to Chicago."

She breathed a shockingly vile curse. "So, you're fleeing back to your prison . . . oh, I mean lair. It's so much safer to watch the world through MTV and YouTube, isn't it, chief?"

His hands clenched into fists at her accusation, refusing to consider the bitter truth of her words.

"Return to Styx, Regan. He'll be able to track Culligan."

"I don't need him or you or anyone else to track Culligan," she gritted. "I already found him."

The defenses he'd been struggling to build were shattered as Jagr jerked his head around to stab her with a shocked gaze.

"What?"

Her eyes flashed, as if pleased at by his sharp reaction. "Where do you think I picked up that handy-dandy little amulet?" Her brows abruptly drew together. "An amulet, I might add, that was confiscated by your friend Tane before he would let me come down here."

Jagr shook his head. Later he would thank Tane for ensuring that Regan couldn't slip up on him unaware, but for now he could think of nothing but the realization that she'd found the imp who had tormented her for thirty years.

"He's dead?"

She shrugged. "He was alive when I left the cabin, but his odds of living through the night are about zero to none. Not once the curs realize he's just as pathetic at being bait as he is at being an imp."

He stepped toward her, his bare feet sinking into the thick carpet, his damp braid brushing across his back. Not that he noticed. He was utterly consumed by the tiny female perched on the end of the bed.

"You found the imp and . . . walked away?"

"I had other things on my mind, as I have mentioned more than once," she said.

Jagr frowned. She was behaving as if finding the demon responsible for her years of misery, a demon who she had risked her life to kill, was nothing more than a trivial encounter.

"Dammit, Regan, you've waited your entire life to have your revenge."

The emerald gaze never wavered. "I'm well aware of that."

"Then why didn't you take it?"

"I told you."

He growled low in his throat as he studied her stubborn expression.

Okay, it was official.

The woman was going to drive him right over the edge.

"There had to be more than just a need to find me, little one." He folded his arms over his chest, refusing to back down. He didn't understand why he had to know. Only that he did. "Killing him would have taken you less than a heartbeat. Tell me the truth."

She abruptly rose to her feet, standing so close to him that his entire body was bathed in sweet jasmine heat.

"Christ, I don't know," she rasped. "I suppose a part of it was the fact that he looked so incredibly pathetic chained in that cabin. For so many years he was my personal boogey-man. He brutalized me for so long I began to think of him as invincible." Her lips twisted as she gave a shake of her head. "But then I saw him as he truly is. A weak, cowardly idiot who crawled through the sewers because he didn't have the talent or intelligence or spine to be a decent man. He just wasn't worth the effort of killing."

He trembled with the need to pull her into his arms as her eyes darkened with a vulnerability that cut through his very soul.

This was more than lust. More than an instinctive need to protect.

This was . . .

Gods, he didn't know what to call it.

He only knew that it had buried so deep inside him that he'd never be rid of it.

"And the other part?" he demanded, his voice thick.

"I realized I didn't need to kill him." She held her arms wide. "The chains are already gone."

A combination of emotions warred through him. Pride, relief, astonishment, and a treacherous sense of regret at the knowledge she no longer had need of him.

Unable to battle his need, he reached up to lightly stroke his fingers down her cheek.

"Regan."

She stepped even closer, sending jolts of agonizing need through his body.

"I understand now," she said, softly. "He wasn't holding me in the past. *I* was. It's time to let it go."

He shuddered at the feel of her soft skin beneath his finger tips. A warm, satin temptation. His thighs clenched in response, his erection painfully hard.

"So you're free," he whispered, ignoring the desire clamoring through him. It was something he was going to have to get used to.

"No, I'll never be completely free. The memories will always haunt me." Her hand reached up to cover his fingers, pressing them against her cheek. "Just as they haunt you."

Feeling as if he'd just been singed, Jagr yanked his hand away and stepped back.

"They do a great deal more than haunt me," he pointed out, his voice harsh.

Her lips thinned with annoyance. "You reacted to your situation. Just like any other human or demon or fey would."

"A blind, killing rage?"

"If it had been a blind, killing rage, you wouldn't have stopped with the curs holding you captive. All of Hannibal would be dead."

Jagr shifted. It was true. In his early days, the rage would consume him to the point he couldn't halt. Only the threat of dawn could end the rampage and drive him back to his lair.

Still, he'd lost enough control to strangle Regan. And that was unacceptable.

His gaze lowered to her throat that was once again smooth and unmarred.

"I hurt you."

She rolled her eyes. "For God's sake, I've tripped over my damned feet and done more damage."

He shook his head. "You don't understand."

"I understand that everyone has moments of insanity." She deliberately moved forward, perhaps knowing he couldn't form a coherent thought when she was so near. "Salvatore told me that Styx nearly destroyed the entire vampire race because he protected some crazed vampire he was sworn to, and your own clan chief tried to kill your precious king. Should they be locked up in their lairs?"

Again he couldn't refute her words. Styx had protected the previous Anasso even when it was obvious the vampire was threatening to rip apart the peace they'd struggled for centuries to achieve. And Viper had been willing to sacrifice his own king to save Shay from death.

It was even rumored that Styx had been lost in bloodlust when he'd been attacked by a band of renegade vampires intent on taking his crown.

"Nothing you say will change my mind," he forced himself to say, although the words didn't ring quite true in his heart.

No doubt because he wanted his mind changed.

"Fine."

Obviously wearied of his stubborn refusal to dismiss the dark fever that lurked deep inside him, Regan took matters into her own hands.

Literally.

Keeping her gaze locked on his tight expression, she grasped the hem of her too-tight shirt, and with one smooth motion had it yanked over her head and tossed on the floor.

Jagr grunted, feeling as if he'd just been hit in the stomach with a sledgehammer.

Against his will his eyes lowered, feasting on the slender limbs that were toned with muscle and covered with flawless ivory skin. She wore a flimsy bit of lace that covered her breasts, but it was no barrier to his greedy gaze. Not when the rosy nipples hardened beneath his hot gaze.

A roaring need to tumble her onto the nearby bed instead had Jagr backing away until he banged into the wall.

"Regan, what the hell are you doing?"

With a wicked smile, Regan casually reached up to snap the tiny clip of her bra, dropping it on top of her shirt.

"You said I couldn't change your mind," she purred. "At least not with words."

His mouth went dry, his brain shutting down as his desire settled into the driver's seat.

"So you think you can manipulate me with . . ."

The words lodged in his throat as she slid down the zipper on her jeans and shimmied them down her body. There was a moment as she halted to kick off her shoes, then the jeans were gone and she was standing there in nothing more than a pair of white panties.

Holy hell.

The things he could do to that exquisite, ivory body. Delicious, sinful, perhaps even illegal things that would include his lips and tongue and throbbing fangs.

As if fearing it might have been forgotten, his cock gave a painful jerk against his jeans, reminding Jagr of just how good it felt to be buried deep inside Regan's heat.

"Is it working?" she murmured, running hands up his bare chest.

Working? He was on fire, being consumed by flames that raged through his body like an inferno. And worse, he was beginning to forget why he shouldn't have her beneath him as he explored every inch of her delectable body.

He squeezed his eyes shut as his muscles clenched with desperate hunger.

"Gods," he breathed, his stomach cramping as he tried to deny the furious instinct to take this woman to his bed and never let her go.

Her soft chuckle feathered over his chest, her fingers skimming down to tease at the waistband of his jeans.

"You're showing your fangs, vampire."

His eyes snapped open as he reached out to grasp her shoulders, careful not to dig into her tender flesh.

"And you're playing a perilous game, Were."

"Should I be afraid?"

"Yes," he growled, although he knew with perfect clarity that there was no genuine danger.

At least not to Regan.

He, on the other hand, was in very serious danger of imploding if he didn't ease the savage need to be inside her.

Soon.

She deliberately licked her lips. "Are you going to hurt me?"

"Keep it up, and I'll devour you."

The green eyes glittered with invitation. "You promise?"

He smacked his hands against the wall behind him, barely noticing the large holes he punched into the paneling. Screw it. Tane could send him a bill.

"Regan, I want you too much and my control is too unpredictable," he gritted, his body trembling. "If I start this, I won't be able to stop."

"Who said anything about stopping?"

He shook his head. This was a mistake. Even if he could be confident his control was trustworthy, Regan no longer needed a champion. Hell, she never truly had.

And no doubt, she was already making plans to move on.

Plans that didn't include a damaged vampire.

So why not enjoy what was offered before he returned to his dark, lonely lair? The voice of temptation whispered in the back of his mind.

Because he was rapidly reaching the point where he would never be capable of letting her go. The voice of reason answered.

Which might explain why he was so anxious to grasp onto the fear that he couldn't be trusted with her.

Already the thought of walking away made him want to howl in pain. How much worse would it be if they became even more intimate?

Barely aware of what he was doing, Jagr allowed his hands to caress the silky perfection of her shoulders, his thoughts occupied with a last, desperate means to cling to a thread of reason.

"Dammit, woman, you've been trying to get rid of me

since I arrived in Hannibal," he rasped. "Why would you suddenly want me to stay?"

She shrugged. "I'm a woman. I'm allowed to change my mind whenever I want, as many times as I want."

"Convenient."

"Sometimes." With a smile, she popped the button of his jeans.

"Stop." Jagr hissed as his hand reached to grasp her wrist. How the hell was he supposed to be reasonable when she refused to cooperate?

She didn't struggle against his grip. Instead she leaned forward to lick a warm, wet path from his sternum to the base of his throat.

"You don't want me?" she whispered against his skin.

Jagr swallowed his shout of pleasure, his fangs fully extended, and his last hope to cling to common sense shattered.

"I . . . yes." His hands grasped her hips and pressed them against his aching erection. "I want you."

Her lashes fluttered down until only a small, smoldering slit of emerald was visible.

"Then what's the problem?"

There was a problem. He'd just been thinking about it. Unfortunately, it was as elusive as a mist fairy and, when she once again tugged at the button of his jeans, it disappeared altogether.

His head lowered so he could bury his face in the curve of her neck, the heated jasmine scent doing nothing to clear his desire-fogged brain.

"Damn you, Regan," he husked, his fangs scraping against her soft skin. "Don't say I didn't warn you."

She shivered at his soft warning, but not from fear. He could already smell the potent perfume of her arousal as she awkwardly tugged at his zipper.

Jagr was swift to help push down the unwelcome jeans, kicking them impatiently aside. Later he would no doubt regret this momentary weakness, but for now nothing mattered but the feel of her soft hands exploring the clenched muscles of his stomach.

"I've told you, chief, I don't need you to protect me," she husked, nipping at his chest. "Not even from you."

Jagr shuddered, the pleasure of even such a light caress nearly sending him over the edge.

"Take care with those teeth, little one," he muttered, his hands compulsively stroking over her back. "Vampires exchange blood for more than food."

Tilting back her head, she regarded him with a hint of curiosity.

"What do you mean?"

"A vampire's blood is the source of our power, as well as our means of claiming our true mate." A rueful smile touched his lips. "Take my blood and I might very well be bound to you for all eternity."

Her eyes widened, uncertainty flaring through them at his blunt confession.

"Jagr . . ."

"If you want to flee, now would be the time to do it."

For a moment, he thought she would. His body tensed and his gut wrenched with a ruthless disappointment.

Why the hell hadn't he kept his mouth shut?

A stark painful silence filled the room, and Jagr braced himself for rejection. Regan might possess more courage than any creature he'd ever known, but the one thing she truly feared was being imprisoned once again.

And in her mind, emotional attachments were just as terrifying as any chains made of silver.

Why else would she refuse to meet with Darcy?

Even as he tensed, however, Regan was giving a slight shake of her head and without warning, she bent forward to scatter kisses over his chest, pausing at each nipple to flick her tongue over the beaded tip. Jagr groaned, one hand burying in her satin hair in silent encouragement.

Later he would wonder why Regan had so abruptly gone from trying to deny the desire that constantly pulsed between them, but for now . . .

Gods, for now he could only enjoy.

Trailing a devastating path down the center of his stomach, she tongued his belly button, making his cock twitch with a silent plea of mercy. Jagr squeezed his eyes shut, torn between the need to flip her onto the bed and take her with a swift, glorious explosion of pleasure, and allowing Regan to continue her seductive torment.

It was at last the feel of Regan's soft lips stroking ever lower that made the decision.

In the past, he'd always been the aggressor during a sexual encounter. His predatory nature preferred being the hunter to the prey. Besides, it made it easier to make the contact as brief and uncomplicated as possible. The last thing he wanted was a clinging woman.

He'd never realized just how erotic it could be to have a woman take charge.

Running his fingers through the strands of her hair as she kneeled before him, he forgot his earlier terror at having been lost in his bloodlust. And even his lingering suspicion of her sudden determination to seduce him.

There was only one thought on his mind.

Getting that warm, wet mouth on his aching arousal.

A pleasure easier dreamed of than achieved.

Although Regan had to be aware of the straining thrust of his erection, she refused to give into his silent urging, instead nibbling a path over his hip bone and down his inner thigh.

Muttering a desperate curse, he tugged her head up to meet his hungry gaze.

"If you intend to punish me, little one, you're doing a fine job."

A tiny smile curved her lips as she held his gaze, her finger tracing a teasing path up the length of his cock.

"Well, I would hate for my efforts to be wasted."

He moaned as she reached the tip, toying with the tiny drop of moisture that had pooled there.

"You're a cruel woman."

"I do try," she murmured, bending down to trace him with her tongue from top to bottom and then back again. He swallowed a shout of pleasure, his hips instinctively arching toward her tempting lips.

"Oh . . . damn that feels good," he ground out, forcing his eyes open so he could witness the sight of her pleasuring him.

He nearly came at the mere sight.

Lost in a sensual haze, his gaze drifted over the strands of hair that shimmered like gold in the pale light, the perfect lines of her profile, and the expanse of ivory skin that stretched over her supple muscles.

Nothing was ever so beautiful.

His tiny Were, with the soul of a warrior and the innocence of an angel.

A warm, poignant tenderness threaded through his hunger. He had warned Regan to take care, already sensing that if she were to drink his blood the mating would be complete, but in this moment he realized that it didn't matter.

She had already claimed him in all the ways that mattered, and whether they ever completed the bond, he would never, ever love another woman.

The thought should have terrified him.

A vampire who found and lost his mate usually ended up an empty shell.

Instead, Jagr felt nothing but a tide of all-consuming peace that chased away the lingering darkness.

The past and all he had suffered no longer mattered.

Regan was like a blast of sunlight that chased away the bitter shadows.

The realization had barely managed to form, when it was abruptly shoved to the back of his mind as his temptress circled her fingers around him and explored the straining length with exquisite care.

His hands instinctively fisted in her hair, his body coiled so tight he nearly shattered when her lips tentatively slipped over the tip of his cock and slid downward.

Paradise.

Complete, utter paradise.

A moan hummed deep in his throat, his world focused on the sensation of warm lips and rasping tongue.

With slow wet strokes, she all too swiftly had him straining toward climax. Damn. He wanted to enjoy the fierce pleasure. To spend the night pressed against the wall as Regan offered him the most intense and blissful sensations he'd ever enjoyed. But even as the sweet release beckoned, he was reaching down to grasp her arms and tug her upward.

He wanted to be buried deep inside her, to watch her beautiful face as she reached her own orgasm.

"I need to be in you, Regan," he groaned, capturing her lips in a rough, demanding kiss before pulling back to regard her with a raw, undisguised yearning. "Now."

"Then what are you waiting for, chief?" she husked, her smile piercing his heart with the ruthless power of a dagger.

The bed loomed behind her, but too impatient for even that small distance, Jagr slid his hands down her pretty little bottom and with one powerful motion had her lifted off her feet with her legs wrapped around his waist.

"You," he whispered, positioning the tip of his erection at her entrance. "I've been waiting for you."

Regan moaned, her body already wet and ready for his thrust.

Clutching her thighs, he captured her mouth in a devouring kiss before he plunged himself inside her, halting only when he was buried as deep as he could go.

"Jagr" she rasped, her sheath clamping around him like a warm, luscious vise.

He momentarily stilled, savoring the sense of completeness that flooded through him. This is what it meant to be with his true mate. This intense connection that went way beyond two bodies indulging in sex.

This was two souls, two hearts, two minds joined as one.

As they both absorbed the sheer pleasure of being so intimately joined, their eyes met and Jagr gently began to thrust into her heat. Her hands lifted to frame his face, claiming his lips in a branding kiss. He moaned his pleasure, his fingers tightening on her thighs.

More. He needed more.

He shifted his mouth to nip at her ear and was rewarded as her body shuddered with undisguised need.

"God, I want taste you," he muttered as he nibbled and stroked a path down her neck, careful not to break her skin with his extended fangs. "Everywhere."

Regan gasped as Jagr licked the underside of her breast. "That's . . . that's a good start."

He chuckled as he thrust even deeper, his tongue finding the hardened tip of her nipple.

"What about here?"

Her legs tightened as he quickened his pace, her head falling back to reveal the smooth, tempting curve of her throat.

Oh . . . gods.

Every instinct urged him to pierce that ivory perfection. To sink his fangs in deep, and take in her essence as he pounded into her body. To mark her as his, and only his.

With a low growl, he wrenched his thoughts from the dangerous enticement and concentrated on surging into her damp heat. A task made considerably easier as her fingernails sank into his back and she moaned in pleasure.

"Faster."

"Yes, my demanding Were," he breathed as he suckled on a tender nipple.

Someday he would know the satisfaction of taking Regan's blood as he took her body. For today this was enough.

More than enough, he acknowledged as his cock sank to the very heart of her.

Her nails dug deeper as he steadily pumped himself into her. "Christ, Jagr, I'm . . ."

His fingers bit deep into her skin, his need an unbearable ache. The flames were beginning to consume him and nothing had ever felt so glorious.

They surged together. Her pants filled the air, mixed with his low moans. Deeper, faster, climbing ever higher.

Then with one last thrust, he heard Regan cry out in release as he climaxed with enough force to shatter the remaining lamp and blast the marble statues in the bathroom into a fine layer of dust.

Chapter 18

Lying in Jagr's arms on the bed, Regan floated in a fog of pleasure.

Sweaty, shivering, sated pleasure.

Good Lord.

That had been . . .

Well, she didn't actually have words to describe what had just happened between her and Jagr. Fierce, certainly. Overwhelming. Shattering.

And insanely wonderful.

With a rueful smile she glanced around the room. There was little left to destroy after their last bout of sex, but what remained was now scattered across the carpet.

"I sincerely hope that your tastes run toward Tupperware instead of Tiffany in that lair of yours, chief," she murmured, unable to keep her fingers from tracing the scars that ran the length of his stomach. "Things could get expensive after a wild night."

He shifted to steal a brief, heart-pounding kiss. "Since you seem to be the only trigger for my more destructive tendencies, I'll be certain to lock away the china when you visit."

His tone was light, but Regan tensed, unable to halt her instinctive withdrawal at his possessive tone. During the heat of the moment, she'd managed to block out his unnerving suggestion that she was his mate. Hell, at that precise moment she would have been able to block out a looming apocalypse.

Now she discovered that the thought made it difficult to breathe. As if she was being smothered.

"You're assuming I'll visit your lair?" she tried to tease, not entirely surprised when his eyes narrowed. He was far too capable of sensing her emotions not to catch whiff of her unease.

"I'm holding you naked in my arms after enjoying the most intense orgasm either of us has ever experienced." He caught and held her wary gaze. "What else would I assume?"

She smiled, weakly. "Who knows what the future might hold?"

There was no return smile. In fact, his expression was downright grim.

"Who, indeed."

"We should get dressed. I promised Styx that I would . . ." Pressing her hands against his chest, she struggled to push away from his hard body, only to have the massive vampire abruptly roll on top of her. "Jagr."

His eyes shimmered with suppressed irritation in the thick shadows. "Why?"

His body pressing her intimately into the mattress did nothing to help her breathing troubles.

She didn't want to think about mates or emotional entanglements or the fear of being expected to offer something she didn't even know if she possessed.

She just wanted to spread her legs and allow pure, uncomplicated sensation to sweep her away.

So much easier.

Unfortunately, Jagr seemed more intent of forcing an unwelcome discussion rather than enjoying their brief time together.

"What?" she at last forced herself to demand.

"Why did you come down here tonight determined to seduce me?"

"I would think that was obvious."

"Indulge me."

She swallowed a resigned sigh. "I wanted you. You said you wanted me. Granted, I've been caged most of my life, but I was under the assumption that was an adequate reason for two people to have sex. Am I wrong?"

"Yes, I wanted you, I *still* want you, but not out of some twisted sense of sympathy."

Sympathy? Her brows snapped together. "What the hell are you talking about?"

His jaw was tight as he glared down at her. "You didn't want me to punish myself for hurting you, so you came down here determined to do whatever necessary to distract me."

It took a second for his words to sink in, but when they did, her temper instantly flared.

"You think this was a pity fuck?" she gritted.

He flinched at her blunt words. "Don't."

"What? You're the one who's implying I'm willing to barter my body for a bit of comfort. Real nice."

"Then why?"

"Does there have to be a reason?"

"No, it could be exactly as you said . . ." He deliberately paused, then with an exaggerated motion he rolled off her and stood beside the bed. "A mindless coupling to relieve a physical urge. Maybe I should be grateful you didn't decide Tane would do."

Scrambling off the mattress, Regan jerkily pulled on her clothes, covertly watching as Jagr did the same. Her stomach did a funny flop as he slid the stone-washed jeans up the powerful muscles of thighs and over his butt. Holy crap. She wanted to spend hours exploring those hard angles and planes.

No, stop that, Regan.

Jagr might be all that was yummy, but he was going to drive her to a loony bin.

Frowning, she watched as Jagr pulled on a black T-shirt that molded to his perfect chest, and bent down to tug on a pair of heavy black boots. Still ignoring her, he collected his daggers and efficiently strapped them to various parts of his body.

"Dammit, Jagr," she growled.

He tucked a handgun in the waistband of his jeans. "I think we've said all that needs to be said."

"God, you're a pain in the ass." Throwing her hands in the air, she stormed to stand directly before him. "Fine. I came down here because I was worried about you."

"So it was a pity . . ."

She'd slammed her hand across his mouth before he could throw her words back into her face.

"I came down here because I was worried, but that's not the reason I seduced you."

Reaching up, he tugged her hand from his lips, his thumb absently rubbing a tender circle on her inner wrist.

"Are you going to tell me why?"

"Because I needed to be with you," she muttered awkwardly. Christ. She didn't do confessionals. They made her feel like a cheap extra on *As the World Turns*. "And it had to be you. Just you. Nobody else." She shook her head as his lips parted. "Don't freaking ask me why, because I don't know."

Bending his head, he stroked his lips over the pulse hammering in her inner wrist.

"If you need me, then the thought of visiting my lair shouldn't send you into a panic."

A renewed sense of alarm had her tugging her hand free so she could step back.

"It wouldn't have if you hadn't mentioned that whole mate thing."

He searched her tight expression. "Are you afraid I intend to trap you?"

"I just . . ." She wrapped her arms around her waist, unable to find the words for her unease. "Are you certain?"

"Certain?"

"About me being your mate?"

"You don't carry my mark yet, but yes, I'm certain."

She shook her head, telling herself it was all some cosmic mistake. This large, beautiful, incredibly sexy predator deserved a mate who could offer untarnished, unconditional devotion. Not a screwed-up Were who was torn between fleeing in utter terror, and a breathless dread of never seeing him again.

"How can it even be possible? I mean, we've done nothing but argue since we met."

"One of fate's little jokes, no doubt."

Ridiculously, she felt a prick of disappointment at his mocking tone.

"You don't sound particularly happy."

"Should I be?" He planted his fists on his hips, the movement stretching the shirt over his massive chest. "After centuries of being alone, I at last find the female destined to be my mate, and she has commitment issues. Forgive me for not jumping for joy."

She tilted her chin, although her gaze kept straying down to the enticing ripple of muscle beneath that damned shirt.

Hey, she might be a demon, but she was all female.

Who wouldn't be distracted?

"I don't have issues, I just . . ."

Golden brows arched as she struggled to find the words. "Yes?"

"I'm just not ready to think about the future."

"You've found Culligan. What else do you have to think about but the future?"

She latched onto the first thing that came to mind. "My sister for one thing."

He frowned. "Darcy?"

"No, the one being held captive by Caine." She met his exasperated gaze with a tight smile. "I think we might have a means to track her."

Levet was not a happy gargoyle.

He'd come to Hannibal to rescue Regan from the clutches of the evil imp. He was supposed to be the hero who won the fair damsel and was celebrated among the demon-world.

Instead, he'd not only lost the girl to yet another devious vampire, but he was now stuck playing babysitter to a bad-tempered cur who couldn't decide if he wanted to be a good or bad guy.

Where was the justice in that?

And to top it off, he was stuck in a cramped fishing cabin that was nearly hidden in a tangle of trees, waiting for Salvatore to make an appearance at dawn.

Kicking a stray rock, Levet negotiated the narrow trail that ran along the Mississippi River.

When Salvatore had commanded Duncan to meet him at a private sanctuary less than an hour north of St. Louis, Levet had held on to the hope the place would be along the lines of Hefner's Playboy Mansion. Salvatore might be a dog, but he was King of the Dogs, and rumors were that he liked the ladies.

Stupid Were.

The splash of water wrenched Levet out of his satisfying bout of self-pity, and with a sinking heart he turned toward the river to watch as Bella's head popped into view, the rest of her body remaining hidden in the murky waves.

"Well, well." A smug smile touched her lovely face. "If it isn't the stunted gargoyle."

"*Sacrebleu.*" Levet threw up his hands in resignation. "Am I to be forever tormented by you? Why will you not go away?"

The water sprite pouted. Oy. She managed to make even that a thing of beauty.

"Until the cur makes his third wish, I am free to roam as I please."

"Then roam somewhere else, you annoying pest."

She swam closer. "You're only mad because I managed to lure you into a trap."

Levet snorted, refusing to admit his pride was stung at having been so easily distracted by the tempting sprite.

"I am mad because you make my head hurt." His eyes narrowed as he was struck by a sudden thought. "Wait. Duncan has wishes?"

"He summoned me," she said, sounding annoyed that he would even ask such an obvious question. "That's the deal. You summon me, you get three wishes."

Of course Levet knew the basics of calling a water sprite. He'd accidentally done it just a few weeks ago. His interest was in whether or not Duncan was playing some devious game.

"Then why didn't he just wish for you to make him impervious to harm?" Levet snapped.

"I'm a sprite, not a god. I can alter physical appearances, as I did with you, or conjure material possessions." She deliberately reminded him of his brief stint as a full-sized gargoyle. One capable of plundering, pillaging, and wholesale destruction. Ah, good times. "But I can't make someone immortal, or influence anyone other than the person making the wish."

"So he couldn't wish away his enemies?"

"Nope."

"Or make Caine forget him?"

"Again, nope."

"So what did he wish for?"

She grimaced. "The usual."

Levet's brief suspicion began to ease. "Riches?"

"Of course. So tedious."

"What else?"

"His own private island."

"Why would he want an island?"

"I believe he has some grandiose scheme to take over the renegade curs and start his own pack, once Salvatore kills Caine for him."

His wings snapped with mocking amusement. "What a titty."

"Titty?" Bella blinked in confusion. "Oh . . . do you mean boob?"

"Titty, boob, whatever," he dismissed. "Salvatore will never allow the curs to escape to some private Garden of Eden. They'll be lucky to keep their hides. The King of Weres might be a pureblood, but he's as rabid as any dog. He should have been put down years ago, if you ask me."

"I don't tell my victims . . ." Bella hastily tried to cover her slip. "I mean, I don't tell my *fortunate masters* what to wish for. I just obey."

Levet wasn't fooled. As a full blooded demon, he was immune to the water sprite's curse, but most men greedy enough to accept the offer of her three wishes, soon learned the truth in the old saying, "If it sounds too good to be true . . ."

"So why hasn't Duncan demanded his last wish?"

Her lips curled. "He's a cur, not a demon."

It took a minute, then his eyes widened. "Ah. So like a human, his last wish will condemn him to the watery depths of your nest?"

"Such a smart little gargoyle," she murmured, swimming forward and stepping out of the river to reveal her full glory.

And what glory it was.

Levet's tail went stiff as the moonlight lapped over the tiny, perfectly formed woman wearing nothing more than a sheer toga. The sprite might be the most dim-witted, annoying creature ever to have crossed his path, but with her white skin, slanted blue eyes, and pale green hair, she was causing all sorts of things to hum and jump and grow.

Grow really hard.

"*Mon Dieu,*" he groaned in genuine pain.

Smiling, she sashayed toward him, her hands running down her generous curves. "Do you like?"

Levet muttered his favorite curses. The damned sprite had made a fool of him once. He was horny (holy bat dung, was he horny), but he wasn't stupid.

"I am a male—I enjoy a good ogle as well as the next— but I am also a gargoyle with powers that make the demon-world shudder in fear," he muttered. "My . . . man parts do not rule me."

"A shame." She closed the tiny space he'd managed to earn, enveloping him in the scent of spring rain. "I've thought about you so often during my long, lonely days beneath the water."

"*Oui,* thoughts about putting my precious testicles into a vise."

"Oh, no. When I thought about your testicles, they were in quite a different place."

She deliberately licked her lips, and Levet nearly swallowed his tongue.

He wanted to be ruled by his man parts.

Actually he wanted to rule *her* with his man parts.

This whole being sensible thing sucked.

"Bah," he managed to croak. "Do you think I have forgotten that you betrayed me at the first opportunity?"

She did another one of those charming pouts. "I will admit I was the teeniest bit annoyed that you condemned me back to my nest after I helped you rescue your friends. Can you blame me?"

A thread of irritation managed to bubble through his raging lust.

"Hell, yes, I can blame you. I was magic-bombed . . . by a cur." He pounded a fist against his chest. "Me. Do you know the indignity I will suffer if that little embarrassment gets back to my family?"

"Oh, pooh. Who will tell them?"

"Well, let me think . . ." He pointed a claw in her direction. "You. You will tell them. What better revenge than to make me a source of mockery among my brethren?"

She studied him with a vacant gaze. "But I would think you were already . . ." She slapped a hand over her mouth. "Oops."

Levet quivered with outrage. "I am already what?"

"Nothing."

"Oh, it was something." He turned his hand over, allowing a small ball of flame to dance in his palm. "Maybe I should just change you into a toad and be done with it. At least I won't have to worry about you flapping your lips."

Rather than trembling in terror, the aggravating pest leaned down to stroke her fingers lightly on the tip of his wings.

"Now, let's not be hasty, my tiny gargoyle."

Ohhhhh. It was good. So good.

"I am not tiny," he denied, his voice strained. "I am majestically petite."

Her fingers dipped and fondled and caressed.

"I like petite."

He groaned against his will. "Stop that."

"Your lips say no, but your wings say yes."

Levet glanced over his shoulder, realizing the treacherous things were glowing like a neon light in front of a cheap bar.

"Stupid wings."

"And what about these delectable horns?" Her hands skimmed up to toy with the stunted nubs. "What do they have to say?"

"Bella . . ." She stroked a particularly tender spot, and his knees nearly gave way. Now this was a sprite who knew the secrets of pleasing a gargoyle. "Oh. *Sacrebleu*. Where did you learn to do that?"

"Here and there." She leaned down to lick the tip of one horn. "Do you want to discover what else I've learned?"

Eyes rolling back in his head, Levet conceded defeat. No, he leaped headfirst into defeat.

If this was a trap, then screw it.

"Yes. Gods, yes."

The great philosophers, poets, and playwrights devoted entire lives to revealing the ironies of life.

Jagr had made a study of their works.

He'd intellectually understood their struggles to make sense of a sometimes senseless existence. But there'd always been a part of himself removed from their experiences.

For centuries he had remained distant from society, watching from the shadows and rarely interacting. Shrouded in peace and solitude, he often considered the portrayals of intimate relationships as nothing more than melodramatic drivel.

How could love, or even affection, offer such uncertainty, such confusion, such downright torture?

Now he understood with painful clarity.

Since Regan's arrival in his world, nothing was the same.

It was like existing in the midst of a whirlwind, he grimly acknowledged, pacing Tane's bedroom with jerky steps. One moment he was drowning in sensual pleasure, the next he was struggling against the bleak tide of resignation as Regan panicked at the thought of being his mate.

And the next . . .

The next he was consumed with pure fury as Regan

revealed her adventures in stupidity while he'd been locked in Gaynor's prison.

"You went searching for Sadie without Tane?" he gritted, his voice dripping with ice as he sought to contain his ravaging emotions.

Standing near the door to the bathroom, Regan jerked a brush through her glorious curls, her jaw set in stubborn lines even though she had to know she was in the wrong.

"He was a little too sun-combustible to join me."

Jagr fiercely refused to remember just how wondrous it had felt to run his fingers though that golden mane.

"Dammit, when you said you found Culligan, I didn't realize you'd been out roaming the countryside alone."

The green eyes shimmered with warning. "Because a pure-blooded Were can't take care of herself without a vampire playing bodyguard?"

"Because if something happened to you, it would send me over the edge," he ground out the brutal truth. "And nothing would bring me back."

He heard her catch her breath, the brush dropping from her fingers as her defensive expression softened.

"Look, all I intended to do was see if I could track the curs. I had no plans to confront them without Tane and Styx."

Jagr stilled, struck by the sudden realization that Regan had managed to do what he'd tried and failed to do.

"How did you track them?"

Her lips twitched at the hint of irritation he couldn't hide.

"Gaynor mentioned Sadie's obsession with his peanut butter fudge. Once I had the scent, I searched until I ran across it again."

"Peanut butter fudge?"

"It worked."

He muttered an ancient curse. "And that's where you found Culligan?"

"He was chained in the shed." She shrugged, but it didn't disguise the lingering revulsion. "When I questioned him, I learned that Gaynor's portal was weak, and that you were probably being held close to where you disappeared. I decided to take his amulet and see if I could find you."

Jagr bit back his harsh words. As furious as he might be, he'd rather cut out his tongue than cause Regan unnecessary distress.

"And Duncan?" he instead demanded.

"We stumbled over each other when I left the cabin."

The thought of the cur not only attacking Regan, but actually holding her captive was enough to make his fangs lengthen and the room fill with a frigid burst of power.

Not bloodlust, just good old-fashioned fury any male would feel at his mate being harmed.

"He could have killed you."

With an impatient click of her tongue, Regan moved to stand directly before him.

"One more word about me putting myself in danger and we're done with this conversation, chief."

Chief. Absurdly, the pet name helped to calm his temper. It reminded him that for all her protests, Regan wasn't as emotionally detached as she wanted to be.

"Fine," he grudgingly conceded. What was the point in arguing? Regan would do what she wanted. Always.

And in some twisted way, it was what he admired most about her.

Irony, indeed.

"Besides, it all worked out for the best," she pointed out. "Now we can at least hope my sister can be rescued."

Well, that was true enough. Jagr scrubbed his hands over his face, feeling weary despite his recent feeding of the cur.

A small part of him wished he'd managed to pack his bag and return to the sanctity of his lair. Every moment spent in

Regan's company was bound to deepen the sense of loss when she disappeared from his world.

But even as the cowardly thought flared through his mind, he was dismissing it.

So long as this beautiful Were had need of him, he would stand at her side.

Pitiful, but true.

With a restless shake of his head, Jagr headed toward the door to the outer rooms.

"We must share this information with Styx."

"Jagr."

Halting, he glanced over his shoulder. "What?"

She licked her lips, strangely uncertain. As if she struggled with some inner demon.

At last she gave a jerky shake of her head.

"Never mind."

Jagr bit back his curse of impatience. He might not be the most perceptive vampire, but he did learn from his mistakes. And trying to press Regan would only make her dig in her heels deeper.

A knowledge that did nothing to ease his temper as he stormed from the rooms and went in search of his Anasso.

Following the unmistakable scent of power, Jagr moved through the surveillance rooms to a large library, complete with plasma TV. Not surprisingly, Styx was engrossed in a rare book on the history of the Huguenots rather than watching Cinemax. The ancient vampire had never possessed Jagr's interest in the ever changing society, and it was only because he was determined to please his new mate that he wasn't still living in a damp cavern without one modern convenience.

As Jagr stepped through the door, Styx was on his feet, his lifted brow revealing he was well aware of his companion's tangled emotions, although he was smart enough not to comment.

Instead he listened in silence as Jagr revealed Duncan's attempted negotiations with the Weres, and the cur's promise he could reveal the location of Regan's missing sister.

As he finished, Styx pulled a cell phone from his pocket and swiftly dialed Salvatore's number.

Absently, Jagr listened to the short, tense argument, his body flaring with awareness as he felt Regan entering the room behind him.

He deliberately kept his gaze on Styx's imposing form as she halted beside him, not that it mattered. She had only to be near for him to drown in her jasmine-scented presence.

With an audible snap, Styx closed his phone and stuffed it into the pocket of his leather pants. Perhaps not surprisingly, Regan took a step closer to Jagr.

Styx was overwhelming under the best of circumstances. With the scowl marring his stark features, and his massive body tense with annoyance, any creature not brain-dead would be wary.

Either unaware, or simply ignoring the prickles in the air, Styx lifted a hand to smooth over the raven hair he'd pulled into a braid that hung nearly to his knees.

Darcy was never going to drag the proud vampire fully into the twenty-first century.

"The meeting with Duncan is set for dawn," Styx revealed, his voice hard. "He refused to offer the location."

"Refused?" Jagr shook his head. "Arrogant dog."

Styx grimaced. "He has proclaimed it Were business and I have no authority to interfere, although Darcy may have a different opinion when I tell her."

"Good God, you actually listen to your mate's opinion?" Regan demanded, her tone overly sweet.

Jagr frowned, but Styx seemed to find the jab amusing. "Believe me, it was a hard-earned talent," he admitted with a low chuckle.

Jagr's frown deepened as he glared at his king. Traitor.

"Do you intend to return to Chicago?"

Styx briefly closed his eyes, testing the air. "It is too late to make the journey tonight," he concluded, opening his eyes. "And I would prefer to clean up any loose ends before leaving."

Jagr gave a dip of his head. "Speaking of loose ends, I have an imp to track down."

"The dawn is only two hours away," Styx warned.

Jagr patted one of the numerous daggers strapped to his body. "This won't take long."

"I will join you." Styx took a step forward. "Once the imp is dead, we can search the cabin that Regan found. It could be the remaining curs have returned there."

"Which means you'll need me if you want to find the place," Regan said, a smug smile curving her lips.

"There's no need. We can follow your trail," Jagr said, unable to halt the futile words even as Regan was sticking a finger in his face.

"Don't even start. I'm coming."

The two stood there, glaring at one another, until Styx moved forward to slap Jagr on the back.

"I would suggest you let it go, old friend," Styx warned, leaving the room.

Jagr didn't concede defeat as much as give into the inevitable. Regan was a force of nature he didn't know how to control.

In silence, he followed Styx out of the lair and to the waiting Porsche parked in the circle drive. He even managed to hold his tongue as Regan climbed into the back, and he took his position in the passenger seat.

He'd barely shut the door when Styx revved the powerful engine and hurtled them through the empty streets, his lips twisted in what Jagr strongly suspected was a smile of amusement.

What the hell happened to vampire solidarity?

Bastard.

At least the car was able to make the trip at a pace just short of light speed, and directing Styx through the back roads, he at last held up his hand.

"Stop here." He pointed toward the frilly house on the corner. "The tea shop is just ahead."

The Porsche came to a halt, and they climbed out to stand in the shadows of a dogwood tree.

A dogwood that was currently decorated with a familiar, albeit considerably worse for the wear, truck.

Styx studied the ruined vehicle with a lift of his brows. "Tane's?"

"It was." Jagr glanced toward Regan, who was looking decidedly guilty. "Your handiwork?"

"Hey, I'd never driven before." She gave an awkward lift of her shoulder. "Besides, it was already a piece of junk."

"I would suggest you keep your keys close at hand, my lord," he said, dryly.

"Ha. Very funny." With a toss of her head, Regan moved down the street, her back rigid.

Styx smiled. "Although I hate to question Regan's skill in demolition, I have to admit she is a mere amateur in destroying cars compared to Levet. That gargoyle possesses an exquisite ability to mangle even the finest vehicle. Just ask Viper."

"Considering Viper's unnatural obsession with his cars, I would rather not provoke any unpleasant memories."

"Wise choice," Styx drawled.

"I occasionally have moments of self-preservation." His gaze was instinctively drawn to Regan as she paced impatiently just across the street from the tea shop. "Although not nearly so many as I might hope for."

Styx laid a surprisingly gentle hand on his shoulder. "I would tell you that it gets easier, but I try to make it a policy not to lie any more than necessary."

Jagr winced as a sharp pang pierced his heart. "Our time together draws to an end."

"Only the Oracles can read the future. Cezar is proof of that."

Jagr's lips twisted. Cezar's mate had turned out to be one of the rare Oracles, a fate that Jagr wouldn't wish on anyone.

Bad enough to have a bad-tempered Were with a commitment phobia.

"I don't need an Oracle to tell me that Regan is determined to remain a true lone wolf."

Obviously weary of waiting, Regan planted her hands on her hips and glared at the two vampires.

"Are we doing this, or what?"

Styx slanted Jagr an amused glance. "Bossy little thing, isn't she?"

"You have no idea."

Throwing up her hands in defeat, Regan turned on her heel and marched across the street to the silent tea shop.

"Maybe we should make sure she doesn't run into trouble," Styx murmured.

"If only it was possible." Jagr was swiftly rushing after her tiny form, a sudden urgency lending him speed as she disappeared through the gate of the picket fence and rounded the back of the house. Even at a distance, the scent of rotting peaches filled the air. "Regan."

She came to an abrupt halt, her expression wary. "I smell it. Is he dead?"

"Yes." Jagr didn't need to see Gaynor's body to feel the violence that shrouded the house. "And his death wasn't pleasant. There's a lot of blood."

Appearing from the shadows, Styx studied the broken French doors. "There are three dead curs, and one unconscious, as well as the dead imp. I sense no one else."

Jagr's gaze searched the dark garden, his instincts tingling with an unmistakable warning.

"That doesn't mean they aren't prowling around," he growled. "Those damn amulets make it impossible to be certain."

Styx frowned. "We should make a quick sweep of the house."

"You go." Jagr continued his wary survey. "We'll stay here."

"Jagr . . ."

He placed a finger over Regan's lips to halt her protest. "No, Regan, this has nothing to do with protecting you."

Styx stepped closer. "What is it?"

"Nothing I can put my finger on. I just think we should keep guard."

The ancient vampire nodded, not questioning Jagr's vague unease.

"I trust your instincts, my brother. I will not be long."

Chapter 19

Regan watched as the very large, very scary Styx disappeared through the French doors before turning to study Jagr with a frown.

She felt strangely numb as the smell of death and violence wrapped around her.

Maybe not surprising after the last few days.

There was only so much a woman, even one accustomed to demon brutality, could bear without going into emotional overload.

That didn't mean, however, she was oblivious to the danger that continued to haunt her.

She had only to glance at Jagr's tight expression to be reminded.

"What do you sense?" she whispered.

"We're being watched." Without even glancing in her direction (a seeming trend this evening), Jagr tugged two daggers from his boots and handed her one. "Here."

Gingerly taking the dagger, she grimaced at the long, lethally sharp blade.

"Silver?"

"Yes. Try not to stick yourself."

"I know where I'd like to stick it."

Expecting a sharp response, Regan was caught off guard as Jagr slowly turned, his expression somber.

"Are we destined to be enemies, little one?"

She floundered at the soft, but inexorable question.

Christ, this vampire tied her knots. Why couldn't he just let her panic and drive him away with her volatile, completely irrational behavior?

It's what any decent demon would do.

Instead, he stood there staring at her with that icily guarded expression that she knew hid just how much her answer meant to him.

"No," she at last whispered, unable to deliver the final, unalterable blow. "I don't want to be your enemy, Jagr. I seem to have enough of them already."

Lifting a hand, he gently cupped her face. "Regan . . ."

She had no idea what he was about to say, nor was she destined to discover, as Jagr abruptly turned toward the house, his body stiff with tension.

"Jagr, what is it?"

"A trap," he rasped, charging toward the French doors with a near blinding speed. "Styx."

Momentarily stunned, Regan watched as Jagr disappeared into the tea shop. What the hell? Regan stepped forward, intent on following Jagr, when there was an audible click, followed instantly by the sound of an explosion that made the earth shake beneath her feet.

The world seemed stuck in slow motion as Regan watched in horror while the flames and smoke billowed through the house. Then without warning, the concussion hit, sending her flying backward as the house shattered from the force of the blast.

Jagr.

Stark panic clawed through her, but she was helpless as she was tossed like a piece of trash through the air, at last crashing into an oak tree with enough force to briefly knock her unconscious.

The blackness came and went with a blazing flare of pain, but Regan ignored the dizziness and urge to toss up what little remained in her stomach. She didn't have time to be sick. Jagr had been in the house. She had to reach him, and by God, if he'd let himself be killed, she was going to . . .

"Alone at last, bitch."

Consumed with her desperate fear, Regan was completely unprepared for the tall, dark-haired, dark-eyed woman who dropped from the branches of the tree to stand directly in her path.

Stumbling to a halt, Regan gritted her teeth as her gaze swept over the stranger, absently grimacing at the leather bustier and pants that matched the high-heeled boots. It wasn't the Sluts-R-Us outfit, however, that caught and held her attention. Instead it was the hard, perfectly toned muscles that revealed this woman wasn't just a local stripper on her way home from a hard night.

That, and the complete absence of scent.

"Sadie," she breathed, her gut twisting with fury.

This woman was behind luring Regan to Hannibal, behind Gaynor imprisoning Jagr, and now behind an explosion that might very well have killed her vampire.

She was going to cut her heart right out of her freaking chest.

"I see my reputation precedes me," the woman taunted, clearly unaware that she was already dead. "What? No snappy banter? I knew you were bound to be a disappointment."

Regan slowly began to circle the cur. During her unexpected flight, she'd dropped the dagger that Jagr had given her. Go figure. And while her instincts howled for an opportunity to rip out her heart, she wasn't stupid.

Now was not the time to take chances. Not when Jagr needed her.

"I don't need snappy banter to kill you," she drawled, hoping to keep the woman distracted.

"You kill me?"

"Yes."

"You're nothing without your vampire, you genetic freak," the woman mocked. "A Were who can't even shift."

Regan's heart twisted at the mention of Jagr, but she grimly kept circling the cur.

"I may be a freak, but I'm a pureblooded freak, which is more than you can say . . . cur."

Reaching behind her back, Sadie tugged free a tightly coiled whip.

A whip?

Who the hell used a whip? Well, who besides Indiana Jones?

With a practiced flip of her hand, the cur snapped her wrist, sending the tail of the whip cracking a mere inch from Regan's face.

Holy shit.

Leaping back, Regan swallowed a curse of frustration. The whip couldn't kill her, but it could wrap around her and hold her immobile.

Not to mention it had enough reach to keep her from easily retrieving the dagger.

The only hope was leading Sadie away from the damned thing so she could try and make a dash for it when the cur was off guard.

"You think you're better than me?" The whip snaked out again, slicing through the flesh of Regan's cheek.

"I don't *think,* I *know.*" Ignoring the blood that dripped down her neck, Regan altered her course as if she were trying to reach the nearby gate. "You're nothing more than an infected human who can imitate a Were but never become one. A pathetic wannabe."

The dark eyes flared as the words hit their mark. "You know nothing."

Regan jerked to the side as the whip flared out. "I know of your psycho plan to use my sister as some sort of guinea pig, in the pathetic hope you can become more than the bottom-feeders of the demon-world."

"It's our destiny to rule."

Regan took two steps closer to the gate, hiding her grim satisfaction as Sadie followed.

"Because some idiot saw it in a vision?"

Crack. The whip cut a deep slice through her abdomen, ruining her new shirt.

Bitch.

"Caine is a prophet," Sadie hissed.

Regan didn't bother hiding her flare of pain as she stumbled, deliberately glancing over her shoulder as if judging the distance to the open gate.

"He's a whack job who should be put in a straightjacket, and you're even more of a whack job to believe him. I suppose the old saying is true—'There's a sucker born every minute.'"

A hard smile curved the woman's lips. A pity really. The cur would have been beautiful if not for the vicious expression.

Well, that and the tart-from-hell outfit.

"Where's your faith, Were?" Sadie demanded.

"When someone starts babbling about visions, my first thought is medication, not hallelujah."

"You see, that's what is wrong with youth today."

"Sanity?"

"Cynicism." A hand stroked up the bustier, cupping a still pert breast. "Look at me, I was a two-bit whore who was regularly raped by my father, and traded my body for the heroin that made my personal hell bearable. Then Caine changed everything, and soon I'll be a queen."

"Queen of Dogs?" She mocked, ignoring the heat of the burning tea house as she managed another few steps. Dammit, she had to get to that dagger and kill the bitch. If Jagr were still alive . . . no, he was alive. She couldn't allow herself to think anything else. And she had to get to him. "Big deal."

"It's certainly better than wasting my time whining and pouting because you think you got a bad break."

"Bad break? Culligan tortured me for the past thirty years."

"Boohoo. So you had a few cuts and bruises." The whip sizzled through the air, striking Regan's neck even as she dove to the side. "Did you have to spread your legs for every disgusting male who couldn't get it up unless he was beating on you? Did you sleep in an alley and pray someone would slit your throat so you didn't have to wake up?"

Regan gritted her teeth. She healed swiftly, but she was losing too much blood.

"Worse, I've had to listen to your entire life story," she taunted, luring Sadie even further from the dagger. "Do you bore everyone with it? Because that might explain why your only friend is an outlaw cur with delusions of grandeur."

"Better than a stunted gargoyle and a walking corpse." The black eyes smoldered with hatred. "Tell me, what's it like banging a cold stiff?"

Regan hissed, her wolf howling with the urge to kill.

"God damn you."

"Ah, did I touch a nerve?" Sadie unwittingly stepped further from the dagger, using the whip to slice another wound on Regan's stomach. "You know, you have no one to blame but yourself for his untimely death. Well . . . second death. If you'd just come along nicely, there'd be no reason for the gorgeous vampire to die."

Shit. Regan pressed a hand to the gaping wound. A few more steps.

Just a few.

"I have issues with becoming a lab rat for a bunch of dogs. Sue me."

"I'd rather kill you, but unfortunately that's going to have to wait until Caine is confident he has all he needs from your sister."

Regan never halted her slow circle, but her eyes narrowed at the mention of her sister.

Just maybe she could kill two birds with one stone.

Or two worthless curs.

"Why does he want me?"

Sadie sneered as she flicked a dismissive gaze over Regan's tattered, bloody body.

"You, my freak, are our backup in case she's so ill-mannered as to croak on us."

"Nice."

"Revolutions are always messy." She lashed out with her whip, frowning when Regan managed to dance out of the path. "At least for the losers."

"Oh, you have that right." From the corner of her eye, Regan could see the silver of the dagger glittering in the moonlight. Time to bring out the big guns. "As your beloved Caine is about to discover. Salvatore is already on his trail."

Sadie snarled, her eyes suddenly glowing with an eerie light as the urge to shift pulsed through her body.

"I suppose this is some pathetic trick to try and distract me?"

Regan managed a mocking smile despite her pain. "You really need to work on that sparkling personality of yours, Sadie. It doesn't seem to inspire the sort of loyalty that successful revolutions are made of." Her smile widened. "Duncan has already turned traitor."

Sadie froze. "Liar."

Regan began to covertly angle directly toward the dagger. She couldn't waste any more time.

"Surely you can't be surprised?" she demanded, inwardly judging the remaining distance. "I don't know what you did to him, but the cur hates you with a passion. He couldn't wait to set up a meeting with Salvatore to squeal everything he knows about Caine and his secret laboratories."

"As if Caine would reveal anything to a mere peon like

Duncan," Sadie scorned, although she couldn't disguise the tightening of her hard features. "They'll never find him."

"Oh, they will." Regan grunted as the whip caught her across the shoulder. She was going to shove that thing up Sadie's ass once this was over. For the moment, all she could do was grin and bear it. "And, if you're as smart as you claim to be, then you'll contact Salvatore and try to make your own deal. If you can lead him directly to my sister, he might be willing to negotiate with you rather than Duncan."

"There will be no negotiating," Sadie hissed, trembling with the need to shift. "If Salvatore interferes, he'll die."

"I hope you're not a betting woman, Sadie, because you're backing the wrong horse."

"Enough," the cur screeched. "We're leaving. Now."

"I don't think so."

Prepared for Sadie's attempt to wrap the whip around her, Regan lunged to the ground, managing to avoid the strike. Remaining on her hands and knees, she crawled the short distance, at long last managing to grasp the dagger.

A surge of victory tingled through her. About freaking time. Sadie was soooo dead.

Closing her fingers around the hilt, she was already envisioning sliding the silver blade deep into the bitch's heart when a low growl filled the air.

Damn.

Regan swiftly rolled to the side, barely avoiding the snapping jaws of the shifted cur.

Obviously Sadie had decided that if she couldn't take Regan alive, then she'd take her dead.

Or maybe she just couldn't control that cur instinct of hers.

In either case, Regan abruptly knew she was in serious danger.

Rolling onto her back, Regan caught her first sight of the transformed Sadie. She was a beautiful wolf. Of course. Large and lean, her pelt was a rich mahogany, with a touch of silver on her muzzle. In the darkness her eyes glowed with a crimson light, sending a tingle over Regan's skin as if her own wolf was struggling to respond.

Something that might almost have been envy briefly flared through Regan before she was thrusting aside the inane sensation and concentrating on more important matters.

Like staying alive.

Growling deep in her throat, Sadie prepared to leap, and realizing that it would be fatal to be pinned to the ground, Regan lashed out with the dagger.

She was too far away to do more than cut a shallow gash through the cur's chest, but the burn of silver was enough to make Sadie leap backward instinctively.

Swift to take advantage, Regan was on her feet, her gaze never wavering from the cur who was moving to the side in an effort to catch Regan from behind.

She stepped in perfect time with the cur, the dagger held at her side. In her current form, Sadie held a distinct advantage, not only in size, but sheer, raw strength.

Thankfully, any common sense tended to disappear when a cur was in full-rage mode.

Sadie continued to circle, snapping her impressive fangs and occasionally feigning an attack. Regan ignored the taunts, knowing the woman was hoping to lure her into overreacting, exposing an opening.

Behind her the fire continued to spread through the tea shop, the smoke and heat spilling through the garden, but wiping away the sweat that gathered on her brow, Regan remained grimly prepared to strike. Sadie wouldn't last long. She was a cur, not a Were. Her emotions would be her downfall.

There was another feint, but as Regan refused to flinch, Sadie laid back her ears and howled in frustration.

Regan shifted her weight to the balls of her feet, her fingers tightening on the grip of the dagger. Any second now. Any . . . second . . .

The howl lowered to a growl as Sadie abruptly charged forward, her jaws parted as she leaped directly at Regan's throat. Prepared for the attack, Regan bent backwards, avoiding the snapping teeth even as she plunged her dagger deep into the cur's chest.

The blade slid in with sickening ease, but the force of Sadie's heavy body sent Regan reeling from the impact. Landing flat on her back, she ignored the teeth that sank into her shoulder and kept the dagger stuck deep into the cur's flesh. Already the stench of burning flesh was tainting the air. It wouldn't be long before the silver weakened Sadie.

She was right.

Only a few minutes passed before there was a shimmer around the wolf form, and Sadie was shifting back to human. A few minutes that seemed like an eternity as the bitch managed to gnaw her way to Regan's shoulder bone.

As the wolf melted to a human shape, Regan forced herself to ignore her pain and rolled over so she was perched on top of her nemesis. Still clutching the dagger that she'd deliberately stuck in an inch above the woman's heart, she struggled to catch her breath.

"Tell me where to find my sister," she rasped.

The pale features twisted with hate. "Go screw yourself, freak."

Regan didn't hesitate as she yanked the dagger free and plunged it back in. This time directly into the heart.

The woman would rather die than betray Caine, and Regan wasn't about to waste any more time.

"This is for Jagr," she muttered as the dagger hit the cur's heart.

She didn't wait to watch Sadie die.

The silver would eventually do its thing, even if the cur managed to pull out the dagger, and Regan was far more interested in reaching Jagr.

Dripping blood from a half dozen wounds, Regan reached the back terrace when she heard an eerie laugh behind her.

Against her will, her feet halted and her head turned to see Sadie, crawling the short distance to her shredded clothing, pulling a pistol from the tattered pile of leather.

Stupidly, all Regan could think about was how the hell the woman had managed to hide a gun. The freaking outfit had been stretched so tight that not even a prayer could have come between leather and skin.

Then it no longer mattered where Sadie had stashed the gun.

Smiling with cruel intent, the cur pulled the trigger. Over and over.

"And this is for me."

Regan was quick, but there was no dodging the bullets that drilled into her torso, shattering ribs and puncturing her lungs.

The force of the projectiles dropped Regan to her knees, her breathing labored, the pain ripping through her with relentless force.

"Shit," she whispered as her life began to drain from her body.

The bullets had been coated in silver.

Chapter 20

Jagr felt like hell.

It might have been because he'd just survived an explosion, had a tea shop fall on his head, and was forced to dig a tunnel to avoid becoming charcoaled.

It might have been.

But it wasn't.

For all his lingering wounds, his current suffering was entirely due to the woman lying on the bed in Tane's lair.

Perched on the edge of the mattress, Jagr gently stroked his fingers through Regan's golden hair, his gaze compulsively running over her too-slender form that he'd stripped down to the tiny bra and panties so he could keep a constant surveillance on her numerous injuries.

The gashes from the whip had healed before they had returned to the lair (not soon enough to ease Jagr's fury at the thought of Regan being flayed by the damned cur), but the bullet wounds remained angry red lesions that made his gut twist with pain.

Silver-plated bullets.

If Sadie hadn't already been dead, Jagr would have torn her apart limb by limb.

Without warning, Regan stirred beneath his fingers, and

abruptly realizing his frigid power was blasting through the room, he hurriedly smothered his fury and leaned down to brush his lips over her temple in silent apology.

"Jagr."

He pulled back just far enough to watch her lids flutter upward, revealing her pain-dazed eyes.

"I'm here, little one."

"The explosion . . ." Her voice was a low, tortured rasp. "I thought . . ."

He tenderly tucked a strand of hair behind her ear. "You thought you were rid of me? No such luck, I fear."

An echo of remembered horror darkened her eyes. "Gods, don't even joke. How did you get out of the house?"

"Vampires possess the ability to call the earth."

"Call the earth?"

His lips twisted. The words made the skill sound pompously grand. In truth, it was a talent that allowed vampires to soften and shift the ground to cover themselves during the day, or more often, to hide the remains of their latest meal.

"We dug a tunnel," he said dryly.

"Oh." Her brows drew together as her gaze lowered to the burns that still marred his neck. He needed to feed and rest before he could fully heal, but his concern for Regan overrode any thought of his own injuries. "You're hurt."

"It's nothing that won't be healed in a few hours."

"You need to feed."

"Soon."

She frowned at his vague reply, but wise enough to recognize the bleak set of his features, she resisted any urge to lecture him.

"What about Styx?" she instead demanded.

"He's recovering."

There was a long silence as Regan drifted in and out of consciousness, then with an obvious effort, she forced her eyes open.

"How did you survive?"

He smiled wryly at the shocking desire to share how he endured the crushing weight of the building as it fell on his head, and how he used his powers to hold off the worst of the flames while Styx carved a path through the hard packed earth.

Like he was a boasting playa in a singles bar.

Pathetic.

"The initial blast knocked out the floor and we dropped into the basement before the actual explosion swept through the house," he murmured, keeping his tone light. "We were able to avoid most of the flames."

Her eyes narrowed, easily able to sense there was more to the story than he revealed, but before she could grill him, her eyes widened abruptly, and she struggled to sit up.

"Sadie," she rasped.

He pressed her back onto the pillow with a gentle but relentless hand.

"You don't have to worry about the cur. She's gone."

"Gone." Her distress only deepened. "She's going to warn Caine. You have to stop her."

He cupped her cheek, his thumb rubbing the satin skin of her cheek in a soothing motion.

"You made certain that Sadie won't be talking with anyone but the grim reaper."

"She's dead?"

"Yes."

There was a beat, then the green eyes flashed with unmistakable satisfaction.

"Good."

Unable to resist, Jagr bent down to lightly brush his lips over her brow. He loved that fire that burned deep inside her.

The fire of a survivor.

"I agree, but I would have preferred you would have

killed her before letting her shoot you full of silver bullets," he murmured.

"Me, too. They hurt like a bitch." She shifted to glance down at her chest, frowning as she caught sight of the lingering wounds. "Are they out?"

The air chilled as he fought back the memories of cutting the bullets from her broken body. The image would be seared into his mind for all eternity.

"I removed them before we brought you back to Tane's."

"How long have we been here?"

"A few hours."

She frowned. "I should be healed, shouldn't I?"

"The silver did a lot of damage."

Shifting, he stretched out on the mattress, pulling her into his arms so he could hold her close. He paused, waiting to see if she would pull away. When she instead snuggled closer, he swallowed a moan.

This is what fate had intended.

This female completed him in a way he'd never dreamed possible.

"Have they found my sister?" she demanded, her voice thick as she tried to hold back the healing darkness.

"I haven't spoken with Salvatore or Levet. I doubt if they've had time to search yet." His hand cupped the back of her head as he settled it more firmly against his chest. "Your work is done, little one. You must rest."

She gathered enough strength to poke him in the side. "You should know better than to give me orders, chief."

"If you don't like me giving you orders, then get well enough to get out of this bed and stop me."

"Bully."

He dropped a kiss on top her head. "Sleep."

"Jagr?" she murmured as her eyes drifted shut.

"Yes?"

"Will you stay?"

His heart clenched. This time with Regan was a moment out of time. He intended to savor every second.

"For as long as you need me, little one."

With a soft sigh, she slung her arm over his body and gave into the inevitable.

Tugging her even closer, Jagr allowed the midnight jasmine to soothe away his lingering pain and heal his wounds. Although he still needed to feed to regain his strength, he realized that the gentle magic in Regan's touch was swiftly healing the last of his injuries.

Yet more proof she was his intended mate.

Drinking in the bittersweet pleasure of simply holding her close, Jagr didn't stir as he felt the encroaching presence of Styx.

His respect for the ancient vampire had gone up a great deal over the past few hours.

Not only had Styx remained unruffled as the house had fallen on their heads, but he hadn't hesitated to trust Jagr to hold back the wall of flames as he calmly blasted a hole in the thick cement and forged a path through the heavy dirt.

It was that trust that had altered something deep inside Jagr.

He hadn't wanted to be a part of a clan. He didn't need brothers, or a leader, who cared whether he lived or died.

He just wanted to be alone.

Now he was forced to accept that he'd felt . . . pride at Styx's faith in his ability.

Not that he was ready to leap into vampire society. Nor had he forgotten that it was Styx who sent him to Hannibal in the first place.

The cunning old Aztec had a great deal to answer for.

Entering the bedroom, Styx leaned against the doorjamb and studied the two lying on the bed. In the candlelight, his face looked like polished bronze, and his massive form was covered in black leather and sharp weapons.

Jagr impulsively shielded Regan with his larger body. Not that he feared Styx would cause her harm. What little brains he had left understood the Anasso had pledged his life to protect his sister-mate. Still, his instincts refused to be denied.

Thankfully, Styx seemed accustomed to deranged vampires, and with a faint smile, he nodded his head toward the half-hidden woman.

"She's healing?" he demanded, softly.

"Slowly."

The harsh expression promised dire retribution on the curs who had dared to hurt Regan.

"So much silver was bound to make her recovery more difficult." His attention shifted to Jagr. "You could speed the process."

Jagr tensed. The urge to share his blood with his mate was a vicious force. The means to heal her flowed through his veins, but because of the barriers she'd placed between them, he was unable to share his gift.

"No."

Styx arched a brow at his sharp refusal. "She's refused your blood?"

"She's refused me as her mate." His icy tone didn't hide the savage pain. "I won't force any deeper connection."

Styx grimaced, realizing that Jagr couldn't share his blood without completing his half of the mating process.

"Of course."

Tucking the blanket around Regan's slender body, Jagr slid from the bed, careful not to disturb his sleeping beauty.

As much as he disliked giving up the rare opportunity to hold Regan without protest, Jagr had a few questions he intended to get answered.

Crossing the room, he stood directly before his king, his arms folded across his chest.

"Why did you send me to Hannibal, my lord?"

Styx met his accusing gaze with a bland smile. "Obviously

to rescue my sister-mate. Which reminds me that I have yet to thank you for your services. You have only to name your price . . ."

"You have a half dozen Ravens who are the finest vampire warriors ever born," Jagr interrupted, in no mood for games. "Why did you send me?"

"Like me, the Ravens have spent the past centuries hidden from society while protecting the previous Anasso. They are still struggling to learn the skills necessary to pass among the humans, including the latest technology." His smile widened with genuine amusement. "You should watch them try to use the remote control. You, on the other hand, have made a study of this era."

Jagr stiffened. He'd never shared his fascination with the MTV generation, and he sure as hell hadn't announced his occasional forays into the human population.

"How did you know?"

"Viper keeps a close eye on his clan." Styx shrugged. "Very little escapes his notice."

Keeping a close eye sounded way too much like spying for Jagr's peace of mind.

"I didn't realize that becoming a part of a clan included losing any right to privacy."

"Viper can be a bit overzealous in his attempts to protect his brothers."

Jagr snorted. "Meddling mother hen."

"At least you know he cares."

"He could care without sticking his nose in my business."

Styx flashed his rare smile, revealing fangs that could rip through steel.

"Perhaps, but it would not be nearly so much fun."

Jagr narrowed his eyes at the deliberate goading, then with effort, he gave a shake of his head.

"No, I will not be distracted," he warned. "Tell me the truth of why I was sent to Hannibal."

Styx silently toyed with the medallion that hung about his neck, debating just how much he was willing to share.

"It was in part because of your comfort in moving among humans, as well as your skills as a warrior," he said, at last.

"And the other part?"

"I knew that you were the one person who would be able to sympathize with what Regan had endured."

Jagr flinched. "Because I've been tortured?"

"Yes," Styx admitted without apology. "You better than anyone could understand the damage that was done during her years of captivity, and offer patience while she struggled to come to terms with her newfound freedom." The ancient vampire grimaced. "Although I'll admit I didn't anticipate quite so much patience."

Annoyance at having been needed not for his strength, but for his weakness, stirred Jagr's temper, adding a sudden chill to the air.

"I beg your pardon?"

Styx blandly ignored the danger prickling in the air. "I assumed you would be eager to be done with your task, and bring Regan directly to Chicago. I didn't consider the possibility that you would actually encourage her dangerous lust for vengeance."

"I didn't encourage her," Jagr snapped.

"No?"

The air dropped another ten degrees. "She's young, but she's capable of making her own decisions. In fact, she insists on it."

Styx grunted, his expression rueful. "That I believe. Any relation of Darcy is bound to have a mind of her own, and a stubborn streak a mile wide."

"Stubborn?" Jagr glanced toward the fragile woman curled on the bed. "She's as obstinate as an emula demon, with the temper of a hellhound."

"Even more reason to return her to her family," Styx pointed out.

Jagr snapped his brows together. Damned if he would be chastised as if he were a fledgling demon. He'd done what he thought best for Regan, and he wouldn't change a thing.

"If you wanted me to treat her as my prisoner, then you should have told me," he said coldly. "As I recall, I was warned to treat her with kid gloves."

Perhaps sensing he'd pressed as far as he dared, Styx shrugged. "True enough, and as the famous bard once said, 'All's well that ends well.' So long as there are no unexpected complications, she should be recovered enough to be moved to Chicago by this evening."

Jagr's scowl only deepened, his heart feeling as if it were being crushed in a ruthless vise.

So this was it?

This was how it was all to end?

Gods.

"Are you so certain she wants to be moved?" he rasped.

The golden eyes hardened with determination. "It will take two or three days before she is back to full strength. Until then she needs the protection my lair can provide. Besides, Darcy will castrate me if I don't give her the opportunity to nurse Regan back to health."

"And Regan might castrate you for forcing her into a family reunion she doesn't want."

"It would seem I'm in a no-win situation, not an unusual place for a mated vampire." Without warning, Styx reached out to place a comforting hand on Jagr's shoulder. "Do not fear, Jagr, we will take good care of your wounded female."

Shaking off his companion's hand, as well as his sympathy, Jagr hid his jagged pain behind a stoic mask.

He'd been alone for centuries.

What were a few more isolated, forlorn, miserable years?

"Have you heard from Salvatore?" He deliberately changed the subject.

"No." Styx allowed a hint of fang to show. "The damned King of Weres has an annoying habit of forgetting that I'm the Anasso."

"I can remind him if you'd like."

The Anasso stilled, his expression unreadable. "You?"

"I may not possess the same hunting skills as your Ravens, but I know Salvatore's scent. Eventually I'll stumble over the dog."

"I don't doubt your skill, Jagr, but what of Regan?"

His jaw knotted as he ignored the clawing need to keep her at his side.

She was his mate, the woman meant to complete his life.

He would rather have his heart cut out than to allow her to leave without him.

But what choice did he have?

Unless Regan accepted his bond, he had no claim on her.

"You said you're taking her to Chicago," he said, his voice as empty as his soul.

Styx frowned. "I assumed you would go with us."

"Regan has no need of me. Not with you to protect her."

"She might not be willing to admit her need, but I saw the way that she clung to you when I entered."

Jagr clenched his fists at the searing memory of Regan snuggled against him.

"Only because she was feeling alone and vulnerable," he muttered, more to convince himself than Styx. The only thing more painful than disappointment was clinging to futile hope. "If she'd been in her right mind, she never would have turned to me."

Styx's sharp laugh echoed through the room. "Bloody hell, I thought I was ignorant when it came to females."

"Do you have a point?"

"A woman doesn't cling to a man like that just because she's lonely."

Jagr took a stiff step back, swallowing the urge to howl in despair. Damn Styx. If he was trying to rub salt in Jagr's wounds then he was doing a bang-up job.

"I will not discuss this with you, my lord."

"Fine." With a weary motion, Styx rubbed the muscles of his neck, reminding Jagr that the older vampire had endured his own share of wounds. "I would appreciate discovering if Salvatore has learned anything from the cur he is meeting. I have only one request." His lips twisted. "No, two requests."

Jagr was wary. Styx's last request had led him to being mated to a woman who didn't want him. He really didn't want any more.

"What are they?"

"The first is that you feed and rest before starting your hunt."

"And the last?"

"That you take Tane with you."

His lips thinned, but he readily dipped his head in agreement. The Anasso was merely being cautious.

"As you command." He took two agonizing steps toward the door before need overcame common sense, and he halted to turn back for one last glance at the woman who would forever be engraved on his heart. "Styx."

"Yes, my brother?"

"Take care of her."

Styx pressed his fist over his heart in a solemn pledge. "You have my word."

Levet was ten feet tall.

Okay, he wasn't *literally* ten feet tall. Not even mind-blowing sex could make him grow seven feet in two hours. But by God it went a long way in making him *feel* that big.

Lying beneath a tangle of bushes, he struggled to wipe the satisfied smile off his lips.

It had been a long time since he'd been with a woman who knew just how to stroke a gargoyle's horns. Oh, and the things Bella had done to his wings. It made his tail curl just to remember them.

Such a naughty water sprite.

A pity she had disappeared so abruptly. He might have been ridden hard and put up wet, but there was a chance he would recover before the sun crested. And when a demon had to wait centuries between sex, he couldn't afford to waste a single opportunity.

Debating the odds of finding Bella before dawn, Levet was floating on a delicious cloud of sated pleasure.

Or at least he was floating until the bushes were ruthlessly ripped aside and Salvatore's angry face was looming over him.

"Levet?"

With a squawk, Levet scrambled to his feet, not at all pleased to have been caught fantasizing like a horny teenager.

"*Sacrebleu,* did your mother never teach you not to sneak up on a gargoyle? I could have turned you into a steaming pile of dog poop."

The Were's lean features were hard with displeasure. Not unusual. The King was always displeased with something or other. Just like a stupid vampire. Only with fur.

"What are you doing skulking in the bushes?"

Levet didn't hesitate. There was a time for truth and a time for lies.

This was one of those lying times.

"I am keeping watch like you commanded, to make certain this is not a trap."

"Keeping watch?"

"*Oui.*"

Without warning, Salvatore grasped him by the horn and

plucked him off the ground, twirling him around as if he were a peculiar rock to be investigated, instead of a dignified demon.

Damned dog.

"Then why are you covered in mud?" the King demanded. "Do you not have anything better to do than barbeque me?"

"Barbeque?" Salvatore's brows snapped together. "*Cristo,* it's grill, not barbeque."

"Barbeque . . . grill . . . what is the difference?" Levet huffed. "Now put me down."

"You still haven't explained the mud." Salvatore leaned his head down to suck in a deep breath. "Or the fact that you reek of water sprite."

Levet folded his arms over his chest. "Hey, a gargoyle has to have some fun."

"Meaning that you allowed yourself to be distracted," Salvatore growled.

"There might have been the tiniest bit of distraction, but nothing could get by me, that I assure you."

"We shall see."

With a flip of his hand, Salvatore rudely dropped Levet back to the ground and turned to make his way easily up the steep bank. Stumbling behind with all the grace of a drunken sailor, Levet shifted through his mind for some spell that would shrink a Were's balls to marbles.

In the distance, he could smell the scent of Salvatore's curs spread throughout the surrounding woods, and something else. Something that smelled like . . . blood.

"*Cristo,*" Salvatore muttered, bolting toward the small cabin with a speed that Levet couldn't hope to match.

"What?" Huffing and puffing, Levet at last reached the open door. "What is it?"

Kneeling beside a lifeless cur that was fully shifted into wolf form, Salvatore turned his head to stab Levet with a glowing gaze.

"Nothing can get by you?" he growled. "How do you explain this?"

"*Mon Dieu,*" Levet breathed, stepping onto the bare wooden floor, although he stayed far away from the corpse.

Salvatore touched the cur's head in a soft benediction. "Duncan, I presume?"

"*Oui.*" Levet's stomach twisted. He hadn't liked the treacherous cur, but he would never have wished this on him. "He was fine just an hour ago."

"How long?"

"Well, perhaps it was closer to two or three hours ago."

"Worthless demon," Salvatore growled, returning his attention to the dead dog.

Levet flapped his wings. He wasn't taking the fall for this disaster. Even if he *was* responsible.

"Do I look like one of your sniveling curs?" he demanded. "No, I do not. I am here only as a favor to Regan, and if you think I am going to stand here and be insulted by a lice-infested, mangy dog, then you have another thing . . ."

"Shut up, and come here," Salvatore interrupted.

"Arrogant bastard."

"Levet."

Throwing up his hands, Levet waddled across the floor. "I am coming. Do not get your thong in a bunch."

Slashing him an impatient frown, Salvatore pointed at the lifeless cur.

"How did he die?"

Levet's tail twitched, warily wondering if the King had taken a recent blow to the head.

"Well, this is only a guess, but it might have something to do with that huge silver dagger sticking in his heart."

Salvatore hissed as he yanked the dagger free and tossed it across the barren room.

"If he'd been killed by silver, he would have shifted back

to human form. He was already dead when someone stuck the dagger in his heart."

Levet frowned. "Why would someone stick a dagger into a dead cur?"

"I'm more interested in how he died."

Holding out his hands, Levet circled the main room of the cabin, pausing at the stone fireplace, as well as the wooden table and chairs that were the only furniture.

"There's no hex marks or magic, at least not a spell directed at him." Sensing a faint tingle in the air, Levet hopped onto one of the chairs and grabbed the half-empty glass of wine that was left in the center of the table. "Can a cur be poisoned?"

Flowing to his feet, Salvatore studied the bottle of wine with a frown.

"Where did that come from?" he demanded.

"It was sitting on the table, along with the two glasses, when we arrived." Levet shuddered as the air thickened with Salvatore's power. "What is it?"

With glowing eyes, Salvatore pointed toward the hidden door that was swinging open near the fireplace.

"A trap."

A low, mocking laugh floated through the night. "And here I thought the King of Weres was all fangs and no brains."

Chapter 21

Drifting in some weird stage between sleep and vague awareness, Regan shifted on the wide bed and reached her hand out.

"Jagr?"

Her voice was no more than a ragged whisper, but there was a movement to the side, and the edge of the mattress dipped down as someone settled next to her.

"Not Jagr, I'm afraid. Just a sister who has longed to meet you."

Cracking her eyes open a bare slit, Regan stilled as she caught sight of the tiny heart-shaped face that was all too familiar.

Christ.

The woman looked just like her. Same blond hair, although Darcy's was cut short and spiked. The same green eyes. The same slender body. Even the same stubborn line of their jaw.

Twins without a doubt, but Regan suspected that the two of them would never be mistaken for one another.

It would take only a glance at Darcy's serene expression and sweet smile to recognize the difference.

There was nothing serene or sweet about Regan.

Careful not to jar her aching head, Regan scooted up the

pile of pillows and glanced around the gold and ivory room that seemed to go on forever.

Holy crap.

Everything was big.

Big and shiny.

Polished marble walls. Gilded furnishings. Cut crystal chandeliers. Hell, there was enough glitz and glitter to please Elton John.

Obviously Darcy liked her bling.

Regan . . . well, not so much.

Maybe it was her years of living in a trashy RV, but she felt unnerved lying beneath the cupids that danced across the vaulted ceiling. Talk about Versailles overkill.

"Where am I?"

Seeming almost as out of place among the elegance as Regan felt, Darcy tucked her feet beneath her as she settled more comfortably on the mattress. Certainly she didn't dress like a queen. Not with those faded jeans and oversized T-shirt.

"Styx brought you to Chicago so you could heal in safety."

"This is your home?"

"Yes." Darcy chewed her bottom lip, studying Regan's tight expression. "Please don't be angry with Styx. He only did what he thought best."

Yeah, big surprise there. Regan had known she was going to be hauled to Chicago the moment she called Styx and requested his help.

Everything had a price.

That didn't mean she had to like it.

"And he didn't consider asking my opinion?" she demanded dryly.

"You've spent the past few days in the company of a vampire." Darcy wrinkled her nose. "When do they ever ask for another's opinion?"

Well, hell, how could she argue with that logic? She rolled her eyes.

"I suppose there's always a chance hell will freeze over."

"A very remote chance."

Regan tilted her chin. "He should have at least waited until I was conscious."

Reaching out, Darcy grasped Regan's hand in a warm grasp. "The blame is mine, Regan. Styx knew how desperate I was to have you here, and he doesn't mind trampling over anyone in his quest to please me. I swear, a mated vampire should have to wear a blinking warning sign for the safety of others."

Mated vampire.

The image of a huge, blond, ruthlessly beautiful Visigoth chief scorched through her mind.

Regan flinched. She'd tried so hard to ignore the looming thoughts of Jagr.

So stupid.

He was a two hundred and fifty pound gorilla squatting smack-dab in the middle of her brain. She wouldn't be able to concentrate on anything until she knew he was all right.

"I suppose Jagr is here as well?" She tossed out the words as if she couldn't care less.

"Jagr?" Darcy frowned at the unexpected question. "Actually, I think he stayed in Hannibal to try and discover if Salvatore has any clues to finding our sister."

"Oh." Her gut twisted with disappointment. He wasn't even in Chicago. She hadn't seen that coming.

As if sensing Regan's distress, Darcy tugged a rolling table closer to the bed, and whipped aside the linen cloth that was covering it.

"I brought a tray. I thought you might be hungry after your healing."

"I'm starving," Regan admitted, knowing she needed to eat to regain her strength. Turning her head toward the tray, she grunted in disbelief. "Good God."

Darcy laughed. "I wasn't sure what you wanted."

Regan studied the mounds of eggs, ham, pancakes, fresh fruit, toast, fried potatoes, sausage links, and warm biscuits.

"So you brought everything?"

"I want you to feel at home, Regan."

Meeting the warm, welcoming gaze, Regan squirmed in discomfort. Dammit. Her sister was the sort of charming, captivating, completely adorable woman you couldn't help but love. But Regan didn't want to love her sister. Or feel the growing connection.

"I . . ."

"Eat," Darcy firmly interrupted. "You'll feel better."

Guilt and something that might've been misery swirled through her heart, reminding Regan of why she avoided emotional complications. She was bound to disappoint Darcy.

And Jagr.

Blinking back ridiculous tears, Regan took a plate and filled it with a large helping of the eggs and ham and sausage. She would need protein to finish healing the last of her wounds that remained an angry red beneath the satin nightgown.

Freaking silver.

She still felt as weak as a newborn babe.

Strangely vulnerable, Regan wolfed down her food, her eyes darting about the monstrosity of a bedroom rather than meeting Darcy's worried gaze.

"Yes, I know. It's outrageous, isn't it?" Darcy murmured, her hand sweeping to indicate the acres of gilt and ivory. "And as hard as it is to believe, the rest of the mansion is even worse."

"It's certainly not what I'm used to."

"Me either. I grew up in the streets, and Styx lived in a damp cave for centuries." She softly chuckled. "The poor man tiptoes through the place as if he's terrified he's going to break something."

Draining a glass of orange juice, Regan shot her sister a puzzle glance.

"If you don't like it, why do you live here?"

"Viper convinced me that the King of Vampires should own a suitably impressive lair. Someday I'm going to repay him for his helpful suggestion." A small, dangerous smile curved her mouth. "Although I might give the honor to Shay. She does a fine job of punishing him when necessary."

"Shay?"

"His mate. She's a Shalott demon and quite capable of keeping her clan chief in line." Darcy's smile widened. "You're going to love her. And of course there's Abby, who is mated to Dante. She's a goddess. Oh, and Anna is an Oracle, she's mated to Cezar."

Regan polished off the last of the food and returned the plate to the tray, sinking back into the pillows with a small sigh of contentment.

Already she could feel her energy returning. Within a few days she would be well enough to strike out on her own.

That's all that mattered.

And that hollow place in the center of her heart . . .

Well, that was one of those prices she had to pay.

"You lost me at Shalott," she said, anxious to distract her dark thoughts.

"Don't worry, you'll meet everyone in time. Including our mother. She's . . ." Darcy paused to clear her throat. "Perhaps I should let you decide for yourself."

Christ, she'd forgotten there was a mother hovering in the background.

"That sounds ominous."

Darcy shrugged. "Just expect more Sharon Osbourne than June Cleaver."

"I don't expect anything." Regan made her tone deliberately firm. The last thing she wanted was meeting a whole posse of vampire mates who were no doubt deliriously happy. Not to mention a mother she didn't want. "I won't be around long enough to meet her."

There was a pause as Darcy struggled to disguise her disappointment.

"Are you going somewhere?"

"Oh, you know, places to go, people to see."

Regan tried to lighten the atmosphere, but Darcy's expression remained somber.

"I hope you'll feel as if this is your home now, Regan. There's no hurry for you to leave."

"No hurry?" Regan couldn't hide her shudder. "I've been stuck in a cage for the past thirty years. I need . . ."

"What?"

"To feel free."

Darcy tilted her head to the side. "And you can't do that here?"

"I don't know."

"Regan." Once again Darcy reached out to grasp Regan's hand, as if she needed the physical contact. "Styx told me about Caine. How he kidnapped us when we were just babies."

Regan stiffened at the mention of the cur who'd ruined her life.

"Bastard."

"Yes, but my point is that you weren't abandoned by your family. If I had known you were out there and in trouble . . ."

"Darcy, I don't blame you for what happened," Regan interrupted the soft words.

Darcy frowned. "Then why do you want to leave?"

Regan sighed, struggling to find the words to explain the annoying sensation of panic that wouldn't leave her in peace.

"Because I've been a prisoner all my life. I'm not ready for any more chains."

"Chains?"

She squeezed Darcy's fingers, sensing her sister's pain at the stumbled explanation.

"I'm sorry, but the thought of a family and home feels like

shackles to me. I need space to discover who I am, and who I can be."

"Then I will try to be patient, dear sister," Darcy ruefully conceded defeat. "But I'm going to warn you that it won't be easy."

Regan licked her lips, studying Darcy's unmistakable air of contentment.

"Don't you ever feel trapped?"

"Trapped? Never." Shock widened the eyes so similar to Regan's. "Styx completes me."

A pang of unmistakable envy clenched Regan's heart. God, why couldn't she let it be that simple?

Why couldn't she just accept what others were so willing to offer?

She restlessly shook her head. "I'm sorry, I have no right to pry."

"You're not prying, and even if you were, you have every right. We're family." Darcy smiled sweetly. "Regan, you have to understand, my childhood was one of constant loneliness and the fear I would never truly belong anywhere. I didn't know what I was or why I was so different, so I could never let anyone close, in case they realized I was . . . abnormal. And then Styx came crashing into my life, and I learned that I was a Were, if a rather dysfunctional one. I also learned I wasn't alone. There are all sorts of wonderful, weird, and wacky demons in the world."

Regan snorted. "We can at least agree to that."

"I, at last, have a family who loves me exactly as I am, and it's everything to me." Darcy leaned down to brush a light kiss on Regan's troubled brow. "I want you to share in that joy."

Regan's heart gave another twist of envy. "Perhaps someday."

"You're tired." Slipping off the bed, Darcy tucked the covers around Regan's shivering body. "We can speak later."

Regan snuggled into the pillows. "Thank you."

Darcy crossed the room, pausing at the door. "Regan, always know you have a place with me."

Regan gave an absent nod, but she knew her place wasn't here.

But if not here, then where?

Wrapped in the icy composure that had held his demons at bay for centuries, Jagr followed Tane's shadowed form through the dark trees that lined the Mississippi River.

It wasn't that his soul didn't howl for Regan, who'd been carted off to Chicago hours ago. Or that his instincts weren't raw with the need to follow her and force the bond that pulsed through his blood.

But his past had taught him the necessary skills to survive even the most brutal pain.

Until he could return to his lair and lick his wounds in private, he would simply endure.

As always.

Walking a step ahead of Jagr, Tane came to a sudden halt, holding up his hand as he scented the damp night air.

"Hold," he warned, his voice audible only to another vampire. "Curs. One of them dead."

Jagr stepped beside his companion. They had been searching for Salvatore along the banks of the Mississippi for the past three hours.

It was about damned time they caught a break.

"Hess," Jagr growled, recognizing the pungent scent.

Tane's nose flared in disgust. The Charon had little love for dogs.

"You know them?"

"Salvatore's mangy courtiers." Jagr sent his senses flowing through the isolated area, a frown touching his brow. "But no Salvatore. Interesting."

Tane grunted as four fully shifted curs came crashing through the trees.

"Or lethal."

Jagr released a blast of frigid power, knocking the charging animals backwards.

"Stand down, dogs," he snapped.

The curs snapped and snarled in frustration, but as they slowly realized they were no match for two powerful vampires, they at last shimmered and shifted back to human form.

It was the hulking, bald-headed cur who took charge, glaring at Jagr as he stood completely naked among the tangled underbrush.

"Where's our king?" he rasped, sounding more wolf than human.

"Do I look like a nanny for a damned Were?" Tane drawled, absently twirling the large silver dagger he held in his hand. "You're his guard. Isn't it your job to keep track of him?"

"Tane." Jagr gave a shake of his head. He wasn't in the mood to play with the curs. He wanted to discover if Salvatore had any information on Regan's sister, and be done with the entire mess. He turned his head to meet Hess's glowing gaze. "What happened?"

Hess gritted his teeth, but obviously judging that Jagr was there to help, he jerked his head toward the cabin set in a clearing just on top of the ridge.

"Salvatore was to meet with Duncan in the cabin. He went in with the gargoyle and never came out."

"Levet is missing as well?" Jagr demanded, his thoughts instantly turning to Regan's bizarre fondness for the stupid beast. "Damn."

Tane arched a raven brow. "I didn't know you cared."

Jagr shrugged. "Nothing would please me more than to send the stunted pain in the ass back to the gutter he crawled out of. Unfortunately, he's a favorite of the Anasso's mate."

"And your own mate?" Tane demanded.

Jagr flinched at the unexpected stab of pain, swiftly returning his attention to the wary Hess.

"A pureblood and a gargoyle can't just disappear," he accused. "You saw nothing?"

Hess gritted his teeth, looking as if he were in dire need of some bloody, mindless violence to take the edge off.

"I saw nothing."

Accepting that Hess was clueless, Jagr brushed past the curs and made his way to the cabin. Tane was quickly at his side, his gaze sweeping the ground with the expertise of a trained hunter.

"Footprints going in." Tane pointed to the two sets of tracks.

"And none going out," Jagr muttered, easily detecting the scents of Salvatore and Levet. They'd entered the cabin together and neither had left. Turning his head, Jagr stabbed the towering cur with a narrow gaze. "Are there any tunnels?"

Hess gave a shake of his head, tugging on the jeans he'd left near the door.

"Salvatore borrowed the cabin from the St. Louis pack master. I don't know about any tunnels."

Jagr growled with impatience. The cur's talent as a king's guard clearly wasn't his keen intelligence.

"Is the pack master a pureblood?"

"Yes."

"Then there's a tunnel. You and your merry band of idiots—keep watch. I won't be pleased with any unexpected visitors."

"Don't give me orders." Hess snapped his fangs, his hands curled into fists large enough to smash a small car. Hell, maybe a midsize. "The others can keep watch, I'm coming with you."

Only Jagr's swift reflexes saved the damned cur's life. Catching Tane's arm as he surged toward Hess, Jagr gave the younger vampire a warning shake of his head.

Once Salvatore was found, Tane could snack on as many

curs as he wanted. For now, they might have need of Hess's considerable muscle, if not his less than considerable brain.

"Fine, just stay out of the way," he warned.

Allowing the grumbling Tane to take the lead, Jagr entered the shadowed cabin, his instincts screaming as he moved toward the dead cur in the middle of the floor. His brows snapped together as a shiver inched down his spine.

What the hell?

It couldn't be the heavy scent of death that made his nerves twitch, or his fangs lengthen. Death was his stock in trade. So what was it?

Bending beside the lifeless cur, Jagr allowed his senses to flow outward, his frown deepening at the strange prickles that filled the air.

It was almost as if lightning had recently struck.

Inside the cabin.

With a shake of his head, Jagr lifted his head to watch Tane circle the room.

"Well?"

"There are tunnels." The younger vampire briefly closed his eyes. "Headed west."

Jagr straightened, gesturing toward the hovering cur. "Start looking for a trapdoor."

In silence, the three scoured the cramped cabin, seeking the entrance to the tunnels. It was at last Tane who discovered the hidden door at the side of the fireplace.

"Here."

Not bothering to seek the lever that would open the door, Tane swung his arm and knocked the panel loose.

Instantly, the scent of Were blood filled the air.

With a howl, Hess charged forward, obviously intent on storming into the dark tunnel with mindless fury.

"Salvatore."

Jagr grasped the cur by the neck and tossed him against a far wall.

"Dammit, if you can't control yourself, then find me someone who can. Salvatore needs his guards to rescue him, not a pack of rabid beasts attracting unwanted attention."

Hess banged his head against the wall, the muscles of his thick neck corded, his eyes squeezed shut as he battled the instinctive urge to shift.

At last he sucked in a ragged breath and rose to his feet. His eyes still glowed with an eerie light, but his expression was one of grim control.

"I won't fail him."

With a snort of disgust, Tane studied the hidden door that led to the tunnel buried nearly six feet beneath the ground.

"There's the smell of curs, and something . . ." The golden features that spoke of South Pacific islands hardened with annoyance. "Else."

Jagr joined his companion near the fireplace. "Witch?"

"Demon."

"That covers a lot of territory."

"That's as close as I can get." Tane shook his head. "I know it's a demon and that it's female, but . . ."

"But?"

"I don't know what kind."

Jagr shrugged. A demon would explain the oddly charged air around the dead cur. There were a few species that could call powers that were remarkably like a jolt of electricity. It might even be what had killed Duncan.

"Maybe it's a mongrel," he suggested. "They always leave a confusing scent."

Tane smiled with a lethal intent. "There's only one way to find out."

Jagr stilled. "You intend to follow the trail?"

"I have nothing better to do at the moment."

There was a growl from behind Jagr. "Not without me and the others," Hess foolishly challenged. "Our lives are pledged to protecting our king."

"And you're doing a real bang-up job," Tane mocked. Then astonishingly, the vampire muttered a curse and gave a wave of his hand. "Shit. Get your dogs and try to keep up."

Hess was smart enough not to press his luck, and spinning on his heel, he ran from the cabin to collect the other curs. Alone with Tane, Jagr leaned against the edge of the fireplace.

"There's no need for you to do this, Tane. Styx gave the duty of finding Salvatore to me."

Tane sheathed his dagger and pulled a leather cord from the pocket of his khaki shorts to tie back his long raven hair.

"Which only confirms my belief that a vampire loses all higher brain functions when he becomes mated," he drawled.

True enough. Regan had stolen any hope of coherent reasoning days ago. Of course, agreeing with Tane didn't mean Jagr was going to stand around and be mocked by a vampire half his age.

"I'm not sure if you're insulting Styx's judgment, or my skills."

Tane shrugged. "Both."

"I always heard that Charons had a death wish."

"Return to Chicago, Jagr. Until the woman takes you as a mate, you're going to be worthless."

Jagr's hard, humorless laugh echoed through the barren cabin.

"Thanks."

"You know I'm right."

Of course Jagr knew. He wasn't stupid, despite his lack of higher brain functions. Regan was a constant, endless distraction. A distraction could mean the difference between life and death when confronting an enemy.

But what the hell was he to do?

Lock himself in his lair and mold into a hermit?

He shoved away from the door and paced toward the center of the room.

"You may be right, but since the woman has no intention of taking me as a mate, I might as well . . ." Cutting off his words, Jagr turned to glare at the young vampire who had tossed back his head to laugh with obvious enjoyment. "You find something amusing?"

Tane met Jagr's burning gaze without flinching. "I'm trying to decide if you're blind or just a fool."

Jagr stepped forward, his jaw clenched. "You really do have a death wish."

"Shit, Jagr, that woman nearly sets the air on fire when she's in the same room with you. I'm afraid I might get singed if I get too close."

Jagr grunted at the painful blast of memories. Regan in his arms. Her nails digging into his back. Her soft moans brushing over his skin.

Tiny slices of paradise that would have to last him for the rest of eternity.

"I don't doubt her desire, but we both know that it takes more than lust to form the mating bond," he said, his voice thick.

"Thank the gods," Tane muttered, referring to his own insatiable desire, before his expression become somber and he reached out to lay a hand on Jagr's shoulder. "Look, old man, there are few demons who have more experience with desire in all its delightful forms than I do, and I know when a female is simply in heat. I've never had a woman look at me the way Regan looks at you. She might not admit it yet, but she's yours." He gave Jagr a smack on the back. "Go back to Chicago and claim her."

Jagr took a sharp step backward, shaking his head against the agonizing need that clamored to heed Tane's words.

God dammit.

Was the vampire trying to send him over the edge?

He'd done everything in his power to earn Regan's heart. And deep in his gut, he was certain she did love him.

But after years of being held captive, she wasn't capable of bonding herself to anyone.

Let alone to an overly possessive, overly arrogant vampire who was consumed with his need for her.

And in many ways, he couldn't blame her. He remembered his own bleak days after escaping Kesi. The last thing he could have endured was a mate who depended on him for her every happiness.

"I can't force her to become my mate."

Tane flashed a wicked smile. "No, but you can remind her what she's missing."

They were thankfully interrupted by the sound of approaching footsteps, and turning his head, Jagr watched the gang of curs troop into the cabin, all fully dressed and loaded with enough firepower to take out the Pentagon.

"We're ready." Hess stated the obvious.

Tane muttered his opinion of working with stinking dogs, but with a wry grimace, he moved toward the doorway and stairs that led into the waiting tunnel.

"Then let's do this."

Chapter 22

Left alone in the cabin, Jagr briefly considered his options.

He could always join Tane on the trail of Salvatore.

The ease that Caine had revealed in kidnapping a pureblood of Salvatore's strength proved the cur (or whoever the hell was behind this latest disaster) was a dangerous adversary. And who the hell knew what damage the unknown demon could cause?

Unfortunately, he knew that Tane was right.

In this moment, he wasn't capable of concentrating on the hunt.

Not with his emotions unstable and his thoughts consumed with Regan.

Humiliating, but true.

His only other option was to return to Tane's lair.

It was far too late to attempt the journey to Chicago before dawn. And if he was being perfectly honest, he wasn't prepared to make his appearance at Styx's and give his latest report.

Not when Regan was bound to be there.

His need was still too raw. If he caught scent of her, there was nothing that would keep him from tossing her over his shoulder and hauling her to his lair, whether she liked it or not.

Something he was trying to avoid.

Besides, he was weary to the bone.

He needed to rest and feed.

His decision made, Jagr followed the trail back to Tane's remote lair, careful to choose a room far from the one he shared with Regan. The aching emptiness was bad enough without being surrounded by the vivid reminders of their time together.

Forcing himself to feed, Jagr endured the worried questions of Tane's servants, and then managed a few hours' rest.

He was pacing the floor by the time the sun at last set again, and the moment he judged it safe, he was speeding out of the lair and heading to Chicago.

The journey was thankfully tedious, and heading directly to Styx's sprawling mansion north of the city, he was taken to the Anasso's private office.

Now he sat on a low leather sofa and watched as Styx paced from one end of the book-lined room to the other.

"Damn. These curs are starting to wear on my temper," the towering Aztec muttered as Jagr finished his report, appearing distinctly out of place among the polished mahogany furniture and delicate Persian carpet. A six-foot-five leather-clad bull in a china shop. "Someone needs to nail their hides to a wall."

Jagr's lips twisted as he considered Salvatore's reaction to being kidnapped. The proud Were was no doubt ready to declare genocide on the curs.

"I would guess that you're not alone in wanting to nail a few cur hides to the wall," he said dryly. "Unfortunately, they constantly seem to be one step ahead of us."

Styx made a sound of disgust, his hands clenched at his side as if wishing he had a weapon to seize.

"Could you sense how badly Salvatore was injured?"

Jagr shrugged. "Not so badly he should have been overcome by a mere cur."

"Was there magic?"

"Tane could sense a female demon, but he couldn't determine a species. It could have magical abilities."

Styx halted near his massive desk, his brow furrowed with frustration.

"I don't like this. Tane could be walking into a trap."

"If you want, I'll return and . . ."

"No, you've done enough, my brother," Styx interrupted. "I'll contact Tane, although I might as well ram my head into a wall as try to convince him to return to Hannibal. The vampire terrifies even me when he's on the hunt."

Jagr didn't doubt it. There was an intensity about Tane that would frighten anyone.

"I assume that's why you chose him as a Charon."

"One of the reasons."

Jagr grimaced. "I don't think I want to know the others."

"Wise choice." Styx folded his arms over his chest. "There was no sign of Levet?"

Surprisingly, Jagr felt a small pang of remorse at the disappearance of the aggravating gargoyle. Not that he actually cared if the beast was dead, he hastily assured himself. He couldn't have gone that soft in the head. It was just that he couldn't bear the thought of Regan mourning for one of her few friends.

"We know he went into the cabin and didn't come out," he admitted.

Styx leaned against the desk, his expression weary. "Bloody hell, Darcy's not going to be happy. Not only have I lost track of her sister, but that ridiculous gargoyle has disappeared. Why she's attached herself to that annoying lump of granite defies logic, but then she's a woman. They very rarely make sense."

Jagr snorted. What was the latest saying . . . preaching to the choir . . .

"You won't get an argument from me," he muttered.

"No, I don't suppose I would." Styx paused, his gaze unnervingly perceptive. "Regan is here."

Jagr clenched the arms of his chair until the wood threatened to crack beneath the pressure.

He didn't need Styx to warn him of Regan's presence. He'd sensed her like a punch in the gut the moment he stepped onto the rolling parkland that surrounded the mansion.

Thankfully, the large office was hexed to ensure privacy, and the familiar scent of midnight jasmine was muted enough to ease the stark yearning that plagued him.

"I know." He turned his head to stare at the leather-bound books that filled the shelves. He couldn't bear to see the sympathy in Styx's eyes. "She's . . . well?"

"She's healing," Styx said slowly. "At least physically."

Unable to halt the biting concern, Jagr snapped his head back to stab Styx with a narrowed glare.

"Is something wrong?"

Styx tugged on the ancient medallion hung around his neck. A sure sign he was troubled.

"I may not possess Viper's skill in reading the souls of others, but I know Regan carries a burden that darkens her heart."

Jagr struggled not to overreact.

Bad, bad things happened when he overreacted.

"She was just released from hell. She needs time to heal."

"Shutting herself off from those who would help her isn't healing," Styx growled, clearly annoyed that Regan wasn't embracing her new family with the eagerness he'd hoped for. "I should know. I spent centuries wandering alone and miserable. It wasn't until the previous Anasso took me as his servant that I could accept the brutality of my past, and begin to consider a future."

Although Jagr had never heard Styx speak of his past, the Anasso was old enough to have endured the chaos and violence that was common among the vampires in ancient times. Back then, a newly made vampire rarely survived more than a few years.

Something that Styx had dedicated his life to changing.

Jagr slowly rose to his feet. He was weary and in need of the peace of his lair.

"Who's to say that if the Anasso had approached you any earlier you would have been prepared to join him?" he demanded with a wry smile. "Perhaps our master was wise enough to wait until you could accept a place as his chosen."

Styx arched a brow. "And Viper told me you were just another pretty face. Obviously all those years of scholarly research wasn't a complete waste."

Jagr's sharp laugh echoed through the room. "I wouldn't jump to any hasty conclusions. I can be remarkably stupid when I put my mind to it."

Styx moved to stand directly before him. "What will you do now?"

"In the next few moments, or with the rest of my existence?"

Styx flashed his rare smile. "You are in a philosophical mood tonight."

"It must be the ambiance."

"Gods, don't remind me." Styx shuddered as he cast a disgusted glance around the ornate, elegant furnishings before returning his attention to Jagr. "Are you returning to your lair?"

"For now."

"There's no need for you to be alone, you know. Viper called earlier with an invitation for you to join him and Shay. And, of course, you are always welcome here."

Jagr narrowed his gaze at the low, almost commanding tone. Why the hell would Styx care where he stayed? God knew he'd been left alone in his lair for years without . . .

Comprehension struck like a bolt of lightning, and Jagr stiffened in humiliation.

"Ah, Regan told you about my bout of madness," he gritted. "Are you afraid I might ravage Chicago?"

Styx allowed a hint of his power to flow over Jagr, the prickle of energy a painful reminder of the Anasso's strength.

"If I feared you were mad then you would be locked in a cell, not sipping my finest brandy in the lair I share with my mate." As swiftly as the punishment began, it came to a halt, and Styx reached out to lay a hand on Jagr's shoulder. "My only concern is for your happiness, my brother."

Jagr gave a shake of his head, spinning away from the disturbing compassion etched on the vampire's face.

Dammit. Just a few weeks ago he'd been a nearly forgotten vampire living beneath the streets of Chicago. An eccentric loner who possessed the nasty sort of reputation to keep others away.

And that was exactly how he had liked it.

Then without warning, he'd been dragged kicking and screaming back into a world filled with clan brothers, vampire politics, and a beautiful Were that had breathed life back into his frozen soul.

He wasn't sure if he wanted to stick a stake in Styx's heart, or fall to his knees and bless him.

Maybe both.

"I need . . . distance," he at last admitted.

"From Regan?"

"Yes."

There was a long silence, then Styx moved to take his seat behind the desk.

"You could leave Chicago if you want," he said smoothly.

"Not without fighting every clan chief whose territory I enter. That's why I approached Viper in the first place."

"As one of my Ravens, you could travel the world without fear of being challenged by other vampires."

Jagr jerked around, meeting Styx's steady gaze with an undisguised shock.

Holy hell. He hadn't seen that coming.

"A Raven?"

Styx leaned back in the chair, his fingers steepled beneath his chin as he studied Jagr.

"It's rare that I find a warrior of your skill and loyalty. When I do, I'm smart enough to insist upon their service."

"Loyalty?" Jagr shook his head, wondering if the man was suffering from dementia. What else could possess the usually intelligent vampire to make such a dangerous offer? "In case you've forgotten, I don't follow orders."

"Loyalty is different from blind obedience," Styx countered. "I often send out my Ravens on delicate tasks. I need soldiers who can think for themselves and make decisions when they can't contact me."

Jagr snorted. "I'm about as delicate as a war hammer."

"Sometimes a mission takes a rapier, and sometimes it takes a war hammer." Styx tapped his fingers on the glossy surface of the desk. "It's my job to determine which weapon is needed."

"And my bouts of madness?" he demanded. "They are rare, but . . ."

"They are no more than any other demon battles, including myself," Styx overrode his argument.

Jagr shook his head.

A Raven.

A part of him wanted to laugh at the sheer absurdity.

He was a half-feral vampire who had devoted his first centuries to hating those who'd tortured him, and the last few centuries hating the beast he'd become.

Now, the King of Vampires was offering him a position of highest respect among the demon-world.

Talk about irony.

But another part of him, the part he'd kept closed off until Regan had smashed into his life, was strangely tempted by the offer.

He'd always depended on his studies to give him a sense of

purpose. The gaining of knowledge was not only fascinating, but it was as lethal a weapon as his sword or daggers.

Besides, there was a quiet peace to be found in his vast library. And of course, the bonus of knowing his books weren't going to try to kill him.

Now, however, he couldn't help but wonder if it was time he put an end to his self-imposed exile.

Without undue vanity, he knew he was one of the most powerful vampires to walk the earth. And his vast studies gave him insights into both the human and demon-world that few others could claim.

Skills that would serve the Anasso well.

More importantly, becoming a Raven might offer an opportunity to devote his mind to something other than mourning the absence of his mate.

As if sensing his conflicting emotions, Styx rose from his seat and rounded the desk to stand directly in front of Jagr.

"Don't answer now. Take your time to consider the offer," he commanded. "It will always be there."

"Thank you, my lord." Jagr offered a dip of his head. "I should go."

"Of course, you must be anxious to return to your lair." Waiting until Jagr had reached the door, Styx cleared his throat. "Be warned that Viper will be intruding into your privacy, along with Dante and Cezar."

Jagr glanced over his shoulder with a frown. "Why?"

Styx shrugged. "Because they're meddlesome mother hens."

"Great."

Knowing the Anasso would do nothing to save him from the impending interference of his brothers, Jagr stepped out of the office, instantly hit with the potent scent of jasmine.

On cue, his fangs lengthened and his muscles clenched in desperate, clawing need.

Shit.

He had to get out of there.

* * *

Regan knew the minute that Jagr entered the house.

Amazing considering that she'd been verging on sleep miles away (or at least it seemed like miles), in a bedroom at the far wing of the mansion.

Or maybe not so amazing, she wryly acknowledged as she yanked on a pair of faded jeans and a yellow T-shirt.

After all, it wasn't the sound of his voice or his erotic scent that had jerked her from her light slumber. No, it had been the cool wash of power that had filled the entire mansion that had her hastily dressing and hurrying through the silent hallways.

It had to be Jagr.

Regan rushed down the long flight of stairs, only to discover that Jagr had disappeared into Styx's private office. With a muttered curse, she plopped down on the last step, prepared to wait the entire night if necessary.

Why she was prepared wait was a question that should have troubled her.

Thankfully, she was developing a fine talent for self-deception, and telling herself that she was simply anxious to know if he discovered anything about her missing sister, she gnawed on her thumbnail and pretended her heart wasn't lodged somewhere in her throat.

Her abused nail was nearly gone by the time the door to the office at last opened and Jagr stepped from the room. Hidden by the carved oak banister, Regan felt as if the wind had been kicked from her.

Christ, did he have to be so damned beautiful?

Struggling to breathe, Regan allowed her gaze to drink in the pale, starkly carved features and golden hair that was pulled into a long braid.

Beautiful, but so terrifyingly dangerous.

In more ways than one.

Lost in the painful tangle of emotions, it took a moment for

Regan to realize that Jagr was headed directly toward the back entrance.

Why, the annoying jerk.

He had to know she was just behind him.

Hell, he could probably close his eyes and hit her with a dart a hundred miles away.

Which meant that he was deliberately ignoring her.

And why wouldn't he, a tiny voice whispered in the back of her mind.

He was a proud, magnificent vampire who had offered her his heart. She, on the other hand, was a totally screwed-up Were who was running scared.

She wouldn't blame him if he never wanted to see her again.

Of course, that didn't stop her from charging after his retreating form.

Screwed up, indeed.

"Jagr, wait."

He halted at her soft call, his shoulders stiff, as if he were battling the urge to keep walking.

Then, with obvious reluctance, he slowly turned to face her.

"Regan." His expression was as coldly aloof as his voice. "How are you feeling?"

She sucked in an agonized breath. God, she would rather he hit her than treat her as if she were a vague stranger.

"I'm fine," she managed to husk. "Did you just return from Hannibal?"

"Yes."

Sharp. To the point.

Emotionless.

Regan licked her dry lips, her gut twisting with sick regret.

"Did you discover anything about my sister?"

"No, I'm sorry." The pale eyes darkened with frustration. "Salvatore disappeared, along with Levet."

"Damn." Regan stiffened in shock, momentarily forgetting her own troubles. "Did Duncan betray them?"

"I doubt it. Duncan was dead when we found the cabin where they were supposed to meet."

Regan pressed a hand to her heart. It was bad enough that the cur was dead, and the powerful Salvatore missing, but poor Levet . . .

Christ, she should never have insisted that he accompany Duncan to that damn meeting.

She couldn't seem to do anything without messing it up lately.

The Mess-Up Queen.

She should have a tiara and sash.

"It has to be Caine," she muttered.

"That's our assumption."

"That bastard needs to have his ass kicked."

Jagr shrugged, his hard muscles rippling beneath the tight black T-shirt.

Oy. He was edible.

Her mouth went dry.

"I believe Styx intends to nail his hide to the wall."

"That'll work."

"Tane's on the trail. I'm sure he'll let Styx know if he discovers anything." With a stiff nod, Jagr turned back toward the door.

Let him go, let him go, let him go . . .

"Are you leaving?" The words bypassed her brain and burst from her lips.

Once again, he grudgingly halted and turned. "I have my own lair. Or at least I did." Without warning, that almost smile touched his lips, making her heart kick against her ribs. "The rats may have taken over while I was gone."

Tentatively she moved toward him, half-afraid he might disappear into the night if she pressed too hard.

"They wouldn't dare."

He arched a golden brow. "You're obviously unfamiliar with the rats native to Chicago. They fear no demon."

"Perhaps no demon, but every creature fears an oversized Visigoth chief."

His gaze deliberately skimmed over her pale face, lingering on the dark shadows beneath her eyes.

"Not every creature."

"Well, I've never been very smart. If I had a brain, I'd no doubt be terrified."

The stunning blue gaze lowered to her lips, his jaw clenching, as if in pain.

"I should go."

Her hand lifted to touch him, only to hastily drop when he took a sharp step back.

"Will you be back?"

"Not unless Styx commands my presence."

She swallowed the thick lump in her throat. "Oh."

There was a tense, awkward silence that made Regan want to ram her head into the wall.

Before tonight she'd felt a lot of things when Jagr was near.

Fury, frustration, searing passion, and heart-melting tenderness.

Never, ever awkwardness.

What the hell had she done?

Slowly his gaze lifted to tangle with hers. "Do you intend to remain here?"

"No. I . . ." She gave a helpless shrug, unable to explain the stupid panic that attacked her each time Darcy tried to draw her deeper into their cozy clan. "No."

"Where will you go?"

For all her determination to leave, she'd given remarkably little thought to the tedious details.

"I can't go far. At least not until I've found a job and saved some money."

His brows snapped together. Regan found herself pathetically pleased by the first real display of emotion.

"There's no need for you to work . . ."

"Darcy's already offered me money," she hurriedly headed off his offer.

"Which you refused."

"I'm not just being stubborn, Jagr."

"Did I say you were?" he snapped.

"You didn't have to," she ruefully teased. "It was written in neon across your face."

His scowl remained firmly intact. "Highly doubtful."

She sighed, running a restless hand through her hair. "I want to see if I can make my way in the world like a normal person. Is that so astonishing?"

The brief glimpse of emotion was wiped away. Replaced by a coating of ice.

"You'll never be a normal person."

"Fine, like a normal demon." She clenched her hands, wishing she could make someone, anyone, understand. "I need to know I can do it."

"Who are you trying to convince, Regan?" he demanded, softly. "Me? Or yourself?"

"I'm trying to explain . . ." She shook her head. "Never mind."

The tightening of his jaw was Jagr's only response as he turned on his heel.

"I must go."

"Jagr."

"Dammit, Regan, what do you want from me?" he hissed, keeping his back to her.

A good question.

Unfortunately, she didn't have a damned clue.

She only knew that watching him walk away was ripping out her heart.

"I . . . I want to thank you."

He stiffened, still refusing to turn. "Thank me?"

"If it hadn't been for you, I would have walked straight into the trap that Sadie set for me."

"Somehow I doubt you would have been so easily captured," he said dryly.

Her lips twisted. Her pride might want to believe his words, but she'd had plenty of time to consider her rash flight to Hannibal.

"I appreciate your confidence in my skills, but we both know I was so consumed with my need for revenge, I wasn't thinking clearly. If it hadn't been for you I . . ."

"I don't need your gratitude, Regan," he unexpectedly intruded, his voice harsh. "Just take care of yourself."

And with that, he was wrenching open the door and disappearing into the waiting shadows.

Stunned by his abrupt departure, Regan grasped a nearby marble statue as her knees threatened to buckle.

Every instinct screamed at her to run after Jagr and wrap her arms around him. To beg him to toss her over his shoulder, and cart her to his hidden lair.

To . . .

With a crack loud enough to wake the dead, the arm of the statue snapped off in her hand. With a muttered curse, she hastily tossed the dismembered limb onto the floor.

"God, I'm such an idiot."

Chapter 23

One month later . . .

The quaint pub near Wrigley Field was the trendy sort of place that attracted locals, as well as a number of tourists who came for the hot wings and stayed for the cold beer.

Regan had quite literally stumbled across the joint when she'd been on the search for a place to live, and before she knew it, she'd rented one of the retro-shabby apartments above the pub and was working as a dishwasher to supplement the money that Darcy had adamantly insisted she take before leaving the mansion.

Not that she regretted her choice.

The owner of the building and pub, Tobi Williams, was a tiny, thirty-something woman with short, spiky pink hair, dark eyes, and enough piercings to make a metal detector explode.

In many ways she reminded Regan of her sister. She was perky, incurably optimistic, and yet a shrewd enough businesswoman to have taken a dilapidated building she'd inherited from her father and turned it into a raging success.

She also had a heart as big as Chicago.

Within two days of Regan moving in, Tobi had not only

offered her a job washing dishes, but she'd badgered and hounded Regan to allow her to sell the drawings that Regan had created to fill her long, lonely nights.

Regan had been reluctant at first.

The simple ink-on-canvas etchings of local streets and various tourist spots were more doodles than masterpieces. Who the hell would waste their hard-earned money on them?

Only a week later, however, Tobi had managed to sell ten of the smaller etchings and four of the larger ones, handing over a wad of cash that Regan had promptly stashed into her nest egg. Now she could barely keep up with the demand.

Stacking away the last of the dishes, Regan wiped down the stainless steel sinks. It was well past midnight and the kitchen had shut down an hour ago. The bar would stay open until three a.m., but Regan's duties were done.

Still, she made no move to climb the back steps to her apartment.

It wasn't that she didn't love her new home, she grimly assured herself.

Granted it was small, with *Brady Bunch* furnishings and the constant smell of hot wings, but it was hers. Completely and utterly hers.

Proof positive of her independence.

Yippee kiyah.

Trying to shake her strange sense of melancholy, Regan jerked off the large apron that covered her cotton shorts and skimpy T-shirt. The Illinois weather had taken a turn toward spring, and standing in front of a hot, steaming sink for hours didn't help. If it wouldn't have shocked the natives, she would come to work wearing nothing.

She'd just tossed the apron into the laundry basket when the swinging doors were shoved open, and Tobi danced into the kitchen waving around a small business card.

"I told you, I told you, I told you," she sang as she twirled to a halt directly in front of Regan.

Regan rolled her eyes at her friend's antics. "Christ, Tobi, you're making me dizzy."

Tobi flashed her charming grin, looking about sixteen in her polka dot sundress that revealed her numerous tattoos.

"I told you."

"Yes, well, you've told me that the old man who lives in 4B is actually an alien who missed his ride home on the mother ship. You told me that terrorists are training sharks to attack our beaches. And that your dead mother communicates to you through tea leaves," Regan said dryly. "You're going to have to be a bit more specific."

"Here."

Taking the card that Tobi shoved into her hand, Regan studied the gilt name etched onto the expensive card paper.

"Charles Rosewood." With a frown, she lifted her head to meet Tobi's expectant gaze. "What's this?"

"He's waiting for you at the bar."

"Why would he be waiting for me?"

"He owns a bazillion tourist shops around Chicago. All in the most primo locations, I might add." She heaved a wistful sigh. "God, I'd kill for his Michigan Avenue store."

Okay. That explained precisely nothing.

Not an uncommon occurrence with Tobi.

She might possess the business acumen of a Fortune 500 executive, but she rambled like a total ditz.

"He's a friend of yours?"

"Not hardly." Tobi ran a hand through her hot pink hair. "He's way out of my league. I only recognize him from the society pages."

Regan shifted, uneasy at the thought some stranger was asking to see her.

Was it another trap? Was Caine still hoping he could capture her?

"Then what's he doing here?" she demanded, openly suspicious. "And why does he want to see me?"

"He's here because he noticed the etchings in the window, and he wanted to be introduced to the artist."

"Why?"

"Holy crap, for such an intelligent woman, you can be incredibly dim." With quicksilver movements that made Regan occasionally wonder if Tobi was more than just human, she grasped Regan's arm and pushed her out the swinging doors. "Go talk to him."

"But . . ."

"Go," Tobi hissed, shoving her hard enough that she stumbled into the main room.

Intensely aware that a dozen customers had turned to look at her with raised brows, Regan had little choice but to smooth back the damp curls that had escaped her ponytail, and walk with as much dignity as possible toward the bar.

Keeping her pace measured, she wound her way through the wooden booths and small tables that glowed beneath the discreet lighting set in the open-beamed ceiling.

Once she reached the open space reserved for bar patrons, it was easy to spot the odd man out.

It wasn't just his hand-tailored suit that fit his lean body like a glove, or the perfectly trimmed silver hair that framed his lined, still-handsome face. It was the way he held himself, and the cool arrogance with which he studied his surroundings.

He might as well have rich bastard stamped on his forehead.

Certainly not one of their usual fun-loving, free-spirited customers.

Angling so she would approach him from behind, Regan opened her senses and breathed in deeply. The stranger certainly smelled like a human. Not even a hint of demon blood. Odd considering most successful business owners were at least part imp.

Of course, that didn't mean she was going to lower her guard.

"Mr. Rosewood?"

The older man turned smoothly, a charming smile already curving his lips. A smile that didn't hide the shrewd intelligence in his dark eyes.

"Please, call me Charles."

"Tobi said you wanted to talk to me?"

"Yes, Ms . . . ?"

"Regan," she said shortly, not bothering to hide her suspicion.

"Regan." He took her hand and lifted it to his lips. "A beautiful name for a beautiful young woman."

Regan allowed his grip to linger before pulling her hand free.

Yep. Definitely human.

"How can I help you?"

He waved a manicured hand toward the etchings in the pub window. "You did those?"

"Yes. Tobi lets me sell them here on commission to make some extra cash. Is there a problem?"

"Quite the opposite. I find them enchanting."

"Thank you." Her voice was polite, guarded. "Were you interested in buying one of them?"

"Actually, I'm interested in selling them."

"Selling?" She shook her head. "I don't understand."

"As I said, I find them enchanting, but more importantly, I'm certain my customers will find them enchanting." Almost as if a switch had been thrown, his expression went from charming to astute. "How fast do you work?"

Regan blinked, sensing she was about to be hit by a steamroller.

"I can do one or two smaller sketches in a day. The larger ones take at least two days."

"So . . . four smaller sketches and two large sketches in a week?"

"Something like that."

"Good." He regarded her steadily. "I want to buy them."

"All of them?"

"All of them, every week. And I'm willing to pay top dollar for exclusive rights to your work. Shall we say—" He reached down to pluck his business card from her hand, and retrieving a pen from his pocket, he wrote on the back. Then with a faint smile he shoved it back into her hand. "How's that as a starting figure?"

Steamroller, indeed.

No wonder the man owned half of Chicago. The poor imps didn't have a chance.

Bemused by the man's brisk, decisive manner, Regan glanced down at the card, her heart nearly halting at the figure he had scrawled on the card.

"Christ."

"Here." Reaching toward the bar, Charles poured a large shot of whiskey into a glass and handed it to her. "You look like you could use a drink."

"Thanks." She downed the whiskey in one fiery gulp. "It's just a shock."

"A good shock, I hope?" he murmured.

"Yes, I . . ." Abruptly, Regan was hit by the unwelcome reminder, that "if it seemed to good to be true . . ." motto. This sudden windfall seemed all too convenient. "Wait. You don't happen to know Styx, do you?"

"Styx?" The man frowned in confusion. "As in the mythical river?"

"What about Jagr?"

He shook his head. "I'm sorry, I've never heard of them. Are they local artists?"

She grimaced. His confusion seemed genuine enough.

"Never mind."

His brows lifted at her odd behavior, but taking the empty glass from her hands and setting it on the bar, he determinedly pressed his advantage.

"So, Regan, will you meet at my office so we can make my offer official?"

"You're serious?"

"When it comes to business, I'm always serious," he assured her. "Call the number on the card and my secretary will make the arrangements."

With a nod of his silver head, Charles turned and walked toward the pub door.

Regan watched his departure, clutching the business card as she tried to decide what she was feeling.

There was surprise, of course. She never dreamed her casual etchings could be worth a dime, let alone a small fortune. And maybe a bit of pride. Hell, she wasn't above a few vices.

But shouldn't there be more?

Satisfaction at the knowledge she would soon have financial security? Anticipation of planning her future? Overwhelming joy and fulfillment?

Obviously spying from the kitchen, Tobi was charging toward the bar before the door had closed behind Charles.

Skidding to a halt, she regarded Regan with an impatient expression.

"Well?"

Regan gave a bemused shake of her head. "He wants to buy my etchings."

"Woo hoo!" Indifferent to the curious gazes she was attracting, Tobi grabbed Regan and gave her a rib-crushing hug. "I knew it. Haven't I been telling you that you're a fabo artist, and that you were bound to be discovered?"

Gently disentangling herself so she could suck air into her collapsed lungs, Regan pulled her lips into a stiff smile.

"I'm not sure peddling art to tourists is being discovered, but I'll admit you've always had a lot more faith than I did."

"Because I know talent when I see it."

Regan's smile became genuine as she reached out to ruffle Tobi's pink spikes of hair.

"You've been such a good friend to me, Tobi. If you hadn't let me . . ."

"Blah, blah, blah." The woman waved her hands in dismissal, then her eyes abruptly widened. "You know, you should go out and celebrate. Drink some bubbly, eat some chocolate, find some yummy stud to spend the night giving you mind-blowing sex." She grimaced, waving her hand toward the bar. "I'd join you, but Carly's a no-show yet again, and I have to close."

That's exactly what she should do.

Go out. Maybe hit the bars. Find some adorable hunk to . . .

Her mind shut down.

It simply refused to go where adorable hunks might lurk, even if it was only in her fantasy.

She heaved a sigh. "Actually, I think I'll just go home and savor my stroke of fortune."

Tobi threw her hands in the air, her silver bracelets rattling.

"Jeez, what am I going to do with you? You're beautiful, intelligent, and sexy as hell, and if I weren't such a nice person I'd hate your guts, but you don't have a damn clue about enjoying yourself." She tilted her head, her smile disappearing as she studied Regan with an uncharacteristically serious expression. "That apartment might as well be a prison, Regan. Go out. Live. You can't be a hermit forever."

Prison . . .

Regan winched at the repulsive word.

Because it was true.

Oh, it was nothing like her time with Culligan.

She could come and go as she pleased. She could wear what she wanted, eat what she wanted, and make her own decisions.

She had her independence. A home, a job, the promise of all the money she could possibly need.

But where was the glorious freedom she'd been seeking?

She worked, she sketched, she slept.

Not precisely the full-throated, guns-blazing sort of existence she'd dreamed about all those years behind bars.

She'd exchanged one prison for another.

And why?

Because every moment of every day she missed Jagr. Hell, she even missed Darcy and the terrifying Styx.

Lifting her hands, she rubbed her aching temples.

For so many years, she fantasized about escaping Culligan and being her own master. It was the only thing that had kept her sane.

And she held on to those fantasies like a drowning woman held onto a lifeline.

Even when a genuine, unmistakable chance at happiness was dangled right before her eyes.

Holy shit.

She really was a schmuck.

"Regan? Is there something wrong?"

Regan was jerked out of her painful thoughts. With a blink she focused on Tobi, not surprised to discover her friend staring at her with a worried expression.

She'd been standing there like a mindless zombie.

"Actually, I'm great." Impulsively she leaned forward to kiss Tobi's cheek. "And you're right. What my night needs is a yummy stud."

Tobi lifted her brows. "You sound like you know where to find one."

"Not exactly, but I know where to start the search."

With a newfound, glorious sense of purpose, Regan squared her shoulders and headed directly toward the front entrance. In a distant part of her mind she heard Tobi call her name, but she never faltered as she stepped out the door and into the dark street.

She'd made up her mind.

And for the first time, perhaps in her entire life, it felt absolutely, completely right.

Jogging down the street without her purse, without her keys to her apartment, or even her cell phone, Regan headed directly south. She didn't know the precise location of Jagr's lair, but Darcy had mentioned the neighborhood, so she at least had a general idea of where she was going.

Of course, a general idea in a city the size of Chicago still meant hours wasted zigzagging through dingy, trash-lined streets, not to mention teaching the occasional mugger the dangers of messing with a pureblood on a mission.

Just when she was beginning to wonder if Jagr had moved, or even left town, she caught the faint trace of cold power.

Slowing her rapid pace, Regan angled across the eerily empty street toward the abandoned warehouse.

Jagr was near.

Even if she couldn't sense his presence, she would know by the fact there wasn't so much as a mouse willing to stray near the place. No doubt it had something to do with the whole *Night of the Living Dead* vibe.

Perfect for keeping away unwanted guests.

Like her?

The dispiriting thought had barely passed through her mind when the temperature abruptly plunged, and a low, familiar voice floated on the air.

"Lose your way, Regan?"

Spinning around, Regan could see nothing but abandoned cars and empty Dumpsters. Jagr was there, but he'd cloaked himself in those damned vampire shadows.

Why couldn't she have some of those freaking Romulan powers?

Warning herself to be patient, Regan ignored the biting need to see him, and spoke in his general direction.

"Yeah, I think I did," she said softly. "I was hoping that I could find someone to give me directions."

"In this neighborhood, you're more likely to get your throat slit. If you want to slum, you should find a less dangerous place."

His voice was cool, distant, but Regan's heart warmed with joy. God, just knowing he was near gave her more happiness than she'd had in a month.

"I'm not afraid."

"You should be." She sensed him move, slowly circling her like a predator on the hunt. "Around here, things really do go bump in the night."

She stood perfectly still, refusing to show unease. She might be a bit slow (okay, a lot slow), but the one thing she was absolutely certain of was that Jagr would never harm her.

"Things like vampires?"

"Among other demons."

Regan shrugged. "Then I should fit right in."

"I thought you'd decided to live like a human."

She frowned at his mocking words. "How do you know I've been living like a human?"

His soft laugh tingled down her spine and clenched her stomach with a surge of awareness.

"You can't be naïve enough to believe that Styx hasn't had a guard keeping constant watch on you."

"Impossible," she breathed, refusing to admit just how much time she'd spent at her window searching for some hint of Jagr, or hell, even Darcy. "I would have sensed if a vampire was near."

"Not all of Styx's servants are demons."

"Humans?"

"Some of Chicago's finest."

Her surprise that the arrogant Styx would lower himself to

deal with mere humans was overshadowed by a hypocritical flare of annoyance.

Okay, she might have been hurt by the thought that she'd been so easily forgotten, but that didn't mean she wanted to be spied on.

"How dare he?" Unable to see Jagr, she glared at the nearest Dumpster. "I'm not one of his Almighty's subjects."

"No, but you are family, and for all we know Caine is still plotting to capture you." His voice sounded closer, as if he were circling ever closer to her. "Darcy would neuter him if something happened to you."

"And he's been reporting my every moment to you?" she accused.

"He mentioned that you had a job and apartment the last time we met. Nothing more."

She bit her lip at his dismissive tone. Christ. Had she made a terrible mistake coming here? Maybe Jagr had decided his life was a whole lot better without her driving him nuts. And who the hell could blame him?

"So . . . you spend a lot of time with Styx and Darcy?"

"More than I expected," he said dryly.

"Oh." She was struck by a sudden thought. "Are you being punished for not forcing me back to Chicago?"

"I suppose that's a matter of opinion." There was a short pause. "He's requested that I become one of his Ravens."

She sucked in a sharp breath. "A Raven?"

"You can't be more shocked than I was."

Regan shook her head. She wasn't shocked. She was horrified.

"Are you considering his offer?"

"Yes." His voice came directly in front of her.

Concern tightened her muscles. "Darcy said the Ravens are sent to keep the vampires and other demons in line. Like some sort of uber enforcer."

"That's part of the duties."

If she could have seen him, she might have punched him for at his cavalier tone.

From what little she'd learned from her sister, the Ravens were Styx's private Secret Service, and regularly risked their lives at the command of the king.

Jagr was supposed to be a scholar. A recluse. A vampire who was too smart to go around looking for trouble.

"It sounds dangerous."

"What's life without a little danger?"

"Safe?" she gritted.

"Every day is a gamble. Something I forgot along the way," he said, not hiding his self-derision. "And at least this way, I'll always be on my guard."

"Jagr . . ." Her words broke off in frustration. "Dammit, why are you hiding from me?"

"I'm trying to decide if you're friend or foe."

She flinched at the smooth response. "I've never been your foe."

"No? I distinctly recall you threatening to shove a stake up my ass."

She remembered, too.

Vividly.

It had been during their first encounter and at the time, she had only wanted to be rid of him.

Now . . .

Now her heart ached to hold him in her arms for an eternity.

"I've warned you that I'm not very smart."

She thought she heard a low hiss at her words. "Why are you here, Regan?"

Knowing that this was it, her one chance to make it right, Regan spoke the words that seared across her heart.

"Because I love you."

* * *

Jagr was centuries old.

He'd watched nations rise and fall. He'd witnessed plagues, fire, and war sweep around the world, decimating everything in its path. He'd endured torture and bloody battles that would turn any demon's stomach.

But nothing had shattered him.

Not until Regan breathed those soft words.

His powers faltered, shredding his protective shadows and lowering his icy barriers to allow the full force of Regan's presence to slam into him.

With a soft groan he savored the midnight jasmine that washed over him.

Over the past month he'd waged an endless war to keep himself from tracking her down and haunting her every step.

It was a vampire's instinct to keep his mate close. Hell, there'd been a time when vampires would hold a reluctant mate prisoner in their lair.

Only the knowledge that his lurking presence might infuriate her into leaving Chicago altogether kept him away.

That, and Styx's constant assurances that she was well guarded and seemingly content in her new life.

Now he stepped close enough to allow her precious heat to warm his frozen heart.

"What did you say?" he rasped, his gaze drinking in her pale, golden beauty.

She licked her lips in a nervous gesture. "Have your advanced years made you hard of hearing?"

"Regan."

She sighed at his warning tone. "I said I love you."

He trembled, desperate to believe.

"Why?"

"Do I have to bring up that whole being stupid thing again?"

He ignored her teasing, needing to be certain.

He couldn't survive losing her again.

"Tell me why."

Without warning she moved forward, her hands lifting to frame his face.

"I love you because you're strong and loyal and tender and honorable."

He shuddered at her gentle touch, his too-long suppressed hunger not giving a damn if she were sincere or not.

"And?"

"Sexy as hell."

He groaned. She wasn't helping.

"And?"

The emerald eyes darkened with all the emotion he'd been seeking. "And when I'm with you, I'm whole again."

His meager restraint snapped. She was here. She said she loved him.

What more did he need?

Leaning down, he claimed her lips in a near savage kiss.

"Regan."

"I've missed you, chief," she whispered against his mouth, her breath catching as he abruptly jerked her off her feet and cradled her against his chest. "What are you doing?"

Without hesitation, Jagr headed into the empty warehouse. "What I should have done the minute you rammed into my life."

She snorted, but a pleased smile curved her lips. "Very caveman of you. And for your information, any ramming was done by you."

Wicked need curled through his stomach at her intentionally provocative words.

"You haven't seen anything yet, little one," he growled.

A delicious blush touched her cheeks. "Promises, promises."

Oh, they were going to be more than promises, he silently vowed.

He was going to put her in his bed and savor her for the next millennium.

Reaching the middle of the decrepit building, Jagr bent down to tug aside the heavy trapdoor. Then, holding Regan tight in his arms, he stepped off the edge and fell the six feet to the tunnel beneath.

He landed without jarring the woman in his arms, and with long strides headed down the narrow tunnel, muttering curses as he was forced to halt at the heavy steel doors that guarded his lair.

As he disarmed the various locks, hexes, and sensors, Regan choked back a laugh.

"Yow. Paranoid much?"

"Better safe than sorry." His gaze swept over her precious face. He would go to any lengths to protect this woman. His woman. "Especially now."

Stepping over the threshold, Jagr slammed the door shut and used his powers to fill the long room with light. Regan gasped at the dozen rows of shelves that were overflowing with leather-bound books. It was only a small portion of his collection. The fragile and rarest manuscripts were kept in a vault beneath his lair. Soon he intended to share his priceless treasures with his mate.

Soon, but not now.

Ignoring her attempts to catch a glimpse at the numerous framed maps that lined the steel walls, he passed into his most private rooms, not surprised by her startled expression as she caught sight of the high-tech computer system that consumed one corner of the carpeted room, and the plasma TV angled toward the sectional couch.

Most who met him assumed he must live in a dungeon, complete with chains.

"Wait, Jagr, I want to see . . ."

He cut off her words with a brief, desperate kiss. "Later."

"But . . ."

He kissed her again. Longer. Deeper.

"Much later," he whispered, pulling back to watch in satisfaction as her eyes darkened with ready passion.

Reaching the back of the lair, he pressed open the thick door to his bedroom and crossed directly to the low, wide bed draped in gold satin sheets and a thick fur cover. On the walls, twelfth century tapestries glowed in the candlelight, hiding the heavy cabinets that held his lethal collection of daggers, swords, spears, and handguns.

Not exactly the most romantic setting, but Regan didn't seem to notice as she smiled up at him with a slow, wicked temptation.

Bracing one knee on the edge of the bed, he bent over her and tugged the ribbon from her hair. Flames licked through his blood as he threaded his fingers through the golden strands, his gaze skimming over her slender curves.

"Blessed gods, you are so beautiful."

Her smile widened as she reached up, and with unexpected strength, ripped the T-shirt from his body.

"Not nearly as beautiful as you," she murmured, her fingers tracing the scars that crisscrossed his torso.

He shuddered, his fangs extending and his body hardening in all the right places.

"I've always heard that love is blind. Now I'm certain of it."

"Don't play coy." Her fingers trailed a path of fire down the hard planes of his stomach, popping the button of his jeans and easing down the zipper. Jagr growled in approval. She was a woman in charge. And he liked it. "You know very well you make women all hot and bothered."

Him?

Well, hell. If she wanted to believe he was some sort of babe magnet, then so be it.

Kicking off his heavy boots, Jagr rid himself of the jeans and climbed on the bed to pull Regan into his arms.

He had once cursed a fate that offered nothing but cruelty and stark loneliness. Now he could only marvel at his extraordinary stroke of fortune.

Skimming his hands over her warm, deliciously shaped body, he removed her far too short shorts and far too tight shirt, briefly appreciating the matching bra and panties before they too were tossed onto the floor.

Once she was exposed in all her glory, he forced himself to slow his pace, his fingers savoring the sensation of her smooth, ivory skin.

"Are you all hot and bothered?" he husked.

Her arms lifted to circle around his neck, her breath unsteady as his roaming fingers stroked up the curve of her breast.

"I'm getting there."

Lowering his head, he brushed his lips down the line of her nose, then gently teased the corner of her mouth.

"Regan, you're certain?" he forced himself to ask. "Once we're mated, I won't be able to let you go."

Painful regret flared through her eyes. "I'm so sorry, Jagr."

"There's no need for apologies. You did what you needed to do."

"No, I was big, freaking coward." She grimaced. "I wasn't proving I could make it on my own. I was running from my feelings because they terrified me."

He pulled back with a frown. "Terrified?"

"I know how to be alone. I'm pretty good at it." A wistful smile touched her lips as her hands glided down his back. "I don't know anything about being a mate or sister."

A groan was wrenched from his throat as he planted a path of kisses down her jaw, and at last buried his face in the curve of her neck.

"We'll figure it out together," he promised softly.

She deliberately rubbed against the heavy length of his erection. "Mmmm. I like the sound of that."

Oh, he liked more than just the sound of it.

He liked the feel and taste and . . .

A vicious hunger gripped him and with an unsteady hand, he tugged aside her hair, baring her throat.

"I need to taste you, little one," he rasped, his voice thick. "I want to be your mate."

He expected her to hesitate. Even to pull away.

After all, he was demanding nothing less than her heart and soul.

Instead, she plunged her fingers into the thickness of his hair and urged him even closer.

"Now, Jagr."

The soft prompting pushed him over the edge, searing away his last trace of common sense.

He'd waited over a thousand years to find his mate.

He wasn't going to wait another moment.

Tilting her chin, Jagr bared his fangs and allowed them to sink into her sweet, vulnerable flesh. Oh . . . gods. He closed his eyes as the rich, potent elixir hit his tongue and slid down his throat.

The taste of Regan's blood was just as erotic, just as intoxicating as he remembered.

But this time it was more.

More than nourishment. More than a means to heal his wounds. Even more than sex.

It was dazzling magic that swirled through his body and tingled through his blood. As if the very essence of Regan was flooding through him, melding and altering him until they coalesced into one.

Beneath him, he felt Regan tremble, her moan of pleasure echoing through the room.

"Jagr." Her nails bit into his back, her voice ragged. "I need you."

Eager and willing to fulfill her every desire, Jagr unlatched from her throat, gently licking closed the two small puncture wounds before scattering kisses down her collarbone and over the swell of her breast.

"Your every wish is my command, my love," he assured her as he shifted to settle between her legs. "For now and always."

Her hands clutched his lips, her creamy skin flushed with need. "A dangerous promise, chief."

He gazed deep into the slumberous emerald eyes, capable of feeling the sharp ache of her desire.

"You don't scare me, Were."

"No? Maybe you should . . ."

Her words broke off with a low groan as he surged into her damp heat. Pure sensation jolted through him, clenching his muscles and heating him to the very marrow. For a moment he halted to simply relish being so intimately bound together.

"I should do this?" he breathed as he lowered his head to plunder her soft lips. "And maybe this?" Slowly he pulled back his hips and once again thrust deep inside her.

"Oh, yes," she breathed.

A growl was wrenched from his throat as she lifted her hips and his cock sank to the heart of her. So close to perfect.

So. Very. Close.

"Regan."

Her eyes were clenched shut as he steadily pumped himself into her. "Mmmm?"

He traced the tip of one breast his tongue. "It's time to complete the ceremony."

"Christ." With obvious effort, she lifted her heavy lids. "Does it have to be now?"

With a soft chuckle he brushed his lips over her cheeks and gently nipped at her earlobe.

"You are a part of me, little one. Now I want to be a part of you."

Her beautiful face softened with a heartrending tenderness.

"You'll always be a part of me, Jagr." Her hands moved to frame his face. "Now and forever."

With a soft kiss, Jagr cupped the back of Regan's head and pressed her mouth to the side of his neck.

"Bite," he commanded softly.

There was a moment of hesitation before he felt her lips part and she dug her teeth deep into his skin.

Jagr shouted in raw pleasure as she gently sucked at the wound, taking his blood into her.

He'd never willingly allowed anyone to feed from him. He hadn't realized just how intimate the exchange could be.

A primitive passion surged through him. This was his woman.

His mate.

Urging her to drink even deeper, he rocked his hips, pumping in and out of her with a growingly desperate pace.

This was it.

This was perfection.

Wrenching her mouth from his neck, Regan cried out in fulfillment, her nails raking down his back with a blissful sting of pain.

Jagr had never seen anything more beautiful than the sight of Regan reaching her peak, and with one last thrust, his climax slammed into him.

Arching his back, Jagr gloried in the sheer power of the explosion.

Nothing ever had felt so good.

Regan struggled to catch her breath.

Yow.

That just gave a whole new meaning to "bringing down the house."

Certainly she felt as if the roof had collapsed on top of her.

In the best possible way.

Sighing as Jagr rolled to the side and gathered her in his arms, Regan readily snuggled against his cool body. She felt sated to the very tips of her toes.

And more than that, she felt . . .

Jagr.

Christ, it was amazing.

He was like a low hum in the back of her mind.

She sensed his glow of peaceful contentment, his stark need to protect her, and overall the fierce love that shimmered through his soul like threads of gold.

Awed by the sensation of being so closely bound to another, Regan stroked an absent finger down a puckered scar on Jagr's chest. Instantly she was aware of his heated response to her touch. And unexpectedly, a hint of vulnerability as she caressed the flesh he'd kept hidden for so long.

Her heart melted.

How could she have wasted even a moment with her stupid fears?

Culligan and the damn curs had made her a captive, but it had very nearly been her own choice to remain a prisoner.

"It's strange," she murmured.

Dropping a kiss on top of her head, Jagr pulled back to study her with a lift of his brows.

"Strange? That's not exactly what a virile vampire wants to hear after making love with his mate."

"I meant it's strange that I can feel you." Grasping his hand, she pressed it directly over her heart. "Here."

The brilliant blue eyes flared with a heat that he reserved only for her.

"The mating bond." His hand shifted to curve possessively around her breast. "From now on you will always know where I am, what I'm feeling, if I have need of you."

"Need of me, eh?"

He teased the sensitive tip of her nipple, his body hardening with an eagerness that made her chuckle.

"Which will be always," he husked.

Regan deliberately glanced down at the full erection pressing against her hip.

"So I see."

The words had barely left her lips when she found herself flat on her back with a smug vampire perched on top of her.

"Would you like to do more than just see?"

Oh, yeah, she wanted more.

She wanted to lick him from head to toe, pausing to nibble at all the most interesting places. She wanted to spend hours exploring the hard planes and angles of his body. She wanted to forget the world and . . .

Almost as if the mere thought of the world allowed it to intrude, her lovely fantasies were suddenly distracted.

"Holy crap," she muttered.

A ghost of a smile played about his lips. "Again, not what a virile vampire wants to hear." His fingers brushed her cheek. "What's wrong?"

"I can't believe I forgot to ask about Levet. Have you heard from him?"

Jagr snorted, lowering his head to sprinkle light, tormenting kisses over her face and down the line of her throat.

"That's a story for later." He easily evaded her question and set about distracting her with delicious strokes of his tongue that were leading lower and lower.

She tried to hang onto a shred of sanity. "But . . ."

"Later, little one." He tugged her legs apart and smiled with wicked intent. "Much later."

And it was.

Please turn the page
for an exciting sneak peek of
Alexandra Ivy's next novel in the
Guardians of Eternity series,
coming in April 2010!

Chapter 1

It wasn't his finest day, Salvatore Giuliani, the mighty King of Weres, had to admit.

As a matter of fact, it was swerving toward downright shitty.

It was bad enough to regain consciousness to discover he was stretched out in a dark, nasty tunnel that was currently ruining his Gucci suit, and that he had no clear memory of how he had gotten there.

But to open his eyes and use his perfect night vision to discover a three foot gargoyle with stunted horns, ugly gray features, and delicate wings in shades of blue and gold and crimson hovering over him was enough to ruin a perfectly horrible mood.

"Wake up," Levet hissed, his French accent pronounced and his wings fluttering in fear. "Wake up, you mangy dog, or I'll have you spaded."

"Call me a dog again and be assured you'll soon be chopped into bits of gravel and paving my driveway," Salvatore growled, his head throbbing in time to his heartbeat.

What the hell had happened?

The last thing he remembered he'd been north of St. Louis to meet with Duncan, a cur who'd promised information regarding his pack leader (a renegade cur with a taste for regicide) and the next he was waking up with Levet buzzing over him like an oversized, extremely ugly butterfly.

God almighty. When Salvatore got out of the tunnel, he was going to track down Jagr and cut out his heart for sticking him with the annoying Levet. Damned vampire.

"You will not be doing anything unless you get up and move," the gargoyle warned. "Shake your tail, King of Slugs."

Ignoring the grinding pain in his joints, Salvatore rose to his feet and smoothed back his shoulder length raven hair. He didn't bother knocking the dirt from his silk suit. It was going in the nearest fire.

Along with the gargoyle.

"Where are we?"

"In some tunnel."

"A brilliant deduction. What would I do without you?"

"Look, Cujo, all I know is that one minute we were in a cabin with an extremely dead Duncan and the next I was being rudely dropped on my head." Bizarrely the gargoyle rubbed his butt rather than his head. Of course, his skull was more than likely too thick to harm. "That female is fortunate that I did not turn her into a beaver."

"It had to have been a spell. Was the woman a witch?"

"*Non*. A demon, but . . ."

"What?"

"She is a mongrel."

Salvatore shrugged. It was common among the demon world to interbreed.

"Not unusual."

"Her power is."

Salvatore frowned. He might want to choke the gargoyle, but the tiny demon possessed the ability to sense magic that Salvatore couldn't.

"What power?"

"Jinn."

A chill inched down Salvatore's spine and he cast a swift glance up and down the tunnel. In the distance he could sense the approach of his curs and a vampire. The cavalry rushing to the rescue. His attention, however, was focused on searching for any hint of the jinn.

A full-bred jinn was a cruel, unpredictable creature who could manipulate nature. They could call lightning, turn wind into a lethal force, and lay flat an entire city with an earthquake. They could also disappear into a wisp of smoke. Thankfully they rarely took an interest in the world and preferred to remain isolated.

Half-breeds . . .

He shuddered. They might not possess the power of a full-fledged jinn, but their inability to control their volatile energy made them even more dangerous.

"Jinn have been forbidden to breed with other demons."

Levet snorted. "There are many things forbidden in this world."

"The Commission must be told," Salvatore muttered, referring to the cryptic Oracles who were the ultimate leaders of the demon-world. He reached into his pocket, coming up empty. "*Cristo.*"

"What?"

"My cell phone is gone."

"Fine." Levet threw his hands in the air. "We will send a memo. For now we need to get out of here."

"Relax, gargoyle, help is on the way."

With a frown, Levet sniffed the air. "Your curs."

"And a leech."

Levet sniffed again. "Tane."

Expecting Jagr, Salvatore's brows snapped together. One vampire was as bad as another, but Tane's reputation of killing first and asking questions later didn't exactly warm the cockles of a Were's heart.

Whatever the hell a cockle was.

"The Charon?" he demanded. Charons were assassins who hunted down rogue vampires. God only knew what they did to lesser demons. And in a vampire's mind, every demon was lesser.

"An arrogant, condescending donkey," Levet muttered.

Salvatore rolled his eyes. "Jackass, you idiot, not donkey."

Levet waved a dismissive hand. "It is my theory that the taller the demon, the larger his conceit and the smaller his..."

"Continue, gargoyle," a cold voice cut through the dark, abruptly lowering the temperature in the tunnel. "I find your theory fascinating."

"Eek!"

With a flutter of his wings, Levet dashed behind Salvatore. As if he was stupid enough to think Salvatore would keep him from certain death.

"*Dio,* get away from me, you pest," Salvatore growled, swiping a hand at the gargoyle even as his gaze was warily focused on the vampire rounding the corner of the tunnel.

He was worth focusing on.

Although not as large as many of his brothers, the vampire was dangerously muscular with the golden skin of his Polynesian ancestors and thick, black hair shaved on the sides into a long Mohawk that fell past his shoulders. His face was that of a predator, lean and hard with faintly slanted honey eyes. At the moment he was wearing nothing more than a pair of khaki shorts, obviously not sharing Salvatore's own fondness for designer clothes.

Of course, the big dagger he was holding in his hands made sure that no one was going to question his taste in fashion.

Not if they wanted to live.

There was the sound of footsteps and four of his curs came into sight, the largest of them rushing forward to drop to his knees and press his bald head to the ground in front of Salvatore's feet.

"Sire, are you harmed?" Hess demanded.

"Only my pride." Salvatore returned his attention to the vampire as Hess rose to his feet and towered at his side. "I remember nothing after entering the cabin and finding Duncan dead. No, wait. There was a voice, then . . ." He shook his head in aggravation as his memory went blank. "Damn. Did you follow us?"

Tane absently stroked the hilt of his dagger. "When we found the cabin empty, Jagr assumed you were in trouble. Since your clueless crew seemed incapable of forming a coherent thought, I agreed to come in search of you."

Not surprising. Unlike purebloods who were born from full Weres, the curs were humans who had been bitten and transformed into werewolves. Hess and the other curs were excellent killers. Which was why he kept them as guards. Using their brains, however . . . well, he did the thinking for them. It solved any number of problems.

"So what happened to our captors?"

"We've been gaining on you over the past half hour." Tane shrugged. "They obviously preferred escape over keeping their hostages."

"You never caught sight of them?"

"No. A cur escaped through a side tunnel a mile back and the demon simply disappeared." Frustration flashed through the honey eyes. Salvatore could sympathize. He was anxious for a bit of blood and violence himself. "There're only a handful of demons capable of vanishing into thin air."

"The gargoyle thinks it's a jinn mongrel."

"Hey, the gargoyle has a name." Stepping from behind Salvatore, Levet planted his hands on his hips. "And I do not think, I *know*."

Tane narrowed his eyes. "How can you be certain?"

"I had a slight misunderstanding with a jinn a few centuries ago. He zapped off one of my wings. It took years to grow back."

Tane was supremely unimpressed. "And that's somehow relevant?"

"Before the demon dropped me and did her disappearing act, she left a little present." Turning around, Levet revealed the perfectly shaped handprint that had been branded onto his butt. Salvtore's laughter echoed through the tunnel and the gargoyle turned to stab him with a wounded glare. "It is not amusing."

"That still doesn't prove it was a jinn," Tane pointed out, his own lips twitching with amusement.

"Being struck by lightning is not a sensation you easily forget."

Tane instinctively glanced over his shoulder. No demon in his right mind wanted to cross paths with a jinn.

"How do you know it isn't a full jinn?"

Levet grimaced. "I am still alive."

The vampire turned to Salvatore. "The Commission must be warned."

"I agree."

"This is Were business. It's your duty."

"I can't lose the trail of the cur," Salvatore smoothly pointed out. Ah. There was nothing better than getting the upper hand with a leech. "He's proven a danger to more than just Weres. I'm sure the Commission would agree that my duty is put an end to the traitors."

A blast of frigid air filled the tunnel. Salvatore smiled, releasing his own energy to counter the chill with a prickling heat.

The curs stirred uneasily, reacting to the power play between two dangerous predators. Salvatore never allowed his gaze to stray from Tane. Few Weres could best a vampire, but Salvatore wasn't just a Were. He was king. He wasn't going to back down from any demon.

At last, Tane snapped his fangs in Salvatore's direction and stepped back. Salvatore could only assume that the vampire had been ordered to keep the bloodshed to a minimum.

"This will not be forgotten, dog," Tane warned, turning on his heel and silently disappearing down the tunnel.

"Good riddance, leech."

Waiting long enough to make sure the vampire didn't have a change of heart and return to rip out his throat, Salvatore turned back to his waiting curs to discover them battling back their urge to shift.

He grimaced. As a pureblood he had the ability to control his shifts unless it was a full moon; curs on the other hand were at the mercy of their emotions.

With a shudder, Hess at last gained control and sucked in a deep breath.

"Now what?"

Salvatore didn't hesitate. "We follow the cur."

Hess clenched his meaty hands at his side. "It's too dangerous. The jinn . . ." His words broke off in a squeal as Salvatore's power once again reached out, striking the cur like the lash of a whip.

"Hess, on how many occasions have I told you that if I want your opinion I'll ask for it," Salvatore drawled.

The cur lowered his head. "Forgive me, sire."

"The cringing cretin is not entirely wrong." Levet waddled forward, his long tail twitching. "It had to have been the demon who killed Duncan and knocked both of us out."

"No one is asking you to join us, gargoyle," Salvatore snapped.

"*Sacrebleu*. I am not going to be left alone in these tunnels."

"Then chase after the vampire."

The damned gargoyle refused to budge, a sly amusement entering the gray eyes.

"Darcy would not be pleased if something was to happen to me and if Darcy is not happy, then Styx is not happy."

Salvatore snapped his teeth. Darcy was one of the female purebloods he'd been searching for over the past thirty years, and while he didn't have the least fear of her, she'd recently mated with the King of Vampires.

Styx he did fear.

Hey, he wasn't stupid.

Muttering a curse, Salvatore led the way down the tunnel, his already pissy mood plunging to foul.

"Get in my way and I'll chop you up and feed you to the vultures. Understood, gargoyle?"

He sensed his curs falling into step behind him with Levet bringing up the rear.

"Mangy dogs can smooch my posterior," the gargoyle muttered.

"A jinn is not the only creature capable of ripping off a wing," Salvatore warned.

A blessed silence filled the dark tunnel and at last able to concentrate on the faint trail of cur, Salvatore quickened his pace.

It was moments like this that he regretted leaving Italy.

In his elegant lair near Rome no one dared treat him as anything other than Master of the Universe. His word was law and his underlings scrambled to do his bidding. Best of all there were no filthy vampires or stunted gargoyles.

Unfortunately, he'd had no choice in the matter.

The Weres were becoming extinct. Pureblooded females could no longer control their shifts during pregnancy and more often lost their babies before they could be born. Even the bite of Weres was losing its potency. A new cur had not been created in years.

Salvatore had to act, and after years of research, his very expensive scientists had at last managed to alter the DNA of four female pureblood babies so they could not shift.

They were a miracle. Born to save the Weres.

Until they had been stolen from the nursery.

He growled low in his throat, his anger still a potent force even after thirty years. He had wasted far too much time searching through Europe before he at last traveled to America and managed to stumble across two of the females. Unfortunately Darcy was in the hands of Styx, while Regan had proven to be infertile.

While he was in Hannibal, however, he'd managed to discover that the babies had at some point been in the hands of Caine, a cur with a death wish who'd convinced himself that he would be capable of using the blood of the females to turn common curs into Weres. Moron.

Salvatore had been in a cabin to meet with one of Caine's pack who'd promised to reveal the traitor's location when he and Levet had been knocked unconscious and kidnapped.

It had to have been Caine who attacked him.

Now the bastard was leaving a trail straight to his lair.

A smile curved his lips. He intended to savor ripping out the traitor's throat.

A near half hour passed as Salvatore weaved his way through the winding tunnel, his steps slowing as he tilted back his head to sniff the air.

The scent of cur was still strong, but he was beginning to pick up the distant scent of other curs and . . . pureblood.

Female pureblood.

Coming to a sharp halt, Salvatore savored the rich vanilla aroma that filled his senses.

He loved the smell of women. Hell, he loved women.

But this was different.

It was intoxicating.

"*Cristo*," he breathed, his blood racing and an odd tightness creeping through his body, slowly draining his strength.

Almost as if . . .

No. It wasn't possible.

There hadn't been a true Were mating for centuries.

"Curs," Levet said, moving to his side. "And a female pure-blood."

"*Si*," Salvatore muttered, distracted.

"You think it's a trap?"

Salvatore swallowed a grim laugh. Hell, he hoped it *was* a trap. The alternative was enough to send any intelligent Were howling into the night.

"There's only one way to find out."

He moved forward, sensing the end of the tunnel just yards in front of him.

"Salvatore?" Levet tugged on his pants.

Salvatore shook him off. "What?"

"You smell funny. *Mon Dieu*, are you . . ."

With blinding speed Salvatore grasped the gargoyle by one stunted horn and yanked him off his feet to glare into the ugly face. Until that moment he hadn't noticed the musky scent that clung to his skin.

Shit.

"One more word and you lose that tongue," he snarled.

"But . . ."

"Do not screw with me."

"I do not intend to screw with anyone." The gargoyle curled his lips in a mocking smile. "I am not the one in heat."

Hess appeared beside Salvatore, halting his urge to rip off the gargoyle's head.

A pity.

"Sire?" the cur demanded, his thick brow furrowed.

"Take Max and the other curs and keep guard on the rear. I don't want anyone sneaking up on us," he commanded.

It was unlikely the cur would recognize Salvatore's disturbing reaction to the female's scent. Hess hadn't even been transformed when the last mating had happened. Not mention the fact he was as thick as a stump. But Levet was certainly annoying enough to let the cat out of the bag.

Waiting for the curs to grudgingly shift back, he gave the gargoyle a shake before dropping him onto the ground.

"You, not another word."

Regaining his balance, Levet glanced upward, his wings fluttering and his tail twitching.

"Um. Actually, I have two words," he muttered. Then, without warning he was charging forward, ramming directly into Salvatore and sending him flying backward. "CAVE IN!!!"

Momentarily stunned, Salvatore watched in horror as the low ceiling abruptly gave way, sending an avalanche of dirt and stone into the tunnel.

Because of Levet's swift action, he had avoided the worse of the landslide, but rising to his feet he was in no mood for gratitude. Hard to believe this hideous day had just gotten worse.

Moving to the wall of debris that blocked the tunnel, he sent out his sense to find his curs.

"Hess?" he shouted.

Levet coughed at the cloud of dust that filled the air. "Are they . . . ?"

"They're injured, but alive," Salvatore said, able to pick up the heartbeats of his pack, although they were currently unconscious. "Can we dig our way through to them?"

"It would take hours and we risk bringing even more down on our heads."

Of course. Why the hell would it be easy?

"Damn."

The gargoyle shook the dirt off his wings. "The tunnel is clear behind them. Once they recover they should be able to find a way out."

He was right. Hess might have a brain the size of a walnut, but he was as tenacious as a pit bull. Once he realized he wouldn't be able to reach Salvatore, he would lead the others back to the cabin and return overland to dig them out.

Unfortunately, it would take hours.

Turning, he glanced toward the stone wall that marked the end of the tunnel.

Whatever exit the cur had used to get out of the tunnel was now buried beneath the rubble.

"Which is more than I can say for us," he muttered.

"Bah." With a flagrant disregard to the thin sliver of ceiling that hadn't yet fallen on their heads, Levet gingerly climbed up the side of the tunnel. "I am a gargoyle."

Salvatore sucked in a sharp breath. A ton of rock and dirt falling on his head wouldn't kill him. Being buried alive with Levet . . . that would be the end. If he had to rip out his own heart.

"I'm painfully aware of who and what you are."

"I can smell the night." Levet paused and glanced over his shoulder. "Are you coming or what?"

With no legitimate options, Salvatore awkwardly scrambled behind the gargoyle, his pride as tattered as his Italian leather shoes.

"Damn lump of stone," he breathed. "Jagr should rot in hell for sticking me with you."

Nearly flicking Salvatore's nose with the tip of his tail, Levet continued upward, sniffing the air. He paused as he reached the edge of the ceiling, his hands testing the seemingly smooth rock until he abruptly shoved upward, revealing the cleverly hidden door.

Levet disappeared through the narrow opening and Salvatore was swift to follow, grasping the edge of the hole and pulling himself out of the tunnel. He crawled through the dew dampened grass, away from the opening before at last rising to his feet and sucking in the fresh air.

Weres weren't like most demons who enjoyed being hidden in damp, moldy caves and tunnels for centuries on end. A Were needed open space to run and hunt.

With a shudder, Salvatore glanced around the thick trees

that surrounded him, his senses reaching out to make certain there was no immediate threat.

"Ta da!" With a flutter of his wings, Levet landed directly in front of Salvatore, his expression smug. "Shove it up your ear, oh ye of little faith. Hey . . . where are you going?"

Brushing past the annoying pest, Salvatore was weaving his way through the trees.

"To kill me a cur."

"Wait, we can't go alone," Levet protested, his tiny legs pumping to keep pace. "Besides, it is almost dawn."

"I just want to find his lair before he manages to cover his trail. I'm not losing him again."

"And that is all? You promise you will not do anything stupid until we have front-up?"

"Back-up, you fool." The sweet scent of vanilla invaded Salvatore's senses, clouding his mind and stealing his waning strength. "Now be quiet."

At a glance Harley looked like a Barbie Doll.

She stood barely over five feet, her body was slender, her heart-shaped face was delicately carved with large hazel eyes that were thickly lashed, and her golden blond hair that tumbled past her shoulders gave the image of a fragile angel. She also looked far younger than her thirty years.

Anyone, however, stupid enough to dismiss her as harmless usually ended up injured.

Or dead.

She was not only a full-blooded Were, but she took her training in combat skills to a level that Navy SEALS would envy.

She was working out in the full-scale gym when Caine returned to the vast colonial home. She continued lifting the weights that would crush most men as she absently listened to his bitter tirade of the ineptitude of his cur pack and the injustice of a world that contained Salvatore Giuliani, the King of Weres.

At last, Harley moved to take a swig of bottled water and wiped the sweat coating her face. She glanced toward Caine, who leaned negligently against the far wall, his jeans and T-shirt filthy and his short blond hair tousled. Not that his bedraggled appearance dimmed his surfer good looks. Even beneath the fluorescent lights that made everyone appear like death warmed over, his tanned skin glowed with a rich bronze and the blue eyes shimmered like the finest sapphires.

He was gorgeous. And he knew it.

Blech!

Harley's lips twisted. Her relationship with Caine was complicated.

The cur had been her guardian since she was a baby, but while he'd protected her and kept her in considerable luxury, she'd never truly trusted him.

And the feeling was entirely mutual.

Caine might allow her to roam the house and the surrounding lands with seeming freedom, but she knew she was under constant surveillance. And God knew, she was never allowed to travel away from the estate without two or three of Caine's pet curs. Caine claimed he was concerned for her safety, but Harley wasn't stupid. She knew his motives were far more selfish.

It might have been tempting to escape her golden cage but for the knowledge that a lone wolf, even a pureblood, rarely survived. Weres were by nature predators and there were any number of demons that would be eager to rid the world of a Were if they could catch them without a pack's protection.

Besides, there was always the fear that the King of Weres was out there somewhere, anxious to kill her as he had her three sisters. Caine might be determined to use her for his own purpose, but at least that purpose meant he had to keep her alive.

Tossing aside the towel, Harley sent her companion a mocking smile.

"Let me see if I have this straight. You went to Hannibal because Sadie created some mysterious mess that you had to clean up and while you were there you brilliantly decided to kidnap the King of Weres, only to lose him when you were nearly caught by a vampire and pack of curs?"

Caine pushed away from the wall and prowled forward, his gaze skimming over her tight spandex shorts and sports bra. The cur was nothing if not predictable. He'd been trying to seduce her for years.

"You have it in a perfect little nutshell, sweet Harley." He halted directly before her, toying with the ponytail that had fallen over her shoulder. "Do you want a reward?"

"And your pet jinn?"

"Slipped from her leash. She'll be back." His smile was taunting. "Like you, she has nowhere else to go."

Harley jerked from his touch. Bastard.

"So now you've lost half your pack, your demon, and you've left behind a trail that will lead the pissed-off King of Weres and his angry posse directly to this lair."

Caine shrugged. "I'll call for one of the local witches. My trail will be long gone by the time the almighty Salvatore manages to get out."

"Get out of where?"

"I collapsed the tunnel on top of them."

"God. Are you even barely sane?"

"Once they manage to heal enough to dig out of the rubble they'll discover the entrance has been completely blocked. They will have no choice but to turn back."

"You're pretty damned cocky for a cur who has just pissed off your royal master."

"I don't have a master," he snarled, revealing a glimpse of his resentment at being a mere cur before he smoothed his expression. "And besides, the prophecies have spoken. I'm destined to transform the curs into purebloods. Nothing can happen to me."

Harley snorted. Caine wasn't a complete loon. He managed to control his large pack he had spread throughout the Midwest with an iron hand. He was a Harvard trained scientist who made a fortune with his black market drugs. He regularly kicked her ass at Scrabble.

But at some point in his very long life he claimed he'd been visited by an ancient pureblood who had given him a vision. Harley didn't pretend to understand it. Something about seeing his blood run pure.

Being a scientist, he naturally assumed this miracle would be performed in a lab, which was why he kept Harley as his permanent houseguest. He thought by studying her blood he could find the answers he sought. Moronic, of course. Visions were the stuff of mist and magic, not glass beakers and microscopes.

"Look, if you want to get yourself killed because of your delusions of grandeur I don't give a shit." She narrowed her eyes. "But I'm not going to be happy if you put me in the firing line."

Caine stepped forward, reaching to trail his fingers over her shoulder. His touch was warm, experienced. She shook him off.

A woman would have to be dead not to find Caine attractive, but Harley needed more than simple lust. She needed . . . hell, she didn't know what she needed, only that she hadn't yet found it.

Besides, her skin was suddenly feeling hypersensitive. As if it had been rubbed raw by sandpaper.

"Would I ever put you in danger, sweet Harley?" Caine goaded.

"In a heartbeat if it meant saving your own hide."

"Harsh."

"But true."

"Perhaps." His gaze dipped downward, studying her sports bra. "I need a shower. Why don't you join me?"

"In your dreams."

"Every night. Do you want to know what we're doing?"

"I'd rather yank out your tongue and eat it for dinner."

With a laugh, he snapped his teeth near her nose. "Naughty Were. You know how it makes me hard when you threaten violence."

Spinning on her heel, Harley headed for the door. "You'd better make that a cold shower or you won't have to worry about Salvatore Giuliani slicing off your balls. I'll already have them dangling from my rearview mirror."

She ignored Caine's low laugh as she headed toward the front of the house.

It was late and she was tired, but she ignored the carved wooden staircase that led to the bedrooms as she entered the paneled foyer.

What the hell was wrong with her?

She felt restless and on edge. As if there was a looming thunderstorm and she was about to be struck by lightning.

Telling herself it was nothing more than frustration with Caine and the mysterious games that were being played around her, she yanked open the door and stepped outside.

What she needed was a walk.

And if that didn't work, then there was always cheesecake in the fridge.

There was nothing in the world that couldn't be cured by cheesecake.

Romantic Suspense from
Lisa Jackson

See How She Dies	0-8217-7605-3	$6.99US/$9.99CAN
Final Scream	0-8217-7712-2	$7.99US/$10.99CAN
Wishes	0-8217-6309-1	$5.99US/$7.99CAN
Whispers	0-8217-7603-7	$6.99US/$9.99CAN
Twice Kissed	0-8217-6038-6	$5.99US/$7.99CAN
Unspoken	0-8217-6402-0	$6.50US/$8.50CAN
If She Only Knew	0-8217-6708-9	$6.50US/$8.50CAN
Hot Blooded	0-8217-6841-7	$6.99US/$9.99CAN
Cold Blooded	0-8217-6934-0	$6.99US/$9.99CAN
The Night Before	0-8217-6936-7	$6.99US/$9.99CAN
The Morning After	0-8217-7295-3	$6.99US/$9.99CAN
Deep Freeze	0-8217-7296-1	$7.99US/$10.99CAN
Fatal Burn	0-8217-7577-4	$7.99US/$10.99CAN
Shiver	0-8217-7578-2	$7.99US/$10.99CAN
Most Likely to Die	0-8217-7576-6	$7.99US/$10.99CAN
Absolute Fear	0-8217-7936-2	$7.99US/$9.49CAN
Almost Dead	0-8217-7579-0	$7.99US/$10.99CAN
Lost Souls	0-8217-7938-9	$7.99US/$10.99CAN
Left to Die	1-4201-0276-1	$7.99US/$10.99CAN
Wicked Game	1-4201-0338-5	$7.99US/$9.99CAN
Malice	0-8217-7940-0	$7.99US/$9.49CAN

Available Wherever Books Are Sold!
Visit our website at **www.kensingtonbooks.com**